C000212742

THE PORCELAIN DOLL

a&b

THE
PORCELAIN DOLL

Kristen Loesch

Allison & Busby Limited
11 Wardour Mews
London W1F 8AN
allisonandbusby.com

First published in Great Britain by Allison & Busby in 2022.
This paperback edition published by Alison & Busby in 2022.

Copyright © 2022 by KRISTEN LOESCH

The moral right of the author is hereby asserted in accordance with
the Copyright, Designs and Patents Act 1988.

All characters and events in this publication,
other than those clearly in the public domain,
are fictitious and any resemblance to actual persons,
living or dead, is purely coincidental.

All rights reserved. No part of this publication may be reproduced,
stored in a retrieval system, or transmitted, in any form or by
any means without the prior written permission of the publisher,
nor be otherwise circulated in any form of binding or cover
other than that in which it is published and without a similar
condition being imposed on the subsequent buyer.

A CIP catalogue record for this book is available from
the British Library.

10 9 8 7 6 5 4 3 2 1

ISBN 978-0-7490-2801-5

Typeset in 10.5/15.5 pt Sabon LT Pro by
Allison & Busby Ltd.

Printed and bound by
CPI Group (UK) Ltd, Croydon, CR0 4YY

For my family

So few roads were
travelled
So many mistakes
were made

SERGEY YESENIN

PROLOGUE

I N SOME FARAWAY KINGDOM, IN SOME LONG-AGO LAND, there lived a young girl who looked just like her porcelain doll. The same rusty-gold hair. The same dark-wine eyes. The girl's own mother could hardly tell them apart. But they were never apart, for the girl always held the doll at her side, to keep it from the clutches of her many, many siblings.

The family lived in a dusky-pink house by the river, and in the evenings, the children liked to gather around the old stove and listen to their mother tell stories. Stories of kingdoms even further away and lands even longer ago, when there had been kings and queens living in castles; stories of how those castles had been swept away into the midnight-black sea. The many, many siblings would drift away to sleep on these stories, and then the mother would take the girl and the doll into her lap and tell tales of the girl's father. He'd had the same rusty-gold hair, the same dark-wine eyes, in some other faraway kingdom, in some other long-ago land.

But one evening after supper, as the stove simmered and the samovar sang and the mother spoke and the children listened, there came the sound of footsteps outside the house. *Stomp-stomp-stomp*.

There came a knock on the dusky-pink door. *Rap-rap-rap*.

There came a man's voice, which had no colour at all. *Open, open, open!*

The mother opened the door. Two men stood there, each carrying rifles.

'You will come with us,' said the men to the mother.

The mother hung her head so that her children could not see her cry. But the samovar ceased to sing and the stove ceased to simmer and the story stayed untold, and in the silence, the many, many siblings could hear their mother's tears fall to the ground. They ran to stop the men.

Stop-stop-stop!

Bang-bang-bang.

The siblings fell like their mother's tears. Their bodies lay as quiet and as still as the doll that the girl held.

'Is that another one?' said one of the men to the other, pointing to the girl, who had remained by the stove.

'Those are just dolls,' said the other man to the first.

The men took the mother with them. Their footsteps began to fade. *Stomp-stomp-sto* . . . The mother's cries seemed far away and long ago. *No, no, no* . . . The girl began to breathe again. *In, out, in*. She stood, with her doll beneath her arm, and she walked, across the blood-red floor, over her blood-red siblings, through the blood-red door, out of the blood-red house, all the way to the blood-red river. She forgot to wash her blood-red hands.

For fear of those men, the girl did not stay at the river, nor did she stay in that land. For fear of those men, through all her years, along all her journeys, she carried her doll. But she carried it too long, so long that she could not tell the two of them apart any more either. So long that she could not be sure if she was the girl at all; if she was the one who was real.

PART ONE

CHAPTER ONE

Rosie

London, June 1991

THE MAN I'VE COME TO SEE IS NEARLY A CENTURY OLD.
White-haired and lean, with just a dash of his youthful
film-star looks remaining, he sits alone onstage, drumming
his fingers on his knees. His head is tilted back as he takes
a hard look at the crowd, at the latecomers standing
awkwardly in the aisles, their smiles sheepish. At the young
couple who have brought their children, a toddler girl
swinging her legs back and forth, and the older one, a boy,
solemn-faced and motionless. At me.

Usually when two strangers make eye contact across a
crowded room, one or both will look away, but neither of us do.

Alexey Ivanov will be reading tonight from his memoir,
the slim, red-jacketed book sitting on a table next to his
chair. I've read it so many times by now that I could mouth
it alongside him: *A hillside falls out of view, and voices,
too, fall away . . . we are like castaways, adrift on a single*

piece of wreckage that is floating to sea, leaving behind
everything that linked us to humanity . . .

Alexey stands up. 'Thank you all for coming,' he says, with the knife-edge of an accent. 'And so I begin.'

The Last Bolshevik is an account of his time on Stalin's White Sea Canal, told in short-story form so that people don't forget to breathe as they're reading it. Today Alexey has chosen the tale of a work party's doomed expedition through a grim, wintry wilderness to build a road that no one would ever take. The holes that the prisoners dug were for themselves. It would be their only grave . . .

My hands feel clammy and heavy, and my toes begin to tingle in my boots. The middle-aged man seated next to me pulls his coat tighter around himself, while just up ahead, the young girl has stopped swinging her legs and is as straight-backed as her older brother.In a lecture hall full of people, Alexey Ivanov has snuffed out every sound.

He reaches the end of the story and closes the book. 'I am open to questions,' he says.

There's a faint shuffling of feet. Somewhere in the back, someone coughs and a baby begins to fuss. A quick shushing by the mother follows. Alexey is preparing to settle back into his chair when the man next to me suddenly lifts a hand.

Alexey smiles broadly and gestures to the man. 'Go on.'

'My question is a wee bit personal,' says my neighbour, in a thick Scottish brogue. He shifts in his seat. 'I hope you don't mind . . .'

'Please.'

'You dedicated this memoir to someone you only call "Kukolka". Is there any chance you will share with us who that really was?'

The smile slides off Alexey Ivanov's face. Without it he no longer looks like the famous dissident writer, the celebrated historian. He's only an old man, stooping beneath the burden of over nine decades of life. He glances around the room once more, just as the baby, somewhere out there, lets out another startled cry.

Alexey's gaze lands on me again for half a second before moving on. 'Hers is a name I never speak aloud,' he says. 'And if I did, I would shout it.'

I leave my row and head for the stage. The audience is filtering out, but Alexey is still shaking hands, chatting with the organisers. I've read all his writing, mostly while hunched over in a reading room in the Bodleian, and this is the effect of those musty hours, that pure silence: no matter how human the man might look, Alexey Ivanov has become almost a mythical figure to me. A legend.

'Hello there,' he says, turning to me. He has a smile like a torchlight.

'I enjoyed your reading so much, Mr Ivanov,' I say, finding my voice. Maybe *enjoy* isn't the right word, but he nods. 'Your story is inspirational.'

I'd planned in advance to say this, but only after saying it do I realise how much I mean it.

'Thank you,' he says.

'My name is Rosemary White. Rosie. I saw your advert in Oxford. I'm a postgraduate there.' I cough.

'You're looking for a research assistant, for the summer?'

'I am,' he says pleasantly. 'Someone who can join me in Moscow.'

I loosen my hold on my handbag. 'I'd be interested to apply, if the position's still open.'

'It most certainly is.'

'I don't have much experience in your field, but I'm fluent in Russian and English—'

'I'll be in Oxford on Thursday,' he says. 'Why don't we meet up? I'd be happy to tell you more about it.'

'Absolutely, thank you. Only I'm leaving tomorrow for Yorkshire to visit my fiancé's grandmother. She lives alone. We visit once a month.' I'm not sure why I'm spewing information like this. 'I'll be back by the weekend.'

'This weekend, then,' he says. His voice is mild. All around us is nothing but people talking and bantering, a pleasing hum, but there is something in Alexey's eyes that suddenly makes me want to brace against a biting wind. Maybe the excerpt he just read out, the details of the White Sea, those barren roads, those long winters, is still too fresh in my mind. Maybe it's all people ever see, when they look at him.

It's past my mother's bedtime by the time I make it back to her apartment, but there's a sound coming from her room, a low moan.

I knock on her door. 'Mum? You awake?'

Another half-smothered noise.

I push the door open. Mum's bedroom is filthy and gloomy, and she matches it perfectly. Unwashed, unmoving,

18

she is sitting up in bed, slouched against her pillows, the musky scent of vodka rolling off her in waves. I drop in on her at least once a month, stay with her a night or two here in London. I've been visiting more frequently of late, but if anything, she seems to recognise me less. Mum carried on drinking even after the doctors said her liver was bound to fail, was failing, had failed. She's drunk right now.

'I was at a talk,' I say. 'Have you been waiting up?'

Her jaundiced eyes dart around the room before finding me right in front of her.

'Well, goodnight then.' I set the dosette boxes on her bedside table upright and wipe my hands on my slacks. 'Do you want me to wake you in the morning?' I pause. 'I'm going up first thing to York, remember?'

She sucks in her bony cheeks and starts to grasp at her sheets for support. She wants me to come closer. I seat myself gingerly at the foot of the bed.

'Raisa,' she mumbles.

Raisa. My birth name. By now it feels more like a physical thing I left behind in Russia, along with my clothes, my books, everything else that made me, *me*. My mother is the only one who uses it.

When she dies, she'll take it with her.

'I know what you're planning.' Her breaths are staggered.

'I don't know what you're talking about.'

'Yes, you do.' Her gaze locks on mine, but she can't maintain it. 'You've been trying to get to Moscow.'

'How do you—'

'I've overheard you on the telephone with the embassy. Why do they keep denying you? Is it because of what

19

you study?' She tries to laugh. 'I hope they never let you through.'

'It's because of the hash you made of the paperwork when we moved here,' I say, bristling. 'I've always wanted to return just once, to see it. I thought it'd be best to go before Richard and I get married. Get it done with.'

'You're lying, Raisochka. You're going to look for that man.'

She must be drunker than she's ever been, to mention *that man*. Fourteen years ago, as our rickety Aeroflot jet took off into a deep-crimson skyline, London-bound, I dared to ask her about him. Mum only stared straight ahead. That was her answer: there wasn't any *that man*. I dreamt it. I might have dreamt all of it.

'If you go away now, I won't be here when you get back,' she says.

'Mum, please don't talk like that. And if you would just let us—'

'You mean let *him*. Him with his proper money. Thinks he's better than me.'

'What? Are you talking about Richard? Richard doesn't think—'

'The dolls.' Her pupils dilate. 'What do you plan to do with my dolls, may I ask, once I'm dead?'

I open my mouth and snap it shut. The vodka's definitely talking now. Dolls? I've never once considered what I'll do with her collection of old bisque porcelain dolls. They're like an army of the undead, with their stiff faces, unseeing eyes. Luckily they're stored on a shelf in the living room, or they'd be witness to this very conversation. To my wavering.

20

After she's downed a few, Mum often sits and speaks to them.

'I don't know,' I say, but she's already nodded off.

At half eight in the morning, Mum is still asleep. Her face is slimy with sweat, but she appears so relaxed, so restful, that she might well have died overnight. I touch her wrist for her pulse, faint as a stain, and then reach over to her bedside table to fix the dosette boxes – she always knocks them over, groping for something to throw back – but the surface has been cleared. No boxes. No crumpled bills, either, and no bottles. All that lies there now is a leather-bound notebook.

It is open to a page as yellow as my mother.

I feel a burst of nerves as I lean over. The cursive Cyrillic writing is a tight, indecipherable scrawl. Handwritten font is nothing like the block letters of published Russian books or street signs. I am able to make out the first few lines:

A Note for the Reader
These stories should not be read in order.

'Raisa?'

'Mum,' I say, with a jolt. 'I was just looking at—what *is* this? You wrote down your stories?'

She claws for me, and I take her hand.

'I . . .' Something, maybe the bile from her liver, is so high in my mother's throat that it cuts off her voice. 'I . . . for you, Raisochka. Take with you. Read, please. Promise me.'

'I promise. Let me get you some water, Mum.' I try to pull away, but she's the one holding my hand now. My palm against hers feels sticky.

'I . . . sorry . . .'

I want to say sorry too. I'm sorry that I'm the one who ended up here with her. I'm sorry that she wasn't able to leave *me* behind, because if she had, maybe she could have left *that man* behind too. But I've had too much practice not saying things aloud. I learnt that from Mum herself. I can't unlearn it now. Everything that has ever gone unsaid hangs in the air between us, as thick as the smell of decay that emanates from the strange, small notebook.

Or perhaps from what is left of my mother.

'Promise,' she says again.

'I promise.'

'I love you, little sun.' Her eyes close to a sliver. 'Sleepy . . .'

'Mum . . . ?'

She lets go of my hand, still murmuring to herself.

As the train pulls out of King's Cross I rest my forehead against the glass. Richard is already in York. It'll be a decent drive out to where his grandmother lives, in a cottage that sits, or floats, in the nothingness of the northern moors. It is where Richard and I will marry in autumn. Mum has never been there, but she'd love how it looks rugged and angry one day, winsome and windswept the next. Like a landscape from her stories.

I've got her notebook in my handbag now. I'll keep my promise. But I've always hated her stories.

They're the single thing about her to become more vivid and not less, after a tipple. Strange little vignettes, fairy

22

tales in miniature, often with a nightmarish tint. They all start with some version of her favourite line: *Far away and long ago.* That line is not a coincidence. Most of my mother is far away and long ago.

As Charlotte shows us where the musicians will be set up and instructs us not to venture anywhere near her rose garden, with a slight huff, a chilly gust of air whisks past. I shudder, and Richard's grandmother glances at me, her smile just as chilly.

'Does it not suit?' she asks.

'No, it's—it's beautiful.'

Richard shrugs off his coat and puts it around my shoulders. We approach the house from the back. Charlotte's dog, some ankle-high breed of terrier, is yapping by the door, jumping up and down on all fours like a mechanical toy. Charlotte's lips are pressed together. Her dog is usually to be found on his living-room cushions, sniffing at a tray of treats. He is not the sort of dog who sneaks out on purpose. He isn't what most people would even call a dog.

'Have you slipped him some coffee?' I joke to Richard. 'Or some—'

Garlic.

The air is laced with the smell of garlic, carrying further than it otherwise might, perhaps, on that brisk wind. For a second I worry it might be *me*, having just spent the week at my mother's, because Mum adds garlic to everything she consumes. Maybe even her drinks. As a teenager, I used to make snide comments: *Was there a garlic shortage or something when you were a kid?* And she'd laugh like I was being funny, and not like she was pissed.

23

I was not being funny.

'Ro? You OK?' asks Richard.

'Is it the roses?' enquires Charlotte. 'Their scent is peaking.'

'I'm just cold, I think.'

The dog is still howling and now sounds deranged.

'I don't know what could be the matter with him.' Charlotte places a hand on the brooch pinned to her lapel. 'Would you go around front, Richie? Someone might have come by.'

I shrink into Richard's coat. Someone is already there, right *there* by the back entrance. A visitor who has drawn the rat-dog from his morning nap; who has likely been watching us meander through Charlotte's garden. A visitor who is often *there* in Oxford too.

Zoya.

Richard walks off. The dog quiets down, appearing satisfied that the racket has got his message across.

'I feel that there's something amiss with you today, Rosie,' says Charlotte. 'You're not altogether yourself.' She makes a *tch* sound.

The sound is everything she thinks of me, rolled into a syllable. I don't know if she envisioned her favourite grandchild ending up with someone like me, but she also probably reckons it could be worse. *Tch, tch.*

Another *tch* at me for not replying straightaway. I try to smile at her, but she doesn't try in return. What does she want, an apology for not being myself? Who is the Rosie who is herself? Rosie, whose name has not always been Rosie? Sometimes there's a glimmer in Charlotte that makes me wonder if she suspects something to be wrong with my story. But she's the one who retreated into a remote, rose-growing widowhood far from everyone she knows, from her old married life. Maybe there's something wrong with her story too.

'It's my mother. She's—she's unwell,' I say.

Charlotte draws herself up. 'Of course. Richard did say. How terribly difficult for your family. Is your mother religious?'

'She has . . . her views,' I say. 'She believes in the soul.'

Mum was once determined to make me and Zoya believe in it too. She'd try to wear us down, evening after evening, sitting at our bedside, smoothing down that favourite nightgown of hers, the only thing she wears nowadays. Some of her claims about the human soul came with solid moral lessons. Others were bits and bobs of morbid superstition, what schoolkids might circulate in the playground.

I didn't believe any of it then.

The dog is glacially silent now.

'No one,' reports Richard, strolling back towards us. 'Shall we go in?'

Charlotte bends with impressive flexibility and scoops up her pet. His tail whacks like a metronome against her arm. Before I can follow, the smell of garlic wafts by again, mixed with that of vodka now. A potent combination. The particular combination that comes off Mum like radioactivity.

My breakfast turns in my stomach, threatens to rise. According to Mum's folklore, there is only one hard rule: after death, the soul must visit all the different places in which the living person has ever sinned.

Didn't Zoya commit sins anywhere other than right behind me?

* * *

25

Mum's neighbour rings from London late in the evening. Mum has died. He brought in her shopping as usual and he could just tell, he says. I want to ask him to check again because Mum's been passing for dead for a few years now, but I don't. I crawl into bed and I think about this tiny ivy-slathered house and the moorland all around, wild and empty, extending in every direction, coming from nowhere, belonging to no one.

Moors. Moored. Unmoored.

Back in London, there is no funeral, no ceremony beyond the cremation. Mum had no friends. She didn't know anyone who wasn't being paid to know her back. I take her ashes with me in a nondescript urn and I decline Richard's offer to stay behind to help.

I'll only be an extra day, I say, because I have to be in Oxford by the weekend.

I try to tidy up her apartment. I start in the kitchen, with her grisly jars of home-pickled vegetables, not one of which I have ever seen her touch. I have a go at the living room next, but the glass eyes of her dolls follow me around like they're waiting for me to turn my back – so I decide to deal with them next time and I open all the windows instead, to let some of the stale, vodka-soaked air out. To let Mum's soul out.

I just have no idea what to do with what's left. Should I put the urn in storage? Or on display?

If I were going to scatter her ashes, it ought to be off the stage at the Bolshoi, over the musicians' heads, as *brava*s ring out from every box. Mum was in the corps de ballet before getting married – before my sister and I came along,

26

obliterating any chance she had of being promoted to principal – and she probably always hoped to die onstage, mid-plié. Zoya and I used to tease her as she practised in the mornings. We'd fall over our own feet trying to go *en pointe* alongside her.

Katerina Ballerina.

Later I swing by to meet her solicitor. He has a smart office and a sympathetic smile. He tells me she's left me the apartment. It's mine now. That can't be right, I say, trying to argue with him. Richard and I have been paying rent on it. We send her a cheque every three months.

I have the mental image of cheques being stashed away, pickled in jars.

Her solicitor feels sorry for me. I can hear it in his voice. He has a posh accent, like Richard's, the kind that can sand glass. He can show me the deed, he says. Katherine White, a property owner. For a second I think, ah, that's it. He's got the wrong person. My mother's name wasn't Katherine White. It was Yekaterina Simonova. *Katerina Ballerina.*

Richard stands in the rain without a brolly, his college scarf around his neck, his hands stuck in his trouser pockets. I step off the coach and look askance at the dark sky, starched and flat over all of Oxford. A raindrop lands on my eyelashes. I used to wonder if Mum chose England because it is so colourless. Because she never wanted it to be able to compete with her old life.

He kisses me lightly on the mouth. 'You're back so soon.'

'I couldn't stand being there a second longer,' I say. 'I'll sort everything else out another time.'

'Should we go get something to eat?'

Inside the dubious-looking eatery on the corner, I peel off my sour, wet layers and shiver. Richard lends me his scarf, which smells of him, of wood and ash and sherry.

'How are you feeling?' he asks, once the food comes.

'I'm fine. Honestly.' I stab with my fork at a mushy mountain of peas. Richard's own mother died daintily over tea at Fortnum & Mason five years ago, the victim of a brain aneurysm. It's almost hard not to be jealous, when Mum deteriorated over the better part of a decade.

Sometimes it felt like she was going to live for ever, that way.

'Anything happening here?' I ask, my mouth half full.

'Not much. Dad rang yesterday, asked if I'm done yet,' he says. Richard's father seems to find it amusing, his son doing a doctorate in Classics, like Richard has to flush it out of his system before he can crack on with becoming a trader in the City, or whatever it is men in their family usually do. 'He's still upset that Henry and Olivia split up,' Richard adds, referring to his older brother and his brother's long-time, if not lifelong, girlfriend. 'I didn't say that Henry told me he's planning to quit his job and travel Europe this summer.'

'Right, about this summer.' I swallow hard. 'I'm thinking of applying for a short-term project in Moscow.'

His eyebrows rise. 'I know you wanted to spend some time there, but – are you sure? Have you talked to Windle?'

'You know how he is. I'll make it up when I'm back. He won't care.'

'I wish my supervisor didn't care.'

'It is the best thing.'

28

Richard chuckles. 'But would you be home in time for our wedding?' he says, half joking. He doesn't sound put off quite yet, but Richard is rarely put off. His sturdiness and his steadiness and his *sameness* are what endeared him to me in the first place. In Richard's world, people die neatly of invisible brain aneurysms. They do not self-destruct. In Richard's world, it is a shock when one's childhood sweetheart is not, in fact, the love of one's life.

'Don't be daft.' The peas taste like bits of rubber in my mouth. Maybe I somehow knew Mum wouldn't be attending our wedding when we first set the date. Maybe I purposely put it just out of her reach, thinking how she'd only arrive late, her face cherry red, how she'd start snoring at the ceremony, arms and legs flung over other guests' chairs, her body draped over her own chair like a dishcloth.

How she'd still be in her nightgown.

'I'll need some extra time in Moscow anyway,' I add. 'You know. To let friends and family know about Mum?' I can't think what people normally do when someone dies. But people normally have *other people*.

I shovel in more peas.

'Where's the position?' asks Richard. 'There's a rather famous university in Moscow, isn't there, what's it called—'

'Lomonosov. It's just an idea, really.'

Richard drops his gaze to his own platter of what might have been a shepherd's pie in a past life. I can see him trying to work it out around the margins. He pushes around a glob of pie and clears his throat. 'Why don't I join you?'

'You just started writing up.' The peas sit like lead in my stomach. 'You're so busy. And maybe I . . . I don't know. I need to get away for a bit.'

'Is that all it is?'

'That's all it is.' If Richard can just hold on for a few more months, then we never have to speak of Mum or Russia again. It'll be a silent addition to my wedding vows: *To have. To hold. To be Rosie and never Raisa, ever again.*

'Well, I'd miss you.' Perhaps feeling guilty, he adds, 'I understand. It was just you and Kate, the two of you, for so long.'

The two of us. He's right. So why did it always feel like I lost my whole family over the course of one single night in Moscow? Like Mum's blood was spilt there too, all over our living-room floor? Or at least her lifeblood, because she never practised ballet again after we left Soviet Russia. Defected, people would say, but we didn't defect. We escaped. We *fled*.

The peal of bells from a nearby chapel tower is a ghostly sound. Bells have rung in Oxford for centuries. That is how long my nights often seem.

Next to me, Richard stirs, but I don't move. I've been an insomniac for years, and often it's the most awake I ever feel. My father would have understood. He often worked late at night, marking papers, doing exercises. Mum blamed the mathematician in him. *It's not good for numbers to run through a person's head*, she would say, *because there's no end to them.*

But if it's numbers that keep *me* up, they don't go very high.

One, two.

Tonight I think about Alexey Ivanov, whom I will meet tomorrow, and how much he and I have in common. *The Last Bolshevik* was published in Europe in the late 1970s and promptly banned in Russia, forcing him abroad for his own safety. But so much has changed in the USSR since 1985, under Mikhail Gorbachev. The era of political repression appears to be over. Alexey's memoir was officially published in his homeland last year. He's being courted by the Soviet government and has even been offered citizenship again.

I could tell him, *Look, see, something had to end in order for me to go back, too.*

In my case, it was Mum.

Richard lifts his head from the pillow, blinking drowsily. He's used to this, seeing me wide awake, owl-like, in the darkness. Before I can say anything, he kisses my cheek, soft as down. Richard's touch is always gentle, always generous; *You're safe here*, he's telling me, in his way, and soon all thoughts of Mum and Russia have faded into the shadows.

Later, the bells are ringing again on the hour. I try to sleep with my face turned into the pillow. Richard won't be there, in Moscow. Only the shadows.

Alexey's choice of cafe is cosy and low-lit, catering mostly to university staff and students. The leisurely atmosphere fits him. He seems to do most things easily, sitting back in his chair, flicking at the label of his teabag, looking out every so often towards the glass front of the cafe. Letting the conversation stall.

31

The quieter and more relaxed he appears, the more harried I feel, like I want to make up for it.

'I'd love to hear about your new project, Mr Ivanov.' I wrap my hands around my mug. 'I know it's not my background, but I'm a quick learner, and I'm keen. I've been doing a lot of preliminary reading this past month—'

'Why?' he asks.

'I'm sorry?'

'I looked you up. You're in the first year of your DPhil at the Mathematical Institute,' he says. 'In cryptography, I understand. Codebreaking. This brings to my mind Bletchley Park. Very exciting. Why are you pivoting to Russian history?'

I was going to lie outright, but I think he'd see through it. I have to hedge.

'I was born in Moscow,' I say. 'My mother has just died. Honestly, it's made me rethink a lot of things. I want to get to know my own culture and history. My heritage.'

He gives me several seconds to elaborate, and when I don't, he simply nods. I suppose he's been surrounded all his life by people who didn't want to share the long history of their pasts. I almost want to ask him: What is it like not only to share the past, but to *broadcast* it? To take a roomful of questions on it?

'Alright. Well, to be frank, I could use a bit of a different perspective,' says Alexey. 'Because the task at hand is very different from my usual work. I'm trying to find a woman I used to know. That's it. That's the project. We'll just have to see if I have enough time. Not free time,' he adds, with a self-deprecating laugh. 'Just time.'

I look down into my tea, let the steam sting my eyelids. Mum's just died at age fifty-three. My father died at forty-four.

Zoya died at fifteen.

Alexey takes hold of his teabag's wilted label, lifts the bag out, then lets it slide back in.

'She went missing years ago,' he continues. 'I like to think she's ended up somewhere in the countryside. She loved the land. She used to say she could bask in it, bathe in it, drown in it . . .' He sits back, as if he wants the line to reverberate. 'But let's talk logistics. You may not be so keen when you hear the pay, though I'm prepared to take care of the travel paperwork and housing. You won't have to lift a finger in that regard.'

That's what his advert alluded to, and exactly what I've been hoping to hear.

'I'll have to do a fair bit of moving around when we get there, so you'd need to be capable of working on your own. You should also continue reading as much as you can. You'll need a . . .' He gestures vaguely. 'An underlying knowledge base. But it's good for young people to be exposed to history. They just have to take care.'

'Take care?' I repeat.

His blue eyes fix on me. 'There is no enlightenment to be found in the past. No healing. No solace. Whatever we are looking for will not be there.'

It rings out like the chapel bells, the way he says this. *Whatever we are looking for will not be there.*

Can a historian really believe that?

It makes me think of Zoya, of how she'll conjure the smell of rust and cheap candles, forcing me to recall

33

my first winter in England, in that seedy short-term apartment. To recall how Mum would stand by the window, looking through the curtains, one foot curled up like she might dance away, lit candles on every surface, like she wanted the whole place to burn down. I'd be seated at the table, working furiously, surrounded by schoolbooks, thinking, *If I can just make it to the end of this problem, if I can find this one solution, everything will make sense.*

But is Zoya just trying to make me remember?

Or is she sifting my old, hidden-away memories, because she's *looking* for something?

'She's the one who was mentioned the other night,' says Alexey, folding his arms over his tweedy jacket.

He's talking about the woman he hopes to find. I rub at my temples. Zoya's not here right now, and I don't want to think too hard about her or she might show up.

'She was called Kukolka,' he says.

Little doll.

I take a sip of my own tea. It's gone cold.

Kukolka. It's an unwelcome reminder of Mum's porcelain prisoners back in London. I'd be happy never to lay eyes on them again, but it's not just because they're uncanny. It's because Mum preferred her dolls to human company. She always did. Of all the things we could have brought with us from Russia – and we weren't able to bring very much – she chose them.

I linger in the cafe after Alexey leaves, finishing the last of my tea, watching the flow of customers. Through the

34

glass I can see rain peppering the pavement, slowly gaining momentum, while the awning flaps in the wind, looking possessed. People burst in holding soggy newspapers, shaking themselves off like dogs.

It rains constantly in Oxford. Nothing ever seems to dry, inside or out. But it doesn't often storm like this, enough to empty the streets. If only I'd brought along some work, or something to *do*—

Mum's notebook of stories.

I ferret it out of my bag. The spine bends with close to a creak.

The more the sky darkens outside, the brighter it feels in here. But that doesn't make the coil of cursive any less excruciating to read. It doesn't make anything clear.

A Note for the Reader . . .

A NOTE FOR THE READER

These stories should not be read in order.

After you have read all the others, in whatever order you like, you may return to the first one. This is, after all, a book of stories for those who know that the beginning can only be understood at the very end.

You must now close your eyes to see what I am about to show you.

If you think your eyes are closed hard enough, then let us begin: In a faraway kingdom, in a long-ago land . . .

CHAPTER TWO

Antonina
Petrograd, St Petersburg, autumn 1915

Tea is served in the Blue Salon at four in the afternoon, every day. Most days there are also cream cakes, custard cakes, and puff pastries, laid out on platters, or buttered bread, freshly sliced, still steaming. Yet Tonya never feels hungry. She tells herself it's because lunch was too recent, too rich. Or because of the hideous silver-blue wallpaper of this room, for which it was given its name, which makes everything within look sickly. Or because Dmitry hardly ever touches the tea service or the display of goodies himself. Today he is counting banknotes at the escritoire beneath his breath: *Twenty, forty, sixty. One. Two. Three.* Everything in this house has a number.

Everything has a price.

The caravan tea is black and smoky. Tonya drinks as silently as she can.

Dmitry puts aside his wallet. He turns to fish a cigar from the sweet-smelling cedar box he stores them in. It's easy to wonder why they bother with teatime at all, except that they might not see one another all day without it.

'Your nightmares are getting worse,' he says.

Her tongue feels thick, twisted against her teeth. 'No worse than normal.'

Dmitry takes a long puff. 'I could hear you thrashing around yesterday, even from my quarters.'

'I dream of home,' she says tightly. 'Of Otrada. Perhaps it's a sign I ought to visit.'

'It's out of the question for you to travel alone.'

'But I could accompany you, next time you go south—'

'I have no such plans for the foreseeable future. There's a situation here with the union.' A sigh, softened by another puff. 'I have several rabble-rousers in my employ.'

Tonya chokes back a reply. Dmitry makes frequent trips out of town, scouring this country in search of pieces to add to his beloved collection of rarities, oddities and other treasures. He sometimes leaves for weeks on end.

She has to be home by teatime.

'Are you bored, Tonya?' he asks. 'Is that the problem?'

'I—I occupy myself,' she falters.

'Perhaps if you cultivated an interest in philanthropy,' he says. 'I was thinking the other day that a tour of the factory, even the barracks, is long overdue. And it should be to my benefit for them to see that I am a married man.' Dmitry works away at the cigar, appearing pleased by the thought. Against the watery hues of the wallpaper, his profile looks sharp, princely. Dashing, perhaps. Tonya has lived in this house long enough to overhear the giggles of the young housemaids, their swoons: how different their master is from the others of his station! He treats his inferiors with such respect, such benevolence! He is no hard-hearted despot, no devious tyrant, no cruel handler! They are right. He is none of those things.

Downstairs, at least.

Tonya is in the middle of reading Alexander Pushkin's *Eugene Onegin* when Dmitry announces that it is time to take a drive. Did she accidentally feign interest yesterday in the idea of a factory tour? She isn't even sure what his factory *makes*. Magnetos, she has heard people say in passing. Things to do with the ongoing war against Imperial Germany. In the motorcar Tonya closes her eyes and tries to recreate the stunning, romantic world of Pushkin, but her husband's voice cuts through it.

'You've let your hair down,' he notes, as if he never instructed Olenka to keep it so. 'I abhor those matronly updos. You might soon be seventeen, but you're only a girl.' Dmitry leans over and touches her ear, pulls on one pearl-drop earring. 'I like you like this. The way you looked the day we met.'

'Should married women look as I do?' she says, trying not to sound morose.

'Nobody looks as you do,' he says.

His tone suggests that he will visit her bed tonight. It would be the first time since his return from his most recent trip. She knows from the chauffeur's whispers to Cook that Dmitry pays regular visits to the docks, when he is here in the capital. That he likes the girls well-broke, like a horse.

Not all the staff are as blinkered as the housemaids.

Tonya turns to the window. The factory is on the Vyborg side, across the Neva, but the driver seems to be taking a long way around. She blinks, refuses to admire the cityscape. It has been nearly a year and a half since she married Dmitry, over a year since he brought her to Petrograd. Still the only thing she likes about the capital is the single aloof spire of the Admiralty, the way it catches the sunlight. The Neva is not terrible, either, though it stinks of cod and seagull. And sometimes she enjoys seeing the laundry hung on lines in the yellow courtyards, hearing it flap in the wind, *flap-flap-flap*. She wants it to blow away. She wants all of it to blow away.

Eugene Onegin, she tells herself. Think of *Eugene Onegin*.

The tour is deadly dull, led by the foreman, a stubbly man called Gochkin. Tonya runs her hand over the tables, tools, machinery for which she has no name. The workers give her hard stares, but then so do Dmitry's society friends. Tonya might come from provincial gentry, her father might be a prince, but to the old St Petersburg elite, she is lowly country stock. Her home village is so deep in the country that it is hardly considered the *same* country.

Young and old, the faces of the workers are slick with grime, and unsmiling. Dmitry seems not to notice. He is friendly with everyone, shaking hands, slapping shoulders. Asking after babies. Tonya knows her husband fancies himself a liberal. He feels bad that his forefathers ever owned serfs.

He does not, however, feel bad for owning her.

After the tour Tonya joins Dmitry and Gochkin on the high platform that overlooks the factory floor. The men retreat to the office of the latter and Tonya strays to the railing. She plays with the ends of her hair, picks over her sleeve for the smallest threads. This stiff-necked dress is horribly stifling. Her jewellery feels weighty. Uncomfortable and restless, she shifts her attention to a group of workers who have gathered below. Young men, laughing, talking amongst themselves.

The rail is suddenly the only thing that keeps her standing.

Tonya doesn't know who *he* is. He was not present during the tour. She would have remembered if he were. He is dark-haired, lean, but they all are, no doubt subsisting on cabbage soup and kasha. And he is handsome. So handsome that she feels itchy, like lice might have burrowed into her stockings.

'You have an audience, Andreyev,' someone says.

'He always has,' remarks another.

He is the one they are calling Andreyev. He looks up, barely, and meets her gaze. His smile is knowing – no, mocking – and her heart races. Perhaps some wealthy do-gooders have barged in here recently, hoping to elevate the sorry lives of the working classes, looking for a purpose for their pampered lives, and he is mistaking her for one of them. One such couple came to call at the house, just the other day. They were horrified at what they'd witnessed in a workers' barracks, nearly foaming at the mouth as they described cockroaches clinging to plank beds, whole families jammed into spaces unfit for livestock, and the smell, oh, the *smell!*

Tonya can only imagine the smell of someone like *him*. Of the revolting hand-rolled cigarettes that the natives of Petrograd love to smoke. Of the smog and soot of the factory pillars. Of the city streets. Of sweat.

They have looked too long at one another. She flushes. He wipes something from his eye, dirt, or just the sight of her, and turns away.

Since the start of summer Tonya has taken early, winding walks, all the way from the house on the Fontanka up to the Neva, one river to another. Dmitry usually sleeps late, and it's a chance to be alone, unguarded, uninhibited, for no one else is about between five and six in the morning, except droshky drivers and soldiers. And a few troublemakers.

People like – *him*.

She is just passing the newspaper offices on Nevsky Prospekt when she sees him. Just by chance, for a remarkably sizeable crowd has formed around Andreyev: a clutch of students, in blue caps; workers with their tarred hats and unwashed heads; drivers in their signature mink stoles. Tonya is able to join the crowd at the fringes. He is the only one speaking: *The old Russia shall make way for the new! And in this new world, all will participate, all will partake, even you lads, even you ladies, even you, comrade, even—*

You.

He sees her now. Smiles, as yesterday, at the factory. She feels shaky, shivery. As if he is nearer than he actually is, near enough for his hands, his mouth, his body, to be all over hers.

42

Mama once warned her of feeling this way. Of inexplicably wanting something, someone, enough that your blood runs hot, until it bubbles. *Everyone feels this when they're young*, said Mama, *but it passes as quick as it comes*, and Tonya only giggled, because it was unthinkable, both the bubbling of blood and such a feeling of wanting.

He is still orating to the crowd: *Can you see the future that lies before you? Will you reach for it? Will you take it for yourselves?*

But he is watching her still.

You will all of you live two lives, comrades! One is finished, and the other is now!

Tonya tells herself that it is easy to adore a performer, and to forget that they perform for everyone. She feels her own lips moving, saying this. But the voice she hears is his.

As the autumn cedes to winter, Anastasia Sergeyevna, Dmitry's widowed mother, grows too weak to continue living in her dacha by Lake Ladoga. She is moved into their house on the Fontanka and decides to occupy the spare study on the ground floor, a wood-panelled, little-used space that stinks of death even with her in it. In her youth Anastasia was a popular hostess, a beloved wife, a saintly woman. At least that is what people say, the few friends who drop by, who depart with their faces drooping, like the branches on the maple trees outside.

Now she lies as still as the heavy, dark furniture of the room she has chosen for herself.

At Dmitry's request, Tonya sits by her mother-in-law's side for an hour every day. After the first few woefully awkward visits, she brings along *Eugene Onegin*, and reads aloud until the woman falls asleep. It is easy enough to do, in here. Anastasia suffers headaches behind her bad eye, and so the curtains are never drawn. The only light in the room, the only life, comes from the fireplace.

Today Tonya begins: 'My whole life has been a pledge to this meeting with you—'

'Have you read Pushkin before?' interrupts Anastasia.

'I enjoy his poetry,' says Tonya, nervously. 'I am particularly fond of—'

'Olenka tells me you spend hours every day in the library. Have you always read so much?'

'There weren't many books in my parents' home.' Tonya tries to avoid looking in Anastasia's bad eye. 'Nothing like—'

'Do you miss home?'

'At times,' says Tonya, trying not to think of Otrada; of the nearby village of Popovka; of the creek gleaming silver, the moon tossed over the trees. Of running barefoot; of breathing deep. 'But I am happy here,' she adds. She tucks in her skirts, turns the page, knows she's giving away her lie with these small movements. Her mother-in-law has fallen silent again. Tonya blunders on, reading until she sees that Anastasia's good eye has closed. The bad eye does not appear able to close, not like that. The lid has petrified in place.

Tonya puts the book aside and stands from her chair with a yawn of her own.

She has been waking up every day at five, to see *him* speak.

She has her hand on the door handle when she hears the rustling of blankets behind her. She dares to take another look at the divan, at the heaping of pillows and deerskins, the withered figure of Anastasia lost amongst them. The flames in the background, flickering low.

'I mean to ask you, child. I know about your displeasing dreams. Your disturbed sleep.' Anastasia's voice is not unkind. 'Is something troubling you?'

'My dreams began in childhood.' Here, at least, there is no need to lie. 'I have suffered them as long as I can remember.'

'Very well.' The good eye is open again, pale, penetrating. 'But if I can help, just tell me how.'

The good weather ends early here. A winter chill slinks through Petrograd like a serpent, without any warning. Tonya awakens one morning blue-lipped and hardly breathing. Unable to fall back asleep, she climbs out of bed. She draws the velvet-tasselled curtains, opens the doors to the balcony. Her bedroom overlooks the Fontanka, and the river is as lifeless as she feels. She inhales. The air bristles in her lungs.

She could ring for her breakfast and take it in bed. Olenka would tend a flawless fire. There is nowhere to go, nowhere she has to be.

Is this freedom? Or a spacious cage?

For a moment, she hesitates, but only a moment. She has become practised at this routine: dressing on her own, not bothering with her hair; tiptoeing out her own boudoir and past Dmitry's rooms and down the central stairs; ignoring the noise of the servants, dim and chattery and echoed in the walls, like mice. All the way through, along every corridor, Tonya keeps her shawled head bent. She goes out the grand foyer, shutting the bronzed doors gently behind her.

Outside, a hostile wind blows, bites at her face. Snow blankets the parquet along Nevsky, and is still falling, soft and sugary. Although the streets are mostly empty, Tonya can hear the quivery jingle of sleigh bells, the whinny of horses. Petrograd is waking up. Her hands buried in her sable, she hurries now to cross Nevsky at the Anichkov Bridge and continue up Liteyny. It is close to a forty-minute walk to the Neva, but by the time she reaches it, she has warmed.

There is an overturned sleigh dug into the muddy slush of the embankment, surrounded by people. *He* stands somehow balanced upon it, on the runners. He gestures to the bridge, to the river, as if he can see across that growing expanse of ice the very future he is taking pains to describe.

She will be no more, this frail Russia! She will be born anew!

He is a Bolshevik.

Tonya has stood in enough of his crowds by now to know that his name is Valentin Mikhailovich Andreyev. That he is twenty years old, a disciple of Vladimir Lenin, a revolutionary. She has learnt far more about their small but vociferous political party than she probably should; only yesterday she found a published pamphlet by Lenin, *What Is to Be Done?*, in one of Dmitry's libraries, and read it aloud to Anastasia, hoping Dmitry's mother might

46

understand everything Tonya could not. *Revolutionary theory. Class consciousness. Social democracy.* A world of strange, new, meaningless words.

She prefers the ones that Valentin Andreyev uses in his speeches.

Tonya wanders now to the rail of the bridge. She will remain until Andreyev has finished. They will exchange a wordless glance. He will smile as he does, and then she'll walk on, and it will all happen again tomorrow and the next day. He is only a silent, secret fantasy, one that she guards. She has nothing of her own in Petrograd. Not her furs, her lace. Not her hair, her skin, her breath. Nothing except this.

She has started to recognise his closing lines, the things he wants people to remember. She removes her muff and wipes a layer of snowflakes off her shawl. The cold seeps into her gloves. Bells begin to ring in the distance, high and haughty, while the wind swoops by, even higher. She leans against the cast-iron cladding of the rail, glancing in the direction of the Kresty Prison, on the opposite bank of the Neva. Infamous home of the Tsar's political prisoners, it is made of faded red brick. Yet today it looks shiny, scratchy-white, like a Christmas ornament.

That is where people like Valentin Andreyev end up.

'You are devoted to the cause, comrade,' says a voice from behind her.

Tonya turns, but fails to reply. There's a slight rush in her ears. *He* is standing there. The other onlookers have dispersed, and the crowd has scattered. She observes him mutely, almost at a gape. His wool jacket is strewn with holes, and the wind from the river must sail right through. The flurries dust his dark hair, his shoulders, even his smile. Yet she is the one trembling.

'I was certain you'd stop coming, now the weather's turned,' he says.

He must know she is Dmitry's wife. He's being disingenuous, but then she has been, too, acting like she is free to be here, standing with him, staring at him.

'What's your name?' he asks.

'Antonina Nikolayevna,' she says without thinking. It's too many syllables. Too formal. He is already too close for that.

'I'll be on the other side of the bridge on Saturday,' he says. 'Will you come?'

'I don't—I don't know.'

'We'll see, then. Antonina.'

He says it like a challenge, like he doesn't expect to see her again, now that they have spoken. Now that he has come down to her level. She doesn't know whether she wants to prove him wrong or not. She watches as he saunters off, hands in his pockets. Modestly, like he was never atop that sleigh, never addressing the people, never promising a thing. Quietly, like maybe there is more to him than that: Valentin Andreyev, the Bolshevik.

At teatime there is a caller: the Countess Natalya Fyodorovna Burzinova, heiress and socialite, mother and widow, friend and foe. Dmitry and Natalya met as children, and the intimacy between them is old and obvious. He calls her Natasha, a familiar name; Tonya

48

doesn't dare. She used to imagine that the Countess would be something of a mentor, an older sister, a replacement for Nelly and Kirill, her dearest friends back home.

By now she knows better.

Dmitry isn't home for tea, which has often been the case of late. More trouble at the factory, if the servants are to be believed. Once the Countess has swept herself into the Blue Salon, Tonya rings for a tray. The two women regard one another until Tonya backs down, looks instead at the wallpaper, at the places where it curls, where the ends do not quite meet.

The Countess is a regular visitor, yet somehow she always catches Tonya by surprise.

Natalya is older, self-assured, sly. She has the habit of rubbing the silver Orthodox cross that hangs around her neck. *Rub, rub, rub.* Today it matches her snake-like silver earrings. Natalya often accessorises with silver, perhaps to offset – or to accentuate – the flaming redness of her hair. People say that the Countess must paint her hair, for everything else about the woman appears deliberate, even the contours of her face. But anyone acquainted with Natalya's two children would know the beetroot colour is indeed a family trait.

Rub, rub, rub.

'I was hoping to speak to you alone,' says the Countess. 'Is it true that you set off every morning and walk the city?'

'I enjoy the quiet.'

'It's not quiet any more.' Natalya taps her falcon-claw fingernails on the arm of her chair. 'It's anarchy. And perhaps you're unaware, being a country mouse, but when

49

a young woman regularly ventures out on her own at odd hours, rumours tend to follow.'

Tonya has heard her own share of *rumours* by now. She's heard, for example, that the young Natalya was desperately in love with Dmitry; that Natalya's scheming, social-climbing parents intervened, marrying their daughter off to the decrepit Count Burzinov. Oh, if only the Count had died earlier than he did! For by that time Dmitry had already departed on a fateful sojourn to the lower provinces, and was soon to return with, amongst other trinkets, his new bride.

Gossip abounded about that too, of course; about Tonya. The only child of a notoriously reclusive family, not seen in the Imperial Court for decades—

There are rumours enough to float a barge, in this city.

'Dmitry knows about my walks,' says Tonya. 'He doesn't mind.'

'He forgets that a wife is different than a pet, a servant or an employee.' *Rub, rub, rub.* 'He's had too many of all those. Anyway, I've come to say that you'd do better to stay home, darling, what with the demagogues, the radicals, the demonstrators on the streets. And you yourself so inexperienced, so young, so provincial . . .'

The Countess is still speaking – *Tonya? Tonya?* – but Tonya is no longer listening. The demagogues, the radicals. There *he* is, every morning, standing up there, speaking of freedom. Looking like freedom. She thinks of the way he said her name, *Antonina*, the way it came off his tongue, his way.

* * *

Anastasia remarks that Tonya looks different lately. Maybe it's the good eye going bad too, seeing things, but Tonya doesn't say so. *Your face is so bright, child*, Anastasia says, *like you don't view me as a chore any more.* Anastasia pats Tonya's hand, says she's glad Tonya is here, says she always wanted a daughter. This makes Tonya think of Mama, who would never keep a room this dark, for then people wouldn't be able to see her. *What good is beauty*, Mama would say, *if it is left to fester?*

Sometimes it feels disloyal to be spending this much time with Anastasia, with Mama gone and never coming back.

'Have you thought of anything I can do for you?' asks Anastasia. 'Anything that might help make you feel more settled?'

'I have everything anyone could want,' says Tonya. What other answer can she give? That she daydreams about someone she has hardly spoken to – though he speaks to *her*, more than she can say? That she has read every book in this house several times over; that sometimes she entertains the incredible idea of crafting a story of her own, perhaps of unrequited love, like Turgenev, or starry skies and gooseberries, like Chekhov?

Her mother-in-law laughs. It sounds odd, a bit tinny. 'You'll think of something,' she says. 'There's always something.'

Tonya has never observed Petrograd from the Vyborg side before. It has obviously been snowing all night, for there are no tracks on the Liteyny Bridge, no boot-prints except her own. The river below is near frozen. It's hard to imagine that people will emerge from their warm beds in the coming weeks to see anyone speak, even someone with a voice like Valentin Andreyev's. But the city must be growing on her, because this view is appealing, even pretty.

She senses someone beside her at the rail, and she stiffens.

'You're not from Piter,' he says. 'Nobody who is born here, looks upon that part of our city as you are doing now.'

She forces herself to glance at him. He is facing the river, away from her, but something has shifted between them, is shifting still.

Her stomach churns. 'What do you mean? What part?'

'Your part,' he says. 'The centre. Nevsky.'

'What's wrong with Nevsky?' Tonya ignores her own heartbeat, loud in her ears. 'It looks a fine place to live.'

'It is a gilded walkway for tourists. And it's not where people live. It's where they go to escape their lives.' He flashes her a smile. 'But we are all tempted there sometimes.'

She bites her lip to keep from smiling back. 'Did you not say this was where you would give your speech?'

'I told you it was.'

'But there is nobody here.'

'There's you. Do you want me to shout, or will you come closer?'

How far will she go? How far has she already gone? They are right next to one another. She moves closer anyway. She hears her own intake of breath, and his, and then she understands that he does not want to be here, along this river, alone with her, wasting his time, his morning, like this. He wants to be amongst the masses, in the noise, in the fervour. In the fire.

And yet he *is* here.

'Don't you think it's been long enough?' His voice is low, amused. 'These past few months, upon seeing you, I would tell myself: She won't come tomorrow. There's no chance of it.

Today is the last you will ever see of her. But recently I've begun to wonder if today is not the last day. If today is the first day.'

These past few months.

These past few months, at night, before falling asleep, Tonya has often closed her eyes and toyed with silly, steamy thoughts of Valentin. Of him lying beside her in bed, murmuring, trailing his mouth across her skin. But as soon as she opens her eyes, the idea seems laughable. Her bed is full of drapey lace and silk sheets and crochet pillows. Her room is painfully crowded, with its wreath-patterned wallpaper, its eighteenth-century Italian landscapes, the gilt vases and the vanity and the rose-oil lamps burning at all hours, so that it always smells like a bath. Valentin Andreyev does not fit anywhere in it.

He is only a dream, just like her nightmares.

'This speech sounds quite unlike your others,' she says unevenly.

'It is less rehearsed.'

'I should go.'

'If you want to go, then go.'

'It's not possible for me to stay,' she stammers. 'You know I'm married, I'm—I've been mistaken. I'm sorry. You won't see me again.'

Valentin bends his head to hers. He tugs at her shawl, and it falls away. She is exposed now to the frigid air. She realises her own hands are reaching up to touch his face, to meet around his neck. It feels exactly as it does in her daydreams. Nobody has ever mentioned that. She almost wants to say so, but only to slow down this moment, to bask, to bathe, to drown in it. Valentin kisses the curve of her brow bone and it burns, worse than the cold.

CHAPTER THREE

Rosie

Moscow, July 1991

DEEP WITHIN A BIRCH FOREST, A ROAD RUNS THROUGH like a scar. Along this road is a young traveller, but she is trapped behind a panel of glass. She can't reach out to touch the supple white trunks of the trees, all aglow in the afternoon sun. She can't feel the wind that breathes across the leaves, that slips between the branches. Instead she presses her face up to the glass and uses her finger to trace the shape of everything she sees.

It sounds like the opening of one of Mum's fairy tales.

But that traveller is only me, and the glass is only the tinted window of the black Mercedes that met me and Alexey at Sheremetyevo airport.

'It won't be long now,' says Alexey.

The birch forest fades as we approach Moscow proper. Decaying tenements and Stalinist architecture spring up on all sides while the traffic builds, slows to a trickle. Our driver, who's on loan to Alexey Ivanov from the government, curses as he changes lanes.

'How are you doing back there?' asks Alexey, glancing over at me.

I smile uneasily. It is sweltering. My shoes have congealed around my feet. I haven't slept in almost a full day, and I'm ravenous. I wish I'd accepted his offer of a snack at the airport, even if all they had were shrivelled sandwiches, reminiscent of the ones Mum used to make for me. She'd slap on the mayonnaise between voracious swigs of vodka: *Thwack. Thwack-thwack.* Even now I can see the mayonnaise flying, hear the pickle slices screaming, taste the vodka in the bread.

'Doing great,' I say.

The driver brakes hard, and my handbag tumbles off my lap.

Alexey taps on his window. 'We're here, Rosie.'

I look up until I can't put my head back any further. The building in front of us is a *khrushchyovka*, one of the dreary apartment complexes built up during the Khrushchev era. Made of off-white concrete, with square windows, it could pass for some kind of urban sanatorium. This can't be right. We're supposed to stay at Alexey's erstwhile home, somewhere I imagined would be dignified and stately, just like him. It would have a smear of Imperial-era glory, of Mum's fairy-tale universe. Like him.

Not this. I grew up in this.

I step out of the car, blinking in the glare of sunlight. I test the pavement. Solid ground. I am back in Moscow. Throughout our journey here I'd hoped, feared, that I would return to my home town and feel *different*. I would instantly reclaim the sense of continuity that comes naturally to most people, because they live their lives as a single thread. Winding and curling perhaps, but smooth and uninterrupted.

But I still have no such sense. For me, there is one thread that starts the day I was born in this city and stretches until one humid summer night in 1977. There is the other that begins the moment Mum and I touched down at Heathrow and stretches until now. And I've never been able to tie the two together.

The driver and I wait for Alexey by the pavement, beneath a peeling sign for a post office. The driver has a sculpted, serious face. He says nothing. His close-cut hairstyle suggests the military or prison time, places where people learn to say nothing. The silence has become almost unbearable. Beads of sweat pop up along my hairline and pool beneath my ponytail. Everything around us smoulders in the visible heat.

'My keys still work!' Alexey's voice. 'Come on!'

I turn away. We loop around the side of the building and approach a half-hidden blue door, choked by weeds. Alexey gestures for us to enter behind him and pulls the door shut, plunging us into darkness.

'Ready?' he says.

There's a flood of harsh light. The long fluorescent tube attached to the low ceiling throws our surroundings into sharp relief: The nasty, narrow stairwell, the shrieking graffiti, the driver's expressionless face. A layer of dust resettles over the ground.

'There's no lift,' says Alexey. 'But it's only a few storeys up.'

I hear myself laugh. It sounds like a gasp. The driver proceeds up the stairs behind Alexey, bags hoisted onto his shoulders. I look down at my holdall, at my fingers around the handle, already white from squeezing too hard. I follow them up the stairs, telling myself I'll catch my breath once we go in, but when I reach the landing and Alexey fiddles with the keys and the door grinds open, I realise that there isn't anything to breathe.

No air, no wind, *nothing*, has disturbed his apartment in all these years.

Alexey opens the first door we see to reveal the kitchen, the shoebox of a fridge, the used plates and mugs on a small table. Dead flies on the sills. Further down the central hallway there is one bedroom and two separate rooms for the bath and the toilet. The toilet has no seat. In the living room, the furniture is buried beneath piles of books, correspondence, film reels, paint cans, and *Pravda*.

All the lights seem to be working, but there isn't a single lampshade in sight.

I hover in the living room by the door to the balcony, feeling an unexpected stab of panic. The driver comes up beside me and places my suitcase on a mound of what could well be the sofa. It is backed against the wall, trapped by the mess. I mumble my thanks and step out onto the balcony, but I can't breathe that well out here either. The air smells dirty, asphalted, like car fumes. Like all big cities.

So why is there a disorienting note of freshness, the pulpy fragrance of a new book?

Zoya.

It is her first visit to me since Yorkshire, and I know immediately what she wants me to remember: I was twelve, maybe thirteen years old. Mum was putting me to bed and lighting another of her candles to read by. I told her that the candles reeked and, worse, they were a fire hazard. Everything's a fire hazard in England, Mum moaned; but she acquiesced. She showed me what she'd bought that day, a copy of Tolstoy's *War and Peace* in the original Russian, and went straight to her favourite passages, including General Kutuzov's advice to Prince Andrei:

There is nothing stronger than those two warriors, patience and time; they will do everything . . .

I didn't hear her at first. I was in my bed, duvet pulled up to my nose, staring up at the ceiling, counting cracks. *One, two. One, two.* Mum repeated herself and suddenly, it registered.

'Rosie?' Alexey's voice, from within.

It's been fourteen years. Patience and time.

To celebrate his first night in Moscow, his victorious return to the land that banished him, Alexey invites both me and his driver to dinner at an upscale restaurant. While the hostess makes an embarrassing fuss over us, I squint at the tapestry mounted behind the driver's chair. It is one of many that adorn the walls. Knights on horseback, weeping maidens, large predatory birds. Fiery scenes. Bold colours.

The hostess sashays away, drawing the driver's attention with her.

'Does she know who you are?' I ask Alexey.

'People assume we have money,' he says. 'We look foreign.'

If this restaurant is Russia, then I have always been foreign. My gaze wanders to a high pillar upon which a marble bust of a man's head has been placed. The faces of most people in here look just like the bust. Wan, bloated, male. Wealthy. Nobody else eats at a place like this. I turn to the raised platform not far from our table, where a floppy-haired youth sits on a stool with an acoustic guitar, crooning away. He sounds like a fur seal.

'Is he the son of the owner?' I ask.

The driver smirks.

'It's been years, but I used to play,' muses Alexey. 'I should ask for a turn.'

He's having us on. He's going to steal the spotlight, right here in the middle of our meal? He's going to sing with a set of century-old lungs, strum with fingers that were once frostbitten to the bone?

'Don't think I can?' He turns to the driver. 'What do you think, eh?'

The driver finally cracks a smile. Alexey rises from his chair. He winds between the tables, finding his way in the modest light to the platform. The guitarist pauses to hear what Alexey has to say, then he scrambles off the stool, offering his instrument as penance, backing away, disappearing by instinct into the shadows. Alexey looks at me and winks. Then he tries out a few chords, strums for a moment or two.

Already the restaurant is going quiet.

'*I wanted to speak, only she had the words . . .*'

I don't know how he does it. We are sitting in the same silence of that lecture hall in London last month. It seems to follow him everywhere he goes.

59

'*And if I was too weak, then she was the earth . . .*'

His expression is casual, contemplative, but there's a distant note in his eyes. He isn't playing for this audience, or any audience. He's playing for someone else, across time and space, across memory itself.

But for whom? Kukolka?

Behind me, the driver makes a sound. I whip my head around. He's fishing in his glass of water for the ice cubes, which he extracts and deposits into his serviette. He's an attractive bloke, dreamy even, but in a sort of hardened, unhappy way. The way of people who have seen and done things they don't talk about.

He senses my stare and meets it.

'How long have you been a driver?' I ask.

'I'm not.'

'I thought Alexey said—'

'He asked for someone for you.' The driver amends this. 'To help you.'

'I don't understand. I'm—'

'You're his employee this summer, no?'

'Um—'

'Alexey Ivanov will be away a lot,' he says, stringing together his longest sentence thus far. 'He was worried about your security. A young girl. Alone in Moscow. With poor Russian.'

'My Russian's not *poor*, it's *rusty*,' I say defensively. 'I'm a native speaker. And I'm twenty-four. I don't need a childminder.'

He shrugs.

'You mean to say you're my bodyguard? Is that what you do professionally?'

'No,' he replies, stone-faced. 'It is not.'

He wants me to stop talking. Stop asking questions. I pin my gaze back on the tapestry. There's a prickle along my arms. This restaurant has air conditioning *and* ice water. Two things I've never encountered in Moscow before.

I *want* to stop asking questions. I *want* not to have to sit here, drenched in a cold sweat, but if I go back to England now, it'll be the same as it always has. This is the only way to stop thinking about *that man* and how he killed Zoya and Papa, in less than the time it took for me to run from the bedroom I shared with Zoya into the living room. How *that man* looked right at me, with his slate-grey eyes, and I believed that he was going to kill me too, but he didn't. He just left me standing there, in a widening pool of blood.

The tangy aroma of it filled the whole room, filled my lungs to capacity. I've never breathed it out.

It's only when we're back at the apartment that Alexey informs me and the driver, whose name is Lev, of the sleeping arrangements. I had assumed Lev would go home for the night, but apparently part of his job description is to live here. Alexey assigns me the roll-out sofa, which he claims is more comfortable, while Lev can take the cot by the living-room door. I'm so knackered that I start laughing. This is what he meant by sorting the housing?

Lev looks over at me, his eyes narrowed, and offers to sleep outside, but I can't banish anyone into that cheerless hallway.

So, after a late-night tea, I am in bed, if this sofa can be called a bed, lying rigid as a plank, with a complete stranger

61

only yards away. He's so silent that I could easily forget he's there, but I can already hear the whisper of insomnia in my ear.

It can make you feel like you'll never sleep again.

I lean over to turn on the lamp.

'You need something?' asks Lev.

Maybe he can't sleep either. The light flickers as I rummage through my bag. 'No, nothing. Oh – before I forget, I know Alexey's said he'll be out of town Saturday.' Where *are* those bloody sleeping pills? 'I also need to make a quick trip. Just out of Moscow. There's no reason for you to come. You can have the day off.'

'I'll drive you.'

'That's not what I meant. I can take a taxi.'

'Why waste the money,' he says. It's not a question.

The lamplight dies. The driver gets out of the cot and switches on the overhead light. Half past midnight, according to my wristwatch. *Tick. Tock. Tick.* The pills are in hand. I'm about to tell him he can turn it off again when something begins to bloom in the air.

The briny smell of the Black Sea.

The Black Sea at Sochi is the only place my parents ever took me and Zoya on a family holiday. Papa liked to tell us how the water of the Sea is unusually oxygen deficient. Almost nothing can live down there. But almost nothing decomposes, either. Buried treasure. Shipwrecks. Bodies.

No one survives but the dead.

Zoya.

Twice in the same day. This has never happened before.

In Sochi, Zoya and Mum would always collapse in the hotel bed after a day on the beach. Once, over the sound of

62

their snoring, Papa dug out his textbooks and said to me: *Look, Raisa, how would you approach this problem? And what about this one?* I was only five, six years old maybe, and I retorted that I didn't want to do maths, not *again*. I wanted to be snoring too. Why didn't he make Zoya do this? And weren't we supposed to be on holiday?

I don't want to be like you when I grow up, Papa!

There are the people who only see the surface, Papa said. *And then there are the people who can see beneath. You know how beautiful it is when it's just snowed, back home?*

So what, I replied, petulantly.

The snow is only a cover, Raisochka. It hides the dirt, the pavement, the rats, the rot. It hides the bodies, the gravestones, the history, all the things people must pretend do not exist, so that they can live. Every time you look at snow from now on, you remind yourself: there's something else there. Something I cannot see.

But, Papa . . .

You've got the knack for this, he said. *Just not the discipline. That is where I come in. I'm going to show you something else, now. It's a puzzle. A cipher. And you are going to break it.*

To go beneath.

'You should get some sleep.'

The memory splinters. Lev says it again, bluntly. I've dropped the pills back into my bag. I need them even more now, to blot out these images, to stop Zoya. Impatiently I dump the contents out on my lap. Passport. Wallet. A few loose coins. A scrunchie.

Mum's notebook.

It's open just a hair, to that first, unnerving page: *A Note for the Reader*. I pick it up, intending to put it away safely, but the feeble light in this room somehow brings out the writing within. I hesitate. At worst, one of her stories would be a distraction; at best, it might actually help to lull me to sleep. Mum always meant them as bedtime stories. They used to be bedtime stories. Before the drinking.

I did promise her.

'Would you do me a bit of a weird favour?' I ask.

'What?' says Lev, unmoved.

'Would you read one of these stories to me? They were written by my mother. They're quite short.'

He shifts his focus to the notebook. 'You can't *read* Russian?'

'I haven't used cursive since I was a kid.' I stand up, reach it out to him. 'The first page took me an hour.'

'Fine. Why not.' Lev takes it and opens the cover. '"These stories should not be read in order",' he recites, impassively. 'Should I start with the first one?'

'It doesn't—' I stop short. 'Let's just do what it says.'

THE WEDDING VEIL

In a faraway kingdom, in a long-ago land, a girl wore a wedding veil so thick that she wasn't able to see the man she was marrying. The wedding was pretty. There were feasts and songs and a crown was raised over her head. The couple were feted with bread and salt, and the girl's single plait was undone. Everything was coming undone. People she didn't know fussed and clucked about her, and she was taken everywhere: from the bathhouse to her bedroom and then to the church, but still she couldn't see what she had married.

Until it was too late.

CHAPTER FOUR

Antonina
Petrograd, St Petersburg, summer 1916

DMITRY IS PRESENT FOR TEA TODAY. HE EVEN SITS IN a chair beside her, instead of remaining at the escritoire. He smiles, a smile that blends in with the silver-blue wallpaper; Tonya cannot really tell which way it is going.

'I'm neglecting you, my Tonyechka,' he says. 'I was away so much. And now I am here, the board is keeping me busy something terrible. There's strife at the factory. There may even be a strike.'

'I've heard that the Bolshevik and Menshevik factions are at odds,' Tonya says, absently.

He gives her an odd look. 'I didn't realise you were so *au fait*, my dear.'

'I only know from Kirov's wife,' she says, referring to the brazenly political spouse of one of Dmitry's acquaintances, holding her breath through the lie.

'Well, she's right.' Dmitry sounds weary. 'Much of the trouble comes from the new Bolshevik Committee of the Vyborg. Their leader is one of mine, in fact. He's well spoken and good-looking. People flock to him without even understanding the politics he espouses.'

'Fascinating,' Tonya says, as she lifts her cup and tries to bury her face in it.

'How do you pass your time nowadays?'

Tonya has grown concerned, of late, that Dmitry will begin to sense Valentin on her. As if her lover is a soap with which she has scrubbed herself, all over her skin, deeper even. But it seems she needn't have worried. Her husband doesn't know her enough to see if she's changed, and he certainly hasn't. The chauffeur still takes Dmitry down to the neighbourhoods where the girls have blanched foreheads and rouged cheeks, rag-doll hair, rag-doll limbs.

Or at least they do after he is finished with them.

'Reading, as always,' she replies.

'You're looking a bit tired, purple beneath the eyes,' he says. 'It bothers me. You should use rice powder on them tomorrow.'

'If you like.'

'It's those nightmares, isn't it? My poor girl.' Dmitry leans over and runs his hand through her hair, makes yet another comment about how much he likes it like this, loose and unplaited, tumbling freely. *Beautiful*, he says, *like waves*. Right now it feels more like rope. Like a hangman's noose.

At five in the morning, the steps leading down to Valentin's cellar room are bathed sweetly in light. The famous White Nights have arrived. Though the skies are lovely, beneath them Tonya feels unpleasantly exposed. She knocks in a hurry, her heart pounding against her ribs. They have not agreed in advance to meet today, and it's possible that Valentin is not home, or even that he is with somebody else. There must be other women in his life, for he has mentioned both in speeches and in passing that people cannot belong to other people. The same as with land or livestock or material goods—

'Tonya?' he says, sounding surprised, as he opens the door.

'Have I woken you?' she asks.

'I was working on a speech.' Valentin is shirtless, holding a cigarette. She sees him through the spiral of smoke, his bare skin, the lean muscle of his torso, which she has never really *beheld* before, in all their stolen moments together. Only felt with her hands. Her mouth feels dry, but of course this cellar is airless and grotty, even without any smoke.

'I was just out walking,' she says, to explain herself. 'And I thought—'

'Come in,' he says. His smile is easy. 'I can practise on you.'

She follows him inside. The room is tragically small and dark, made smaller still by a partitioning of plywood down the middle. Friends of his often need a place to stay.

To hide from the Okhrana, the Tsar's secret police.

Not even the White Nights can penetrate underground. But the dimness is comforting, makes it easier to surrender as he pulls her close to kiss her. It is slow and quiet. His hands linger by her waist, by the small of her back, and she feels the tickle of a blush. She has never fully undressed in

68

front of him. They have rarely even come indoors. Valentin touches her idly, her face, her cheeks, her lips, and her skin seethes.

He takes her hand, turns it so her palm faces him, and runs his thumb over her wrist. It is so light, so airy, that she scarcely notices as he rolls her sleeve up further.

'How did you get these?' he asks.

'What?'

'Your scars.'

She pulls away. 'I don't know. I was born with them.'

'You have the same all over your legs,' he comments, offhand. 'At first I thought perhaps a burn, or a childhood disease. But I've seen many such scars. These are different.'

'I told you, I don't know.'

He wants to ask more, but he won't. She can tell just by the rawness of his gaze, same as when they see one another on the streets, over the heads of so many strangers. They can speak without speaking. She had never known this to be possible.

'There's a reading circle tonight, at a friend's apartment,' says Valentin, after a short silence. 'Why don't you come with me?'

'But the risk. If someone recognises me—'

'They won't.'

Tonya tries to smile. It's likely somebody will. It's her unusual appearance that is to blame. Everyone in Popovka, the villagers, her friends, even her own family, had a nickname for her: Kukolka. It was not spoken with affection. There's got to be something wrong with a girl who looks like that, something *unseen*, people would say,

69

behind her back, just loud enough to be heard. Maybe Tonya's own father believed it too, for Papa was always so eager for her to marry, to be taken away from Otrada.

To be sold.

But people cannot belong to other people.

'I trust my friends with my life,' says Valentin, as if he hears her thoughts.

'Yes,' she says, shocking herself. 'I'll come.'

A handkerchief that Tonya has never seen before is laid out on her mother-in-law's bedside table. So delicate it is almost ghostly, it is threaded with gold, beaded with pearl, and around the edges is a raised, intricate design of pale blue flowers. Anastasia catches her looking and proffers it with one limp hand. Tonya holds it by a corner, reverently, wistfully.

'It's yours if you want it,' says Anastasia.

Mesmerised, Tonya weaves it through her fingers. It is soft as snakeskin.

'Are we continuing with *Marxism and the National Question* today, child?'

Tonya looks up. 'If you find it dull, Anastasia Sergeyevna, I am happy to—'

'Not in the least. We read a lot of political material these days, but I am glad that you've found something to care about.' Anastasia smiles with the half of her mouth that still works. 'The people's cause is worthy. When I could, you know, I always tried to better the lives of those below me. But you must ease Mitya into it. My son means well. It's been difficult for him, the tensions with the workers, all the discord.'

Tonya tries to picture Dmitry *easing* into something. It does not work. He takes things crudely, by force. He does not show it, of course. Or rather, it does not show on him.

'Tonight, I . . .' she begins. 'There's an event I would like to attend. An evening of reading.'

Anastasia's eyes widen, even the bad one. 'Who is hosting?'

Tonya's face feels buttery with sweat. 'Kirov's wife.'

'Kirov the Catfish?'

'She often joins the women's marches. But if Dmitry were to ask—'

'I understand.' Anastasia reaches out, pats Tonya on the cheek. The touch of the old woman's hand is wispy, like the handkerchief. Anastasia is dissolving. Disappearing. 'I'll tell him you are on an errand for me, if he asks. Anything, little one, so that you are happy here.'

Valentin's friend lives on Zagorodny, not an unfashionable area. The building is new-looking, sleek as a ship and topped by a cupola. Inside, Valentin is waiting for her by the stairwell, slouched against the wall. He lifts his hand in greeting, but she is struck again by the difference in their stations, for even this empty, half-painted entryway is grand compared to the basement room where he lives. What would he think of the foyer of the house on the Fontanka? The marble staircase, the floors lushly carpeted, the mirrored walls? The glass cabinet of porcelains and ceramics? The chandelier of hand-cut crystal, the way it ripples, looks like water from below?

Tonya finds Anastasia's handkerchief in her reticule and dabs her cheeks with it.

'Shall we go up?' he suggests.

There is not very far up to go. Tonya wishes it were further and higher, but Valentin is already knocking on one of the doors. 'Vika?' he says, through the closed door. 'It's me.'

The person who opens up is a smiling young woman with a severe, scraped-back hairstyle and huge doe eyes, or perhaps the eyes are only the effect of the hair. 'Valya, hello,' she says, kissing Valentin once, twice, three times on the cheeks, before turning to Tonya. The smile turns slim, hanging by threads. 'And who is this? You didn't say you were bringing anyone.'

'This is Tonya,' he says. 'Tonya, meet Viktoria Pavlovna.'

'Vika will do,' says the stranger brightly. 'How nice to meet you. Valya has not said a thing about you.' She laughs. 'Well then, come in! I have slippers enough for everyone. Do you want . . . ?' Her gaze drops.

Tonya looks down too, searching for whatever mistake she has already made, and then she realises that Viktoria is staring at her reticule, her sterling-silver bag, engraved with birch branches. In the same hand she still clutches Anastasia's fancy, floaty handkerchief, the gold glinting obscenely against the drab background of everything around.

'Perhaps you would prefer to keep on your shoes,' says Viktoria.

'Vika,' says Valentin, an almost inaudible word.

'I will take the slippers,' says Tonya. 'You're very kind. I have also something for you, that is, as thanks for your hospitality, only a small—'

'Keep it,' says Viktoria, and this time there is no denying the coldness. 'There's no need for that here.'

A wooden folding table is brought out to what appears to be the main room of the apartment. A soup with a shaky mound of lard in the middle is passed around, and they share spoons. Gamely Tonya lifts a spoonful of soup to her mouth. It has a grainy texture that reminds her of bathwater. All around her there is heavy-handed political discussion; names and dates are flung back and forth like insults. In Dmitry's circles, people never speak of politics in these tones, and in Popovka, nobody knew how.

Tonya has picked up from the conversation that Viktoria is the daughter of the well-known writer Pavel Katenin, while Viktoria herself is a classical pianist. It is not just penniless workers who believe in the Bolshevik cause.

'Which writers do you enjoy most, Tonya?' Viktoria asks her, leaning over.

Tonya is about to answer honestly, but then she thinks of her copy of *Eugene Onegin*, with its stiff, starchy pages, its velvet-bound covers. Of course Valentin's friends do not read Pushkin for pleasure, as she does. She knows precisely what they read; she has tried her best to comprehend it. Marx. Chernyshevsky. Radishchev. Lenin. They must find Pushkin soppy, slobbery, romantic mush by comparison. Weaker than the soup.

'Will you not read to us tonight?' Viktoria presses, and Tonya realises she's not given any reply.

'I'm afraid I've never read to others before,' she says, flushing. 'We didn't have reading circles, back home. Though

73

people *would* tell stories around a table like this. Fairy tales and fables, mostly,' Tonya adds, seeing more heads turn her way. 'I am from the country. From Tula.'

'The country,' someone remarks, with the disdain of any of Dmitry's friends. The *country*. Like it is an infectious disease.

Tonya has the fleeting feeling that she may never belong anywhere.

'You must tell us one,' says Viktoria, pointedly.

Beneath the table, Tonya turns the beaded handkerchief in her hands. She has heard countless stories told around countless hearths. And over the past few months, she's begun to have a few half-formed story ideas of her own, silvery spiderweb strands, though she's yet to commit any to paper. Why *shouldn't* she tell a story? Why *not* try, in a setting like this, custom-made for such an endeavour? Expectant faces, sceptical strangers, a breathlessness in the air?

'In a faraway kingdom,' she says, relying on this well-worn phrase, 'in a long-ago land . . .'

As she speaks, she sees their faces change, but how she can't say.

'A princess lived in a palace by the sea, far from the city, far from the . . .'

Their silence is smothering, and in it, her mind is suddenly clear. What has she done, coming here? What has she hoped to prove, to herself, to Valentin? She is everything that these people despise most. Everything that they hope to destroy. She has upended their evening with her intrusion, her ignorance, her country-ness. Too humiliated to continue, Tonya stands up, her chair scraping. She brushes away someone's question, another's concern, an offer for another drink, and she catches a toe on a chair leg as she breaks out of the room.

She halts just outside the door, breathing hard, trying to regain her composure.

Let her go, she hears someone say, Viktoria maybe. *Why would you bring someone like her, Valya? Who's next, one of the grand duchesses?*

Someone like her.

The words are chilling. Tonya grips the splintery wooden rail of the stairs as she goes, confused by how badly she feels.

Valentin catches up to her downstairs.

'It's getting late,' she says, her hand already on the door. 'I'm tired.'

'Too tired to say goodbye?'

Outside, the night sky is bright and glowing. There is no cover in this city, nowhere to hide. Tonya looks back and forth at the intersection of traffic, still busy with late-night revellers. Valentin stays a distance away from her, and she resents him, resents him because before it was only imaginary, and now she *knows* what it is like to be with him, knows what it is like to be the one he looks for, in those crowds.

How will she be content with fantasies now?

'I didn't know you told stories,' he ventures.

'I don't,' she replies, curtly. 'As you could see.'

'My friends were rude to you.' He hesitates. 'I'm sorry. They are wary of strangers.'

'Have you never taken anyone along to meet them before?' She regrets the question at once. It is bourgeois of her to ask this. Possessive. Base. Tonya herself is married, and no matter how Valentin may speak of the future in his speeches, there is no future for the two of them.

'No,' he says simply. 'Come, *milaya*, I'll walk you home.'

When their love affair first began, they were meeting only once a week, and they would depart together, surreptitiously, from the Liteyny Bridge. Only by the stairs leading down to his room would he turn to her, that smile of his balanced on his perfect lips. But soon they were meeting twice a week, and soon after that every other day, and by now they no longer even arrive at those slippery steps. It has been nearly half a year. Nowadays Valentin pulls her down some back alley, some lonesome byway, and his hands find her garter and he whispers against her hair and she buries her cries in his shoulder. Afterwards she has to shake off her skirts and ravel her shawl like a ribbon.

Sometimes, as she's walking home on wobbly legs, Tonya remembers Mama's cautionary tales, about boys like him, about girls like her. Of the diseases, pregnancy, broken hearts, tears, bitterness, but most of all—

Imagine that you are a pair of white gloves, Mama would say, pulling one of her gloves between her hands, too far apart. *Any stain that falls on you becomes part of the fabric. No matter how much you wash, you will never be pure white again. And if the stain seems to fade on its own, it's because it's sunk into the thread; because it's gone even deeper.*

CHAPTER FIVE

Rosie

Moscow, July 1991

I STAND AT THE RAIL OF ALEXEY'S BALCONY. THE NIGHT IS warm and sultry, and the dazzling spray of stars reminds me of the time Mum took me to watch a Guy Fawkes celebration by the Thames. She was holding a bottle of something as pungent as insecticide; back then I didn't know what it was. She was smiling a lot. Too much. It hurt to look at her, so I looked up instead. The fireworks lasted for some half an hour, and then they stopped, and when they did, it was like I was seeing darkness for the very first time.

So that's what's been here all along.

Now Mum's stopped.

What's been here all along?

The gas meter and the geyser are broken. I pay a visit to the landlady and she says that a frozen pipe burst last winter, but that she's in the midst of getting everything fixed. She looks shiftily away from me and I can't help thinking that this place is disintegrating on every possible level: the apartment, the building, the country.

When I get back to the apartment, I find Alexey humming to himself as he adds a dollop of jam to his tea. His glass sits in a nickel-plated holder, the kind I have not seen since leaving Russia. He swirls the liquid with his spoon.

'Did you see the reading list I left for you?' he asks. 'Most of those books should be here somewhere.'

'Should I get started right away?'

'Not quite yet.' More swirling. 'First, I've had Lev unearth my old map box. You're looking for a village called Popovka, in Tula, and I'm telling you now, it's not the Popovka in Aleksinsky District. It's a different one, much smaller. It might not even be on any of my maps – in which case I'll send you to the state archives.'

'No problem,' I say, curiously. 'And what should I do once I—?'

'Kukolka was born at a nearby estate called Otrada,' he continues. 'It would be worth making the trip, to see if anyone's left who knows anything.'

I pour my own cup of tea. When is Alexey going to tell me who Kukolka really is? For someone whose entire life has been about describing the indescribable, about revealing the unimaginable, he's a bit *cagey*, isn't he? Oh, and now the milk's gone off. I've poured too much already, and the tea is covered with ropy white strands.

'Sod it,' I say, under my breath, and I dump it out in the sink.

Does anything work in this bloody country?

Alexey catches my eye and smiles. 'It'll start to hurt,' he says, 'coming home. Because you meet your old self when you do. And the one has to kill the other.'

A group of young men in grey-blue camouflage fatigues are gathered in front of the GUM department store in Red Square, leaning casually, gracefully, against its archways. They talk in low voices, occasionally pausing to eyeball passers-by. They have small metal badges pinned to their chest pockets and oval-shaped patches with a yellow insignia on their sleeves. Alexey's driver is the only one in civilian clothing, but he doesn't stand out. Whoever he is now, he used to be one of *them*.

Military? Some kind of police?

He peels away from the others. 'You said ten,' he says as a greeting.

'I'm sorry. I missed the metro stop.'

'It's some distance to the car.'

'I really appreciate this,' I say.

We walk without talking. I feel lopsided from staring up at the coloured domes of St Basil's Cathedral and have to double my pace to keep with his. To calm my nerves, I dip my hand into my bag and find a solid shape, the curve of small feet, the sandy feel of artificial hair. The only doll that isn't part of Mum's collection. The doll that has been in the dark as long as I have.

Lev doesn't say much in the car either. He pushes the Mercedes hard, the tyres squealing as he changes gears.

'I was born here,' I offer. 'I just haven't been back for years.'

He nods to indicate he's heard me.

'I answered an advert Alexey posted at my university.' I let my bag drop between my feet. The weight of it settles against one ankle. 'Have you read any of his work?'

'The Last Bolshevik.'

'I went to a reading he gave. It took my breath away.'

'I didn't like it,' says Lev.

'Oh. Is it really a question of liking? It is a memoir.'

'It's well written,' he concedes. 'But too careful. There is something missing. I think he left things out, things that didn't fit.'

'Maybe he had to. For it to make sense.'

Lev shrugs. 'OK.'

'Well, my mother didn't like it either,' I say. 'Someone gave her a copy once. She actually burnt it, page by page. By candle flame, of all things.'

'Really?' he says, and I feel encouraged.

'I think she had this idea that he was making Russia look bad. She was quite a patriot, always getting upset when people criticised the government. It's ironic, because we ended up moving to—'

Mamulya.

Zoya.

Mamulya.

It is unmistakably my sister's voice – but she has never spoken to me before. Not once. All I can think of, though, is that I don't consider our mother to be 'Mamulya' any more. Mamulya was beautiful, soft, fluttery, with a youthful, lilting voice. Mum sounded like whatever was destroying her liver was crawling up her trachea. Mamulya would pirouette in front of the mirror every morning, checking every angle. Mum had no angles any more, in that shapeless nightgown that eventually became her second skin.

Mamulya died fourteen years ago. Mum died in June.

'Moving to?' says Lev.

'Sorry. I just . . . I heard . . .' Nothing comes to mind but the truth. 'I'm being haunted.'

'Haunted,' he says.

'By the ghost of my sister.'

Lev looks at me for the first time on this drive, his eyes solemn, like a fox's. 'How did she die?'

My confession is still echoing in my head: *I'm being haunted.* I've never told anyone, not even Richard. How could I explain that I just knew it was Zoya, from the very first time she made me smell something? Smells; now voices. Richard would think I'm having some kind of psychotic break.

Maybe I am.

'She was shot. Point-blank,' I say.

Our fledgling conversation cannot sustain this final blow. He lets it lie and I hunker down in my seat. *I'm being haunted.* I wonder if I've even said it to myself, before. I give directions to Lev. This way. That way. *I'm being haunted.*

The words don't go away, not even as we reach the section of the double-lane Rublyovskoe Highway that zips together what looks like large swathes of forest. This area is riddled with the homes of Moscow's most powerful and influential people – and people who like to live behind high walls. As we turn off the highway, we start to see a few of those walls crop up.

Lev glances at me as he pulls out a new cigarette. He knows that we're not supposed to be here.

'It's that house,' I say, pointing to a towering gate and the soldier standing in front of it, holding an assault rifle. As our car draws in close the soldier motions for Lev to pull over. A patchwork of red and white can now be seen through the black bars of the gate. I remember a three-storey brick house with elaborate window detail from my first visit. At the time, I kept my eye on that window detail, told myself not to look anywhere else.

Lev rolls down the driver's window.

'What are you, lost?' demands the soldier.

I lean over. 'I'm here to see Ivan Vasiliev.'

He scowls. 'The colonel knows you're coming?'

'Tell him it's Raisa Simonova.'

The soldier pulls out a two-way radio and barks into it. The radio rumbles in reply, and then, with a harassed grunt, he begins to open the gate. Lev eases the Mercedes through, pulling up alongside a fleet of black BMWs. He drums his fingers on the steering wheel. He hasn't lit the cigarette.

'I thought your name was Rosie,' he says. 'And why are we here?'

'It is Rosie. But you can use Raisa, if you like it better,' I say, because I can't answer the other question.

'Do *you* like it better?'

I don't have an answer to that either.

As I'm unclipping my seat belt, I see a lone figure making his way along the house's wrap-around white porch. Down the stairs now, towards our car, towards me. He's as small and slim as I remember from childhood, and he still exudes an aura of terrifying power. He doesn't need the gate or the armed guard or the bulletproof German vehicles to seem invulnerable.

This is the kind of power that people might literally die for, and he's just spilling it behind him as he walks, like a petrol leak. As he approaches, I can see the dark, raccoon-like circles around his eyes.

Ivan Vasiliev. The man who got me and Mum out of Russia; who saved us. Or at least that's how it felt at the time.

In his study, the colonel seats himself behind a large desk and puts on his eyeglasses. Lev has been made to wait out in the living room.

'I'm glad you've come,' Colonel Vasiliev begins. He doesn't sound it. 'There's an important matter you and I must discuss. Are you in Moscow long? Where are you staying?'

'For the summer. I can give you my information. I've come to ask a favour,' I say in a rush, before I lose my nerve. 'I'm looking for Eduard Dayneko.'

'Eduard—' The colonel pulls up short. 'No. No, Raisa. I won't help you find that man.'

I'm almost relieved to hear the colonel say *that man*, like it's *that man* to him, and to everyone. Like it's normal, that I think about this person every day, like it's fine, that I never sleep a whole night through, like it's OK, being haunted by a dead sister.

'He left something behind,' I say.

In 1977, Eduard Dayneko was a well-known hitman for a burgeoning criminal organisation. He'd been in and out of prison for years. He'd been spotted earlier in the day in our

83

neighbourhood, and the lady who let him into our building later picked him out from a series of mugshots. Indeed, identifying him was never the problem. The problem was that the police seemed to hold him in unreservedly high regard. They spoke of him as if we'd been graced with a rare sighting of a god, as if he'd taken human form for just that one night, to commit those murders.

I still don't believe they wanted to catch him.

Ivan Vasiliev was the one who created that god, or at least taught him to kill. In his youth, Dayneko had been the colonel's gifted protégé. He'd been trained as a sniper in the GRU Spetsnaz, the Special Forces. Vasiliev posted him all over the map before letting him slip into the clutches of a criminal *bratva*.

I know the colonel still feels responsible for what happened. I try not to hold him responsible. I try to think it isn't his fault any more than it is mine, just because I didn't enter the living room earlier, or do something differently.

Just because I survived.

Vasiliev is looking unconvinced, so I try again. 'That night. Dayneko saw me and he left something.'

He sighs. 'Why didn't you tell the police? Or me, when I approached you and your mother?'

'I didn't trust the police not to destroy it.' I reach for my bag. 'But most of all, I guess, I didn't want my mother to take it away. She has, she had, this thing about dolls—'

'Dolls?'

I place it flat on his desk.

The colonel frowns. He picks up the half-a-foot-long toy and pulls at one strand of the golden mohair, which curls sharply around his finger. He examines the painted rainbow-arch eyebrows, the lacquered sheen of the porcelain, the brocaded white dress hiding the booted feet. The doll's hands are bare, stretched too far, as if it wants to be held.

It has never been held. I've been keeping it in a box for a decade and a half.

'So you will chase a professional assassin around Moscow, just because of this thing,' says Vasiliev, untwisting his finger from the grotesque grasp of the doll's hair.

'If Dayneko wanted to kill me, he would have done it that night, but he didn't. It was different than all his other jobs. You said yourself that the motive had to be personal, that he was after us, that he'd never stop coming after us. That nobody knew why. Well, I know it had to do with my mother! He knew her – he left this for her. I just want to understand, that's all. Why he did what he did.'

'How do you know it was for Katya? Why would he leave her a *doll*?'

'She had a collection of dolls just like these!'

'Why didn't you just ask her, Raisa?' Ivan Vasiliev plants the doll face down on his desk. He might be a colonel in the Soviet Armed Forces, he might have fought guerrilla rebels in Afghanistan, he might know how to go a week without sleep and walk with his boots on backwards to leave a false trail. But even he is no match for a child's plaything whose dead eyes never break contact.

'I tried. She refused to talk about that night. She pretended it never happened.' I push the doll back into my bag. 'And now she's dead. She died last month of liver disease.'

'I am aware,' says Vasiliev, in a measured tone. 'And very sorry. But I still don't see—'

'*You* told us that we had to leave Moscow. You told us that we had to be different people. Well, it worked. My mother became so different that I didn't even know her.'

And me, is what I want to add, but don't. Can't you see what's happened to me? I became this.

Ivan Vasiliev takes off his eyeglasses, sighs again. Behind him the window is half open, letting in a murmur of sound. The trebly chirp of summer crickets; the caterwaul of an animal; the stifled static of his soldiers' radios.

'You're not a child any more,' he says. 'It's your choice. I can tell you how to find him.'

Alexey's maps are stored in a birchwood trunk with a brass clasp. The maps are large and unwieldy. Disorganised, too, as much so as the rest of the apartment. As far as I can tell, there aren't any Popovkas besides the one Alexey mentioned.

Just how small *was* this village?

While Alexey is out at dinner with friends, Lev joins me on the floor. I spread out one of the remaining maps that include Moscow and Tula provinces and ask him to have a look, because my brain is swimming. He bends his head to read off the quaint, quintessentially Russian names of the towns that dot the area, and I catch myself studying him.

Attractive, very much so, in that unnerving way. A sliver of sunlight through the window falls across his face, and the effect is almost transfixing. Trying to look elsewhere, I notice a scar on his neck, along the hairline; thin, white and deep, it stands out more now that he's no longer clean-shaven.

'Combat knife,' he says.

My own neck feels hot. We stare at one another for a moment.

'Have you ever been to Tula?' I ask, awkwardly.

'To Yasnaya Polyana.'

Yasnaya Polyana. Leo Tolstoy's former home, now kept as a museum in his honour. My mother and father used to argue about making the trip out there. Mum worshipped Tolstoy, had read everything he ever wrote. Papa only ever wanted to take our one annual holiday to the Black Sea. He would not waste time looking at a dead man's dinner plates, he would say to Mum, before leaving for the secondary school where he taught, putting a real damper on the row.

I think Mum would have rather he heaved some of our own dinner plates at the wall to make his point, but my father was not that kind of person. He never shouted, never snapped. Mum had double the emotional charge of most people and he had none.

'What are you looking for?' asks Lev.

'Popovka, in Tula, but not the one in Aleksinsky,' I reply, pointing to the map. 'That would have been much too easy.'

'There is part of a map of Tula in your mother's notebook. It shows a different Popovka.'

'What?'

'It fell out while I was reading to you the other night,' he says, stretching his legs.

'My mother's never been to Tula,' I say blankly.

87

'People sometimes keep maps of places they've never been.'

Was that an attempt at humour? I look at him, but he's unreadable. Worse than Mum's cursive. 'Why didn't you show me?'

'You had just fallen asleep.'

I rise, scrambling a little, reaching for the bedside shelf I have made of the coffee table. The notebook is underneath several of the maps I've just gone through. I brush off the leather binding and blow across the cover. As I turn it upside down, experimentally, a page comes loose. Lev is right. It's an old map, with marked creases and serious browning, torn in a way that suggests it once belonged to an atlas.

Something feels tight in my chest, and I fold the map back up. 'It's weird. Alexey is looking for a place called Popovka but I can't find it on any of these other maps, and then this just happens to show the way?'

'Coincidence,' says Lev.

'I don't believe in coincidences. What, you don't think it's unlikely?'

He sits back, rubbing his neck. 'I think your work for the day is done.'

CHAPTER SIX

Antonina

Petrograd, St Petersburg, February 1917

IN THE ENTRY HALL OF THE HOUSE ON THE FONTANKA, beneath the twinkly, tiered chandelier, Tonya stops to stare at the cabinet that contains Dmitry's collection of Gzhel ceramics and Lomonosov porcelains. She presses a hand against her flat belly. Mama's warnings seem to float around her eyes, like black spots.

She has not bled since Christmas.

She knows what that means. She remembers the first time she ever bled, only months before she met Dmitry, the way Mama leapt upon the mess. The look on Mama's face was all bled out too. *You can have children now*, said Mama. Mama who lost so many babies over the years, or not quite babies. Stops and starts. Tightly bound bundles that had to be whisked away at midnight while the malevolent midwives whispered to themselves: *Lucky that it did not survive, sad mite . . .*

Tonya was the one who survived.

* * *

The weather is warm for February. It feels like a fever. The whole city has somehow, without explanation, without impetus, poured out of the houses and offices and cafes and restaurants and schools and museums, and onto the streets. Men, women, children, workers, shopkeepers, bankers, taxi drivers. There are police, and there must be secret police too, but they can do nothing. There have been plenty of political demonstrations this year, but something is different today. Something that sings.

She fights her way up the embankment to the Liteyny Bridge, only to see that protestors are swarming the length of the river. Streaming in from the Vyborg side, they spill onto the ice of the Neva, which cracks and creaks beneath their weight.

People of Russia, the skin of our city is on fire, and soon the body will know . . .

'Soldiers!' comes the shout.

Tonya turns and nearly trips. A mounted brigade of the Tsar's Cossacks is forming a half-moon by the bridge. A chunk of ice sails through the air with a shrill whistle. It lands a yard from her feet. Someone pushes her from behind and she falls forward, skids on her knees, crawls to standing. Ice and stones and sticks fly overhead. The Cossacks' horses are spitting froth, their ears pitched forward, their noses running.

A red ribbon lands on her shoulder, hooks into her hair. She tugs at it, and there is a sharp jag of pain as it comes away. Damp hands slide off her, rough clothing scrapes against her as she forces her way across the bridge, against the tide. On the Vyborg side she stumbles along the embankment, onwards until the protests fade to a distant murmur, but even here, on these tranquil side streets, she can tell that Petrograd is bursting at the seams. Hungry and heaving. Pulsating. Pulsing. *Alive*.

She swallows to stem her growing nausea.

Valentin's courtyard looks empty, but then she sees him emerging, stopping at the top of the cellar stairs. He calls out to her, but his voice is hoarse. His lips are pale. He looks as if he hasn't slept for days.

'Do you see what's happening?' he says, in a single breath. 'You must join the cause. Join us.'

Join him.

'You should sleep,' she says, going closer. 'You'll make yourself ill.'

'I can't rest. The people need me. And they would need you too.'

She laughs. 'You wouldn't want someone like me in the underground. I'd give in straightaway to the Okhrana.'

'You might last longer than you think,' he counters. 'Everyone has strength that they don't know exists, Tonya, until the moment comes. The right time and place.'

'Have you given this speech before?' she asks, trying to tease.

'Not this.' He reaches for her, kisses her on the forehead. Speaks against her skin. 'This is the very first time.'

It is teatime, even in the midst of citywide chaos, and the Countess Burzinova has come again to call.

Tonya entertains Natalya and Natalya's daughter, Akulina, in the Blue Salon. Akulina is eleven years old, skinny, mopey, often scratching at a fingernail, hiding behind her shock of red hair. It is only that hair that suggests she is related to Natalya at all.

Dmitry is out of the house. Tonya sits perched on the edge of her chair, doing her best to pay attention to the Countess. There is a layer of gunpowder hanging over the city so thick that she can taste it in her mouth, even in here. She nibbles at a slice of linseed cake, the only pastry they have left. She can't banish the taste. Where is Valentin now? What does he think, how does he feel, as people throw themselves against the sides of buildings, scurry across the intersections? Is he safe? Is he alive? Is he—

'Are you listening?' The Countess Burzinova is looking at her with one eyebrow raised, like a fish hook.

Tonya lowers her plate.

'I was saying what a scene it is out there,' remarks Natalya. 'Soldiers at all the intersections and machine guns in all the squares. Weren't you frightened, Lina?'

Her daughter gives something of a nod.

'What about you?' Natalya throws at Tonya. 'Have you been deterred from taking your morning walks?'

Tonya has to proceed cautiously here, as she would on the weary spring ice of the Fontanka. Natalya is too much a stranger to be trusted, and too close an acquaintance to be rebuffed. 'At times,' she says. 'But I never feel in danger.'

'Please, darling.'

Tonya licks her lips, does not respond. Akulina has bowed her head, as if in prayer. They are both children in the presence of the Countess.

Natalya dusts the crumbs off her fingers. 'You've been seen with Valentin Andreyev.'

'Valentin is a friend of mine.' Tonya keeps her voice bland. 'I admire him.'

'Admire,' says Natalya. 'What a word for it.'

Natalya knows.

A denial of wrongdoing springs to Tonya's lips, but no further. There is something delicious, delectable, about the truth. She has been with Valentin for over a year now. She was with him yesterday, and the day before that, and the day before that and before that. They are still careful, of course. She is always home by teatime. But she wonders now if she has been *waiting* to be discovered, for upon discovery, a choice must be made.

This life, or him.

This palace, or that cellar.

Royalty, or revolution.

Something turns, twists in her gut.

'I understand a certain infatuation. The boy turns heads.' Natalya makes a sound. A resigned laugh. 'Many of his past – let us call them admirers, as well – have donated handsomely to his cause.'

'I have not given him a kopeck,' says Tonya stoutly.

'Oh, darling, he doesn't love you. Men like him, they are in love with something greater, something more perfect, than any one person could be.'

'And if I love him?'

Natalya's smile widens, splits at the edges. 'So that's how it is.'

A sharp silence descends.

Tonya's hand on the plate is unsteady. The cake is sawdust in her mouth. Still she wills herself not to avert her eyes from the Countess; not to stand down.

'I will not let you hurt Dmitry. You will not see Valentin Andreyev again,' says the Countess softly. 'Never again. And in return, I will not bear any grudge against you. Fair is fair.'

Tonya waits by the cellar steps, toeing the dirty snow with her boots until they are streaky with it. The sky is shedding light. Valentin may not show up today at all, with everything that goes on now. She straightens, prepares for the walk home, and finds herself unable to take that first step.

Would she leave Dmitry to be with Valentin?

No. It cannot be. She and Valentin might want each other now, but what happens when the passion ebbs? When the shouting on the streets turns to normal conversation, when there is no longer any cause to set him on fire? Living in squalor, ageing too rapidly, they would both grow haggard and broken. Disillusioned and embittered. They would turn on one another. She would regret giving up so much to be with him. He would despise her for regretting.

'Tonya!'

She looks up, flinches at the happiness in his face. He knows none of her turmoil.

'I knew we would see this in our lifetime,' he says. 'I knew it.'

This is the way Valentin often speaks to her. *Our lifetime*, in the singular. As if it is already the two of them against all else.

'I have to get home,' she says. 'I should not have come at all.'

94

'Stay with me tonight, Tonya.'

Tonya feels something cramping up, seizing in her lower belly. He might invite her to stay, but for how long? Valentin is always in action, always on his way to something exciting and important. She pretends to understand his desire to overthrow the monarchy, to rebuild the world upon its ashes, or however he puts it in his speeches. She *wants* to believe what he believes, and there are times, when he is speaking to the crowd and his every word brings her to her knees, when she *almost* does.

But when she is alone, she knows she is no socialist. She is no revolutionary. She has no cause. She is only Kukolka, the little doll of her home and village. She has never stood for anything. She has never even stood on her own.

'I can't,' she whispers.

'Tomorrow then, *milaya*.'

She searches for something else to say, perhaps in jest, to lighten the mood between them, but none of this is light-hearted any more.

'Can I see you home?' he asks.

'You can come with me as far as the river,' she says. The Neva, the boundary between their worlds, his and hers. Their *world*, Valentin might say, but he is a Bolshevik. He is a dreamer.

In the bath, Tonya hugs her legs to her chest and sighs. Taking baths is one of the most indulgent luxuries of her marriage. At Otrada, as a child, Tonya would stand in a tub hardly larger than a bucket, sniffling, while one of the maids would dump creek-water over her head, with Mama looking on critically, silently. Now the tub is long-legged and made of silver, and the water is pleasant, soapy, scented with perfume.

Now the only person who keeps her company does not look her way at all.

Olenka comes from a village outside Petrograd and sends most of her money home. Sometimes Tonya feels a funny urge to say that *she*, Tonya, comes from a village. That *she*, too, is friendless in this town. But the lady's maid always turns away just in time.

It's surely for the best. The servants do love their gossip. That's how Tonya knows, for instance, that Olenka used to work in the textile mills, that there's enough fluff in the maid's lungs to make a full set of bedding. One day many years ago, as the story goes, Dmitry's mother happened to be visiting Olenka's workplace on a charitable mission. The hour was lonely enough for the girl's weepy cough to be discerned over the sound of grinding machinery. The kind-hearted Anastasia *rescued* Olenka, installed her as a servant in this very house.

That is what the Lulikovs do. They rescue people.

Tonya should treasure that beaded handkerchief, what will soon be the only remaining piece of her mother-in-law. But she realises now that she has not seen it for months. She has no idea where Anastasia's handkerchief has gone.

Its loss is a small thing, but somehow foreboding, and despite the comforts of the bath, to which Olenka will add new, warmer water at any moment, Tonya feels cold.

* * *

96

In the early morning the sound of volleys and machine guns is deafening. It rattles in her bones: *Rat-a-tat-tat! Rat-a-tat-tat!* Valentin halts to look down the embankment. He is close enough for Tonya to reach him, to touch him, but it often feels too hopeful to take his hand. As if they are facing the same way.

He once told the crowd that they will live two lives, but she is already living two lives.

'The police districts have all fallen,' says Valentin, turning to her. 'The courthouses are on fire. All that's left is for Nicholas to abdicate the throne. It's time to take a side.'

Tonya clutches at her shawl to keep the wind from tearing it away.

'You could go home and pack a case, meet me later,' he says. 'And never go back.'

He was never going to be satisfied with alleyways and ducked heads. She knows him well by now, and he does not do anything in the half-light. Valentin Andreyev believes in absolutes, in right and wrong. It is what separates the Bolshevik Party from the other revolutionaries, the Mensheviks, the Social Revolutionaries, the Anarchists. There will be no compromises.

His Bolsheviks will have all, or nothing.

'I am in love with you,' he says. 'Will you come? Will you take *my* side?'

There is no trace of uncertainty in his face. Whatever is overtaking the city, it has found them. It is between them, like a third party. It is unavoidable.

'I'm not like you,' she says, at half-volume. 'I don't have your strength of will—'

'Do you not feel the same about me?'

'I could never fight for anything, not as you—'

'Do you not,' he says, 'feel the same about me?'

Valentin has said often enough that people are wrong, that the real war is not with Germany, not with the Kaiser; the real war is within. Russia against herself. But he is wrong, too. It is *her*, Tonya, against herself. Maybe it has always been.

'I do,' she says faintly.

He lets his breath out slow. 'I'll be there tonight. By our bridge, from eight o'clock. I won't leave until you come.'

In the distance, the machine guns still fire: *Rat-a-tat-tat! Rat-a-tat-tat!* It is the music of revolution. Petrograd is collapsing around them. He kisses her, whispers: *Until tonight, Antonina.* He makes her feel grown-up, worldly even, but this is an illusion, because she is young. *Too young for a soul to know itself*, Mama would say. Never mind another's. Tonya slips her shawl over her face. Valentin is striding away. He turns to wave at her and she waves back, her insides rippling, her heart racing. She sees, in the street beyond, a serene line of the Tsar's Cossacks on horseback. Their lances gleam in the sunlight and their horses' tails dance in the wind.

When Tonya goes to check on Anastasia, she finds Olenka inexplicably present, standing motionless by the fireplace. The curtains are as firmly shut as always. They have made this place an early grave. The Lulikov matriarch is propped up against her pillows, her eyes going to glass. She sounds as consumptive as Olenka, every breath a labour.

'Shall I read to you today, Anastasia Sergeyevna?' Tonya asks, unsure.

'I wrote to my son, you know,' says Anastasia, her lips barely moving. 'I told him not to marry you. Especially without his own mother there to witness it.'

'I—'

'But when he brought you here, I saw how he was fixated. My Mitya is just like his father.' Anastasia's good eye blinks hard. 'I tried to make you feel welcome. How I've tried, and *this* is my reward!'

Tonya does not dare approach. Olenka is still standing by, hovering like a sandfly.

'Did the Countess Burzinova tell you?' Tonya says, dimly.

'She advised me to have Olenka follow you this morning. You have been indiscreet indeed, child. But it's obviously over now.' The words are brandished like rapiers. 'Shall we send your – this despicable person – some money, to make sure he leaves well enough alone? Write a letter, perhaps, to inform him of this development?'

'He won't take your money,' Tonya says, and before she can stop herself: 'I am going to him. I am leaving.'

She hardly believes she has said it, but she has, and now she cannot unsay it. Cannot undo it. She feels queasy, quite peculiar, but she's been feeling worse and worse recently. Her appetite has been wretched, though of course the offerings have been meagre. Shortages, as people say. The room spins, sparks a little. She has forgotten how quiet it can be when nobody speaks, when one cannot hear the gunfire from outside.

She starts again: 'I am leaving Dmitry.'

'Oh, my dear.' Anastasia's upper lip furls.

Tonya's cheekbones twinge with nausea. 'I am not coming back.'

'How dare you speak to me like this. Leave me at once!' thunders the old woman, with new fury. Her eyes appear to part company, the good one glaring at Tonya, the bad one shrinking away. 'Olenka, get this girl out of my—Tonya, what's the matter with you? Tonya!'

Tonya's field of vision begins to curl inwards. The world blackens. She is going to faint. She saw Mama faint many times, in the early months.

Pregnancy it is.

Tonya watches from the bed as the doctor rearranges the items in his vinyl-lined bag. Hollow tubes. A stethoscope. What appear to be devices of torture. There is a throb in her temple, but no feeling in her body. When she looks down at her hands, they might as well be someone else's. She thinks of asking if there is a way to confirm her pregnancy, or if there is something she should do or not, but Dmitry's presence at the foot of the bed silences her.

'What time is it now?' she asks thickly.

'Just past six,' Dmitry answers.

'Women are prone to such spells,' says the doctor. 'You must look after her,' he instructs Dmitry, with a tut.

Dmitry kisses Tonya's hand. His mouth on her skin is cold.

The doctor says to Dmitry that he will look in on Anastasia before he departs. He is as slow-moving as tar.

Tonya waits until the doors click shut behind the two men. Alone at last. She gets out of bed. Her slippers slap against the floor. There is no time to pack, to prepare. She will just have to go as she is.

She has chosen.

She knows what kind of father Dmitry would make. He would buy the most expensive pram in the city, would order bonnets and ribbons from Paris, handcrafted wooden toys from Germany, baby bath soap from England. She knows, because he pampers *her* in this very way, as if she is a statuette, one that he must take down from its shelf, and brush off daily. At teatime.

But he could also drop her at any moment. Crack her open.

She ties her hair back with a ribbon, wraps her thickest shawl around her neck. She pauses, listens, and then she moves the door handle. Again, and then once more. The shawl begins to feel tight, even sweaty. She braces her body against the frame and pulls, then pushes. If she were more familiar with curses, the classy kind that Dmitry uses when he reads the papers or the colourful kind that Valentin speaks right into her ear, she would try them now.

Instead she sinks to the floor and puts her head between her knees.

The door is locked.

Tonya sleeps only an hour or two during the night, but it is long enough for one of her nightmares. When she wakes up she is choking on her own saliva. She lights a candle and sees a smear in the sheets and thinks despairingly that this is it, this will be *her* sad, small bundle of almost-baby, but it doesn't come from between her legs. It comes from her arms. She tore into her own skin in slumber with her nails. She turns on her side and cries, and when she is fully conscious again, it is already morning.

Olenka enters with a tray and a newspaper. Tonya looks blearily at the headlines. Tsar Nicholas II has just abdicated the throne. The three-hundred-year dynasty of the Romanovs is ended. The people of Russia have been set free. Olenka curtseys, coughs, and goes out again, locking Tonya in.

CHAPTER SEVEN

Valentin
Petrograd, St Petersburg, March 1917

A S THE LIGHT BREAKS OVER THE RIVER, IT IS A MORNING unlike any other. The stone eagles of the Romanovs lie smashed on the ground, and the red flags of revolution are visible through the plumes of smoke that fill the air. It is everything Valentin has wanted, has worked for, has dreamt of. And yet it is not enough.

His eyes sting as if he spent the night buried in sand. He looks again over the bridge, but he is seeing double, likely from sleeplessness.

Double of everything and everyone. And none of Tonya.

While waiting for her last night, he tried to compose in his head. *Comrades, as the Imperial regime recedes into oblivion we are left with a void. A void that stretches from here where I stand to the Winter Palace – and someone will rise to fill that emptiness! Will that someone be us? Will it be you?*

But there is nothing that can fill this emptiness.

He is not sure how, but he begins to leave the Liteyny Bridge behind. He wants to smoke, but he cannot bear to breathe.

Valentin knows where Tonya lives, in one of the many wealthy enclaves along the Fontanka, rows of corniced mansions whose reflections shimmer in the river like a mirage. Maybe a mirage is all she ever was, because he can't believe she came this far, every day, so many days, just to see *him*.

The street sweepers are the only ones out at this early hour, and they look at him as if he is litter, as if they might brush him away too. Valentin has never been inside the house, but he's seen it from across the water, pastel-pink and proud-looking. It was built not too long ago, replacing an original structure, according to Tonya. She has said the house is like a museum. It has several libraries. It has bedrooms devoid of people, full of furniture. It has galleries for displaying the knick-knacks, trifles, novelties, from her husband's travels.

The bourgeois do love to own things.

There is only one balcony, curving around the central window on the second floor. Behind it, there is a shadow of movement, and quickly Valentin turns away, pulls up his collar. He'll go around back. Every house like this has a front door, an entryway for family and guests, people with calling cards, and another separate, sordid entrance, for everyone else.

A maidservant opens the back door. She has a frown that looks permanent and deep lines etched into her forehead, disappearing into her white cap. 'Delivery?' she says.

'I have a message for your mistress,' Valentin says. *Barynya.* These affectations should be outlawed. 'Antonina Lulikova. Or is it possible she might see me?'

'I doubt it. Who are you?'

'My name is Valentin Andreyev.'

'Wait here.'

The small courtyard behind the house is very still. He turns the corner, lights a cigarette, tries to inhale normally. When he first laid eyes on Tonya, he had that shameful, secret, *sinking* feeling he gets when he looks through the gates of the Winter Palace; the feeling that all he wants is to keep looking. The feeling that, no matter how loudly he proclaims otherwise, he will never be equal to what lies before him.

When will that feeling end?

'Is someone there?'

Valentin ducks back into the yard. A different maid steps past the threshold, this one in a plain black gown and no cap. She is ageless in a bad way, and she keeps her hands behind her back. This must be Olenka, the lady-in-waiting, the one beholden to Tonya's invalid mother-in-law. She is the kind of person who will be hardest to liberate, when the real revolution comes; who has been in servitude so long she won't know how to look up even when there's no one holding her down.

'Sir,' she says, in a strange, froggy voice, 'Antonina Nikolayevna does not wish to see you ever again.'

'Just get a message to her from me,' he says. 'Please.'

'I have been told to inform you, sir—'

'Told by whom?'

105

Wordlessly the girl produces whatever she had been fumbling with behind her back. Not just her hands, but a piece of paper torn from personal stationery, with Tonya's initials embossed in the corner. Only two lines are written upon the sheet:

> *I loved you; maybe the love in my soul has not faded away*
> *But let it not trouble you any longer*

It is from the famous poem by Alexander Pushkin. Tonya's favourite. Valentin looks from the lines to the frayed-looking maidservant and back to the lines again. Whatever he is feeling right now, whatever this agony is, it is new. There is no word for it, and Valentin always has the right word for everything.

Words have often been all he has. And now he is left with nothing.

'A girl like that only wants what she can't have,' declares Viktoria. She is faced away from him, peering into her looking glass, tying her tawny shoulder-length hair into a knot. 'You should have foreseen this. You can't have honestly thought she would live in a basement!'

But he had. Valentin had convinced himself of something impossible, because all around him the impossible was already occurring. The promise and the glory of revolution had blinded him; he'd let himself believe he could have everything he wanted.

'She was seeking a diversion,' says Viktoria, turning around. 'And you make a good one.'

'I should get home, Vika.'

'I meant it as a compliment,' she says. 'I understand why she wanted you. You are—you are the ideal to which the rest of us aspire. I need a piano and all my years of practice to move people the way you do.'

He stops to consider her. Viktoria is smiling at him in a way that he once would have given anything to see. When he first saw her, he was only ten years old, and she was an unfathomable fifteen. Three years later, watching her perform, dazzled by the sight of her fingers flying over the keys, he decided he would one day woo her, perhaps even win her. At sixteen, when Viktoria, herself age twenty-one, came home from a tour of Europe, Valentin blurted out his feelings. She turned him down with such gentleness that he can still conjure the embarrassment of it, if he tries hard enough.

Now he is twenty-two, and he has not thought of her that way since.

'Why don't you stay over tonight?' she says lightly.

'No,' he says. 'I should probably be alone.'

One morning Viktoria's father, Pavel, is waiting outside Valentin's door, his cane already poised to knock. The pepper-haired Pavel cuts a clean and respectable figure, and when he removes his hat and looks squarely at Valentin, his voice, too, is clean and calm.

'I have to talk to you, boy,' says Pavel.

'I'm on my way out,' says Valentin, but half-heartedly. Valentin owes Pavel everything and can refuse him nothing. As a ten-year-old Valentin had just run away from his uncle, a notorious drunk, and he'd been sleeping in a box by the wharf, pickpocketing to survive. Pavel was there handing out political pamphlets and poetry to the sailors and street-sellers. He took Valentin home, fed him, clothed him, taught him, found him a factory job. Introduced him to the underground.

'Vika's told me what's happened with the girl,' says Pavel. 'But you've disappeared on us. You still have your duties, Valya, your responsibility to the cause and to your fellows. And to me.'

Your life begins here, Pavel said then. *You are in. And if you are in, you are in for ever. You will do anything for us, and we will do anything for you.*

'It's good that this has happened,' says Pavel. 'At your tender age. Now you know better.'

'It was a mistake,' says Valentin flatly.

'A companion for the life you're going to lead, boy, had better be one of us.'

'I understand.'

'Good.' Pavel motions with the cane for Valentin to come close. The older man's embrace is firm. 'Mistakes or not, you're my son,' he says. 'I'm so proud of you.'

'Thank you,' says Valentin, a slight crack in his voice. He grips Pavel hard in response. He was reborn, after meeting the Katenins, after joining the Party. But he remembers that he had another family once, a mother with warm eyes and a babushka with wrinkled hands; remembers growing up with them in an apartment with so many cockroaches that he often mistook those bugs for the ceiling. He knows that he used to be somebody else, someone other than a Bolshevik, someone with things to say that were not rehearsed.

With Tonya, he was that someone again.

He doesn't know *why* it felt like that, with her. He doesn't know how. But Valentin does know this: he may never be rid of the past, but nor can she, or anyone, bring it back. Tonya, in the end, is nothing more than any other petty bourgeois. She will have to pay. They will all have to pay.

CHAPTER EIGHT

Rosie

Moscow, July 1991

I COMPOSE A LETTER TO RICHARD THAT IS FULL OF DEFT LITTLE touches. I explain how our resident cockroaches frolic in the cocaine-like powder that is meant to kill them. How the electrical voltage meltdowns are more reliable than the current. How the supermarket meat runs like it was just sluiced off the animal; how the cashier uses an abacus to calculate my total. I can imagine Richard, wonderful Richard, reading this, smiling, enjoying the glimpse into daily life in Moscow. But it is a superficial, touristy view. I could send a blank postcard of Red Square. It would have the same effect.

But what should I write instead?

I'm being haunted.

I read and reread my words. I gnaw on my pen until the cap falls off.

'Ready to head out?' Alexey pokes his head into the kitchen.

I turn the paper over. 'Yup, let's go.'

* * *

I awaken to feel a soupy wind in my face, the open car windows letting in a puzzling mix of aromas: pine trees and wildflowers, wood-tar and petrol. I must have fallen asleep on the motorway, because we already seem to be crossing the precise spot where the city and the country meet. As we drive on, the undergrowth thickens, throttles the landscape. The trees are taller, packed together.

Lev manoeuvres the Mercedes down the potholed lanes with disregard, one arm dangling out the window as he smokes. The road is degrading into an unpaved path. Alexey indicates a turn, and the car shrieks in protest as Lev pulls it up short.

The first sign of human habitation is a small log cabin, but it seems long abandoned. The door hangs off its hinges. Planks of wood are missing from the frame and porch rails. A noisy family of sparrows occupies the roof, and something dashes by, a blur of brown. More cabins appear, further down the way, all in the same state, a tableau of decay.

'These villages often die off, as young people move to the cities,' says Alexey.

The so-called village has a prying stare, even without eyes. I edge away from the window. Mum had quite a few stories that took place in the countryside, but her idea of rural Russia was troikas and teahouses, silver bells and painted windowsills. Like a massive Christmas gingerbread display. There was always a manic quality to these details, like she *knew* it was too much, but she just couldn't help herself.

'There's somebody there,' notes Alexey.

An old man is seated in a rocking chair on one of the porches. The chair moves, back and forth, to and fro. He cradles something in his arms, too straight, the way you might hold someone else's baby. He turns and I see that his face is sallow, saggy with time. He might be younger than Alexey, but he has aged worse.

'Let's stop for a moment,' says Alexey.

Lev obeys. The car engine shudders and dies. I smooth down my summery frock, which sticks to the back of my legs as I step out of the Mercedes. I am not dressed for trekking through bramble. The mushrooms beneath my feet make a crunching noise as I go closer, and now the object in the man's grasp begins to take shape: it's nothing more than some kind of kitchen rag or cloth, compressed into a ball.

Nature is reclaiming all of this, the land, the village, the villager, but it will never have that rag.

'Good day to you, friend,' says Alexey. 'We're looking for Otrada. Could you help us? Direct us from here?'

The old man's eyes are filmy with cataracts. He gestures for us to follow him inside, keeping the rag-ball stowed beneath his arm.

The interior of the cabin is cramped and dismal. One corner is overflowing with Orthodox icons and candle stubs; pushed against another is a thatch-covered bag of dirt that I suspect to be a bed. Beside the long, silent stove stands a slanted table, and beyond that is a pyramid of food jars not unlike Mum's own collection. Their pickled contents appear monstrous, the white sweet onions like human eyeballs, the gherkins like foetuses.

112

'There is nobody at Otrada any more,' says our host.

'But could you help us find the way?' says Alexey.

'There is no way.' The old man's voice sharpens. 'Not in, not out.'

Alexey gives a small sigh.

I look down at the table, at what appear to be some old letters. *Dear Kirill Vladimirovich*, begins the one on top. The smell of wet earth is beginning to eat at my good humour. I glance through the window, impatiently, towards the car.

And then I smell something else.

Charcoal.

Zoya is here. But no matter how I trawl my memory, I can't think of anything that matches the smell. What's coming to mind is entirely foreign, shaky and blurred as it takes shape: it's not a memory at all, but the image of a house. Not a house, only a lifeless shell, its remaining walls in the grip of greedy vines. Behind these ruins lie blackened fields, a few weeds sprouting through, and looming beyond, a white-birch forest, the trees stripped of bark, like people stripped of . . .

Until now, Zoya was never able to make me *see* anything besides my own memories; anything beyond the borders of my own life. This is different. I've never been to this place. I've never stood amongst this charred wreckage.

I turn around. My mouth feels funny. 'Did Otrada burn down?'

'What was that, Rosie?' asks Alexey.

'Did it . . . did the house burn down?'

The old man's pupils grow large in my direction. It

113

doesn't help him see me. 'Take this,' he commands, and lets the ball droop from his hand. The rag is so ratty, so disgusting, that it can't shake itself loose. He says, louder now: 'Take it, *take it!*'

I don't know what else to do besides take it.

He opens his mouth and I think he's going to ask for it back but instead, he *sings*. He sings a line from a famous wartime ditty that Mum was always fond of, 'The Blue Kerchief', and then he sings another, another. Somewhere in there, beneath the leathery skin and the cataracts and the dementia, is someone who desperately wants to do more than sing. I can almost hear that person screaming from within.

As he warbles on, the only thing I can think with any certainty at this moment is that the cloth he has just handed me is not blue. It is in that no-man's-land of colour. Too long faded.

'Alright,' says Alexey, 'thank you for your hospitality—'

The old man whirls on him. 'I know who you are! Don't think I don't!'

Alexey's face goes as grey as the rag.

The old man spits and crosses himself. His eyes roll back in his head. Then he stops. A smile appears on those crusty lips, so vacant it is almost sinister. Whatever chance there may ever have been is gone. He has withdrawn to the refuge he has found for himself in his mind.

The sky is a resplendent, radiant purple, heralding the romantic stretch of evening before the light will fade and turn this village into a graveyard. Alexey finally admits defeat. We've driven, we've hiked, we've even got briefly lost. We can't find Otrada. It's in the forest somewhere, and not on any map, he says tiredly, and he closes the one I gave him, the one from Mum's notebook, and tucks it into a pocket. The Mercedes growls as Lev forces it back onto a cratered path, the wheels catching, the gears grinding. Alexey does not say another word.

After some forty minutes of driving, I can tell he has gone to sleep. We are still a ways out of Moscow.

'Are you OK?' Lev asks, from the front seat.

'I'm fine,' I say, and regret it. I'm not fine. That's just the British layer of me talking; the top layer. It's one thing for Zoya to force me to remember things, but what happened in that cabin was a worse violation. She grabbed hold of my mind not to pull out something old, but to shove in something new.

'Will we take another trip to see your GRU colonel next weekend?' asks Lev.

'You could tell he's GRU?'

'I was in the Moscow OMON. Until a few months ago.'

I glance at him, but he's still facing the road. The OMON? They're crowd control. Riot police. Part of the repressive machinery of the Soviet state, designed to keep the people down and at arm's – or better yet, sniper's – length. I know them only by reputation: the 'Black Berets'. It's all anybody would want to know.

'Your friends are too,' I say. 'When we met at Red Square.'

'Former colleagues.'

'You quit?'

'I've been temporarily reassigned,' he says, a little sourly. 'To this.'

To *me*, is what he means. 'Why?'

'Why did you visit the colonel?'

Fair enough.

We're on the motorway now. The noise, the traffic, can just about replace conversation. I don't have to say anything else. We can leave it at that impasse, at the same line I always draw on this subject. Lev tries the radio, managing to snag onto a recording of *Swan Lake*. The orchestra is approaching a climax.

As it does, as the notes spill like a river over a collapsing dam, everything just spills out of me too.

'My sister and father were killed in 1977,' I say. 'By a man named Eduard Dayneko. He was a sniper working for a mafia *bratva*. All his previous victims were criminals.' I look down at my hands. They're clenched into fists. 'He murdered my family execution-style.'

'Your father wasn't a criminal?'

'My father was a schoolteacher. I'm sorry to tell you all this, I . . .'

'You don't need to keep saying sorry.'

We're almost back in Moscow, and night is falling. The less I see, the more I hear: the clanging of tram bells, the honking of lorry horns, the shouting pedestrians, the barking dogs. But I feel calm, balanced against the noise and activity of the city. I released a valve, speaking out loud about my family. Some pressure must have lifted.

'I was involved with someone, a journalist,' he says. 'She was using me to get information on my superiors in Internal Affairs. She was exposed. Our relationship ended. Now I am here. Out of the OMON until the Ministry can decide whether I'm trustworthy.'

116

'It's not too bad, I hope.'

'It was a light punishment.'

His eyes meet mine in the rear-view mirror. I rally a smile. When I think of the OMON, I think of them as one being, one entity. They are always faceless and featureless, behind their shields and balaclavas. It's strange to imagine them as individuals. As people.

What will Zoya show me, now that she can show me anything? Where will it end?

I should have got to know her better when she was alive. Maybe then I would know what she wants from me now. But we were never close, as children.

In our neighbourhood there was a playground where every piece of equipment was made of metal, the slides, the hoops, the bars. I often wanted to stop, to play. Zoya never did. She always had to go meet friends, or eventually, some new boy. She'd tell me to play on my own. She'd run off and I believed I saw it in her too: something metal. My sister, underneath the winning smiles, the glowing skin, the glossy hair, was made of metal.

Tick, tock, tick, tock, says my wristwatch. I've switched off all the lights, but I can't make anything go dark: that husk of a house, the grasping vines, the naked birch. I pull my blanket higher, wishing I could pull it over my head.

'Can't sleep again?' asks Lev, shattering the silence like glass.

I had no idea he was awake too. He can stay so still for so long. Like some kind of animal playing dead. 'It's

always rubbish being haunted, but especially at night.'
I pause. 'My sister's name was Zoya.'

'Not too common,' he remarks. 'Like Raisa.'

'My mother named us. She liked to stand out.'

'You don't?'

'Names are just labels.'

'But they can have a lot of power.'

Tick, tock, tick, tock.

'I think Zoya wants me to uncover the truth,' I say thinly. 'To understand what happened the night they were killed.'

'Or else she wants to keep you from it.'

I can't tell whether he's being serious. 'I think she knows that if anyone is going to figure it out, it's me.'

'Are you a detective, in England?'

'A PhD student. I study codes, encryption.' I eyeball the ceiling. 'My father was an amateur cryptographer. He trained me to perceive unusual patterns, breaks, pieces of a puzzle, and how to move them around, hold them in my head, put them back together.'

'That does sound convenient for solving mysteries.'

'Yeah, but as a result, I'm often bothered by tiny things. Patterns that don't matter. Or that aren't even there. I've become hypersensitive, I suppose.' I make a face, even though I know he can't see it. 'Maybe *that's* why Zoya chose me, to communicate with, because I'd be the one to sense her. But also she knows . . .' I pause, and then a bit hoarsely: 'I'll never give up. There's an answer, to what happened to my family, and I'll keep going until I have it. However long it takes.'

'Ah,' he says. 'I see now why you don't believe in coincidences.'

I turn my head. I shouldn't burden Lev any further. I'm here to purge myself of my past, not poison others with it. And he must have his own demons. No one ends up in the OMON by accident.

Besides, it's not just Zoya's interference that's keeping me up. It's not even the map, or any 'coincidence'.

I might not have read History, and I know this isn't a normal research project, but something about my role as Alexey's assistant feels off. Alexey still isn't telling me much, and bar today, he's barely been around. My note-taking on generic textbooks, meanwhile, is obviously just faff. Alexey *lived* through all the things in those books. He doesn't need my help understanding them.

Why does he need me at all?

'Hey,' says Lev, 'do you want me to read you another story? From your mother's notebook?'

The Great and Terrible Monster

In a faraway kingdom, in a long-ago land, the townspeople were afraid of a monster said to live underground, in the sewers. They whispered to themselves of his hunger, his cruelty, how his teeth were like needles and his eyes as yellow as yolks, how his fingers were sausages, his fingernails meathooks.

One day the monster burst out of the gutters and began his rampage. He seized and slaughtered. He was worse than the people had feared, because he did not look the way they had feared. He looked like one of them. He did not have meathook fingernails or needles for teeth. When the king's soldiers came to defend the city, they did not know whom to kill. So the monster was free to do as he wished, and everything that the townspeople had ever prophesied came true.

That was when a woman who lived in the town murdered her husband. She stabbed him with a knife and threw him over a bridge and into a river. Her husband's body disappeared into the water, and she thought of how, at any other time, she wouldn't have been able to get away

120

with it. But now, even if he did resurface downriver, he would do so alongside a hundred other blubbery corpses. Dukes and duchesses, schoolmistresses and ship merchants, cheesemakers and undertakers.

He would be one more body that no one would notice.

CHAPTER NINE

Antonina

Petrograd, St Petersburg, spring 1917

THE SERVANTS HAVE STRIPPED TONYA'S BEDROOM BARE. Her furniture is removed, her shelves, her vases, even the rose-oil lamps. The only things left are a chamber pot and a few books, for entertainment. Didn't she always enjoy *Eugene Onegin*? The doors to the balcony are now locked too. Olenka brings newspapers and meals on a tray, but Tonya eats so little and vomits so often that even if she did make it out to the balcony, the wind might carry her off.

She reads *Eugene Onegin* at night, reads aloud until her lips are so dry that they crack.

My whole life has been a pledge to this meeting with you . . .

She must get a letter to Valentin. She knows she can't appeal to Olenka. But perhaps if she threw a letter into the street, a stranger might come upon it, might find some sympathy for her. She could write around the margins of *Eugene Onegin* if she only had a pen. She will use her own blood, if that is all she has.

Dmitry still takes tea with her, every day at four, only now the tea service is brought into her boudoir. Every day Tonya falls at his feet.

'Just the balcony,' she pleads. 'I need the light!'

'It's almost summer,' he says. 'It'll never be dark at all then.'

'No, please! Please, I beg of you!'

But he only sips his tea and smiles. Then he leaves, and she claws at the door behind him. She shreds the skin off her hands, vomits, falls asleep in her own stomach bile, but it hardly matters. By now she has not had any bath, let alone a perfumed one, in weeks. She is sticky and sour, her hair as matted as wool.

At some point the family doctor drops in and pronounces her hysterical. Dmitry mentions Tonya's nightmares and the doctor recommends no more books or newspapers. They will only cause further mental disturbances.

Every day, Tonya screams until she loses her voice. There is not very much left to lose. Perhaps *that* is why the balcony is locked. Perhaps Dmitry thinks she would jump.

Tonya's only permitted visitor is the Countess Burzinova. Natalya has defied the doctor and brought news of the outside world: there is now a Provisional Government ruling Russia, one that contains many of the same ministers and officials as the Imperial regime. The Countess doesn't sound perturbed, merely intrigued, that Nicholas and the rest of the Romanovs have been banished to the Alexander Palace at Tsarskoye Selo.

Tonya sits up in bed, rubs at her puffy eyes.

'The only reason you bemoan your current situation, darling,' says Natalya, 'is because you haven't seen enough.

123

Better to be comfortable, if – controlled – than to be free, and struggling, starving, selling yourself for a loaf of bread. You are a hand-fed lapdog who dreams of hunting elk in the wild, Tonya, who has no notion of what it takes to survive.'

Tonya blows out a strand of hair, breathes it back in.

Natalya sighs. 'Well, Dmitry's mother is on your side.'

'It was . . .' Tonya struggles to speak. 'It was Anastasia who told him about my affair. She does not care for my well-being.'

Natalya rubs her silver necklace. 'Maybe she regrets the telling.'

'Or was it you who told him?' Tonya asks, in a croak.

'Certainly not, darling. I go about things more quietly than that. Perhaps it was your lady's maid, the one who sounds like she swallowed a shoe? Wasn't she the one sent to follow you?'

'Please,' Tonya says, her tongue twisting on the plea, 'would you help me?'

A throaty laugh. 'With what?'

'Would you find Valentin Andreyev, and tell him what's become of me?'

'I will do no such thing,' says the Countess, who is no longer laughing. Even if the events of these few months, the founding of the new government, the Tsar being run out of the city, the masses rising up, are amusing to people like Natalya, it's clearly not amusing to such people when it happens in their households. A revolution on the streets, that's as may be. But a revolution inside, in *here*, that is an entirely different thing.

* * *

Dmitry is in the doorway. Groggy with sleep, Tonya somehow notices that her husband is dressed in an evening jacket, like he has just come from a show at the Mariinsky. His hair is groomed and slicked, his cravat high and tight. The cloying stench of liquor seems to form a cloud around him.

'I heard you from downstairs, Tonyechka,' he says, approaching the bed. 'Did you have another nightmare?'

The day Tonya first met Dmitry, she was fifteen years old. It was spring and the orchard trees at Otrada were beginning to bloom. Tonya was coming in from the creek with Nelly, the two of them holding up their skirts and bast shoes, giggling madly. She was carrying a spray of wildflowers in her free hand. And then she and Nelly turned, just at the place where Otrada comes into view, and a stranger was standing there.

Right now, he is her only nightmare.

'I'm not feeling well. Could we speak in the morning,' Tonya says, not able to raise her voice, to turn it into a question. He is already lifting her bedcovers. He hasn't come to her like this in months. Longer. Maybe he's been revolted by the rodent-nest of her hair, the bruised tint of her lips, the bald desperation in her eyes. She's become something he might scrape off a shoe.

But tonight it appears he has drunk enough.

He removes his cravat. His breath is strong and tarty.

'Of everything I have ever brought home, of all my collections,' he says, 'you are the crowning piece.'

Three years ago, after Nelly ran off, still giggling, the stranger introduced himself. He was from the capital. He

125

was visiting the area and had come to pay his respects to Mama and Papa. His name was Dmitry Lulikov, and someone in the village had told him about Kukolka, the girl who looked like a doll, only he hadn't believed. He believed now, he said. He offered Tonya his arm.

In taking it, she remembers for the first time, she dropped her wildflowers.

She wonders how they must have looked later, abandoned in the soft earth, the stems broken, the colour faded, the petals crushed into nothing.

The study is darker than ever. The fire has long died, though the grate still shudders. Anastasia lies flat beneath her blankets. Even the pillows no longer elevate her head. She begins to hum, off-key. She has had too much morphine. The body strums, with too much morphine. The brain slows. Tonya saw it with Papa, after Mama died, the way a person's eyes glide over everything, catch on nothing.

Anastasia's gaze rotates her way. 'My son has let you come.'

'He says you asked for me.'

'As my dying wish. Oh, child, just look at you.'

'I've been unwell, Anastasia Sergeyevna.'

'I shouldn't have told him. Natalya was right. She said to put Mitya's feelings first. I only thought it would be best . . . for him to know . . .' The old woman's voice is full of holes. 'Olenka tells me that your menstruation has ceased, that it has been months now. Dare I take this to mean you are pregnant?'

'I think so,' Tonya says, looking away.

'Why haven't you told my son? A baby does so much for a marriage—'

'It's not his.'

'How can you know?'

'He left in December, Anastasia Sergeyevna, and was gone well past a month. I last bled around Christmas.'

He has not gone away since.

There is a long silence in which Tonya thinks Anastasia may have already died, but then the old woman lifts her head from the pillow. 'You must pretend that it is his, Tonya. You must not say otherwise.'

'Why shouldn't I?'

'For everyone's good. The baby's good.' Anastasia's head drops once more. 'Mitya is like his father. You never knew my husband, but he lacked—I daresay he lacked the ability to care for others, or even to think of others. When we were first married, I thought it was merely his upbringing, his privilege; had I known his temperament, his traits, would pass to his offspring, I would have done much differently! But now it's too late, and once you're a mother yourself, you will understand. You'll see how helpless we all are, in loving our children. Whoever your child is, you will forgive him anything.'

'No,' says Tonya hazily, 'I won't.'

'I promise you, you will.' One tear falls, out of the good eye. 'Now read something to me, child, as you used to, before you go.'

Tonya agrees to read, but mostly because she doesn't wish to return to her room. There are no books here, and the light is too poor for her to read anyway, so she closes her eyes and recites Pushkin from memory instead: *You appeared to me in dreams . . . in my soul, your voice resounded . . .*

She looks to see if Anastasia is still awake. Anastasia's eyes are open.

The bad one is clearer than the good one.

It's not such a bad way to die, listening to Pushkin, and Tonya keeps going, in case her mother-in-law's spirit is still in the room and wants to hear more.

Dmitry motions for her to make space in the bed. He's been drinking more and more lately. Perhaps as a replacement for travelling. Tonya slides over, already feeling numb. He says he wants to tell her about Anastasia's funeral, about how they had a small *litia* in the church by her dacha. Few people attended. Most of Anastasia's friends and relations are dead. The rest have fled Russia in the wake of revolution.

Dmitry pinches her chin gently, turns her face sideways.

'My mother's last request,' he says, 'was for a grandchild.'

It is not a question and Tonya does not answer.

'Do you not desire a baby? My baby?'

My baby. It would be his baby and not hers. He can't even think otherwise, because everything else *is* his. Even if Nicholas II is no longer in power, there are many more in this city who have not given up their thrones, who still rule their own kingdoms. Perhaps there will have to be yet another revolution before the people can truly have anything of their own. Even their babies.

'I'm not overly fond of children, but I like the idea of someone to inherit everything I've amassed, in my time.' Dmitry wipes something off her cheek. 'Once you're stronger, and back to yourself again, we can talk about it some more. Should I have Olenka run you a bath? Or shall I brush your hair for you? Whatever you want, Tonyechka. You're the only lady of the house now.'

Anastasia was the bulwark, Tonya realises, that kept the most savage part of Dmitry at bay. But Anastasia is gone now, and with her, all pretences. Tonya has never been a wife. She has always been a prisoner. Dmitry has always been her jailer, and he will find out one way or another.

'I'll leave you to sleep,' he says.

'I am already pregnant.'

Dmitry looks at her as if he hasn't understood.

'It is Valentin Andreyev's.' Tonya finds herself revelling in each word. 'Do you know who Valentin is? He is the leader of the Vyborg Committee. He is their speaker in the union. He is head of the workers' militia—'

He hits her hard, across the face, and then again, this time drawing blood from her nose.

'I love him,' she shrieks, 'and no matter how long you keep me in here, you will never be able to stop me! I will never be yours! I will never belong to you!'

The alcohol in his system has dulled. She can tell by the way he climbs astride her, the way he might move a chess piece. With painstaking care. He straddles her and she begins to spread her legs, wanting it to be over with as quickly as possible, but he holds her in place. Tonya opens her mouth to scream but no sound emerges, her voice is too weak, so she clamps down on her tongue until it's bleeding too and the pain bursts out of her eyes instead – but still she doesn't make a sound, even as the blows are different, deeper, intended to lay waste.

She begins to feel muddled and muddy, and now she couldn't say a thing even if she wanted to because she doesn't know where her mouth is, where anything is, or whether she is in too many pieces ever to be repaired.

'Please drink, Antonina Nikolayevna.' It is Olenka. 'You have gone a day without.'

Tonya turns in bed with a moan. She accepts the cup and spills water down her nightgown, but there is already wetness in the bed sheets. She submerges her hands in it, this plummy liquid, and then she holds her fingers up. They are webbed with blood.

'It is less now,' says Olenka mournfully.

'Why am I . . . ?'

Olenka hangs her head. 'The doctor thinks you have lost your pregnancy.'

Tonya gazes at her hands. Dmitry has killed the baby. It couldn't have had a good hold in there to begin with, given Mama's history, and he jarred it loose. He cracked her open at last and something fell out. Yes, Dmitry killed the baby – but she was the one who waited too long. She should have run away from him before any of this. Instead she let herself and her unborn child ripen, mould, split like summer fruit gone to spoil.

It is her doing, too.

She looks back at Olenka, who appears terrified and has begun to cough.

'Olenka,' Tonya says, 'you must help me.'

The maid only coughs harder.

'Olenka,' says Tonya, 'I will die, if I stay here any longer. You must help me. You must unlock my door for me tonight.'

'Oh.' Olenka's eyes are wide and pained. 'I can't—'

'Was there never in your life,' says Tonya, just above a hiss, 'a time when you needed one person to take pity on you, when no one else would? Have you never been snatched from the brink, through the kindness of one other soul?'

'I can't, Antonina Nikolayevna,' is the meagre reply.

'You *can*,' Tonya insists. 'Anastasia is dead. There's nothing to keep you here either. You should take everything you can carry that's of any value and leave this house. Go home to your family.'

Olenka begins to weep, but is still coughing. Together it makes a wretched cacophony. Tonya thinks for one wild moment that she can overpower the maid with threats, that she must look like a madwoman, a murderer, in these stained sheets, with these stained hands, and it does happen, that women come apart after they lose a baby. It happened, a little, to Mama, over and over again. *Leave the door unlocked, Olenka, or the first life I will take for the one that has just been lost is yours!* She feels it, even without saying it, the swell of insanity.

'You and I,' she says softly, 'we should never have left the countryside, that's the trouble. Those were our real lives, Olenka, and all this, it is only a bad dream. Let us wake from it at last.'

It must be near midnight, but the night sky is only a deep maroon, marred by fog. The season will tip soon into summer, just as Dmitry said. How long has she been in here? Weeks? Months? She should have kept track of the

131

days; should have marked the walls with her nails instead of breaking them off trying to scratch through the door.

Tonya tries the door handle, not daring to hope.

It is unlocked. Olenka has left it unlocked, and Dmitry appears to have made no other provisions for an escape attempt. There are no trapdoors in the parquet floors, no barricades in the corridors. Tonya's legs are unsteady, and as she descends the stairs one ankle lands badly. Her body feels unbalanced. She makes it through to the front foyer and looks behind her, and there is a slinky stream of blood leading up to her heels.

She plods on like an injured animal. Outside, the moon shines through the fog, illuminates the way. It is crisp but not cold. She will keep to the Fontanka embankment until she reaches the Neva, will stay close to the water all the way into the Vyborg. Once Valentin's cellar room reminded her of a mole's burrow, or of a dungeon, but it no longer does. It will be lighter, lovelier, than anywhere else in the world.

There is little sound on the streets except for the cry of birds, the lapping of the river.

'Tonya!' somebody shouts, from behind.

She feels light-headed, loose-limbed. She keeps going.

'Tonya, stop!'

Dmitry. How can it be? How could he know? How could he have heard? Or does he never sleep these days, never cease his watch? Her panic flows, ebbs just as swiftly. She wills herself to run, to fight, but her surge of strength is over. She has bled all the way from the house. She has led him directly to her.

132

'Tonya.' Dmitry has her hard by the shoulder.

His grip is iron. She tries to go limp, hopes he will loosen his hand. He doesn't.

'Come home,' he says. 'You're weak, Tonyechka. You need to be looked after.'

She is about to reply, to ask him to kill her, because she would rather die than return to that house, but before she can speak she sees movement in the mist. A flash of red. Bright, blazing, as a bonfire. There is somebody coming.

Now she hears a new voice. It is her own.

'Help,' she shouts. 'Help me!'

'Be quiet,' says Dmitry. 'Come on. Let's go home—'

'Help me! Please, help me!'

She doesn't know if they will help. She doesn't know who they are. But she sees them approaching. Roving, as if they are on the lookout for prey. Young men, rail-thin and flat-eyed beneath their wayward mops of hair. She sees the red again: the bands of the Bolsheviks, tied around their upper arms. One of them carries, extended in his hand, a hunting knife with a birch handle, the kind that a peasant might use to gut a goat. He is clearly their leader.

'What goes on here?' he asks.

'A private matter,' says Dmitry roughly. 'She is my wife.'

Tonya sees the youths steel themselves. They don't believe in *private*, or possibly even in wives. Dmitry may not understand them, but she does; she has seen one of them up close, close enough that there were times when she didn't know where her own body ended, where his began.

I didn't know you told stories . . .

133

'He is my husband's employer,' she cries, 'and he's murdered my husband, to have me for himself! My husband is one of you! Please, comrade! *All Power to the Soviet!*'

It is enough. Maybe it's what they have been looking for. The young men encircle her and Dmitry and two of them grab Dmitry by both arms, and Tonya is instantly free. She watches as the one with the knife plunges it into Dmitry's side. Once, hard. Deep.

Her mouth tastes coppery. Dmitry sways like a pocket watch on a chain before he falls. Stillness for a moment, and then the others drag her husband to the side of the rail, leaving him in a heap. Tonya asks if they can pull the coat off the body. She puts it on over her sullied nightgown and turns away. The youth with the blade is wiping it off on his armband, red against red. *When the true socialist revolution comes, blood will run through this city like any other river*, Valentin said to her once. A warning. Or perhaps just a promise.

She will sleep when she gets there. She only has to make it there. She tells herself on every corner to go one block further. One by one. She has no idea what time it is, only that it's darker now, that the moon has slipped behind streaks of grey clouds. Rain begins to fall as Tonya turns into Valentin's courtyard. She exhales through her teeth. The stairs leading down are the most difficult. The streets have torn holes into her slippers.

She knocks on his door. No answer.

'Valentin?' she calls out, feebly.

The rain shows no sign of slowing. There's a tide rolling in that will bring up everything from the depths, Valentin

134

used to say. And it will drag down all that has ever lived on the surface. Thunder rolls, rumbles overhead. She can feel another rivulet of blood on her inner thigh.

The door opens halfway.

'What are you doing here?' Valentin asks. He sounds not at all pleased.

There is rain in her eyes, on her lips. 'I've come to speak with you,' she babbles.

'Why?'

Tonya can't begin to explain everything that has happened since they last saw one another, everything that has happened only tonight, and yet she must. He will understand, of course. She steps towards him, but he steps back, away. 'That night in February,' she says. 'I wanted to—'

'Don't,' he says. 'It doesn't matter any more.'

The rain pummels everything around them, punctuates his words. Her throat closes hard. She doesn't want to talk any more, only wants to be near him, to kiss him, to never let go.

He hasn't invited her in. She is soaked. Nearly wilted.

'It does matter,' she insists. 'I have to tell you – I have to explain—'

The door opens wider. Standing there, hair sweaty-damp, arms and shoulders bare, a sheet pulled over the rest of her body, is Viktoria Katenina. Viktoria doesn't venture as far as Valentin, perhaps to remain sheltered from the rain, and her smile is syrupy, dripping down her face.

'Oh,' Tonya says dumbly. 'Oh.'

'How can you leave her standing here, Valya?' Viktoria chastises. 'Tonya, you look like a drowned rat! You must come inside and get warm. I'll go put something on.'

'No,' Tonya says, 'thank you,' and it is all she manages. She shakes her head as Viktoria offers again, keeps shaking her head so that her wet hair falls in her face and she can't see through it well enough to tell if Valentin is even still there, or if he has already gone inside. She backs away, up the cellar steps, turns and compels herself to keep going. The same way she came, one foot in front of the other. Now the rain falls hard as bullets. If he calls for her, says her name, if he says *anything*, she'll turn around, but he doesn't.

Valentin Andreyev, the great Bolshevik orator, silent at last.

Everything she was going to tell him, Tonya tells herself instead, on the lonely journey back to the house on the Fontanka. That she misses him. That she thinks of him every day. That they might have had a baby, in *their lifetime*. But they were never going to have *their lifetime*. Or else it has already passed.

In the days that follow, Tonya prepares to depart for Otrada. She sells, barters as much of Dmitry's precious collections as she can. She uses the income to pay the servants advance wages, and then she tells them to gather their things and go. She gives no explanation for their master's absence. There's no need. She's read the papers now. All of Petrograd is in such disarray that people often pack up and depart in the middle of the night. The wealthy have left in droves.

The Countess Burzinova and her daughter Akulina come to call shortly before Tonya is set to leave. Tonya has nothing to offer her final pair of guests. This very morning she ate her last slices of rye, soaked in sunflower oil and thickened with water. She may not eat again until she is back in her village.

'Where is your husband?' asks Natalya sharply, with a glance to both ends of the Blue Salon, as if he might be hiding in the corner.

'Gone,' says Tonya. 'Dmitry left overnight, a week ago.'

'Gone?' the other woman repeats.

Tonya nods. Natalya's presence is both abrupt and yet entirely predictable, for the Countess never fails to turn up when Tonya is least prepared to receive her. She focuses, steadfastly, on the waves painted into the wallpaper. It is meant to look like the sea. People are supposed to be able to submerge themselves in it. She does feel a little like she is underwater.

'He did not say *where*?' Natalya asks.

'I woke up and my door was unlocked. I heard from the servants that he'd gone. They didn't know any more than that.'

'This beggars belief.' Natalya's voice is like a horsewhip. 'Dmitry wouldn't leave without telling me. We discuss all his travel plans. Let me talk to the servants myself, then, and see if I can't scare it out of them. Where are they? Or have they all run off too?'

'I had to dismiss them—'

'*Dismiss* them!'

This conversation is slipping from Tonya's grasp. She is fumbling for words, mishandling what she does say. She looks over at Akulina, who sits with her arms crossed, looking churlish. Tonya breathes in, draws herself up,

137

for the things that once underlaid her world, that seemed like laws of nature – the Tsar, Imperial Russia, Mama, her marriage – have proven man-made and destructible. One by one they have come crashing to her feet. Everything that has ever stood may be torn down this summer.

Even the Countess Burzinova.

'You've been indisposed, darling,' says Natalya, 'but did Dmitry share with you anything of the trouble at the factory? The strikes, the violence?'

'I know some,' says Tonya.

'The foreman has been run out of town. The union is up in arms. Many have joined the Red Guards.' Natalya's fingers knead her silver necklace like dough. 'It's happening everywhere, but it's worst in the Vyborg. My sense, Tonya, is that something has happened to Dmitry. Because he would not leave like this. He would not. He is meticulous in his methods.'

'I don't understand—'

'His workers,' is the lash of a reply. 'They might have kidnapped him.'

'You think they would . . . hurt him?'

Natalya's eyes have narrowed into pinpoints. 'Or perhaps just one worker, with his own reasons.'

Tonya hides her trembling hands in her lap.

'If it *was* Valentin Andreyev, if he's dared to lay a finger on your husband,' says Natalya, with sudden tranquillity, 'he will suffer for it. If anyone has hurt Dmitry, I will repay.'

'Valentin would not kill for me,' Tonya says in a whisper, 'if that is what you mean. He might kill for his principle. But not for me.'

'You leave it to me, darling. I have my ways for getting at the truth. In the meantime, what's to become of you? Come and live with me. Look at you. You're already thin as paper.'

'I'm leaving for Otrada,' says Tonya.

'Where on earth is that?' says Natalya, with distaste.

'My family's home. In Tula.'

'And how will I reach you there, if I need to?'

There are no telegraph machines at Otrada. The post is inconsistent at best. Most people fetch newspapers from the nearest *selo*, or the much larger town of Kalasy. Tonya retrieves one of the atlases, tears out a map of Tula province, and indicates the village of Popovka. Natalya takes it, but Tonya doubts the Countess will ever think of her again, after today. Natalya offers some money and Tonya accepts even though money is mostly useless now, with inflation, and she escorts her guests out to the foyer. She sees Natalya staring at the cabinets where the ceramics and porcelains used to stand.

Everything is empty now, Tonya wants to say. Just like her womb.

Petrograd has changed from what Tonya remembers. Scarlet banners and ribbons hang out of every window, strung across all the rooftops. Breadlines wind around whole city blocks. Many who wait have brought footstools to rest upon. The streets are covered in sewage, and at all the corners, prostitutes advertise openly. They might be younger than her, but they walk like old women.

Tonya continues on foot to the train station.

The outside world, Mama said years and years ago, *is little but suffering*. Mama was seated at her easel-backed vanity as she spoke this. The table and its glass were gilt-edged with silver, like Mama's hair. Tonya remembers noticing the silver for the first time, a sign of age, visible in the childlike blonde ringlets. Mama was noticing it too.

That was probably why she was thinking, at that moment, of human suffering.

Mama pulled her own cheeks upwards, sighed, and let them fall again.

Pain and sorrow will stick to your skirts as you walk through this world, like pollen grains, said Mama. *You think you can shake them off later. But this is only what you think.*

That's why, no matter what your father says, you are better off here. At Otrada. With me.

CHAPTER TEN

Rosie

Moscow, July 1991

O N A SUNNY SATURDAY MORNING, THE OPEN-AIR Vernissage market at Izmaylovo is overpopulated with tourists. Their cameras swing from their necks and their maps flap in the wind. They gawk at the Cheburashka plush toys and birch-bark baskets and milky bottles of Stolichnaya as the more experienced shoppers, the native Muscovites, haggle with the vendors. The scent of coffee and roasting chestnuts moves swiftly to fill in any gaps in the narrow lanes.

Mum often brought me and Zoya here as kids.

She seemed to know everyone well: one couple who sold samovars, for example, who were aficionados of the ballet. She'd take us by their stall and chat with them, laugh with them, as if *she* were selling something, rather than the other way around. But that was Mum. She was always curtseying low as her fandom showered her with praise. Always holding her breath; seeing if their applause could outlast her.

Lev and I pass an array of baggy shawls and move on to a gleaming collection of watches, followed by trays of faux diamond earrings; bracelets and necklaces in robin-egg-blue enamel; wooden Khokhloma handicrafts.

'That might be it,' he says, pointing to the next table.

A plump, broad-featured woman with dark chin whiskers spreads her hands wide to indicate her wares, a selection of lacquer miniatures and matryoshka dolls. She picks up a matryoshka and steadies it on her palm. The face looks standard, with bright blue eyes, two dots for a nose, ruby-red lips. But the scene depicted below the face, on the doll's body, is painted in excruciating detail: The Firebird, bursting with burgundy and orange plumage, about to take flight.

'Can I see?' I ask.

She places it in my hand. I flip it over: *E. N. Dayneko*, in block letters. Murderer and mafia contract killer – and woodworker and painter. No wonder the sumptuous red colour of the Firebird's wings looks so much like blood. I turn it over and over again. What sort of person has as much talent for creation as for death? Who paints fake faces with such care and eliminates real ones without a second thought? Does each object represent someone he killed, a life he took? Is he trying to resurrect his victims in some macabre way?

'He is from Fedoskino, so the lacquer boxes are very authentic,' says the woman. 'It's in their blood, you know. Just look at this paintwork, here!'

Fedoskino, indeed. They'll say anything to make a sale. 'I'd like to meet him,' I say, with confidence I don't quite feel. 'I might even have something he painted.'

'What's that?' she says, a bit unhappily.

The doll is already poking one chubby leg out of my bag. I smooth everything out and hand it to the vendor for inspection.

'I don't think so.' The woman frowns, the liver spots around her mouth quivering. 'But I can ask. Come back next weekend. What is your name?'

'Raisa,' I say. 'Raisa Simonova.'

'And will you buy something today?' The woman selects a different matryoshka. This one is carrying a basket of strawberries. I've opened enough of these to know that every doll inside will be holding something different: a bouquet, a tea kettle, a baby. The final doll might be holding something only the artist can see.

Little does this woman know, I've recently inherited enough dolls to open my own stall. I hand her a wad of roubles, which she pockets eagerly, her sun-beaten mouth arranging itself into a smile.

'You're sure this is a good idea?' asks Lev, as we fall back in line with the passing crowds.

'I've waited fourteen years. I think I can last another week.'

'Things are different now than when you left,' he says, cryptically. 'It might not happen as you expect.'

I've noticed over the past few weeks how different things are. There were no parliamentary debates on telly when I was a kid. No liberal politicians like President Boris Yeltsin daring to take on the hard-line communists; no independent newspapers for sale at the kiosks. Only *Pravda* and *Izvestiia*, state-owned and state-controlled. But I'm sure there are other sides to it, as well. I did not grow up in a world dominated by *deficits* or shortages of basic foods and goods. The lines were never this long.

We've come to the edge of the market. A group of European tourists is blocking the wooden bridge that leads to the small kremlin. Lev doesn't say anything more, but I know what he's thinking: I'd be better off as a tourist too. But I can't be a tourist here in Moscow. It's either this, or I would be already back on Aeroflot, using my bag as a pillow, seeing the blur of lights below as the aeroplane begins its descent into Heathrow. Richard would be at the gate to meet me.

Welcome back to your real life, Ro.

I ache with homesickness at the thought of it. But I'm doing all this for Richard's sake too. For the sake of our future together.

'If it's what you have to do,' Lev says, grimly.

'They're the ones that died,' I say. 'I should be the one living.'

Alexey sits down at the kitchen table across from me. He's in black-tie, doubtlessly headed to some formal function, some other celebration of his life. Since we arrived there has been an unceasing flow of invitations and engagements and phone calls. Alexey Ivanov made it possible to talk about the Gulag in Russia, and now people expect him never to stop.

'You've been reading?' he asks.

'I've done four on the list so far.' I gesture to my spread of books and paper. 'Do you want my notes?'

'I hate to divert you, but I have something else in mind.'

I put down my pen. I can tell that it's going to be something mysterious and tedious. More maps, maybe.

'I spotted this by chance the other day.' Alexey pulls out yet another book. Its dust jacket is sparkly new, garish compared to the covers laid out in front of me. 'It's a Civil War memoir by an aristocrat called Natalya Burzinova. She was famous – infamous – at the time. You know the years of the Civil War?'

Now I do. '1918 to 1922?'

'I've only read the introduction. She was arrested for smuggling and speculating by the Petrograd Cheka in 1920. She wrote this memoir in jail.' Alexey sounds faraway for a moment, drifty. 'I read as many memoirs as I can, you know. There are so many interesting people forgotten to history.'

But *he* rose above the fray, didn't he? Alexey Ivanov will never be forgotten.

'This text – the original handwritten copy of it – was apparently discovered in someone's basement a few years ago.' Alexey turns his attention back to me. 'Find out whose basement it was.'

'Oh,' I say, unable to conceal my surprise. 'I should contact the publishers then?'

'I already did. It was given to them by Natalya's daughter. Her name is Akulina Burzinova. She lives here in Moscow. I want you to go in person and talk to her.'

Why? is what I want to ask, but his voice is too bland, his expression as burnished as the book's cover. He's not going to tell me.

'I'm off.' Alexey smiles at me. 'I have to be out of town this weekend, I think I mentioned.'

Lev reads aloud again from Mum's notebook, this time without asking. Tonight's story, 'The Silver Queen', is about a queen who wore a magical silver necklace that enables her to live for ever. Without it, she would die. The tale is short, and though this too goes without asking, neither of us are ready to fall asleep afterwards. The night feels too soft, too summery, like we should be having drinks by the river, smoking, even though I don't smoke. Laughing, even though I don't do that too much either.

'You know Koschei the Deathless, the fairy tale?' asks Lev. 'This story, with the necklace, it reminds me of it.'

Every schoolchild in Russia has heard of Koschei the Deathless, the immortal who stores his life in objects, who gets up to nasty tricks, stealing women, slaying rivals.

'My mother liked to tell her own version of Koschei,' I say. 'He falls in love, or something.'

'You don't enjoy these stories,' he says. 'I can tell. Why are we reading them?'

'I promised her I would. And it's not that I don't enjoy them, it's that . . . you know, what's the point?'

'The point of what?'

'Of stories. Fiction. Fantasy. Mum was always reading novels, daydreaming, making things up. She preferred to spend all her time in this world that was fake. That's probably another reason she didn't like *The Last Bolshevik*.' I lie back, playing with my scrunchie. 'Because it was true.'

'Maybe you're interpreting too literally,' Lev says. 'The stories could be allegorical. Perhaps she is writing about real ideas or even real people, and not about monsters and queens.'

'Maybe. But Mum wasn't a subtle person. I think her stories were mostly for entertainment. For escape.'

'She chose her words with care,' he points out. 'I see

146

many places where it looks as if she erased the original word she used and wrote another.'

'That *really* doesn't sound like my mother.' I wrap the scrunchie back around my wrist. 'Erased? It's in pen.'

'Only the first page,' he says. 'The note to the reader.'

I go silent as he switches off the light. Pencil. Mum didn't often use pencil; the rubber erasers made her eyes itch. Some kind of allergy.

'I used to be an avid reader,' says Lev, neutrally. 'In school. Before I joined the military.'

My eyes have adjusted enough to the darkness that I can find him across the length of the room, see him sitting up on the cot, back against the wall, looking away. I know now that he's twenty-seven years old; that he's spent the last nine years in the military, the last five in the Moscow OMON. What did he do most days, I wonder? Climb through the windows of burning buildings? Tear down barricades with his bare hands?

I already know the answer. He did whatever he was told.

Years ago, here in Moscow, my family had an elderly neighbour who collected samizdat, illegal dissident material circulated by the anti-Soviet underground. Sometimes, when Zoya and I were home from school, he would share it with us. Poetry, novels, even diaries. And though I was too young to understand most of it, I gleaned the message that emanated from his every pore: there is *them*, and there is *us*.

Lev is one of *them*.

In the year 1895, Natalya, future countess, is an awkward and socially stunted six-year-old, with – in her words – carrot-red hair and a breathy lisp. Her only friend is a little boy whose parents attend a party at Natalya's home one day, who joins her in hiding by the stairwell. That year, Natalya's already frail mother dies of consumption, and her father hastily remarries. Her new stepmother is an opium-addled woman who hosts raucous salon parties and desperately wishes to get into the good graces of the Imperial Family. Natalya comes into her own, over the years. No longer awkward, she discovers by late adolescence that she's in love with that first friend, no longer a little boy. Her stepmother, getting wind of this, responds by arranging a union with the much older, twice-married Count Burzinov.

It was not out of weakness that I gave into my stepmother's wishes. It was out of fear.

I could not confess my feelings to the man I loved.

Natalya's most cherished possession is her mother's silver Orthodox cross, which she wears on a necklace. Given her relationship with her stepmother, I can understand why she would cling to this small piece of her birth mother. To the idea of a parent she lost, and a life of which she must have felt robbed.

I'm no countess, but I feel a sudden camaraderie with her.

The next few chapters of the memoir deal with her family life. The Count is a dreary man. They rapidly have two children. Natalya, though she loves her children, is bored and unfulfilled by motherhood. She throws herself into the whirlwind of St Petersburg society, and finds herself empathising with her stepmother, of all people.

It is when everyone else's attention is upon us, that we can forget the one person whose head we fail to turn.

She is bitterly lonely. Natalya struggles to connect with her children, in particular her daughter Akulina – the two of them are very different – while the Count's health declines. She takes lovers, but she never stops longing for her friend. He has no romantic interest in her, and I start to suspect that this unattainability is partly why she focuses all her intense feelings on him.

She doesn't know how to be loved back.

Lev comes in as I'm reading. He's just dropped Alexey off at a train station.

'Something to drink?' he asks. I nod.

In the summer of 1914, there is an unwelcome if foreseeable turn of events: the man Natalya loves finally marries someone else.

His new bride was the most ornamental-looking creature you will have ever seen.

But there was something in her eyes that I did not trust.

I was reminded that rare diamonds are kept behind glass not only to preserve them, not only to prevent thievery.

Also because they are cursed.

I read on until I reach 1918, the start of the Civil War, which forces Natalya to wake up to the reality of what is happening in Russia. All this time, she has been firmly convinced that the Tsar or his brother would be brought back as a constitutional monarch; now she seems frightened. She joins the effort to aid the White Army, which eventually lands her in prison, and here the memoir reaches her present moment: it is 1920. The Countess is writing out of a jail cell in Bolshevik-controlled Petrograd. She has negotiated with the guards for various favours, including paper. They don't treat her badly, but she has just been told she faces execution.

They have taken my belongings, my children, my home,

my freedom. I have nothing but the silver cross around my neck. When they take that, they will have killed me.

A silver necklace that she will wear until death.

Like in 'The Silver Queen', the story of Mum's that Lev and I read just last night. *Another* coincidence?

I look up and Lev has returned. I explain as best I can: first the map of Popovka, and now this. In a way, I prefer when things are obviously wrong, blood everywhere and your mother sobbing and the police shouting and the shoe-prints of a mafia killer all over the apartment.

This is what I can't stand. When you can't tell what's wrong, but you just know, nonetheless, that it's there.

'I believe in coincidences,' says Lev.

'How's that?'

'Sometimes things that seem too improbable, even impossible, just happen.' He holds my gaze. 'It's funny. You are the one who believes she is being haunted, but you are also the more sceptical of the two of us.'

'You really think it could be random? Meaningless?' I ask.

'I didn't say meaningless. Perhaps your mother heard of this woman, this countess, if she was so famous. Or even read this memoir.'

'I told you, Mum wasn't keen on non-fiction. Something else is going on here.'

Lev half-smiles. 'I see how you are always trying to fit things together,' he says. 'Not just what happened to your family, but everything, all around you.'

I don't know what to say, so I look down at my hands, twist them together.

'I didn't say it was bad, Raisa.'

I look up again and this time, he treats me to a real smile. To my shock, I feel a light frisson down my spine, the unravelling of a knot in my stomach that I wasn't even aware of.

Oh, *no*, no, no.

'I'm going to pop out to make a few phone calls,' I say quickly.

'No problem. I should run to the supermarket,' he says.

Alexey's telephone sits on a three-legged stool in the entry hall. I cradle the receiver as Lev puts on his shoes. The frisson tapers off with the sound of his footsteps. I need to step more carefully. I'm doing so much digging into the past; I don't want to overturn anything else. I tell myself, more than once to reinforce it, that it wasn't because of Lev, that whispery little feeling. It was just hearing my former name the way he said it. Like I have never been Rosie at all.

The operator puts me through. Thankfully it's the weekend and Richard is at home, and I tuck myself into the space between the stool and the wall and I tell him all the things I was going to say in my letters. He laughs at the idea of merry-making cockroaches, says he's discovered a mouse in our apartment. It's eaten a hole through one of the cupboards and he wants to call the exterminator but at the same time he feels bad. Maybe he'll hold off until I come home.

Home: that existence in England that's sitting there on ice. Waiting for me.

Without Rosie, there's nowhere to go from here.

CHAPTER ELEVEN

Antonina
Tula province, 1917

THE TRAVEL BY TRAIN IS MORE THAN A DAY'S WORTH. As the hours pass, Tonya finally begins to enjoy the spicy scent of coal, the incessant rhythm of the wheels. She lies down on her wooden bench to sleep and as she does, there's a twitch in her belly. A strange sensation, almost unearthly. She turns, and there's another. Cautiously she runs a hand over her dress, down her ribs, past her belly button, towards her hip bone. But whatever it was has already gone.

The last leg of her journey is a coach that leaves her in Popovka, at the house of Kirill Vladimirovich. Kirill once worked at Otrada as a stablehand, back when Papa could afford that many horses. He is one of her closest friends, the other being Nelly.

But to Tonya's astonishment, he and Nelly are now *married*.

The slight, silly Nelly has been replaced by a real wife of a woman. One who offers Tonya soup and honey tea and a place by the *pech'*, the masonry stove, and announces breathily that Kirill is out at the windmills.

'I've always adored him,' Nelly says, untying her scarf. 'You know that.'

'I thought the same way I did,' says Tonya stiltedly. 'As a brother!'

'I already have a brother,' Nelly says, matter-of-fact. 'And he doesn't look like Kirill.'

Tonya cringes. 'I plan to go on to Otrada tomorrow,' she says, to change the subject. 'Papa doesn't know I'm coming. How is he managing, Nelly?'

Nelly doesn't answer. Tonya notices that Nelly is wearing a peasant's *panyova*, a long, chequered skirt. The material is coarse, ungainly, unbecoming. It is the costume of grown women. This whole scene is surreal and yet familiar, the simple wooden home with its thatched roof, the animals making noise outside in the yard, the way Nelly seats herself at the wheel. She spins hemp, round and round and round, while the oil lamp gives off a moony glow.

These are the sights and smells of home; *this*, right here, is surely where Tonya belongs. They sit without conversing further, and Tonya begins to feel sleepy.

'Is that you, Tonya?'

She jerks upright, nearly spilling her tea. Kirill comes to where she is sitting and gives her a kiss on the head. He is still broad-shouldered, beaming, the same boy who taught Tonya to ride, to fish, and even her sums, when Mama and Papa declined to send her to the village school. Who was once dreadfully infatuated with Mama, so that all Popovka knew.

'You have such a beard now,' says Tonya, with affection, but Kirill only pulls out a chair at the table beside her.

A new scent is keen in the air, overcooked and overdone. Nelly has stopped spinning.

Something is wrong.

'I must tell you about your father,' says Kirill.

Tonya looks back and forth between them. She's had no word from Papa in years, but that didn't come as any surprise. Papa just about stopped speaking altogether after Mama's death in childbirth, mere months before Tonya married Dmitry, and there was no proper goodbye when Tonya left, only a hand lifted briefly as he looked up from his hothouse roses. It could have been to reach for his pruners.

Quietly Kirill explains that a few village mobs banded together just after the revolution in February. Armed with nothing more than farm tools, they began marching on the estates of the landed gentry, hanging the inhabitants of those estates, setting fire to library collections older than Russia herself. Enacting one thousand years of revenge in one night.

'They ransacked Otrada,' says Kirill. 'But they left it standing, at least. They killed the Prince.' He sounds strangled. 'Gutted him. In the conservatory. His handprints were all over the glass.'

Tonya wants to ask what happened to Papa's body, where it's buried now. Even if Papa never wanted anything to do with her, she'd rather know. But the words don't form right, and even as Kirill and Nelly's faces fill with sympathy, something else begins to brew in Tonya's mind. The family at Otrada is old and noble, yes, the villagers always used to say; their line can be traced back to the days of ancient Muscovy. But their blood has curdled. Something is rotten. That's why the Prince and Princess have had no more children, after Kukolka. Why all the babies end up dead. *The family is cursed.*

Such gossip never bothered Mama the way it did Tonya, of course. *They are simple, superstitious folk, the muzhiki,* Mama would remark, while staring into her own black-opal eyes in the mirror.

They are jealous of anything beautiful. They are afraid, and all they have is their pitchforks.

Mama was right, but still there are times when Tonya wonders if the village knew her family best. If there was a curse Mama would have seen, if she'd only turned around.

The weeks drift along. Tonya sleeps poorly, spends hours lying in the crawl space above the stove. For the first time in her life, she begins to awaken *inside* her nightmares. She often finds herself, in these dreams, close to the veranda behind Otrada; in the orchards. She can hear the barking of Papa's borzois. The French doors are open. Something soft slinks between her legs. It is the family cat, Sery. There is an outline of someone in the doorway.

Mama.

Tonya's eyes fly open.

There it is again, that twinge at the base of her abdomen. She presses up and down her stomach and the more she does, the giddier she feels. The strange dream is instantly forgotten. She's felt a hard ridge like this before, but from the outside. It was as big as Mama ever got.

The baby?

Could the Lulikov family doctor have been wrong? But if so, what could she have lost in all that blood, clotty as kasha?

Nelly, who confides that she is hoping to fall pregnant herself, says that they should ask the village midwife. Tonya's sure that Mama once said pregnancy makes you smell things stronger than normal, and the burnt-leaf scent of Nelly's candles does make her want to retch. Sometimes she can even smell the unharvested orchards of Otrada, fervent and filthy, the stink from the estate hanging over the village. It reminds her of Dmitry's cologne. As if he has followed her here.

The midwife touches Tonya's belly, says, *Oh, look, I think your baby is awake*, and Tonya pitches forward, trying to capture the movement within. The midwife says, *Have you never felt a baby, and don't you know that they swim like that*, but Mama's babies never moved like this. The midwife isn't certain of the source of the bleeding a month before, but she says she's seen it happen. The bursting of some sac in the early to middle weeks, but the baby is fine.

'Wonderful news,' exclaims Nelly. 'Imagine if we could have little ones close in age, Tonya!'

Tonya keeps her hands spread like fins across her midsection.

'Before you go, Shura,' says Nelly, addressing the midwife, 'tell us. *You* would know – you speak with everyone. Has anyone been by Otrada recently, or seen the state it's in?'

The midwife nods. 'Some kids said they saw a curl of smoke from the chimney.'

'A squatter? A malingerer?'

Tonya listens only vaguely, her thoughts fluttering like the baby, her heart pounding. If she is still pregnant, should she write to Valentin? Should she let him know? But how could she say it? How could she not say it?

'Kids telling tales, is all. They said they saw someone in front of the house, by the willows. A woman holding a pair of infant mittens, half stitched. No baby in sight.' The midwife's tone is resentful. It is terrible luck to prepare gifts for a baby before the birth, and nobody would know it better than a midwife. 'The woman had curling hair pinned up with flowers, they said. Wore a flax dress with trimmings. They're telling people it's a ghost.'

The midwife says it like she doesn't believe in ghosts, but they are all raised to believe in ghosts, around here. In witches, wood-goblins, talking animals, water-spirits, house-spirits. In magic.

Tonya moves her hand over her belly again, which feels tighter, tauter than before, and she feels the baby's flurry of kicks, as if in reply. She grew up here too, but she never believed in any magic. Not until now, at least. Not until today.

The summer passes slow and hot. Valentin doesn't reply to any of her letters, but the pregnancy has put Tonya into a kind of trance. Under its spell, she is unaware of feelings other than the baby's kicks, her hunger, the throb in her arms and legs as she works the harvest fields for the first

157

time in her life. She will think about Valentin later, after the spell breaks.

It happens, abruptly, on a pale evening in September. As Tonya stands from the rocking chair, there is a soaring, gripping pain across her body. Nelly looks up from spinning. The room is spinning too. The baby has been unusually still all day, and a band of fear tightens around Tonya's chest. Maybe she worked too long today. But peasant women all work until they give birth; some even try to work through labour. Mama never worked, barely even left the bedroom while she was pregnant, sometimes not even the bed.

That is the other thought Tonya has not fully allowed herself, all these months, alongside the thought of Valentin.

Mama's babies.

The pain again, sharper now, like fingernails scraped across a wound, and Tonya gasps. Kirill is not home. The midwife could be anywhere from here to Kalasy.

Nelly's eyes turn to beads. 'Is it coming?'

'I don't know,' Tonya says, in a pant.

'I'll go for the midwife,' says Nelly. 'Lie down, dearest. I'll be back right away.'

Breathlessly Tonya does as she is told. It cannot be the baby, but of course it is, it's time, even if Valentin has answered none of her letters, even if she hasn't yet chosen a name, even if she's only a child herself, not quite nineteen. But these doubts are soon blasted away by another wave of agony, and she groans. A moment's relief, and then again, and then again.

No, not yet, not yet—

It only gets worse. The pain, and the terror. Tonya has no idea how to have a baby, at least a live one. She saw all those dead ones come out of Mama, of course, too many, and they are all she can see right now, the way they were bluish, furry, with their cords thick and grey and hung round their necks. The midwife would tie off these flaccid ropes with flax and blow on the tiny faces, on the hands, the feet, while Mama would flop over like a fish, like she was the one who could not get any air.

No, no, no—

'Let me help,' says a voice. A male voice.

Tonya squeezes one eye open.

'I was passing by outside, and heard your cries,' says the stranger. 'It's easier if you sit up and brace yourself against me.'

She has no presence of mind, no time to wonder who he is. She lets out a sob, swipes at the sweat on her face.

'Breathe,' the voice continues. '*Tishe edesh', dal'she budesh'*. No?'

Tonya looks blindly at him, trying to absorb the meaning of this old village phrase, *The slower you ride, the further you go*, trying to express that every baby she ever saw was dead, but instead what emerges is a roar, a primordial sound. He looks as if he understands. She has the unclear sense that she knows him from somewhere but before she can think of where, it is happening again, she is ripping open.

She screams loud enough to unseal the windows.

'Here's the head. It won't be long.'

Something breaks, surges. Tonya falls back against the bed, feeling her tongue roll out of her mouth and back in again. *Is it alive?* she tries to ask, but the stranger is smiling.

159

'Baby girl,' he says. 'There is still the afterbirth.'

'Afterbirth?'

He is already wrapping the baby in cloth, and it begins to wail. Tonya reaches out for her daughter, and then Nelly is there, suddenly, and the midwife too, and soon Tonya doesn't know who is crying any more and who isn't. She feels clumsy and careless as she looks down at her own child for the first time. She never knew newborns could be like this, red-faced and furious, but also milky and warm, with hummingbird-breaths.

'Oh, Tonya,' says Nelly, brushing a finger over the baby's slippery head. 'Oh, I must have one too, I must.'

'Who helped me?' Tonya says hoarsely. 'I want to thank him.'

Nelly looks away. 'No one I know,' she says. 'Must have been a good Samaritan just passing through.'

Tonya decides to call the baby Lena. In slumber Lena looks ethereal, like a fairy, but awake she never stops crying. Nelly is able to calm her much better than Tonya, clucking and cooing, whispering how soon she will have a baby too, hopefully, a friend that Lena can play with.

In winter the world is swept white. The trees wear the snowfall like queens. New papers finally make their way into Popovka, and Kirill reads aloud in a sombre voice: There is no more Provisional Government, no more Imperial ministers, no more links to the reign of the Tsar. There has been another revolution. Another coup.

The Winter Palace itself has been taken.

Petrograd belongs to the Bolsheviks.

Soon after the spring thaws, a brigade of Chekists arrives in the village. The Cheka are said to be the new Bolshevik secret police, but nobody knows what this will mean. The brigade sets up camp in the village and Tonya sees them in the lane sometimes, in their matching leather greatcoats, a washed-out quality to their faces, like a piece of laundry gone over one time too many.

Every night, Tonya remains slack atop the *pech'*, as the baby rustles angrily on her belly, roots for a nipple. She feels her bowels burning, her breasts leaking, maybe her heart breaking, whatever is left of it. If Valentin has indeed received her letters, he has still not deigned to answer. Valentin Andreyev has reached the future, *his* future, and she is in the past, and the space between them is infinite.

There is shouting from outside, but no knocking. Lena is on her hands and knees in the crib, sobbing, and Tonya has to scoop her from the basket, hoist her onto a hip. Nelly rolls to one side on the mattress nearby. Nelly has been crankier than normal. Kirill and Nelly are trying to have a baby, and Tonya takes long walks with Lena every day to avoid their lovemaking.

She needs to find her own place to live.

'Open up, comrades,' comes the command, but Chekists are already barrelling in. Their leather coats make them look like flayed animals.

The deputy declares that they are here for grain, for the surplus grain, that is being hidden in this village, in every home. His soldiers begin to overturn the farm tools, the horses' harnesses. They rip and rummage through everything they find: the kettles, the pots, the churn. They pilfer a bottle of barley liquor. Aside from the deputy himself, they are all clearly drunk, so drunk they wouldn't see surplus grain if it fell on their faces like snow.

Lena is still hollering. Wearily Tonya takes her to the rocking chair, lowers her blouse, and tries to latch the baby on, but Lena, worked up to a fury, only writhes on the breast.

Nelly sits up and stares across the room. She is whey-faced. 'Get out of my home,' she says, in a snarl.

For a second Tonya feels that Nelly is looking right at *her*.

'It is not normal times. We are at war,' the Chekist deputy replies, without emotion.

'You mean with Germany still, with the Kaiser?' Tonya asks, over Lena's howling.

'No.' He spits. 'We've just signed a peace with Germany. We are at war with the White Army, comrade, the forces who fight for the Tsar. Vladimir Lenin has called upon the Russian people to help weed out all enemies of the revolution.'

Tonya removes the baby from her breast. Having fed for hours, Lena has sniffled and snuffled herself to sleep at last. The room is quiet. Nelly is at the wheel, spinning hemp, eyes large and unfocused. Kirill stands, head lowered, in front of the small shrine to St Nicholas. He says the same prayer again and again, one of the Psalms: *De profundis clamavi ad te, Domine.*

From the depths, I have cried out to you, O Lord.

Nelly has started her monthly bleeding. It was a week late, giving rise to such high hopes. Tonya wants to tell her friend

162

to eat more. To smile more. To cease the weekly gatherings with the village ladies, who burst with new suggestions for what Nelly needs to do to get pregnant: Consume these herbs and not those ones. Stop sitting on cold surfaces. Spin your wheel a certain number of times before you stop.

Tell Kukolka to leave your home for good.

'Let us alone for a moment, Tonya,' says Kirill, without looking.

Lena appears settled in her blankets, so Tonya throws her shawl around her shoulders and slips outside. The night sky is slung low, and the moon casts the village in an icy light, but the air is fresh, tickly. A sign of spring. The timing must seem cruel to Nelly, for spring is symbolised by eggs. New life. New beginnings.

Maybe next month.

Behind the houses of Popovka, beyond the trees, lies the path that leads to Otrada. Once it was wide and cleared away enough to allow carriages and sleighs, and once there were harvest parties and dinners with neighbouring gentry families and music and merriment. The change took place gradually, over Tonya's childhood. The fields turning muddy. The forest turning darker. Mama turning inwards.

One person, or two people, could live off the land at Otrada easily. The vegetable plots, the orchards, the deep larders; Tonya knows it all better than anyone. And nobody would bother her.

People may soon forget that the estate was ever there.

New beginnings.

There is a sound. Someone dressed in a sheepskin coat is walking along the village lane, leading a horse by the nose. It's the stranger from the day Lena was born. He doffs his hat, showing a glimpse of short, white-blonde hair. His eyes are light, startling. He is younger than she remembers, perhaps not quite thirty.

'It's you,' she says plainly. 'I didn't know how to find you.'

'Were you looking for me?' he asks.

'I wished to thank you. My daughter is six months old. I don't know what I would have done without you. I'm Tonya,' she adds.

'Sasha,' he says. 'Sasha Ozhereliev.'

He bids her a good evening and Tonya returns it, his name flickering in her memory. Sasha Ozhereliev. A village outcast, rumoured to have murdered his wife and her lover, years ago, it would have been. He'd been banished into the wilderness, coming into town rarely, only to be sneered back out again.

But perhaps the presence of the Cheka has emboldened him. The villagers are not the only authority around any more.

'Sasha Ozhereliev has been coming around since before the Chekists,' says Nelly, in snipped tones. 'Since the Tsar abdicated at least. I believe he has something to do with the attacks on the estates, Tonya. I wouldn't be surprised if he's the one who killed your father!'

'Is there reason to think that he killed Papa?' Tonya asks.

'He's a killer! What more reason do you need?'

If Nelly were her usual self, and not this facsimile, Tonya would confide right now that she, too, is nearly a killer. That

164

Dmitry died because of her. But there are already whispers enough about her in Popovka, by now more so than about Sasha Ozhereliev. *No baby will be born to Nelly and Kirill until Tonya leaves,* is what the villagers say; *maybe Kukolka wants Kirill for herself! It's wrong that he lets her live with them, but he was always weak, wasn't he, when it came to that family! Poor, poor Nelly!*

'There may be more to his story,' Tonya says instead.

'There isn't,' retorts Nelly. 'Some people just don't belong here.'

As spring turns to summer Tonya works the fields again with the others. The soil is shuddery-soft, like fresh clay. She binds, threshes, weeds until the skin comes off her hands. Lena is an early walker who stays at Tonya's heels like a sheepdog. Refuses to be left behind with anyone. The peasants are increasingly rankled, rubbed wrong by the demands of the Chekists. Tonya can feel the anger coming off the others as she works, and out here, now that the hours are long and the fields are long too and the people are tired, the murmurs become raised voices: *It's because of Kukolka, all of their bad luck! And where is Nelly, why does she not come to work? Where is Nelly?*

Tonya asks herself that question too when she sees Nelly at home, sewing a shawl that never seems to end. Nelly will look at Lena and then at Tonya and the look says, *Some people just don't belong here.*

At last Tonya receives a reply in the post. *Valentin has gone away to the front,* it says. *I will pass on all messages to him when he returns. Yours sincerely, Viktoria Andreyeva.*

Tonya stares down at the note, the loop of letters. Viktoria Andreyeva. She remembers Viktoria Katenina, with those eyes like milk saucers.

She doesn't remember Viktoria Andreyeva.

Valentin is married.

Sasha Ozhereliev seats himself at the table but declines the offer of bread or tea. Lena is eating a baked potato, shoving it in with both fists, and Sasha reaches into his coat, produces a wooden miniature sleigh for which the baby lunges. He catches her and sets her gently on the ground. Lena wobbles away, prize in hand, and Tonya hides a smile.

Kirill's at the granary and Tonya knows, just knows, that Sasha has chosen *this* moment, that he wanted to catch her on her own.

Relatively, of course, for Nelly is there, pricking away at the shawl that nobody needs.

'People talk about you,' says Sasha. He glances at Tonya and she catches herself thinking that his eyes are luminous. There is an impenetrable aspect to his face, but he isn't murderous looking. He doesn't seem like someone who came across his wife and a neighbour against the wall of a cowshed, the cows lowing only yards away, masking their gasps. Someone who had a scythe and a flash of rage so fast that the pair had no time to make another sound, of pleasure *or* pain.

Tonya dusts specks of potato off the table. 'There's not much to talk about in Popovka.'

Nelly makes the closest thing to a laugh Tonya has heard from her in weeks.

'I often think of leaving,' says Sasha.

'Where would you go?' Tonya asks.

'I'd like to live in a house by a wide river. I have some cousins in Saratov.'

Saratov. Saratov is on the Volga, that mighty river that divides this country into east and west. Valentin spoke often of the city, the birthplace of many famous radical writers and revolutionaries. *There is a rich black soil unique to that region*, was what he said, *the richest soil known to man. In such fertile earth, anything can grow, even a cause as unlikely as ours. All it takes is a single seed.*

But that was always the way Valentin explained things. Turned simple facts into poetry. Twisted them.

'We will live, we will see,' Sasha answers, obliquely. He reaches for his hat, as if this was all he ever planned to say. 'The Chekists are interested in Otrada,' he adds. 'They're searching for a place they might requisition for their own . . . purposes. Do you wish for me to direct them elsewhere?'

'Why would they listen to you?' she says crisply.

'I've helped them with a few things.'

'Then tell them to leave Otrada alone.'

A corner of his mouth lifts in a smile. 'I shall.'

When Sasha has gone, Nelly begins to reel in the shawl. She finally breaks her monkish silence: 'You should stay away from him.'

'Why?' asks Tonya loudly. 'Because the village hates him?'

'Because there's something wrong with him. You can tell just by looking. He's cold-blooded. Inhuman.'

'He helped bring Lena into the world. He can't be evil.'

'He murdered his wife!'

'Did he?' Tonya snaps back. 'Was her dead body dragged through the village? She and her lover disappeared, Nelly. For all we know they ran off together.'

'Leaving behind her child? That was the *first* baby he delivered, you know! And where is the child now? Nobody knows. No one has seen the boy in years. A lot has happened in Popovka, Tonya, since you flitted off to the capital!' Nelly is shouting. The windows are rattling. 'But you think you can just come back, swan in, win everyone over—'

'I've done no such thing! They loathe me!'

'They don't loathe you, you idiot. They envy you. Desire you. You are still a princess and always will be. And what has it been like for me, all my life, to stand beside you? Can you begin to understand? I was *happy* when you left! I wish you'd stayed away for ever!' Tears stream down Nelly's face. 'Everyone knows Kirill was in love with your mother. If he can't have her, why not you? Our little Kukolka?'

Silence.

Lena drops her new toy and begins to cry.

Nelly returns to the shawl. Tonya is left shaking. Kirill's affection is familial, there is no question of anything else, but she feels exhausted, bruised. Tonight her sleep will be fraught and fleeting, and tomorrow she will be out on those fields again, feeling the gaze of the village on her back, hotter than the low-lying sun.

Nelly has fallen asleep, and Tonya is fixing a hole in Nelly's *panyova*. She tugs on the thread, pulls it through. Every so often the thread breaks. Tonya remembers that just after their betrothal, Dmitry took her to the fields to watch the village folk at work. Instead of sunflower nubs to snack on, he said, she would have Antonovka apples and plums. Instead of the stink of her own sweat, she would have perfume water from Paris. Instead of country dress, she would have ball gowns to rival the Tsaritsa Alexandra.

Yet here she is, fixing a hole in a *panyova* because it is the only thing she can fix.

Kirill comes in and sits by the shrine. Tonya can tell how troubled he's become. It's not only his beard that is now crested with white. Also his hair, the look in his eye. He doesn't say anything as he lights a candle to the saints.

De profundis clamavi ad te, Domine.

'I've stayed too long,' says Tonya quietly.

'You don't have anywhere else to go,' Kirill says, his eyes now closed.

'I do,' she says. 'I'm going home.'

Tonya senses that something awaits her in her nightmares, only the figure of Mama is always blocking the way.

I am dreaming, this is only a dream, she reminds herself, as she approaches Otrada from the back, through the orchards, just as she does every time. Ducking the branches. The veranda is up ahead. Dream-Sery is by her ankles, purring so low it is only vibration. If Tonya goes closer, she will see Mama; she already knows that. Tonight she tries something else. She goes around the rotunda, towards the conservatory.

The door to the conservatory is open. Dream-Sery follows her inside, though the real Sery never wandered into this glass house. Once filled with Papa's exotic flowers, it was steamy, sickly-sweet all the year round. There are no flowers in here now. The ground is covered in ivy. Papa did not grow ivy. The ivy has climbed the walls, strangles all the beams. It is still growing even as Tonya stands there watching it.

Someone is coming into the conservatory through the other entrance, from within the house.

It is a girl, a young girl, with white ribbons in her plaited hair. With a dullish sense of horror Tonya sees that the ivy covers the girl, too, but from the inside, like darkened veins. Showing through the skin.

The girl looks at her.

Help me, she says to Tonya, but as she opens her mouth, the ivy slithers out.

Tonya begins to scream.

CHAPTER TWELVE

Valentin

Southern Russia, 1919

THEY ARE LEAVING BEHIND THE PLAIN, PARCHED grasslands of the steppe. No more peasants plod by leading scrawny livestock by the nose; no more shaky caravans pass, heaped with too many belongings. Here the land has not yet been ravaged by occupation and conflict, and here it has a shape: hills and furrows and shallow valleys that distinguish it from the flat, unbroken sky.

In the late afternoon they make an encampment atop a small hill, and Valentin stops to survey a Russia he has never known.

'What are those white things over there?' he asks the man beside him.

'Chapels,' his fellow prisoner replies, looking at him strangely. 'Do you want to know what that blue line is, too?'

The line is a river that snakes up another hill, between a sprinkling of wooden houses. Valentin stands still, lets the wind blow against him. His feet and legs are coming back to life. He feels heavy and flushed. A horsefly buzzes by his ear, and he looks over to where the other war prisoners are sitting, their faces chalky with dust, just out of range of the campfire's warmth. A jug of water is being passed from hand to hand. Valentin's throat feels lined with that same dust. He is always thirsty now. He could drink that whole river beyond and not quench it.

'Something you're trying to see out there, brother?' the other man asks wryly, the emphasis on *brother* a mockery of the way the Don Cossacks address each other.

Valentin shakes his head. A sound begins to rise, above the scuffling of the horses' hooves, the agitated swarming of insects. It is the White officers, *singing* again. How many times can they sing the same folksy ballads of Maria and her true love? How many times can he hear them before his ears start bleeding? But the singing is over quickly tonight, and they have begun to make elaborate, impassioned toasts: The greatness of the Tsar! The glory of the empire! That prima ballerina onstage three years ago, her pale, slender neck!

The smell of honey from the bird-cherry trees; the sight of home in the corner of one's eye from around the curve in the road . . .

Valentin wipes something wet from his cracked lips. He is *crying*. What little hydration he still has, he is wasting on them, on the enemy, but he can't help himself. He can envision it too, that world, in all its decadence, an obscene mask of beauty obscuring the ugly, steaming, seething masses below, and in the middle of it all, himself and—

Tonya.

The toasts are turning to curses, the drunken cheers to indignant anger. Home is no longer there, not as it was, because the peasants have looted the estate; the bird-cherry trees are a smoking ruin. The Tsar has fallen.

'Let's go into the village,' comes the furious cry.

The mood of the prisoners shifts. They know what this means; what will happen. They will be gathered up, too many to a wagon. Human cargo. Down in the village they will be locked in barns and left to suffocate in the miasma of horse manure while the Whites storm somebody's home. Whatever they find, whoever they find, they will take.

The sound of one child screaming will be louder than all the warring armies of Russia put together.

Valentin shuts his eyes. He gropes for a thought, a line, a philosophy that will comfort him, but all that comes to mind tonight is that countryside and the light wind that swept through, brushing up against him, out of nowhere, carrying her touch with it.

His throat begins to itch, especially at night. He no longer participates in conversation with the other prisoners. Their number include locals, stragglers, deserters; they are all tired of war. Many recall seeing their home villages burnt by the Whites, their wives and daughters raped, their Jews and Tartars beaten to bone. Others claim the Red Army does all these same things.

Valentin wants to defend his side. The Reds act out of principle. If there is violence, it is the necessary kind. In the annals of history, centuries from now, the rightness of the communist cause will be obvious to all. *The past cannot be allowed to defeat the future!*

But he is too thirsty to speak.

Valentin has been a prisoner since last winter. Before his capture, he was a commissar of the Red Army, tasked with boosting morale amongst the peasant conscripts in his regiment who did not identify with the Reds or even with Russia herself. He failed in this.

He had never failed before.

The prisoners sleep most nights out in the open now, because of an outbreak of what the bivouac officer calls the *flu*. The longer he spends out here, living like the nomadic hordes of the steppe, looking up at that canopy of stars, the more that failure weighs on him. The more he loses his bearings. The more he wonders how he came to be here in the first place.

The more his throat hurts.

The local flu is typhus, they say. Valentin is quickly transferred to the special barracks, and cannot go haul loads on the railways with everyone else. Nobody seems to know how many recover from typhus. Maybe the people who do know are all dead.

He fights a high and hungry fever for weeks, in the care of a nurse with a foreign accent. You are in Samara, she explains. East of the Volga. He doesn't even remember crossing the Volga. He suffers delirium, visions, convulsions. His lucid moments grow fewer and further between. The nurse's voice sounds like someone playing on the frets of a balalaika. Sometimes he thinks he hears the men to either side of him plotting over his head their escape from these barracks, from Russia altogether: *past the bridge, into the village, onto a stolen horse . . .*

174

He is trapped in the space between night and day. *Between*. Valentin did not even believe in the existence of *between*, before. Only in the one and the other. In opposites. In opposition.

Valentin.

He suddenly feels a cool hand on his hot forehead. He sees Tonya in front of him, her white shawl tied over her hair, like a halo. The moon rises above her head, and when she smiles, he cannot tell if she is standing in the light, or if she is the one to give light. If she is all the light he has ever known.

'Take a bite. It's kefir.' The nurse is waving a spoon in his face. 'I'll write to your sweetheart, lad, if you tell me how. Her full name . . .'

Valentin coughs, gags on the syllables. The image is fading. He wants to run after it, catch up to it, but his feet are leaden. You cannot chase light, anyway. You cannot even hold it.

It is too late.

'Tonya,' prompts the nurse. 'You've been asking for her.'

No, he tries to respond, *my wife is called Viktoria. My wife and I share a joint calling. My wife is the woman I love* – but even as he thinks it, shapes it with his lips, he knows that it isn't true. Maybe it didn't matter before, that he doesn't love her. It didn't matter the day they married, when they went down to the Registry Office and Viktoria was on his arm saying how perfect they were for one another, how much sense this made; and there was no arguing with that, nor with her happiness on the way home. He cares for Viktoria. He wants her to be happy.

But if it didn't matter then, it matters now, now that Valentin is going to die.

I've made a terrible mistake, he tells the nurse, but he only hears a murmur of sympathy in reply, a whispered promise, maybe in Russian, maybe in her native tongue: *It'll be over soon, lovely lad.*

CHAPTER THIRTEEN

Rosie

Moscow, July 1991

I MAKE A NEW CUP OF TEA AND DRAG ONE OF THE KITCHEN chairs into the foyer, next to the stool. I can't imagine that the daughter of a countess could actually be living somewhere in this city, but when I call Moscow Information, the operator gives me a phone number for Akulina Burzinova. With a name like that, it's unsurprising that there's only one. I rotate the dial carefully. My tea sits, long steeped, and I'm just about to hang up when somebody picks up. She has a crackly voice, a log on a fire. I tell her that I'm a historian's assistant, researching her mother's era, and would she be willing to answer some questions about the memoir?

'If you can come to me,' Akulina says, with a harsh cough. 'I don't travel.'

That's when I hear it.

A laboured rendition of a classical piano concerto. Tchaikovsky's First. Not coming from any room in the apartment, not through the walls or from the stairs outside, not down the telephone wire. Just there, like I'm sitting in the orchestral pit of Moscow's Symphony Hall.

Zoya.

She can make me smell things, see things *and* hear things now. None of my senses are safe.

I am not safe.

'Ms Simonova?'

This was my father's favourite piece of music. He used to play it on the wine-stained keys of our upright piano while Zoya would put her hands over her ears, moaning that the music was too depressing, too old, too wordless. Mum would be in the kitchen, humming along, smiling as she waited on the *ukha*, Papa's favourite oily fish soup, because classical music was the one place where my parents' interests touched, like the meeting of two electrical wires. Papa would later ruin the mood over supper by launching into his monologue about how music was only mathematics, and Mum would get upset: *How can you say that, Antosha! Music is art, it's beauty, it's nature, it's life!* And Papa would say that all those things were only mathematics too, and then they would stop arguing, but the silence would always be worse.

Zoya tried to jump in once, by saying, *If that's true, Papa, why don't you write music?*

One day I'll try, he said. *I like to try new things. New mediums.*

You could even put a code in it, said Zoya, sensing an opportunity to please.

Yes, he said, looking straight at me. *I could.*

A code.

'Hello? Hello!'

The soar of a crescendo, the climax, and then, as discreetly as the chords began, they fade to nothing. I feel the weight of the present moment settling back onto my shoulders, the way it does after I've watched a long film.

'Is anyone there?' Akulina Burzinova barks.

'Pardon me,' I say. 'Yes, I can come to you.'

I lean over to grab the pen, to take down her address. My cup of tea tips over in front of me, spontaneously, just off the rim of the stool, splashing on my bare feet. The lukewarm liquid dribbles between my toes. Akulina is telling me she lives in a peripheral suburb just barely in Moscow. Just barely. Just barely. I must have just barely touched the cup.

Unless Zoya can now move physical things—

No. No. She can't. That's not possible. I click my pen, bite my lip. I take down the address. Click again. No.

Zoya was my sister, my only sibling. No matter what, I loved her, and I believe that she loved me. I wish she hadn't died.

But at the same time, I also wish she would.

Through the slits of alleyways, I glimpse a few playgrounds and open spaces, but nothing that tells me where to go. If Lev is as lost as I feel, he isn't showing it. He stays in the background, blending too well into the silent high-rises, the dark tower blocks, that dominate this neighbourhood. I step into a puddle, less than two inches of water. It feels like more. I may never find my way out of this monolithic sprawl.

'There must be somebody to ask for directions,' I say uselessly, looking down the street, but there's only kids, kicking at some discarded tyres. Too young to know. Too young to be playing alone. The breeze picks up a chill somewhere and nicks at my thin coat. I feel small, straitjacketed into the passages between these lofty buildings.

Is this how Zoya feels, in the afterlife? Is this what she does? This endless circling? No street signs, no identifying marks? No people?

I button up my jacket as high as it goes.

We are an hour late by the time we find Akulina Burzinova's door, steel and spray-painted with obscenities. There are several doorbells, none of them marked. The door opens, revealing a grey-haired woman whose face is a road map of grooves and ridges. She is chewing on something, a repetitive, almost maniacal chewing, a cow with a cud.

'I saw you coming from my—' She stops. She is staring at me with green eyes set deep in their sockets. 'You,' she says. '*You're* the girl who called me?'

'I'm Raisa. Thank you so much for meeting with me,' I say. 'I'm so sorry we're late.'

'Not too late,' she says. 'Come in.'

The lobby of her building is stuffy and dingy. Akulina shakes her head at the rows of postboxes as if she finds the whole lot unseemly. We ascend the stairwell, with Akulina coughing every few seconds, moving like she's in pain. A calico-coloured cat is keeping watch at her open door, and its tail loops around my ankles as I go by.

'By the window is best,' she says, leading us into her living room. 'I breathe better.'

The cat follows, watchfully. I peek out the window to see the streets below, those deflated tyres, the heaps of

180

rubbish, looking different from above, sparkling in the sun. When I was down there, I couldn't perceive any light at all. Lev is right behind me, taking a look for himself, and I duck quickly beneath his arm, remembering too well the heady moment between us the other day. The way he smiled. The way my stomach plummeted.

I present Akulina with a box of chocolates, tied up with ribbon, and she nods, her jaws still working. I should have brought chewing gum.

Akulina invites us to sit on her sofa. She's prepared more than the usual smattering of Russian hospitality fare: breads and rolls and biscuits with jam. She disappears again to fetch drinks. The cat stretches out by my feet, its tail tight as cuffs around my calf. I sit with my back ramrod straight.

This is her. The Countess's daughter. We are about to take tea with Imperial nobility.

Akulina is absent for a noticeably long time. By the time she returns, I feel jittery. She takes the armchair. Her cough is a hard, brassy rattle. 'You said this was about my mother,' she says. 'You should have told me the truth.'

I feel Lev tense up beside me.

She coughs some more. I feel like I might have something lodged in my windpipe too. I await an explanation, but she only goes back to chewing. Her whole face is coming unhinged.

I take a deep breath. 'I'm not sure what you—I'm a research assistant to a historian. He's interested in your mother's memoir. Specifically, where the original was found. In somebody's basement?'

'It was mailed to me,' she says coolly. 'A few years ago.'

'Mailed? You mean in the—'

'In the post.'

'By whom?'

'Whomever found it, I presume.' Akulina spits something into her hand. A piece of toffee. 'I thought maybe, after the book was published, I'd hear again from this anonymous donor, but I never did.'

'Forgive me for asking this,' I say, trying not to sound cynical, 'but if you received the manuscript in the post, anonymously, how could you know it was genuine? And not a forgery, a fake? Your mother being a relatively well-known figure of the Civil War—'

'Because,' she replies, matching my tone, 'they sent my mother's necklace along with it.'

'You mean the silver one? The cross?'

'The cross was a locket. Inside there was an inscription. My mother showed me, once. Perhaps one could fake a memoir, though I don't see why anyone would. But there would be no faking that necklace. And the part about someone's basement, that was just the publisher's idea, you see. Books are always being found in basements these days. It is a selling point. Makes it seem like the material was hidden on purpose. Maybe illegal or illicit.' Akulina clears her throat. 'Have you read the whole memoir?'

I'm still taking in everything she's said. 'Yes. She was a beautiful writer—'

'She was a terrible mother.' Akulina pauses, and then, calmly: 'After the revolutions, when my brother and I were still only children, she began to work, to conspire, against the Bolsheviks. I begged her to stop, for our sake. It was dangerous. But she did not stop. She was eventually arrested.

I thought she was so, so selfish. I vowed never to forgive her.'

The cat leaps into my lap, pinioning me in place.

'But now you have?' I ask.

'The memoir helped me to understand her. My mother had a great, impossible love. I myself have experienced the same. And some women are just not meant to be mothers. Again, I am among them. So the two of us, we did have some things in common, in the end. I also realised, for the first time, how it must have been for her, belonging to a world that ended in a heartbeat with the October Revolution.' Akulina speaks without reservation. 'Thus I am grateful to the person who sent me her writing and her necklace.'

'How did your mother die?' I ask, and then wince. I already know; it's in the editor's foreword to the memoir. I've been thrown off balance by our conversation. I'm not thinking straight.

'She was executed,' Akulina says, with a scoff. 'By the Cheka, in 1920. Your historian doesn't know that?'

'Right. Of course.'

'There *is* no historian, is there?'

'Excuse me?' I say nervously.

'You're lying about why you're here. You want to talk about Tonya.'

'I'm sorry. What?'

Akulina reaches into the pocket of her mousy jumper vest. 'I've just dug this out for you. I hope you appreciate.'

I reach over her cat, who is still sitting on me, feeling a bit like I'm reaching into a museum display. Akulina drops an object in my hand. A small wooden frame, not too much larger than an icon, brittle and blemished. The photograph within is black and white, behind glass that looks new, showing four people: two kids, a frizzy-haired teenager who bears a whimper of a resemblance to Akulina, and a young woman in a whitish frock, brought in at the waist.

The young woman is me.

'What . . .' I start to say. The picture gives off vibes, electricity. It can't be me. I don't own any ankle-length dresses. I've never worn my hair cropped just below the chin, curls held in place by a lace band. I've never even laid eyes on these children.

Whoever this is, she smiles into the camera in a way that tells me she doesn't mean it. I wouldn't mean that smile either.

Lev takes the picture from me. He lets out a low whistle, not an admiring one.

'It's yours now,' says Akulina promptly. 'I'll tell you what I know. Tonya and my mother were acquainted well before the revolutions. Later, after my mother's death, Tonya adopted me and my brother, and took care of us for a few years. See, he's that young boy there.'

'Who is Tonya?' I stammer.

Akulina dissolves into coughing. When she looks at me again, her eyes are red-rimmed. 'Obviously a relation of yours. Just look at the two of you! Was Lena your mother?'

'Lena?'

Her nostrils flare at us. 'Tonya's daughter. She's there in the picture too.'

My jaw clicks. 'My mother's name was Katya. You're mistaken. This is all some kind of mistake.' My voice is rising. I didn't come here to be confronted by something like this picture. To be blindsided. The cat's velvety fur suddenly feels like needles. 'And I don't know any Tonya. I don't know why she—I don't know why this is—I'm—'

'Can I pour anyone more tea?' asks Lev, in a more polite tone than he's ever used before, and Akulina responds, smiling, displaying a row of coffee-browned teeth – but I see it as glee, like something's lit up behind her features, like the glint of gold leaf beneath lacquer.

Alexey told us not to take the Mercedes on this visit, so as not to draw too much attention to ourselves in this area of town, but now I'm wishing we had done. I need to close my eyes and clear my head. Instead, Lev and I have to board a minibus, have to endure the return journey through the jungle of apartment complexes. Akulina's photo frame is in my bag, the strap singeing my shoulder. I'm in Moscow to find Eduard Dayneko. And nothing else matters – not the map, the silver necklace, the picture of Tonya. It doesn't matter if I have no idea why Alexey really sent me to Akulina.

Nothing matters except getting *my* answer, and leaving for ever—

'You're thinking too hard,' says Lev. 'I can almost see steam coming from your ears. I have friends who live just around the corner. Let's get off here and say hello.'

'Do people do that?' I ask, swallowing.

'Have friends? Yes,' he says, with a straight face. 'And social gatherings. And even food.'

It's already early evening. The day has leached away, and I'm grateful for the distraction. The friends' apartment used to belong to a renowned dancer, Lev says, on the way. It does look like the kind of place Mum would have liked – high ceilings, a lot of windows, plenty of space. Enough to put on a show. Lev's friends, a talkative pair, show us every room, with modest pride, and then they lay out more spirits than even Mum could comfortably imbibe.

The wife asks me questions about life in England while she puts out snacks that sear your tongue: gherkins and salty fish. I sip raspberry kvass as she talks and the alcohol begins to hum in my veins. I might have been just like this woman, if not for *that man*, that one night. I might be chatty and cheerful. I might not mind living in a place that once belonged to a dancer.

On the metro home the seats and people are a blur, and when we emerge, the night air is unusually fresh. The cosiness of the friends' apartment is a distant memory. We reach Alexey's building. My skin feels sandpapered.

At the door Lev turns to look at me. There is a sizzling kind of silence, like he's preparing to say something important. He bends his head, so that his forehead nearly touches mine, and suddenly I know what he's going to say. I don't know how to stop him. I don't know how to stop myself.

'I think my father wrote the notebook of stories, and not my mother,' I blurt out. It's the first thing I can think of.

He smiles. 'Tell me.'

'I think he wrote them in some kind of ciphertext. Maybe he suspected that someone was going to kill him. Maybe he even knew why, but he was scared to put me in danger by saying so outright, so he encrypted these stories just in case, wrote them down in the notebook, knowing that one day I would be able to break the code—'

'But he wasn't the one who gave it to you,' says Lev.

'Maybe my mother found out. She could have hidden

the stories. She could have had some reason for not wanting me to know the truth, only her conscience got to her at the end. She had to let me have it before she died.' I know how fanciful, how impossible this sounds, but I keep going. 'Anyway, my point is, I have to look at the notebook again. I have to—I have to . . .'

'I understand,' he says. He brushes a strand of hair away from my face. His hand lingers. 'You have a lot to do.'

Silence again.

Now he doesn't have to say it.

I might be a bit tipsy, but I'm not drunk enough to be able to blame the alcohol. I want to lift my chin, kiss him, give in completely. I don't think I've ever done very much *wanting*, or else it just hasn't felt like this. Like it's breathing underneath my skin. Like it could eat me alive.

This is the opposite of how I feel with Richard—

Richard.

I feel laughter bubbling up in my throat. There's the tipsiness, right there. No wonder Mum was always laughing at nothing. Everything looks funny upside down. 'I'm engaged,' I say.

'You're . . .' Lev stops.

'I'm getting married in September.' I show him my left hand. 'It's smart, I know. A family ring. I should probably be more careful with it.'

'You're wearing it on the wrong hand,' he observes, tonelessly.

'In England we wear it on the left, not the right.'

'Mmm,' he says. 'I didn't know that.'

'Why should you?'

187

Lev doesn't reply. He pulls out the key and lets us in, and we have to make it all the way up those stairs. The funny, fizzy feeling in my skin doesn't go away, not when I collapse on the sofa bed, not when the lights go out. I'm tempted to crawl into the cot beside Lev, to lose myself to the feeling, but of course I don't. I turn towards the wall, dizzy with disgust at myself. Lev doesn't speak to me again.

As I close my eyes, I realise I haven't felt haunted this evening by the past, or even by Zoya. Mum had it right, back in England: alcohol does have a way of expunging things, at least for a little while. Only she forgot to stop at a little while, and couldn't get anything back.

I open half an eyelid to see Alexey in the living room, sitting in the upholstered armchair. I blink hard, and he comes into focus. There's a niggly, spicy taste in my mouth. I forgot to brush my teeth last night. Alexey is sifting through some magazines and doesn't seem to have noticed that I'm awake. He sighs, places them on the low table, and moves to grab one of the sofa cushions I have relegated to the floor.

Beneath the cushion is the framed photograph of the young woman named Tonya, and the children.

I don't recall putting it on the floor yesterday. I open my mouth to say something but Alexey's holding the frame, staring at it, and his expression drains like someone's pulled out a bath plug. He quickly plants the frame back beneath the cushion. He dusts off his hands and stands up, but it's too late.

Now I'm sure.

There's something *behind* that smooth surface of his, that public persona. Something with serrated edges. It's shifting around, like Nessie in the depths of Loch Ness, never so much as making a ripple up above.

'It's not the vendor from last time.' Lev holds up a hand to block out the sun that blazes over the Vernissage. 'But somebody is waiting there.' We've stopped far away enough to be able to turn back without being seen.

'We could just go,' he continues. 'We could get ice cream instead.'

'I left Moscow when I was ten,' I say. 'I'm not ten any more.'

The man standing by the matryoshka stall is silhouetted against the sun, so I can't make out his appearance clearly, but it's a good sign. Eduard Dayneko will have sent one of his lackeys to investigate, some gangly gang member who will be young and ill-tempered, who will ask who I am and why I want to meet *the artist*. The colonel warned that it would take pressing, patience and pocket money to secure meetings higher up the food chain, but I will get there.

'Good morning,' the man says, as we approach.

This is all wrong.

Lev steps in front of me, as if he can sense that too, but my mind is already unspooling. I *am* ten. I'm still ten years old, after all these years; I'm still standing in that living room. I'm still looking at a man dressed in dark clothing, his gloved hands holding a pistol, himself an island in the middle of all that blood, his gaze resting on me as if he wanted me to see him. As if he wanted to get caught.

He must still want to get caught.

'You may not remember my face,' he says. 'My name is Eduard Dayneko.'

PART TWO

THE NEW KING

In a faraway kingdom, in a long-ago land, rain began to fall. The new king stayed dry in his castle, and he gave special coats to his soldiers so that they could protect themselves. But the townspeople were not given coats. The townspeople learnt not to look into each other's eyes, in case they should get rain in their own.

One day a soldier stopped to talk to one of the townspeople. 'I'm sure the rain will be over soon,' the soldier reassured her.

'I have heard,' she said, 'that even soldiers are not safe now. That our new king will take your coat when he has a fit of temper.'

'That is true,' said the soldier.

'I have heard,' she said, 'that the only way for someone like me to gain a coat is to betray someone else to the king.'

'That is also true,' said the soldier.

'Why is our rain so red?' she asked. 'Is all rain, in every country, as red as this?'

The soldier only smiled at her. He was already telling her too many things, and it would not help her to know the truth. The rain was red because the new king made the rain. He made it from the people.

CHAPTER FOURTEEN

Antonina

Tula province, spring 1924

THE BIRCH FOREST HAS MORE JACKDAWS THAN EVER before. Their eyes are so dark Tonya can't make out the pupils. A bit like her own. They perch on the house at Otrada, on all the edges, and sometimes when she opens a window, there is an explosion of black feathers. But this only happens during the day. Every night before bed she goes outside to the balustrade, sees the marble of a moon overhead. And at night, the jackdaws do not move.

'Tonya?'

Sasha walks on kitten-soft feet, and he is suddenly right behind her, putting his arms around her, resting his chin on the top of her head.

'Do you want me to stay?' he asks.

'I'm only restless.' She twists around. 'Go ahead home.'

'I hate these birds,' he says. 'I'd shoot them, if I didn't think they were already dead.'

For some reason this makes her smile. Sasha kisses her goodbye and he heads back inside, picking up his things as he goes, his shirt, his coat, his shoes, sweeping the bedroom of all traces of a visitor. Though she shouldn't consider him a visitor any longer, should she? They've been together since she and Lena first moved into Otrada, years ago now.

The house had been standing empty for so long the wood was rotting, and it had been gouged out from the inside by the mobs. Like a melon. Sasha was the one to help her make it liveable again.

So why is his place not in it?

Tonya turns for one last look at the view, but all she sees are the jackdaws, sitting there, staring at her with her own eyes, like they are all the siblings she almost had.

'Mama!' Lena has appeared on the veranda. At six years old, her eyes are bright as she speaks, starry, like Valentin's. 'Mama, somebody's here to see you!'

Tonya stands up from the garden plot, wipes her hands. It could be Nelly, but Nelly never calls. No matter how much Tonya apologises, Nelly comes no closer. *Such a long friendship can't have been destroyed so quickly*, Tonya has said to Kirill, *it's not possible*, and Kirill agrees, which makes Tonya think it was destroyed years before. Destroyed when Tonya was not even looking.

'From the village?' asks Tonya, despising her own hope.

'She says she's from the capital,' says Lena sunnily. 'Do you know people in the capital, Mama?'

Tonya follows where Lena leads. Lena has stashed their visitor in the front parlour, like a proper hostess. The

194

front parlour of Otrada, of course, is nothing like the Blue Salon in the house on the Fontanka, with its portraits and chandeliers and Savonnerie carpeting. Here, the original furniture was looted, and Tonya has furnished the room simply, with wood-backed chairs to go with the hazelnut wall panels, and a table that Sasha carved by hand.

This is why, perhaps, the visitor stands out like a skin rash.

It is a tall, voluptuous woman, sheathed in lace that hangs off her arms and waist. The woman turns, and her mane of red hair turns with her, now pearly at the roots. From her fingers is draped a long, yellow-tipped cigarette in a holder. She looks as if she has stepped out of a dinner party from ten years ago.

'Honestly, darling,' says Natalya, 'the look on your face! It's only me. Do you know, the locals told me this place was haunted. Earned yourself a reputation, have you?'

'It's haunted *now*,' Tonya retorts, though she can't help the way her body bloats with anxiety. How is this possible? Will she *never* be rid of this woman? 'You're supposed to be dead.'

'Oh, yes, that is what they say about me.'

'It's what your children said about you.'

Natalya's smile turns wary. 'My children?'

Tonya's alarm begins to subside. The Countess Burzinova that she knew in Petrograd did not smell fishy and did not have skin like the sides coming off a cabbage. The yellow-tipped cigarette is not even lit. It is for appearance's sake. Just like the sardonic laugh, the pointed barbs, the *darlings*.

The old Natalya would have pulled every white strand from her hair. Would have worn a wig.

195

Tonya asks Lena to go fetch some tea and invites the Countess to sit. It is a story that she never thought she would have to tell: Akulina and Little Fedya were put in a state facility for orphans after Natalya's arrest in Petrograd in 1920. They endured a year there, and then escaped. In their innocence, they returned home, only to discover that the Burzinovs' former mansion on the Zakharevskaya had been converted into housing for some twenty-odd families, none of whom felt like adopting two runaways.

It was Akulina who found the map of Tula, hidden at the back of a drawer in one of the bedrooms, with Tonya's home town circled upon it.

'They thought you'd been shot by the Cheka,' Tonya says. 'People were singing about you in the streets of Petro— of Leningrad. How you were a symbol of the old empire.'

Natalya's free hand finds her silver necklace, closes around the cross. 'The Cheka let me go,' she says. 'We struck a deal. They wanted money. I thought it would make things – easier, if people believed me dead, and they were very happy to oblige.' She makes a soft, guttural sound. 'I looked for Little Fedya and Akulina. I looked everywhere.'

'Akulina's travelling now, in the east,' says Tonya. 'But we get occasional letters from her. I'll give you the latest address we have.'

'What about my Little Fedya?'

Tonya hesitates. 'Fedya never fully recovered from his time at the orphanage. The conditions there, as Akulina described them to me—'

'Never recovered? What do you mean?'

'He died two years ago.'

196

Natalya's hands fall into her lap. 'I see.'

You *don't* see, Tonya wants to respond. You don't see that it isn't 1916 any more, and I'm no longer Dmitry's Fabergé egg of a wife. You don't see that you can come at teatime if you like, can bring yourself back from the dead if you like, but you can't bring everything back.

'It was painless,' says Tonya. It is a lie. She's not even sure why she says it; perhaps she gained too much practice lying to Natalya, years ago. 'He was at peace.'

'You're good to have taken in my children,' says Natalya. 'I'll return the favour. I promise you. Fair is fair.'

'That isn't necessary.'

The door to the parlour opens, and Lena comes in, moving as she does, like a gust of wind. She places the tray on the table and claps, long dark hair swinging, the large bow hanging.

'I'm Lena,' she says, sounding thrilled. 'Do you want tea? Are you a princess?'

Natalya lifts a teacup, and Lena pours. 'I'm not the princess,' says Natalya. 'What lovely dark hair you have. How different from your mother's.'

'I got it from my father,' chirps Lena.

'And where is your father, Lena?'

'Far away,' Lena says simply. 'But I have never met him either, so don't feel sadly.'

'I won't,' says Natalya. 'Aren't you charming. Come back once more before I go, will you?'

Lena beams and flies back out of the room, dashing down the hallway, footsteps quickening, disappearing.

'She's got Andreyev's eyes, too,' says Natalya. 'More luck her. I assume he doesn't know?'

197

Tonya pours her own tea. 'It's not a secret. He went away to the war; I've not had any word since.'

'I see my opportunity to return your kindness,' says the Countess. 'I had a recent and unexpected encounter with Valentin Andreyev, in fact, in Leningrad. He isn't well, Tonya. He had a bad bout of typhus during the war, it seems, which weakened him. And now – you know how the winters are up north.'

'He is ill?' says Tonya evenly.

'You should go straightaway, darling, if you have anything to say to him.' Natalya waves the cigarette holder in Tonya's direction. 'Perhaps about his daughter? You will not have another chance.'

The moment that follows is peaceful. Too peaceful, like the eye of the storm. Akulina said, when she and Little Fedya first showed up at Tonya's door, that the Cheka executed Natalya Burzinova over a ravine. They sprayed her with bullets, buried her in a mass grave. Only they didn't do it, it seems, with enough bodies piled on top to keep her from climbing back out.

'Thank you for letting me know, Natalya Fyodorovna,' says Tonya, deliberately keeping to the more formal address of first name and patronymic.

'Call me Natasha,' is the airy reply. 'We're equals now, aren't we?'

It is only hours later, when the Countess is long gone and Lena is helping to set the table for dinner and the jackdaws are landing on the sills, that Tonya realises she failed to ask why Natalya had come all the way to Otrada in the first place.

At night the lake between the birch and pine forests is misty, the fog as thick as dust. The water dances against

198

Tonya's bare feet, feels like a cat's tongue.

Love should not be a frenzy, Mama said once. One of the few times Mama looked right at Tonya as she spoke. You will know real love by how quiet it is. How it grows over time, every day a little bit more, a little bit stronger, without anyone noticing, until it's all you can see, like the White Nights of St Petersburg. Until it is just a fact of life.

Why hasn't Tonya fallen in love with Sasha?

Sasha was there the day that Little Fedya died. Lena, not quite five years old, spent hours crying in Sasha's embrace, vowing that she would never let anybody else die, ever, in the world. She'd grow up and find a way to end death. *Nobody, never, and don't all of you believe me? You believe me, don't you?* And Tonya said yes, but people spout all kinds of nonsense when someone is dying, like how after Mama died people said that Mama was finally going to be with all her half-formed babies.

Just before the boy passed, Sasha was at his bedside, and Little Fedya was saying, *I'm so scared, please don't let me die*, and Sasha said: *Have you ever dreamt of being a sailor, Fedya, of steering your ship up the Neva and into the Baltic and seeing the wide, wide world out there? That's all dying is. That's exactly what it is.*

It was a beautiful turn of phrase, and the way he said it, Tonya knew it wasn't his.

It was someone else's. Maybe he'd read it somewhere. Heard it. Stolen it, requisitioned it, just as the Chekist brigades do, the ones with which he is still so friendly, even now. Sasha often speaks in idioms, phrases, quotations. Tonya finds it a harmless habit, even an endearing one. He is full of pithy provincial wisdom. But on that day, with Little Fedya slipping away in front of them, she hated that he had none of his own words. That he was not actually *saying* anything.

And shame burnt low in her belly, because she was comparing him to Valentin.

Tonya has been at the water so long that her feet have gone numb, but she doesn't move. The Countess might try to find Akulina in the vastness of the east. But Tonya remembers that the night they lost Little Fedya, something went missing from Akulina too, something that had always been there before. Something that would be buried the next day alongside her brother, in a coffin that was already much too small.

Akulina cannot be found. Not by Tonya, not by Natalya. Not by anyone.

Finally Tonya rises from the bank. She has made up her mind; she made it up the moment *his* name was spoken. She only had to sit here long enough to be able to admit it. Mama never liked it out here, once tried to forbid Tonya from coming. Mama used to say there are no waves, no tide, in such lakes as these. *Only the currents people make for themselves.*

The moon burns like a gas lamp in the sky. Tonya takes turn after turn until the stone lynxes of Otrada are visible, poised atop the black gate-pillars. The symbol of her family. The guardians of the estate, keeping the dangers out, or holding the dangers in.

She stops at the willow tree avenue to look at the house from the front. It glows blue by starlight, for the floors, the roofs, the window treatments, the fretwork, are all carved out of birch. Close-grained wood, Tonya knows now, that is not really suitable for making whole houses. Maybe that's why the villagers used to say that Otrada was like the bloodsucking ticks out in the forest. A living, breathing thing, looking for a host.

Once the serfs were enough, but without them it is always hungry.

The walls shiver as she enters. Tonya put Lena to sleep hours ago, but she hears noise from the rosewood room, once her family's private drawing room. It must be Sasha. That room is his preferred place to relax, read and smoke, and the stewed-prune scent of his makhorka tobacco is strong.

'I was getting concerned,' says Sasha, as she shuts the door behind her.

'I was by the lake.' Tonya drifts to the window, draws one curtain. 'I had a visit today from someone I used to know. She informed me that Valentin Andreyev is dying. I must go now, to the capital, if I wish to see him.' She ignores the heartbeat that starts, skips over. 'I don't know whether I'll have the courage to tell him about Lena. But I must try. I must say goodbye.'

'If you wish to go, you should.'

'With the travel, it won't be the simplest trip.'

'Would you take Lena with you?' he asks.

'I don't know. I don't know what's wrong with him, what it would be like. And Lena, you remember how she was after Fedya. She's so afraid of death.' She hesitates. 'I could leave her here with you. You know how she'd love that.'

'I can stay however long you like.' He rises to join her at the window. 'It means a great deal that you trust me enough.'

Tonya does trust him. She believes that his wife ran off, took their child with her. She has seen his tenderness, the way his large fighter's hands soften when he handles his animals, whom he openly prefers to people. And Lena adores him. He's the only father she's ever known. Lena speaks of the one who gave her her hair, the one who is *far away*, the way she speaks of princesses. Once they were true. Now they are only pretend.

'There's something I have to show you,' says Sasha. 'I found it in the forest.'

Tonya has been with Sasha for four years, long enough to know anyone all the way through. But maybe that's the problem. 'In the forest?'

'I think I saw someone.'

He sounds so grave that Tonya laughs. 'Did you kidnap them?'

'I wish I had.' He picks up a rumpled-looking sack that was balanced against his chair, and he reaches both hands in at once, like he'll need both to grapple with this thing, and as soon as he withdraws the contents, she lets out a short, cut-glass cry.

'Have you ever seen anything like this?' asks Sasha.

She has, in the toy emporiums of Petrograd, but not quite like *this*—

'One of the villagers must have left it out there to scare you,' he says, and she knows that he will be asking his Chekist friends to pay a visit to Popovka, and what that visit will entail. The brutality of the Cheka towards the villagers doesn't bother him the way it does her. *After the way the village has treated the two of us, Tonya, why do you care what happens to them?*

For the first time, Tonya may agree.

It is a small porcelain doll. Sasha brushes aside the thick yellow hair, sweeps up the spider-leg eyelashes with his finger. Its eyes are black.

It is a doll that looks like her. That was made to look like her.

CHAPTER FIFTEEN

Rosie

Moscow, July 1991

E DUARD DAYNEKO HAS CHOSEN A HOLE-IN-THE-WALL, a place where the seats are pale and plasticky and a tape player on the counter is chewing up a cassette. There are piles of dirty dishes on every table. I am suffocating in second-hand smoke. After Dayneko waylaid us the other day at the Vernissage market, he said it would be better for him to meet me today, like this, to talk properly.

Today Lev is out on an errand with Alexey. I always needed to do this alone.

Dayneko pushes a plate of ungarnished pelmeni, dumplings, across the sticky tabletop. They look like a nest of bird's eggs.

'So you still have the doll.' He rolls up his sleeves, revealing a vivid landscape of tattoos. 'But no, it's not my handiwork.'

Sweat slides down both sides of my face. Every night for the past fourteen years I've gone to bed with hatred for the man sitting in front of me stewing in the pit of my stomach. Determined not to become Mum, determined not to fall into her self-medicating, self-immolating haze, I've held on to that hatred. It's spread to every part of my body by now, disseminated through my bloodstream, and I feel a rush of it as we look at one another. He wants this to be civil? Does he think the passing of time has rinsed away any of the blood he spilt?

'Why did you leave it?' I ask bluntly.

He leans over and saws through one of the pelmeni with his knife, as if he thinks the reason I haven't started eating is that I can't use the cutlery. In my mind, *that man* has always been fixed in time. Like the people he's killed, he never ages. But now that he's closer than ever before, I can see that the real Eduard Dayneko has an age. Fifty, maybe. Fifty-five. Threadlike lines sprout from the corners of his eyes. His hair runs grey at the crown.

'I left it for you,' he says, putting down the knife.

'Me?'

'You're my daughter.'

I hear myself laugh. That's impossible.

'Katya and I were having an affair,' he says. 'One that had lasted almost twelve years, by that time. You're my child.'

I turn away and I see sudden sparks of light, going off like cherry-bombs. This is the man who murdered my sister and my beloved father. Two innocent people. He murdered Mum too, it just took longer. We don't share a bloodline.

We can't.

'I didn't intend to kill anyone, Raisa,' he says. 'If I had, you wouldn't have seen me. No one would have seen me.

I was there to demand that Katya finally make a choice, between her husband and myself, and I brought the doll because I didn't know what her choice would be. I wanted you to have something from me. Either way.'

'But why a *doll*?' I say groggily.

He looks surprised. 'Katya told me you collected them. I saw your collection myself, in the apartment. Many times.'

What he saw was *her* collection. And it means he was in *our* apartment. Many times. I blot my face with my serviette. I can feel a terrifying migraine looming at the edges of my consciousness.

'I didn't know she would be away that night. Visiting friends, or whatever it was. When I arrived, there was a confrontation with your father, and . . .' He sighs. 'Your sister ran in. It got out of hand.'

Out of hand, he calls it.

'It was a tragedy, Raisa.'

A tragedy.

He's making it sound like something that happened on the news. To other people. Something that we could both walk away from. I can't walk away from it. But I can't go on sitting here at this moment, either. I stand up, and then I'm grabbing my bag, I'm shoving my way out of the restaurant, pushing through the humidity and the smoke and the other patrons.

Outside, in full view of several horrified onlookers, I begin to vomit.

I heave and gasp until there's nothing left, and then I run. I don't know this area very well, but I run like I'm being chased, and people give me flummoxed glances as

I go past. They must think from my clothes and my panic that I'm a foreigner. That this is my first summer in Russia. But it's not.

I lived eleven summers of my life here. I'm still living that last one.

Into the metro. Down the escalators. Underground. I can't stop, or I might start *thinking*, and if I start to think, it might start to make sense. What he's said might start to feel true. The migraine is a vindictive one, pinching me at the temples as I reach Alexey's building. I cut myself on the keys trying to open the door. It seems that Alexey and Lev aren't back yet, so at least I won't have to explain why my clothes are covered in vomit, why there's blood on the stairs, why I can't even take a breath.

Upstairs, I grope for the telephone, smear it as I start to dial. The operator puts me through.

'Hello?' Richard picks up.

'It's me. It's me.'

'Hi, Ro,' he says affectionately. 'Wasn't expecting to hear from you today.'

'Richard, I—'

'Sorry, Dad's just got here,' he says. 'We're off to London. I have to dash. Could we do tomorrow rather? I'll—'

The line is dead. The connection from here to Oxford has always been uneven. It hardly matters, because it's not Richard's reassurances or even somebody to talk to that I need. What I need is a reminder that I can reach out and touch something of Rosie's anytime I want. That I haven't been sucked into the vortex of my former life so fully that I may never get out again.

Raisochka . . .

Zoya's never said my name before.

This isn't happening. None of this is happening.

'Go away,' I say, to the empty foyer. 'Please – I don't know who you are. But please, just leave me alone—'

Raisochka . . .

'Be quiet!' I pick up the telephone, handset and all, and throw it at the far wall. 'I can't do this any more! Go away! Go!'

Everything is quiet. I drop to my knees and retrieve the phone. Thankfully it's still intact. I open the door to the kitchen, my headache screaming. I make myself a cup of tea and drink it while it's still too hot and begin to feel even worse. Because of all the vomiting, maybe. I have to lie down. I pull out the bin and I'm about to dump out the tea leaves when I notice something in the rubbish.

The photograph of Tonya. Crumpled up.

Tonya. I'd forgotten about her. Eduard Dayneko has always had that effect. Of obliterating everything else. I grab the bin and overturn it, shake it all out. Bits of glass fall like beads. This isn't the result of dropping the frame. Somebody took a hammer to it. Destroyed it, physically, with violence.

There's another photograph trapped in the debris.

I sink to the floor. This picture is made of a weaker material, cut out of newspaper it looks like, and it shows a young man addressing a huge crowd from a high, street-side balcony. He is striking, starkly handsome. It must have been hidden in the frame, behind Tonya and the children. I can't think where else it could have come from. I can't really think at all.

Valentin Andreyev, Moscow, 1921, reads the caption.

Valentin Andreyev. I don't know the name, but there's definitely something familiar about this fellow. Not in the way that Tonya is familiar; a subtler, subliminal way. The line of the jaw? The ridge of the brow? Just how he looks in a dark suit and tie? The quality of the photograph isn't too high, but that's how imagination can take over. I can almost make out one voice above the crowd, a voice trying to change history, cutting through all other sound . . .

Just like Alexey's.

Alexey, the only other person besides me and Lev who knew about this frame – and who has been alone in the apartment since.

He must have done this.

But *why?* And who would do something like this?

I need to sweep all the glass back into the bin. I need to clean up the tea leaves. I still need to lie down, but I can't even move. I feel something on my cheek and hear a sound and then realise that it's me. Crying, even though I never, ever cry. I'm crying all the tears I didn't cry for Papa and Zoya, the tears I didn't cry when Mum and I arrived in England, the tears I didn't cry when I heard my mother was dead. They've become backlogged, like orders at a restaurant, and now they're all coming at once. They might never stop.

I lie on my side, pretending to be asleep. Lev and Alexey are back. I can hear them talking in the foyer, Lev saying he thinks I'm not feeling well, Alexey expressing concern.

Tomorrow Alexey leaves on a four-day trip to Novosibirsk. More lectures, more talks, more pages in the literal book of his life. Here he is, *The Last Bolshevik*, for all the world to see.

I turn over and blink up at the ceiling. *The Last Bolshevik* is short. Alexey never gives any glimpse into his life before he was arrested, yet that life must have been derailed. Nor does he describe how he felt when he got the news that he would be sent to the White Sea Canal. He supplies readers with the visceral details of his existence in exile, the day-to-day, the difficulty of mere survival in a place never meant for humans, and his writing is lyrical. It carries you along.

But this evocative picture only serves to distract from what's not there: he, himself, the person.

Where is he, in his own book?

Alexey Ivanov's façade is charismatic and compelling. No doubt it's one he cultivated over time, and no doubt it represents some part of him, maybe the part he most wants to be, but it's a façade nonetheless. Whoever he really is, it's still lurking.

Or else he destroyed it, the way he did that frame.

'Ah, you're awake.'

I sit up slowly. My face feels brittle from all the crying. When Lev hands me a glass of water, I have to force myself to take a sip. It's flat and sour as lime, Moscow tap water, but it washes down the remnants of my nausea.

'How did you leave it yesterday with Dayneko?' asks Lev.

I tell him everything: the tattoos on Dayneko's arms, the dolls he thought were mine, the reason Papa and Zoya died. The more I turn it over, the less sense it makes. Maybe Eduard Dayneko killed my father in a jealous rage during a heated confrontation. A crime of passion. I might believe that. But why Zoya? A professional hitman, accidentally murdering a teenager? It doesn't feel right. And it's not like he was afraid of leaving witnesses. He left me alive, after all, daughter or not. He left the lady who let him into the building perfectly alive.

Why? Just to be cruel? To be neat?

'You have what you wanted,' says Lev. 'You know why he was there.'

'Yes, but now I think . . .' My cheeks feel warm. 'I want more.'

'Like what?'

'His story was like – disinformation. Like he's headed me off at the pass. I feel even further away from the truth.'

'You care a lot about the truth.'

I thought I'd used up all my tears by now, but apparently not. I may have busted a pipe yesterday behind my eyes, and I'll just keep on leaking.

'My whole family is dead,' I say forcefully. 'The truth is all I have left!'

'I didn't mean—'

'So yes, I do care, and I'd do anything to get it!'

A pause.

I press a hand against my forehead. I'm burning up. 'Sorry for shouting.'

'That's not shouting.'

'It is in England.'

Lev smiles.

'I want to look at my mother's notebook of stories again,' I mutter. 'I want to investigate my theory. About

211

my father. And a code. Can you teach me to read cursive? I have to break down the letters first—'

'You're running a fever so high that I can feel it from here,' he says. 'Get some more rest. Everything else can wait.'

I am hot, but also cold, a sensation of cold that penetrates down to the bone, and then I feel something – someone – tracing a circle around my elbow. You're delirious, Ro, I tell myself, you're imagining things, feeling a fingertip, Zoya's fingertip. She used to do this when we were children, just before she'd scream into my ear to *wake up, Raisa, wake up right now!*

It's got stronger here in Moscow, my fear of her.

Zoya has also got stronger.

In England, it was like she lived in her world and I lived in mine, and sometimes they overlapped and sometimes they didn't. But now she's here, in mine, all the time. She's *present*. She could be sitting on the other end of the sofa, playing with her hair, chin resting on her palm. Zoya, with her short and sarcastic laugh. Zoya, with her impatient sigh: *Hurry* up, Raisa. *Stop* doing *that, Raisa. I'm* busy, *Raisa, go play on your own!*

Come on, Zoya. Come on . . .

She's there. I know she is.

I believe in you now. I do . . .

She can hear me.

Raisochka, she says, and for the first time since her death, Zoya fills the room with *her* smell – the smell of that two-in-one Ivushka shampoo that she used day and night, that came in a squat glass bottle and foamed like it was rabid, always using so much that the rest of us had to skimp – and as she does, I am bursting with childish yearning for the sister I didn't quite have. Mum was the ballerina, but Zoya might as well have been. She was always higher than my arms could reach.

I could reach her now, if I wanted. She is real.

Which way do I go, Zoya? I was wrong, thinking I could do this. I don't know if I can do it at all. I don't know anything. I'm not sure of anything. I need you.

But she's already gone.

CHAPTER SIXTEEN

Antonina

Leningrad, St Petersburg, spring 1924

THE TRAMS RUN SLOWLY, THE STREETS HAVE FEW CARS or carriages, and there is a hush over the city. Where there were once bustling basement shops, a grocer's, a baker's, a watchmaker's, there are only darkened windows, empty railings. It feels late, even though it's only midday, as if the city is already asleep.

Tonya turns onto a smaller boulevard and checks the address that Natalya gave her. Yes, it's this one, four storeys high, charcoal-grey granite, adorned with balconies. The gate to the courtyard hangs open. Her pulse is galloping. Many of the homes of the Imperial elite have been butchered since the Revolution and turned into communal apartments; she knows this, yet she still can't fathom that Valentin would live in a building that looks like a palace.

'You there,' someone calls out from a low balcony, 'who are you for? The bell's broken!'

'Valentin Andreyev,' she says, squinting.

'Be right down!'

He must live here after all. Tonya paces as she waits. She is plagued by the suspicion that all this is Natalya Burzinova's trick: that of course Valentin doesn't live here, of course he isn't dying. She hopes it's so. Natalya and her games. The Countess must be bored, everyone thinking she's dead, no one calling her by her title any more—

There is little light inside and no way to tell where this stranger will take her. They climb the formal staircase. The man talks as they go, saying that the whole top floor formally belongs to the playwright-poet-writer Pavel Katenin, but he has moved to Moscow. It is now being inhabited by Comrade Andreyev and his limpid-eyed wife. *Comrade Andreyeva plays piano like a goddess*, he enthuses.

Tonya had forgotten about Viktoria, about the famous father. She keeps trudging upward, step after step, the marble banister icy beneath her hand, wondering how high the Katenins have risen by now. Above all these other families. Above all the darkness.

The woman who opens Valentin's door has the narrow face of a borzoi. 'Can I help?' she says briskly. Hands on hips. *You can always tell a servant by the hands*, Mama used to say. *So coarse they cannot feel a feather in the palm.*

But Valentin would never employ a servant.

'Does Valentin Andreyev live here?' Tonya stutters.

The woman clomps away. She returns quickly, says that Valentin is in. Tonya is guided to a sitting room. There is a chaise longue in the middle, surrounded by other decorative chairs. Shelves line the wall above the fireplace,

215

each one studded with porcelain pieces. The wall hangings are spring-green silk, and the carpet is woven with wreaths.

It's a room that belongs in the house on the Fontanka.

Tonya's hands begin to shake: the old nervous habit. She sits on them. When she looks up at the doorway, she feels her face go rosy.

Valentin is standing there.

'Tonya,' he says, like he's pulling her name through a loom. 'It's really you.'

Her mouth goes dry. She stands too, unevenly, wringing her hands behind her back. She prepared for this moment, rehearsed, just as he used to. She used to envy him his confidence, that he could speak to a thousand people, but it can be harder to speak to one person alone. Nothing emerges, not a single word. All that she sees, thinks, knows, is the sight of him.

His hair is shorter than she remembers, without that slight curl, and he has a brush of shadow along his jaw, a line or two in his face. He has grown into more than just the boy Bolshevik, but he still has that air of unspent energy about him. Of dreams unfulfilled.

Something floods her, something horribly familiar.

They stare at one another. His gaze cuts her resolve to ribbons, tells her that he has thought of her too, before this; that he has forgotten nothing. That he carries their history with him, just as she does.

'The Countess—' she attempts.

He says nothing.

'Natalya Burzinova,' she says. It's strangely difficult to breathe. 'She told me . . .'

216

'There are no more countesses in Russia,' says Valentin.

His voice is calm, but contains an undercurrent of – what? Dislike? Scepticism? The wish that she'd never shown her face here? Her eyes search his and just as she's thinking she has erred, inexcusably, that she should not have come, he smiles. Her stomach lurches. She knows how she still feels, how she has always felt; he knows it too. It was never the brightness of White Nights that made her feel vulnerable, naked, raw. It was only him.

Valentin isn't unwell at all. He has never looked better. Tonya recalls Natalya's sudsy face powder, the lips like bread crust, the white hair snaking through the red. The Countess must have been driven mad, years ago, by the presumed loss of her children; that is the most generous explanation one can think of for this bizarre rigmarole.

Valentin takes a seat on the ottoman across from her, pours a drink for them both.

'So you thought I was on my deathbed?' His tone is casual, the words tossed.

She sinks lower into the chaise longue. 'I feared it.'

'What was it that you came to say, if I were?'

She holds back the answer, tries to exhale through it. 'I saw a photograph of you, a few years ago,' she says instead, hearing the whiff of desperation in her own voice, 'on the cover of *Krasnaya Gazeta*.'

Valentin yields to the change of subject. 'Revolution Square in Moscow,' he affirms. 'That was when I'd just come back from the war.' He leans back with a sigh. 'I don't make speeches any more.'

'What do you do?' she asks politely, her heart thundering in her chest. Look at him, as if no time has passed at all! Dressed down, collar up, button askew, still looking the part of the factory worker, the revolutionary, even if they're sitting in an apartment with silk hangings and porcelain novelties and a servant in the background, flapping about like a bat. He is the Valentin she knew, only he now belongs, somehow, to somebody else.

The reminder is prickly, painful. She pushes it away.

'Officially, I work for the People's Commissariat of Education,' he says.

'And . . . unofficially?'

'I oughtn't to say.'

'Why not? Have you become a counter-revolutionary?'

She meant it to tease, to sound carefree. Valentin lights a cigarette in response, cups his hand around it. The smoke obscures his face, makes her eyes water, but his expression is one she recognises. She's seen it turned on her too many times. Here he is again, never content with the status quo, always dreaming of the next impossible thing. *Don't*, she wants to cry out, *don't*. He will make her want impossible things too.

'You aren't,' she says aloud.

'Forget it,' he says.

'You have everything now. Just look at this place.'

'This isn't my place, it's Pavel's. And it doesn't matter what I have. It matters what the people have.'

'Forget the people, Valentin! Live your own life for once!'

'Is this why you've come, then, after all these years?' he says, more harshly than before. 'To tell me what life to live?

218

Are you not satisfied enough with the one *you* chose?'

The undercurrent has risen to the surface at last, and now she understands. Even if they can behave in a polite manner in one another's company, he will never think of her fondly. But she can change this yet – she can explain that she never chose that *other* life. She never chose Dmitry. She was kept against her will; she was a prisoner. And when next she saw Valentin, he was with Viktoria, and—

'Forgive me,' he says, drawing on the cigarette. 'I forget myself.'

'It's not my business,' Tonya says hurriedly, backing away from her own thoughts.

'I love the Party,' he says. 'It's because I believe in true socialism, that I do what I do. They've betrayed the Revolution, Tonya. I thought there might be hope, earlier this year, when Lenin died. But Koba has succeeded him, and now there is no choice but to act.'

Betrayal. Of course – Valentin's favour, once lost, is gone for ever. But he is treading dangerous ground; thanks to Sasha's friendship with the Chekists, Tonya knows precisely how dangerous. Lenin's Red Terror is supposed to be over; the grain brigades no longer swarm the countryside; the lists of traitors no longer appear in the newspapers. But the Tsar's Okhrana were amateurs, role-playing children, compared to the Bolshevik Cheka, now known as the OGPU. It is anything but a game.

'Valya?' A voice rings out from the hallway. 'Where are you?'

'In here,' he answers, putting out the cigarette. 'It's my wife,' he says to Tonya, and at the sound of this word, this

219

unmoveable, unassailable fact, Tonya finally permits herself to wonder, for one long moment, if he would have married *her*, in *their lifetime*. If it would have been without any ceremony, feast or crown around which her hair would ravel. Without singing guests, a lazy turn in the bathhouse, or anxiety in her stomach.

But when you let yourself wonder, as Mama used to say, *a thousand more wonderings unfold and unfurl, like flowers in the sun. They will be unstoppable.*

The fireplace purrs and the candles on the linen-covered table are lit, throwing dancing shadows upon the walls. The dining room is dominated by large mahogany bookcases containing leather-bound encyclopaedias. Tonya touches the glass, leaving smudges on purpose. Pavel Katenin clearly likes matching sets. Collections. Just as Dmitry did.

She feels an intense wave of loathing, even though she has never met Pavel.

'Feel free to borrow anything you like.' Viktoria speaking, from behind her. 'My father never makes use of any of it.'

Tonya peers into the bookcases. 'Are there only encyclopaedias?'

'There would be Alexander Pushkin, somewhere.'

Tonya has never told Viktoria of her love of Pushkin; she is certain of it. 'Thank you,' she says, without looking back.

'You broke his heart. With that poem.'

Now she looks. 'Poem?'

'*I loved you* . . . I don't know the rest.'

Tonya goes a little cold. 'What are you talking about?'

'When Valentin came home from the war,' says Viktoria, tightly, 'he told me we would never—that he did not love me. Our marriage has existed since in name only. He wanted to divorce, but I begged him. Mostly for my father's sake. Heaven forbid I disappoint Papa.' She smiles, without humour. 'We live here as good friends, but only friends.'

'I didn't come here to—'

'I read the letters you sent,' says Viktoria. 'I know you have a daughter. Valya's daughter.' Her voice wavers. 'I burnt them.'

'Burnt them,' says Tonya.

'I can't say how—' Viktoria stops talking. Valentin has come into the room. He glances between them, inquisitive, but Tonya turns back to the bookcases. She closes her eyes hard before opening them again. She can see Valentin there, reflected in the glass. She can overhear the conversation about his journey to Moscow tomorrow, Viktoria suggesting that he should travel down with Tonya, together, as Moscow is on the way to Tula. *Burnt them*. Her mind has gone blank. *You broke his heart*. The only Pushkin she associates with Valentin is from *Eugene Onegin*, the book she was reading when they first met. She may never untangle the two.

'What will you do in Moscow?' Tonya asks, when they are on the train. An hour has already gone, maybe two. So many more lie ahead, but she can feel herself counting down the seconds. At some point she will have lost her chance to speak up. *Scream it*, she tells herself, *tell him what happened, tell him everything*, but some other part of her only answers: To what end? What about Sasha, who has been taking care of Lena all this time? And what about Lena, when will you tell him about Lena? *How* will you tell him about Lena?

And with all this floating in her head, nothing makes it to her lips.

'Meet someone,' says Valentin. 'Unofficially.'

'Does Viktoria know you are working against the Party?' she asks.

'Vika, yes, but not her father,' he says, with a touch of bitterness. 'Pavel remains in denial. If he were anybody else, I wouldn't bother any more, trying to make him see. But all our old friends and allies have been persecuted, Tonya. Hunted. Disappeared off the streets. Meanwhile the only lights on in Piter are in the Astoria – though they call it the First House of the Soviet now. For the Party elite, just as they once were for the rich.' His smile is wry. 'For your husband.'

'You idolised Pavel,' Tonya says softly.

'I almost died in Samara.' He looks right at her. 'But I didn't. I was given another chance to live, and I vowed to be true to myself, wherever that would take me. You see, I already knew things were not as they ought to be, before I was ever assigned to the front. I knew that, but I went anyway. I was living a lie. In more ways than one.'

Tonya falls silent. She cannot be sure what she might say, if she spoke.

'There are many who feel the same. Maxim Gorky is so disillusioned he has left for Europe.' Valentin's tone is no longer introspective. Now he sounds as he always did on the podium, every word a weapon, every sentence ammunition.

222

'But I will never go. No matter what happens, I will always stay to fight. I will always believe in the people.'

The train is pulling into the station and there is hollering, shoving, jostling for position. This is Moscow! Alight for Moscow! The passengers begin to flow onto the platforms. Moscow is already more alive than Leningrad.

'Are you hungry?' Valentin reaches for his briefcase. 'There isn't a train to Tula for a while.'

'Just—wait.' Tonya can hear people rushing by outside, the clamouring, the clattering. Her heart beats hard, like bird wings. Now that they're here, about to part for good, with the trains arriving, leaving, axles firing, wheels grating on tracks, she knows what has really stopped her from speaking, all this time. Now that the whistles are blowing so shrilly she can't hear her own thoughts, and someone is shouting political slogans above all the noise: *Comrades! Workers and peasants of Russia, hear ye, hear ye!*

'What is it?' he says, with a sideways smile.

'I tried to come to you,' she says. 'That night, when we were supposed to meet on the bridge. I tried. My husband stopped me. He locked me in my room. He kept me there.'

'I don't understand,' he says. The smile is gone.

'I would have gone to you,' she says. 'I chose you.'

'You wrote that letter – the poem.' His voice is low.

'I didn't write it,' she whispers. 'I don't even know what letter you mean. But I don't need any poem to be able to tell you, Valya, what it is I feel. You once said we would all live two lives, and you were right, for it started then, *this* life, in which I love you as I have never loved anyone, and never

223

will. You asked why I came, why I'm here – that's why. I came to be with you.'

He stands, his shoulders moving slightly, as if he will leave, but he doesn't.

Tonya stands too.

She cannot believe she is doing this, cannot believe she has found the courage. She goes up to him and reaches for his hand.

They have never held hands before.

He turns halfway.

I have never stopped thinking of you . . .

She isn't sure which of them says it. He lowers his head, lets his mouth sweep against her cheek, skim her skin. He goes no further. He held her like this once before, years ago, on a tram that was so full of people it seeped at the corners like a rolled pastry. Money and tickets were making their way over the passengers' heads and the tram thudded hard, propelled her forward, tipped her into his arms. He did not quite let go.

It was the moment she first understood how he felt. That when he looked over the masses, she was the only one he saw.

They say goodbye outside the station. Valentin has said he will come to Otrada after he is finished in Moscow, and of course it is better that Tonya returns alone first, so she can talk to Sasha, so she can prepare Lena. Yet all of a sudden, without any good reason, she wants Valentin to travel on with her. To come with her now. Never to leave her side again.

'I can't,' he says. 'The person I'm meeting is taking some risk.'

'But there's something else I must tell you,' she says wildly. She hasn't yet mentioned Lena, thinking that it

224

would be better done at Otrada, when his mind isn't on his *unofficial* business, but now she will. Now she'll do anything to keep him here. Without even knowing why.

'I gave them my word,' he says patiently.

'I just don't know if you can have both—' What is she saying? What does she mean? What is this furry feeling up and down her arms, like something has just brushed her by?

'Can't live two lives, you mean?'

'Be serious, Valentin!'

'I'm more serious than I've ever been.' Valentin takes her hands, turns them over, smiles at her. 'We'll be together soon. Nothing will keep me from you. And you've recited the directions to Otrada so many times now, I feel I could make the trip there in my sleep.'

'Alright.' She feels something wet, filthy, on her eyelashes. 'But promise me—'

'I promise, *milaya*. I'll be there. Just wait.'

The sky is white. A few gulls circle the clouds, but they only remind her of the jackdaws. He kisses her lightly at first, then deeper, harder. Another promise. Valentin was always full of promises, she thinks now. As he walks away he looks over his shoulder. *Wait for me, Antonina*, he mouths, and she musters a smile. The sun has come out at last. The light reaches her, staining everything it lands on, even her hands as she presses them against her face, holds everything in. She does not let the tears fall.

To Tonya's surprise, Sasha doesn't take the news hard. *Long farewells mean needless tears*. He says he will always remember her, and that maybe he will now move to a new

225

town, to a house by a wide river, just as he always wished to do. Lena, however, is violently upset to learn that Sasha will not be coming by any more, and remains gloomy for days.

Valentin's arrival will surely help.

Tonya waits, waits some more. She waits for a week, two weeks, three. Nobody comes. She goes to Kalasy to post a letter. Nobody comes. The day a courier finally drags his sorry wagon-cart into the relay station, she is already there waiting. She has grown accustomed to waiting.

There is a letter for her. Valentin has changed his mind, she thinks. He doesn't want her.

But it is not from Valentin.

And now you will know how I felt.
Fair is fair, darling.
Until the day we meet again –
Natasha.

CHAPTER SEVENTEEN

Valentin

Solovetsky Islands, White Sea, summer 1925

THE ORDERS HAVE COME FROM THE DEPUTY CHIEF: the prisoners will dig holes in a straight line. They will carve out a highway with little more than shovels. Five hundred thousand cubic yards of excavations.

The smell of the nearby Black River is salty and putrid. The mosquitoes are the size of a human hand. A swampy mist hangs across the valley, and the guards shout at one another through it. The prisoners sit in the convoy, waiting for their tools.

'I'd like a spade,' grumbles the man next to Valentin.

Valentin is handed a spade. He offers it to his neighbour, who has been given a pick, and the man's mouth falls open.

'Think you're better, do you?' he snarls. 'Think you're not like the rest of us?'

Valentin knows he is just like everyone else. Like everyone else he will work as sweat oozes from his body, as those mosquitoes drain his blood. Like everyone else he will cut logs and stone and level mountains by hand to make a road that starts nowhere and goes nowhere. He is just like everyone else even though he was a commissar, a communist, even though he knows Joseph Stalin personally. Even though he has been a Bolshevik since they were the smallest and unlikeliest of all the parties in Russia.

Valentin does not consider himself lazy or idle. He took well to factory life as a youth. He still likes working with his hands. But this is not work. Prisoners often drop to their knees, die in the ditches, rot away there, and two months later, when the Black River Valley project is abruptly called off, it is not sand or logs or earth or rock that forms the unfinished road.

The Solovetsky Special Purpose Labour Camp is known as Solovky, and also by its acronym, SLON, which happens to mean 'elephant'. Valentin likes this play on words. He misses words. He writes at night in the barracks, by the faithless glow of the sixteen-watt bulb that swings creakily overhead. He keeps short notes, like a diary. Yesterday: *Planted trees along the central avenue. Fifteen hours.* Today: *Woodcutting. Eleven hours.*

He also writes letters. *Dear Tonya*, he writes, *please wait for me*, and then he rips it up, and starts again. *Dear Tonya, I will survive, I swear that I will come home—*

Everyone knows these letters are never sent, even if they are collected. There is no meaning to anything that happens in Solovky. Many prisoners do not even know why they are here. They are told they will be reforged, reformed, remade, into proper Soviet citizens. Most never get the chance. They are beaten to death by the guards. Murdered for their rations. Left to die if they cannot keep up with the others.

Newcomers to the camp sometimes know who Valentin is, and call him the Trotskyist. Leon Trotsky has fallen completely out of favour. It's a crime just to have known the man. Valentin argues that it's not possible to have been a Bolshevik in 1917 without having known Trotsky. They all fought together. They were all on the same side.

But there are no sides. Not in Solovky.

There was once a monastery here on the Islands, which only reminds Valentin of how he lost his own faith. In the Party, in Lenin, in the true socialist revolution. When he returned to Piter from the Civil War, he learnt of the Red Terror, of the widespread repression, the execution of old friends. And he found himself face to face with the reality that the Party had betrayed its own ideals. The October Revolution had not overturned society. The proletariat would never rule.

He joined the new underground. He told himself that he could do better fighting on the inside, secretly, from a position of privilege. But in the end, this was only a new way of running from the truth. He should have publicly cut ties with the Party. He should have screamed until his throat tore, the way he once did.

Instead he kept running.

He doesn't know who found out what he was doing, or who turned him in to the OGPU. His trial was only fifteen minutes long, and nobody bothered to explain how he had ended up in the prisoner's dock. Valentin confessed readily to his crimes because he was *ashamed*, ashamed of all those years he'd spent running. Always running. Still running. Yes, now he sees—

The road he ran along has led him here, to this place.

There are only two seasons in Solovky. At summer's end the last ribbon of daylight disappears, and winter begins. The years pass, but Valentin is losing all concept of time. He can no longer recall images from home. All he sees when he closes his eyes are the dead, lying in ditches. Snow blindness, is what the others call this, with irony. The real snow blindness.

Dear Tonya, he writes, but sometimes he cannot even remember her name.

Dear . . .

Wait . . .

Please . . .

One day he is packed onto a transport ship that sets sail from Solovky into the nothingness of the surrounding waters. He sits in the cargo hold with his head between his knees. The prisoners around him claim that they are headed not for home, but for the White Sea Canal. But there is no such thing as the White Sea Canal, others protest.

There will be.

In this new place, wherever it is, whether it exists or not, the winter storms are so overpowering, so pervasive, that even when the weak paraffin lamps are lit or a storm briefly lifts, Valentin still sees and hears nothing. The only thing he knows is that he is dividing into parts: One part is filling wheelbarrows, stumbling through ice floes, subsisting on gruel and foul water. The other part is pulling away. Try as he might, he cannot reunite these two halves of himself. It is such a complete separation of mind and body that he is losing hold of both.

CHAPTER EIGHTEEN

Rosie

Moscow, July 1991

I WAKE UP FEELING MUCH BETTER. NORMAL TEMPERATURE, clear head, tear ducts intact. I want to get my mind off Eduard Dayneko, to let his explanation marinate, so I try the next book on Alexey's list, a history of the Bolshevik Revolution and its aftermath. It is dull and dry. I miss the Countess's memoir.

But it is in *this* book that I see the name Valentin Andreyev mentioned, the young man from the old newspaper cut-out. And not only that, the image itself: *Valentin Andreyev addresses a crowd in Revolution Square, May 1921.*

I jot down some notes. Valentin Mikhailovich Andreyev, born in St Petersburg in 1896. In 1906, he encountered the radical writer Pavel Katenin. Under Katenin's tutelage, the young Andreyev became prominent in the revolutionary underground in his own right. Following the Bolshevik victory in 1917, Andreyev married Katenin's daughter, the pianist Viktoria Katenina; two years later, he returned from the Civil War to a hero's welcome; in 1924, he was stripped of Party membership and exiled to a new kind of penal colony in the Solovetsky Islands, in the north. In the White Sea.

The first stirrings of the Soviet Gulag.

Valentin Andreyev was never seen or heard from again.

In the central knoll of Dzerzhinsky Square is a tall, imposing statue of Felix Dzerzhinsky, original head of the Bolshevik Cheka. Behind *Iron Felix*, above the traffic going around in circles, looms the infamous Lubyanka. The home of the KGB, the Soviet secret police, it is made of a soft-yellow sandstone. It looks pretty benign.

'Raisa Simonova?'

A man with an impressive moustache waves to me as he approaches. This must be David Antonovich, from the human rights organisation Memorial. He told me on the phone that his mother died of exposure in Kolyma, in eastern Siberia, as part of a logging brigade, while his father was shot at Butovo. Unmarried, childless and highly educated, David Antonovich has dedicated his life to the memory and recovery of victims of political repression, particularly under the Stalinist regime.

Both his parents were processed here, in the Lubyanka.

Across the street, David shows me the Solovetsky Stone, a rock that made an arduous journey from the Islands all the way here to central Moscow. Its placement last year was organised by Memorial, in honour of the lives lost in the camps. It is small, unremarkable, sitting atop a slab of granite.

Yet it stands out against the Lubyanka.

We head down Teatralny. David tells me about the research he does, the material he goes through. He's seen his own father's prisoner file, a plain manila folder containing a photo and a few interrogation records. Name card, prisoner number, stamp in the corner. The full archives of the Lubyanka are not yet public, but Memorial hopes they will continue to open up.

'It's hard to cross the line, between the Soviet Union and the camps,' says David. 'Every time we do, each of us, we fear to vanish into the ether. I've stood where you are now, Raisa. On the line.'

I do feel a bit wobbly. 'No one's ever found anything on Valentin Andreyev?'

'Unfortunately not,' says David. 'Only as much as you'd find in any history book. He was arrested right here in Moscow. He's believed to have died in the Solovetsky Islands. But who can say? So many records were destroyed in the decades to follow. So many people fell off the map.'

Alexey's said something similar to me, about people disappearing. Lost to history. But what about people *reappearing*?

What if Valentin Andreyev was sent into exile, and Alexey Ivanov came back?

I still have trouble reconciling Alexey's placid, room-temperature personality with the act of smashing a framed photograph, but it has to be him. So clearly, something about the picture set him off.

Did he somehow *know* Tonya?

Could she be the woman he's trying to find?

I assumed Kukolka was a long-lost love, family member or friend, and that any reunion would be joyful. But it could equally be that he wants to confront her. Or even harm her.

233

Oh, blimey, am I turning paranoid? Have I spent too long in Soviet Russia?

'Viktoria Andreyeva, Valentin's wife, gave a few magazine and newspaper interviews late in her life,' says David. 'I can see what I can get my hands on, if you're interested.'

My thoughts must show on my face. David gives me a fatherly pat on the shoulder. 'Some people say that the north is white because it's made of human bone,' he says. 'You're not the first to wish those bones could speak.'

My memory of seeing Alexey's advert in Oxford is clear. I ducked into a cafe one afternoon to avoid a hailstorm. While waiting it out, I glanced at the public notice board, and I couldn't believe it. *This* would be my way into Russia, if I could nab it, and it'd be undoubtedly fascinating, three months with Alexey Ivanov. I stepped back, ecstatic, but I also felt a quiver go up my spine. The chill from outside, maybe, or a runaway hailstone in my jumper. I shook it off. But what was it? What did I feel at that moment that I've refused to feel ever since?

What if I've had it the wrong way around this whole time? What if I didn't choose this job at all?

What if *he* chose *me*, because I look like *her*?

Lev shows up just before supper, having spent the afternoon at his parents' dacha. He watches from the doorway as I try to make pelmeni how Mum used to make them when I was little. At the end she'd add flourishes, sprigs of garlic and sour cream. I never gave it a second thought until she began making nothing but sandwiches.

'So you met with the researcher today, from Memorial?' he asks. 'How was it?'

'Interesting,' I reply. 'He thinks that eventually there'll be full public access to the Lubyanka records.'

'Not everyone will want to know what's down in those tunnels.'

'Wouldn't you?'

'No,' he says.

'Why not?'

'None of it matters now. I can't absolve anyone.'

'Like your family, maybe?'

'My family?'

I turn to face him. 'A journalist chose *you* as a way to get dirt on the Ministry of the Interior. And the MVD have let you off easy, with this period of probation. We all know how things work over here. Someone's got your back. A parent? An aunt, an uncle? Family friend?' I turn back to the counter. 'You don't have to tell me. But don't judge my need to understand the past, either.'

A long silence. I think I've offended him.

I put down the rolling pin. 'Can you help me put the filling in the dough?'

He sits down without a word and gets to work. He's obviously done this before. No one has fingers that quick if they haven't.

'How was it, with your parents?' I ask, just for something, anything, to say.

'Only my mother,' he says. 'I wanted advice.'

'Advice on what?'

He smiles. 'My father is a general,' he says, like this answers my question.

'Oh. Wow.'

'He's a security advisor to the Kremlin.'

'*That* kind of military family.'

'He's also an old-school communist who despises Gorbachev. He wants things to go back to the way they were under—'

'Stalin?'

Lev laughs. 'I was going to say Brezhnev. But yes, my father is unhappy about how much control the Party has lost. How much power. That's what he blames for a lot of the hardships the past few years. He doesn't like change.'

'That's what your journalist was after, then? Access to your father?'

'*My* journalist?'

'You know what I mean.' I prod the dumpling into shape.

A muscle in his jaw twitches. 'It was my father who secured this assignment for me. He hates Alexey Ivanov even more than he does Gorbachev. I think he hoped I might do some spying.'

'And here you're stuck filling dumplings with me.'

'It's not that bad.' His voice is neutral. 'I brought you something, Raisa. From my mother's garden.'

Lev reaches inside his jacket and pulls out a small, single pink rose. I can only stare. People are well versed in the language of flowers here in Russia, but I've been away too long. All I recall is that red roses signify deep feelings and that a bouquet should always, always, *vsegda*, contain an odd number of flowers. But for all I know, this is the only thing his mother grows. It doesn't have to mean anything.

236

He is looking at me intently.

'It's lovely.' I reach for the rose, cough a little. 'Thank you.'

'Do you want a cursive lesson tonight?' he asks.

'No, I—I don't think so. Maybe next time.'

'You're avoiding it.'

'I guess I am.'

'Why?'

When I don't answer, Lev says, 'You have been avoiding me too.'

'I should find a vase.' The spices are making my eyes water. I can't do this. I just can't. 'And then I've got to get to cooking these.'

David Antonovich passes on multiple interviews given by Valentin Andreyev's wife between 1950 and 1980, when she died at the ripe old age of eighty-nine, right here in Moscow. In these interviews, Viktoria Katenina – she went back to her maiden name after World War II – talks mostly about her early piano career, daily life during the mass purges of the thirties, and the dramatic rise and fall of her famous playwright father.

She never talks about her husband.

David puts me in touch with Viktoria's daughter-in-law, who is a physics professor. Her name is Marina, and when I contact her office, she agrees to meet in person. We find one another at a small cafe off Pushkinskaya Square and she shakes my hand, a gesture I've never seen a Russian woman use. She's in her fifties or sixties, with a frosty smile and short hair. We order at the counter and as soon as we sit down, she takes command.

'My husband, Mikhail,' she begins, 'is tired of journalists and historians trying to bite off pieces of his family's carcass, as he sees it. He doesn't even know that we're meeting today. But I'm happy to answer any questions you have about Viktoria. She was so good to me.'

'I'm grateful for your help,' I say. 'Let's start with your husband, if that's alright. Mikhail Katenin. He took his mother's family name. What about his father?'

'What *about* his father?'

'Was his father Valentin Andreyev?'

We sit in silence as a waitress puts a pot of tea on the table.

'Your Russian sounds strange to me,' says Marina.

'I've been living in England.'

'Shall we speak in English?'

'Sure. But I—'

'You're barking up a bad tree,' declares Marina in English. She has a precise, posh accent, one that makes me feel like we might be just around the corner from Oxford. 'Mikhail never knew his father.'

'It wasn't Viktoria's husband?' The English words seem to stick to my teeth as I say them. I'm out of practice. 'Valentin Andreyev, the Bolshevik who was sent to the Solovetsky Islands in 1924, and never returned?'

'My husband was born in the thirties.'

There goes that theory, then.

'What is your interest in Valentin Andreyev?' Marina asks, begrudgingly.

'Did Viktoria ever mention him to you?'

'Again,' she says, 'why?'

How can I say that I'm now convinced that Valentin Andreyev became the historian Alexey Ivanov? How can I say that Viktoria's husband might well have penned one of the most famous memoirs of the past century, or that he shares his life story – one chapter of it – with hundreds of strangers at least once a week?

'I think I know him,' I say.

'You think you *know* him,' she repeats.

I feel myself blush. 'It's just a hunch.'

Marina glances around the cafe as if she thinks someone else may be listening. 'Why do you think this?'

'If I'm right, he's living under a different name. I believe he's looking for someone who may be in my family, who is connected to me, only I don't know how. I don't know what he wants, either. I only know he's due back in Moscow soon. So if you can think of anything that might help . . .'

Her eyes have narrowed into slits.

I will myself to keep drinking tea.

'Valentin Andreyev survived exile,' says Marina. 'He came back in 1933. The family didn't tell anyone.'

'What?' It comes out as a yelp. 'Why not?'

'Viktoria's father, Pavel, was popular with the regime. Perhaps he thought welcoming an ex-convict would be dangerous, or just look bad. But it was also the 1930s. People tried not to talk too much in general. Everyone was hiding one thing or another.'

'But couldn't Viktoria just divorce him? Why go to the trouble of *hiding* him?'

'Viktoria was a good person,' Marina replies. 'Valentin returned home traumatised. He needed help. He couldn't be taken out in public anyway, so they just pretended that he never came home. Something like this.'

'Viktoria told you this?'

239

'Not directly. But I have put together that much on my own, over time. My generation, we know how to listen.'

I'm so close to an underlying grain of truth I can almost rub it between my fingers. 'Why didn't Viktoria reveal any of this, in her interviews? Historians still believe Valentin died in the camps—'

'Viktoria tried her best, in those interviews,' says Marina tersely, 'to give everyone the glimpse they wanted into such terrible times. But she was a person too, with her own heartbreak, her own sorrows. She was not a living archive.'

Maybe I do have the tendency to forget, sometimes, that these are real people, real lives, and not just numbers in an equation, pieces in a puzzle I'm trying to solve. The waitress stops by again and I drop my gaze to my lap.

'Valentin left the family years later, after Mikhail was born,' says Marina. 'Abandoned them. But as I said, Valentin was sick in the head, after so many years in the gulag. So, to conclude, it is possible that you are right. That he took a new name and just – became someone else.'

'Do you know when he left?'

'No. I don't have all the facts, as my husband finds the subject so difficult,' says Marina, switching back to Russian. 'But if his father were alive now, Mikhail would want to know. I am absolutely sure. That is why I am telling you all this. I hope I can trust you.'

I start to say that she can, but she shakes her head. She clearly knows more than she's saying, but our discussion is over. At least there now seems to be a way to crack Alexey. It's been too easy for him to avoid hard questions all these years, I reckon, because every time he speaks, he renders everyone else speechless.

If he is in fact Valentin Andreyev, I doubt he could keep denying the truth while looking his own *son* straight in the eye.

'Should they . . . meet?' I ask.

'I will talk to him,' she says. 'I can telephone you, after.'

Upon his return from Novosibirsk, Alexey is not his usual sanded-smooth self. He sits me down in the living room and he keeps giving heavy sighs, as if they're supposed to be breaths. He asks if I made any headway with Akulina Burzinova. I tell him that I went to see her and learnt that the manuscript of the Countess's memoir was mailed to her.

'There was never any basement,' I clarify.

Alexey visibly deflates. He does seem like a person who would enjoy basements full of old manuscripts. Like his apartment, only even more crowded, with even greater possibility of being dragged under.

'You'll need to go back to Akulina,' Alexey says. 'Ask her – ask her if she still has the original.'

Still has the original? What is he *doing*? Keeping me busy, just as a lark? Like the incessant note-taking? No. I'd wager he *knew* that Akulina would notice my resemblance to Tonya. He must know she's the one who gave me the frame. What is it he wants her to do?

'Why?' I ask, bluntly.

'Primary sources are always worth the effort,' he replies. His eyes flash in my direction, but they stay unfocused, like he's looking at somebody just behind me. Alexey Ivanov is haunted too, only his ghost won't say his name, and he won't say hers.

* * *

241

'Now you are ready to speak with me,' says Akulina, who sits on her sofa half swallowed by a large blanket. 'Last time you couldn't get away fast enough.'

Her cat manoeuvres between my crossed ankles. 'I'm sorry to say this,' I begin, 'but the frame you gave me has been destroyed.'

'Destroyed! How could you be so careless?' she demands, a bit shrilly.

'The photograph is OK. The glass, the frame – it was broken by the historian I'm working for. I think he knew Tonya. I thought I'd ask you.'

'What is the name of this historian?'

'Alexey Ivanov.'

'I do not know of him.' Her voice is rough again, papery. 'What does he look like?'

'He's old,' I say, and she chuckles, more like a goat's bleat than a laugh. 'Here. I've brought this along – that's him.'

Akulina pulls eyeglasses from her breast pocket. A moment ticks by as she contemplates the back cover of *The Last Bolshevik*. She shakes her head. 'If I ever met him, it was too long ago.'

'So what happened to Tonya?' I ask, returning the book to my bag.

'I don't know that either,' she says. 'I wish I did. I told you last time, how she took us in, my brother and me. At the time, I never even thanked her. We lost touch after I went east. She was still living at Otrada. By the time I made my way back, she was gone, and now all I have left of her is that one picture – or at least I did.'

'Otrada,' I say, rolling the *r* as Akulina has done. It feels light on my tongue. I've still been using the English *r* all this time. No wonder Marina thought my Russian sounded strange.

'Tonya's family seat, in Tula province.'

'It's her. Alexey Ivanov is searching for Tonya.' I can't believe how normal I sound. 'She's the project.'

'Well, good luck to him.' Akulina sounds unimpressed. 'Tonya had many admirers.' She pauses, and then realisation dawns. Our eyes meet, hers glassy with age. 'But you. You look just like her. Is that why he—'

'I think so.'

'Did he say so?' she exclaims.

'No.'

'Then you should leave Moscow,' she says, with a wet-sounding cough. 'You must get away. What if he tries to hurt you and not just photo frames? Let me see that book again, to make sure it's not the partner she had when I lived with her. I didn't like him at all. I just can't remember his name. No, I do. Sasha.'

Dutifully I hand *The Last Bolshevik* back over to her.

'No,' says Akulina, sounding relieved. 'It's not Sasha.'

'I honestly don't think Alexey could move fast enough to hurt anyone. And he doesn't seem dangerous,' I say. 'He seems lost.'

Akulina harrumphs noisily. 'I would still leave, if I were you.'

'But I hate unanswered questions.' It tumbles out. 'I have this pathological need to understand. You spend your life around people who seal everything off, who hoard the real story to themselves, and you can't help it, you'd do anything just to know, and nothing is scary or too risky if you can just get at the answer. It's like Alexey—'

Like he knows that about me.

'The original manuscript of your mother's memoir,' I say tremulously. 'Do you still have it? May I see it?'

'I'm not going to live for ever,' says Akulina, in an almost eerie voice, one that tells me she knows how much time she has. 'You can take it with you, girlie. Just keep it safe. Don't let the historian anywhere near.'

When I return to the apartment, nobody is home. Night falls. I'm already tucked into a blanket when I hear a key in the lock, the front door squawking in the way it does when someone is trying to stay quiet. It's Lev. He enters the living room without turning on any lights. He smells different, a bit soapy.

'You're still awake, aren't you,' he says, sitting on the cot and stretching.

'I want us to be friends again.'

'Is that what you want?' But he doesn't give me a chance to answer. 'I thought you'd be here this afternoon.'

'I went to see Akulina Burzinova. I can tell you everything tomorrow.'

'Tell me now,' he says, switching on the lamp.

I kick aside my blanket and reach under the sofa. 'Akulina has given me the original manuscript of Natalya's memoir. I need to decide whether to show it to Alexey, as he's asked for it, or hide it away, like she wants me to do. Have a look.'

Lev opens the small box that Akulina gave me, containing hundreds of loose-leaf sheets. He turns them over, one by one, as I look over his shoulder. At the piece of paper he's holding. At the handwriting.

I spent a full hour in a cafe in Oxford examining this same handwriting.

I go over to my pillow, find Mum's notebook, sit down again, turn to the first page. *A Note for the Reader. These stories should not be read in order.*

The same person wrote these.

The notebook, and Natasha's memoir.

'Are you OK?' asks Lev.

'Yeah, yeah. Why?'

'You're crying.'

'Oh. It's just that—' I wipe my cheek with the back of my hand, but it doesn't help. 'You know you asked why I've been avoiding Mum's notebook recently, well, see, I had this hope, this idea that my papa might have actually written these stories, that I was going to crack this cipher of his, and somehow – hear his voice again—' Now I can barely speak through my hiccupping. 'But now I know he didn't write them. Now I *know*. Papa couldn't have and he didn't, and it was stupid to begin with, because this isn't what encrypted messages could possibly look like, and now it's like I've lost him all over again. He's dead. My father's really dead. He didn't leave me any secret message from beyond the grave. He's dead.'

Lev puts the notebook down and takes me into his arms. At some point, I'm not sure when, I stop crying. Back in England I never cried. Now it seems like it's all I do.

'The handwriting's the same,' I say unsteadily, pulling away. 'I can barely read it, but I can tell.'

He considers this. 'Yes, I see it,' he says. 'But wouldn't that be a good thing? If it *were* code, you have two samples of it now. That would make it much easier to break, to understand.'

My breath shudders in my chest. 'I think you were right.'

'Right about what?'

I often have this feeling when I'm working on a problem, right when it seems almost impossible to solve. You look up from endless pages of figures, from dead ends and futile attempts, and instantly you see that the solution is there, in front of you, but you have to reach for it at just the right moment, in just the right way, or it slips past, and the problem is impossible again.

'My father used to tell me that a code is only a cover,' I say, feeling for the words. 'Like snowfall. These stories are another kind of cover. They're hiding something, but there's still a way to go beneath. You said that you could see the original words, the ones that were erased?'

'Yes. Why?'

'Because,' I say, 'I want to exhume them.'

PART THREE

THE BOY AND THE WAVES

In a faraway kingdom, in a long-ago land, a boy was swept out to sea. The waves carried him further and further, until he was so far from the shoreline that he could not see it any more. He did not know if it was still there. He did not know if he had already drowned. He began to weep. *Hush*, said the waves, *and we will help you, since you have made us stronger with your tears.*

Hush, and we will carry you home.

The waves kept their promise, but when the boy stepped onto land again, he was already an old man. He did not recognise anyone, even his own family, and they did not recognise him. He went back to the waves and he shouted at them: *You've brought me to the wrong place. This isn't home.* And the waves replied: *Home is not a place.*

CHAPTER NINETEEN

Antonina
Moscow, spring 1938

THE INTERROGATOR DOES NOT BELIEVE HER. HIS JOB IS not to believe anyone. He leans back, long enough that Tonya wants to squirm in her chair, but she remains demure, lowers her eyes. The Interrogator's office is cosy, intimate. They have been meeting like this for half a year, and every detail to the meetings still feels staged, purposefully added. A radio broadcast plays in the background, describing the latest machinations of Hitler, the German Chancellor. The hallway outside thrums with life.

They are in the Lubyanka building, headquarters of the NKVD, Soviet state security, the most recent incarnation of the Cheka. The Lubyanka sits on busy Dzerzhinsky Square. *Stop a moment*, people often say, *to have a drink at the corner-tavern, or to admire the bowl of Vitaly's central fountain. Take one last look around, before you go inside.*

* * *

The season has not yet turned. People hurry home from work dressed in their warmest wools, with their earflaps pulled low. Darkness drips down from the sky, settles in over the city by late afternoon, and the cobblestones are quickly glazed with frost, though there may not be any cobbles much longer. Many streets have already been asphalted to accommodate an increasing number of automobiles, like the Black Crows of the NKVD, though *they* only come out at night. Nocturnal hunters.

Tonya, heavily pregnant, walks carefully. There is a specific route she takes on the way back from seeing the Interrogator, just past the cafe that has recently opened, past the mouths of the new metro stations, all lit up from the inside. She's never tempted to use the metro. That light may be blinding, but you are still going underground.

On the way, she worries.

Five years ago, in 1933, Viktoria Andreyeva arrived at Otrada looking for her. Viktoria's news was astonishing: Valentin had come home. No, he'd been *smuggled* home, via Pavel Katenin's contacts, in secret, from the White Sea Canal, where he had spent two years, well past the end of his original sentence.

Eight years of hard labour, in total.

Viktoria had broken down, been reduced to tears, explaining how difficult it was to cope with Valentin's bizarre, erratic behaviour, his sudden, volatile temper, his memory loss, his long periods of something she called blankness. Her father had secured new identity papers and medical treatment, but none of it was making much difference, and Pavel's latest ideas for helping Valentin were beginning to concern Viktoria. Untested medications. Experimental treatments. Surgery. Meanwhile, the only thing Valentin ever said clearly was Tonya's name – and an intricate and precise set of instructions for finding Otrada. The very instructions Tonya had given him the day of his arrest, in 1924.

Viktoria wanted to return to Leningrad, so Tonya agreed to move to Moscow. She brought fifteen-year-old Lena with her, of course. They took over Viktoria's apartment and Tonya found a job at a residence home for children. Lena enrolled in school and helped take care of her father. In the first year, Valentin was much as Viktoria described.

It took time, energy, tears, but eventually he recovered.

Almost.

It wasn't their presence that helped him most, if she's being brutally honest with herself. It was the rediscovery of his politics. Pavel Katenin is the only other person in Moscow who knows that Valentin is here – except for the few people Valentin is in contact with, *unofficially*. There is a quietly burgeoning anti-Soviet, anti-Stalin resistance here in the capital. Tonya doesn't dare to take Valentin away from it, because he is finally healed.

Almost.

It was sustainable, once, living like this. But the atmosphere has shifted over the past year, now that Stalin has begun arresting, persecuting, executing, members of the Old Bolshevik Guard, of which Valentin is one; purging the Party and the country. The danger remains hidden, but it is palpable. Like the baby that Tonya carries.

If the NKVD arrest Valentin a second time, it will be for good. He will not make it back again.

* * *

Tonya locks up from the inside. *Click-click-pop-clack*. Like a symphony. 'Hello?' she calls out, and her voice bounces back. It's in the echo that she hears her own fear. She never hears it at the Lubyanka. 'Where are you?'

The door to the kitchen opens.

'Back at last,' he says. Valentin drops a kiss to her forehead, soft as cricket-legs, his hands coming to rest on her distended belly. There is a Maternity House up Leontyevsky that Tonya will have to visit in just over a month, an ugly brick building with a sign like a foghorn: *in-patients*. Valentin will not be allowed in; should probably not show his face in public much anyhow.

She will give birth to their child without him, like last time.

'I wonder what he wants from you,' murmurs Valentin. 'Why any interrogator would do this, bring you in week after week, for months and months—'

'You're safe as long as it keeps going,' she whispers.

Valentin sighs, deep enough that he has to clear his throat. He's had that baby's rattle of a sound in his chest since the day he came home from the White Sea Canal. *That's what blasting through one hundred and forty-one miles of solid granite for two years will do to you*, he's said, like it's a joke. *All of it has to go somewhere*. 'It's not necessary, Tonya. The NKVD don't have anything on me. If they did, I'd already be in the Lubyanka. As before.'

'It's different now. They don't need evidence.'

'You can't do this for ever, *milaya*.'

'If you would agree to leave Moscow, I wouldn't have to.'

'I just said you don't have to.'

'Let's not fight,' she says, placing a hand on her stomach. If she says more, all her fears will fall out of her, fears that he'll leave the apartment one day when she's at work at the orphanage and he'll go to the Lubyanka himself, go straight up to an NKVD officer and he'll say, *Yes, I am an Old Bolshevik, yes, I am an anti-Soviet enemy of the people who is working to overthrow this regime and everything it stands for, yes, I will continue to do so until the day I die.*

That *will* be the day he dies.

She'd never speak it aloud, but that's probably how Valentin *wants* to die. On the grand stage; making one last stand. He has probably already written the speech he plans to make, and when he is alone, he mouths it to himself, the way he once did when they were little more than children, before the October Revolution, before the demise of the Romanovs. Before he and his Party got everything they ever wanted.

The Interrogator has a name, but she refuses to use it. Tonya prefers to think of him as a character, because she's determined to turn this into a story when it's all over, maybe another one she can tell to the younger children at the residence home. She'll draw him in detail, his meaty peasant's accent, the one he tries to disguise. His slicked-back hair, his pencil-thin smile. The way he carries his personal ambition such that the higher he rises, the more he achieves, the heavier the load.

The Interrogator plucks people off the streets, like insects off a picnic blanket. They are shepherded into his personal vehicle, a black Emka touring car with a red stripe down the side. At the start he tries to make it sound exciting, meaningful: how much we depend on such brave, valiant citizens like yourself, to aid our great nation in identifying wreckers and traitors!

Only sign this sheet of paper.

Sign.

Sign.

Sign.

He never says that to be an informant is to be half a prisoner and half a guard. To live the worst of both. He never explains that the state is consuming itself, turning the people against the people. He never says what will happen if you don't sign. He assumes you already know, and she does.

Tonya never wakes up screaming from her nightmares any more, not as she used to. No matter what happens, she keeps her mouth shut. She keeps it shut so tight that in the mornings her lips may be dotted with blood. But she's not alone. Everyone in Moscow knows the dangers of opening one's mouth by accident. To tell the wrong joke. To speak the wrong name. To confess.

'Your daughter, Lena,' says the Interrogator. He cocks his head, examines Tonya off-angle. Like this, his eyes appear large, bulbous, like those of a fish. Today the radio is off, but the small gramophone in the corner plays a folksy song, something a muzhik might tap a felt-booted foot along to. 'I've learnt that she studies at the State University in Leningrad. Biology? Medicine? You've said nothing about your Lenochka.'

The word *Lenochka* is drawn out, so that it billows.

'She doesn't know a thing about her father,' says Tonya. 'He was sent to the Solovetsky Islands before they had a chance to meet.'

The folk tune is still playing. It goes on and on, this kind of peasant music. Designed to last a feast, a wedding, a celebration in the fields. She wonders how the Interrogator can stand it, whether it reminds him of a faraway childhood, of his father smoking a goat's-leg pipe, of his mother embroidering the pillow slips.

'I can't give you more leeway,' he says, 'when you haven't given me anything.' The Interrogator pulls his hands out from behind his desk for the first time. He is holding a bundle of letters, tied with string. He undoes the string and pretends to look for something, but he knows what he's looking for. Just as he did that day on the street, six months ago, when he first plucked *her* off it.

'These arrived from the Investigative Section in Solovetsky,' he says. 'And I imagine there's much more we don't have.'

He slides one across the desk to her.

'See for yourself,' he says.

March 1925

Dear Tonya, milaya moya

They say that [indecipherable] *will come to visit us here, so perhaps I can appeal to him. The lighting is poor, they keep it dark, so I keep this short* [indecipherable] *the only light is my memory of you—*

Valentin

The Interrogator takes the letter back, tweezes another one from the bundle.

July 1926

Zvezda moya

Hands are hurting from today's work but I will write to you as long as they stay on. There are other politicals here like me, Party members from the first. Does Koba know what is happening here? They ask me. But I am going to find out. I am going to survive, I am going to come home, I am going to tell the world the truth about this place. Take care of yourself – I believe you will read this, I send all my love with it – wait for me—

Your Valentin

Tonya's throat constricts. Koba is Joseph Stalin. Valentin was writing to her about Comrade Stalin. It's treason enough, and it's only one line from one letter.

'I've enjoyed our sessions,' says the Interrogator. 'You have an astounding gift for telling stories. From the very first one, I've wanted to see how many you had. If you would ever run out.'

The first story had been an accident. He'd asked for information on anyone she knew. She hadn't known what to say, so she'd made it up, the way she does for the orphans, knowing what would appeal to him. A peasant's tale. She'd seen something unexpected cross his face at the end, as if through her words he had perceived a different, uneventful existence for himself, one in which he'd raised his animals, tended his fields, never left home at all.

'But I am trying to build a career, you know,' he says. 'And the pressure is increasing.'

The song is over. The record has finished. The Interrogator has planned this, timed it perhaps. He pulls out a new sheet of paper. He writes her name at the top. The mention of her daughter was strategic. He will say Lena's name again if Tonya does not sign. Say it in that gruesome, gluey way he did, like he was moving it around with his tongue. *Lenochka.*

'Save yourself, Tonya,' he says softly. 'Valentin Andreyev is past your help. He belongs to the State. But you, your circumstances . . .' He makes a small gesture, up and down. 'Sign against him, and when he is arrested, you will be spared. You have my word.'

He speaks of her pregnancy as if he's seen *into* her. Same as he has the letters. There is no violation too obscene, because there is no such thing as a private life.

He opens his palm, reveals a pen.

'Wait. Just a moment, wait.' There is a droplet in Tonya's eye. Sweat, maybe. It must not fall, or he will think he has made her cry. 'What if I can give you somebody even better? Someone who can make your career?'

The Interrogator laughs aloud. He doesn't believe this either. 'Find somebody better quickly,' he says. 'Make my career.'

The Trials of Nikolay Bukharin and the others have ended. They have been found guilty of conspiracy and treason against the State. Comrade Stalin will see all his former Party compatriots lined up against a wall and shot. Tonya watches Valentin read about the verdict over breakfast. Valentin says nothing as he folds up the newspaper, again and again, so that it ends up as hard as an overbaked biscuit. He once knew all these long-standing members of the Politburo. Bukharin and Rykov. Zinoviev and Kamenev, who were executed last year.

Valentin seems to sense her watching, and looks over. He has that expression on his face he always has when Tonya asks him about the White Sea Canal. He is willing to talk about the six years he spent in Solovetsky, but he never speaks of his two subsequent years on the Canal. He only ever makes that one quip about solid granite.

That is what the expression is, too. Solid granite.

Valentin is the editor of an anti-Stalinist news-sheet, and Tonya reads through a few of his typewritten pages while sipping on a thin root tea recommended for pregnant women.

'What are you looking for, *milaya*?' Valentin asks, over Tonya's shoulder. 'You've never shown this much interest before.'

The tea is unsweetened, burns in her mouth. 'Nothing in particular.'

'You're stuck? You can't think of anything else to say to the Interrogator?'

'Is all this funny to you?' Tonya knows she sounds as bitter as the tea. 'If you're not afraid for yourself, then at least for me, for Lena, for the baby—'

'If the NKVD come, then they come, Tonya.'

'*If?* They are coming! They could come tonight!'

'How does my fear save me then? What good is it to sit here and shake?'

'To show me that you care. That you care about your life, our lives! Don't you see? We should have left Moscow months ago, years ago, only you had to carry on with all *this*!'

His expression darkens. 'I lived through the camps. I have a duty to the people to share that experience, to speak and to fight. I have to make the moral choice.'

'Then you leave *me* to make the immoral one!' She breaks, begins to shout. 'You and your politics, Valentin! Yes, you might be against it now, you might swear it's your enemy, but you are still choosing the Party. You will *always* choose the Party and I am the one who will always choose you!'

Valentin gives her a slanted smile before he leaves, goes into their bedroom, slams the door behind him. He should have fallen in love with Viktoria, she thinks. Or he shouldn't have fallen in love at all. Maybe he wishes there was nothing he cared about other than a better world, a utopia for the masses.

Other than the godforsaken people.

Tonya holds her nose, lets a gulp of tea sit in her mouth. If she calls him back now, it can be like the fight never happened. But this time she needs him to stay away, so that he doesn't see her take several of the sheets, press them flat with her hands, and tuck them into her bag.

Tonya curls up on her side like an inchworm, eyes open, ogling the darkness. She lets out cloud-puffs of breath, sucks them back in. She hardly hears the sound of Valentin's footsteps, or the swish of bedcovers. He has been working for hours.

'Let's go to Leningrad,' he says.

'To visit Lena?'

'To live there.'

'But you've always said you are too involved in what's happening here.'

'I am.' A wry laugh. 'But I'll find something. And I know someone who can arrange a propiska for settling there. It does help to have friends in the underground.' He shifts to sling an arm over her belly. The baby rolls in response. It's always most active at night. 'We don't have to,' he adds. 'It's up to you.'

Valentin is always building sandcastles in the sky. Tonya half believes him. She half thinks this is wild-eyed nonsense. But at least he has been listening. He must know she would rather live in the country, of course; the further you get from the cities, the safer you are, the less the NKVD can do. But Leningrad is a compromise. A middle ground.

'You were right to accuse me,' he says. 'I've put other things above our safety. And I am sorry.'

Tonya is not lucid in her dreams as often as she used to be, but tonight she walks through her nightmare world, towards the conservatory. Usually there is a moment of solitude within, before the girl with the ivy-veins enters from the house, but as Tonya opens the conservatory door, the girl is already there. She is standing *right* in front of the door. The girl's mouth is open, and the ivy is instantly everywhere, circling Tonya's legs, pinning down her arms, fastening around her neck—

Wake up, wake up—

Tonya moves so fast she hits herself on the headboard.

She is awake.

She thinks woozily that she should get a drink of water, turn on some lights, perhaps even rouse Valentin. But as she starts to get off the bed, she feels the sticky stretch of something between her legs. She lifts the duvet.

A gamey, horsey smell lifts with it.

Pink, bloody fluid. It's early, too early. The spring thaws have only recently come. Tonya pictures the rivers of Russia all running at once, a great, gushing torrent of water, and then she feels it on her thighs, streaming down her legs. She sees it on the floor between her feet as she tries to stand. It is the last thing she sees.

People speak over her head. It's an emergency. It's not just one baby, they're saying. They didn't know until now. They begin to cut and she thinks she is turning into shreds of flesh. Then somebody shows her a glimpse of a tiny, dusty face, maybe two faces, and she is told that her twins will be taken to a special hospital for premature babies and will stay there until they are strong enough to go home.

You're lucky, they say. If you'd arrived at the Maternity House any later than you did, your babies would already have gone. And if you were out in the country and not in the middle of Moscow, with the help of professionals, you'd likely have joined them. And if there were no special hospital with special tubes for feeding babies as immature as these, they'd only last a day or two. Lucky, lucky girl.

Tonya has never been called lucky in her life.

Cursed, yes.

Someone asks if they should send for Tonya's husband and she says that she killed her husband and they laugh, say all the women feel that way but he's very much alive, he brought you in, but we don't permit visitors obviously and the first person says, *OK, rest now, my dear*, as if anyone can *rest* when there are a dozen other women in the ward shrieking, screaming, begging for relief.

Luckily the Interrogator was not here this time, because Tonya is sure she would have confessed to anything, that they would all confess to anything, that there is no torture like childbirth.

'Tonya?' A hand on her shoulder. 'It's me. Vika.'

Tonya struggles up to an elbow. Now in her mid-forties, Valentin's ex-wife has a face that is round as a coin, and soft features that only come to life at the piano bench.

'The twins are doing well.' Viktoria's voice is soothing. 'Come on. I've had them ready your bag.'

'Valentin?' Tonya says, more a wince than a word.

'He's at Papa's summer dacha. It's not too far outside Moscow. The NKVD have been at your place. They've gone through it a few times already. They're looking for him. If you both could only leave right now – but of course, the twins need to stay in hospital. So I am taking you to my father's apartment – my father has agreed – and there we will just have to wait.'

262

'Valentin hasn't seen the babies? Yekaterina and Mikhail?'

Viktoria shakes her head. She smiles. 'Beautiful names.'

Outside the Maternity House, Pavel Katenin's chauffeur is waiting. The car's engine is running. The leather interior is slippery-sleek, like Tonya's insides. Viktoria speaks to the driver and he throws the car into gear, jolting them down the road. With every turn there's a fierce ripple down Tonya's torso, through her womb. She has not yet been to the new Moscow residence of Viktoria's father. She has met Pavel several times now, and knows he cares for Valentin, but she can't imagine him doing something so mundane as *living* somewhere, because nowadays Pavel Katenin is everywhere all at once.

He is simply so famous. Nearly as famous as Comrade Stalin.

Pavel doesn't seem to appreciate the danger that Valentin is in. He seemed much more alarmed and cautious when Valentin first came home from the Canal, but perhaps his own position was more vulnerable then. Now Stalin has been to each of his plays. Now Stalin would know him on the street.

But that's not how it works, Pavel, Tonya wants to say. The better Stalin knows you, the more vulnerable you are.

She has learnt much indeed, from the Interrogator.

Pavel announces at breakfast that Bukharin and Rykov were traitors. Along with everyone imprisoned in the Lubyanka. He waves his cane in the air before he sits down to make his point. He calls them the *enemy within*, and there is something furtive in his face as he says this. He must have signed somebody away himself. Maybe a friend. Maybe one of his actors from the theatre. Maybe his own soul.

'But so many are being arrested nowadays,' says Tonya, 'that surely some must be innocent.'

'When the forest is cut, the chips will fly,' he says, as his maid, Annushka, shreds a jelly candy for his tea. Viktoria, at the end of the table, says nothing. Tonya has always had the feeling that Viktoria is cowed by her father, or by the figure of him, now larger than life. 'But on the whole,' he goes on, 'the system is designed to be discerning.'

'And if Valentin is a chip again?' Tonya counters.

'Aha!' says Pavel grandly. 'You make my point for me! Our Valya was *guilty*, was he not, at the time of his arrest! But now he's learnt his lesson. Also, now Comrade Stalin knows me. Knows my family. No harm will come to any of us in the end.'

Tonya lacerates her pancake with a fork. It's like Pavel sees all this as one of his stage plays. It isn't *real*, Antonina Nikolayevna! Silly girl!

Viktoria is the first to excuse herself from the table. Pavel looks at Tonya in a way that suggests he thinks they are now alone. Annushka is only another piece of furniture to him. But this is also a mistake. Furniture do not have eyes and ears.

'There is nothing to fear, Tonya,' Pavel says, reaching for his cane. 'Any interest in Valya will blow over soon. I'm sure he's enjoying himself at my dacha in the meantime. When the babies are strong, your family can summer there; you can all get fat on the native strawberries!'

The most dangerous stories are the ones people don't realise they are telling. Tonya smiles along with him, as if she can already taste the succulent sweetness of wild strawberries, can imagine the juice running down their faces like blood.

The interrogator does not say a word as he reads. When he looks up, his face appears anaemic by lamplight, or perhaps it's because his usually reliable bulb is weak today, beneath its silk-scarf lampshade. 'I've heard you gave birth to twins,' he says. 'Congratulations. Don't they run in families?'

'I know of no twins in mine,' she says.

'More village folklore.' He smiles, bares his fangs. 'This is excellent material, what you've brought me today. You've done your duty at last.' He swivels in his chair, swings his legs to one side. 'You did keep me on your tenterhooks, but it seems it was all worth it. A good informant is infinitely valuable to our—'

'You've done a lot for me, Sasha,' she says. 'Not just now. Also back then.'

His smile dims like the bulb.

'But I saw this,' she says, sweeping a hand across the table that sits between them like a breeze block. 'Back then. I saw this part of you.'

As Sasha himself would say, *Chemu byt', togo ne minovat'*. *What will be, cannot be escaped.*

'It's time to sign against Andreyev, Tonya,' he says.

'You misunderstand. These papers I've brought you have nothing to do with Valentin Andreyev,' she says. The lies flow like water. She is a storyteller. She has always been a storyteller. 'I'm staying in the home of Pavel Katenin. I found them there. They are his. And if you raid his apartment, you will find even more. I am sure of it.'

As Tonya walks to the hospital to stop in on the twins, it starts to rain, but there isn't enough water in the world to wash away what she has just done. After all these years she has learnt to live with fear, to stay laced into it like a bone-corset; she can learn to live with other things too. Even this. She will always remember the night Dmitry lay bleeding at her feet, the way that young Bolshevik's carving knife went in, and whenever she does, she remembers that the choice in this country is not between right and wrong. It is between life and death.

CHAPTER TWENTY

Valentin

Outside Moscow, spring 1938

PAVEL'S DACHA IS MADE UP OF THREE FLOORS. VALENTIN'S room is on the second floor, near the kitchen. There is a bedstead with a mattress, but he will sleep on the ground.

The house is poorly insulated, built for summertime living. Valentin goes through the kitchen drawers and cupboards looking for tins and can openers. He can't find any food, so tomorrow he'll have to go down into the local village, a pimple of a place. It'll be better to see people, though; not to be alone all day long. It's when he's alone that there's trouble, that things come back that shouldn't. He's found a drink in one of the cabinets, some vodka, and that'll do, it'll fill the river in his mind so that he doesn't reach out for another log floating on the surface, believing it is a log, thinking abstractly of logs, only to discover that it is not a log at all, but a person.

That person is him.

Valentin's thoughts often spiral at night. *My name is Valentin Mikhailovich Andreyev. I was born in St*

Petersburg in 1896. My father worked in the Kirov factory. He died when I was four. I was raised by my mother and my grandmother. They died when I was ten. My name is Valentin Mikhailovich Andreyev. I was born in St Petersburg in 1896 . . .

Spiralling, spiralling, until they go to darker and darker places. To the White Sea.

He holds his breath now and he can still smell the bilge, the saltwater, the wet wood. The mould. He gasps for air. Usually Tonya is sleeping beside him. But tonight of course she isn't here. What if she doesn't exist? What if she is only a delusion? What if he is sicker than he knows, and he never came home at all?

What if he is still there right now?

At home, he knows how to break out of the spiral. Sometimes, not wanting to disturb Tonya, he wanders the apartment. He smokes, touches the spines of books, spends hours at the typewriter, because every hard clack of the keys keeps him in the present. He does anything that requires a physical sense other than vision.

Vision is the least trustworthy of all of them.

The bedroom in the dacha is lightless, but nothing would push these shadows away. Everything is in his head: The blinding storm. Blood being spit through his teeth. The lighting of a paraffin lamp to reveal the shivering body of a bunkmate. Someone clipping off the dead tips of his fingers. Heavy bandages. More blood, trickling down the side of his neck, hot and fetid.

Someone did say there would be no escape from the camps. It's not like they were in the East. It's not like they were on the moon. But no one has ever escaped. Even the people who are released do not escape. Valentin will never escape.

CHAPTER TWENTY-ONE

Rosie

Moscow, August 1991

THE BREEZE IS AS LIGHT AS THE EVENING SKY OVERHEAD. I walk without any destination until I find myself standing in front of the Bolshoi Theatre. This building is neoclassical, impressive, iconic, but not entirely beautiful, marked by the hammer and sickle that sits at the apex. I still remember the way Mum spoke about this theatre: *You sink into everything*, she would say. *The floors, the champagne, your seat. There's a gravitational pull to the stage. And the people on that stage, they are other-worldly.*

I've never been inside. My mother was a dancer here, in the most famous ballet in the world, yet I've never attended a performance.

There's a faint hum in my ears, a splash of champagne in the air.

Zoya is back.

I don't resist. I *sink* into the image she shows me, just as Mum said to do, and the famous white foyer of the Bolshoi appears in my mind's eye: a cascade of red carpeting, a double staircase. People everywhere, dressed for the occasion. There is the main stage, and the audience is quiet and the orchestra strains and the lights are turned low, and I know I have been drawn into the past. I nearly expect to see Mum step out of the wings.

But she's seated in the audience.

She looks young. My age. Maybe if she turned, she would somehow see *me*, our parallel universes might intersect, but I can tell that she won't turn. Nothing exists to her at this moment but the ballet.

There's something odd about the rapture in her expression. It's not the look of someone who is already a dancer, because *that* person would know that all this is a fantasy. Everyone up there is human. Their toes are taped. Their bones are being ground to powder. Beneath their pretty costumes, they are gaunt, probably underfed. It is a profession, and a brutal one at that. Not a dream world.

My mother is in a dream world. She looks up at that stage as if she were never there. As if *Katerina Ballerina* was just another fairy tale.

The image is gone. I am standing alone in front of the Bolshoi, staring up at the façade.

I understand my mother's notebook.

The real story is in the white spaces on the page. The real story is unwritten.

'*Bozhe moy*, you're hard to get rid of,' Akulina says to me over the phone. 'What is it this time? Has someone lit my mother's memoir on fire? Would you like to take my pet cat home?'

270

I smile at this, but I stop when I hear her cough again. She's not just coughing out, she's coughing *up*. 'Tell me,' I say. 'Did Tonya like to tell short stories, fairy tales, that sort of thing?'

A drier cough. 'Yes, to her daughter Lena. And to my brother, before he died. But I wouldn't call them stories. Too bulky. More like she sprinkled them around like sugar and if you listened, you might catch a speck of it, and then it was over and you're not even sure what you heard.'

'I have a notebook of stories that belonged to her.'

Akulina guffaws. 'Never saw Tonya with a notebook.'

'I took a sort of – forensic look at it. She wrote in pencil—'

'Never saw Tonya writing. I'm not even certain she could.'

'Pencil,' I repeat, 'I think because there are so many corrections for spelling and grammar. But I found something on the back of the cover. It looked blank at first, but the words *For Lena, beloved daughter* have been erased. It's unmistakable.'

I had intended to tell Akulina that her mother's memoir is in the same handwriting as the notebook, but I hesitate. Suddenly I don't think she's supposed to know that. I think the memoir answered questions about Natalya – and Natalya's choices – that Akulina spent her whole life asking, and I can only imagine how that feels.

I can't take it away.

'For Lena,' Akulina says, digesting this.

'My mother gave me this notebook,' I say, 'and I'm starting to think her mother might have given it to her. That Tonya is my grandmother.'

271

It's scary to say. Family members don't just pop up like that. It's not like Mum's died and now the factory is sending a replacement.

'That was my first thought, when I saw you,' says Akulina. 'But then I realised you couldn't be Lena's child. Lena was born before 1920. You're too young.'

'Yes. I was born in 1967.' My insides are as tangled as the telephone cord. 'And Mum wasn't even thirty when she had me. But do you have any idea where Lena is now? How I might find her? My mother never, ever spoke about her family, not siblings, nothing. She said they were all dead.'

'Unfortunately, no.' Akulina sounds wistful, almost sad. 'Lena was a lively little girl. Ambitious, even as a young child.' Her tone shifts, loses the sadness. 'She'd go around saying she was going to be a doctor and live in a house by a wide river. Though I think the last part was put into her head by Sasha.' A gravelly laugh. 'Tonya's boyfriend. He was ambitious too.'

'A house on a wide river,' I say. 'That's . . . quite interesting. Sasha wasn't Lena's father?'

'Oh, no. Lena's father was a Bolshevik that Tonya knew in Leningrad. Tonya herself used to live on the Fontanka, you know. Speaking of houses on rivers.' Akulina sounds fully herself again. 'I still recall the room where they served tea, in that house. You cannot know the grandeur of that world, Raisa! The chandelier. The paintings. This strange blue wallpaper. It all feels now like a dream.'

'I'd like to see that house,' I say. 'Do you remember the address?'

'If I look at a map first.' She's chewing and chomping again. Those jaws might keep working even after she dies, whittling her teeth down to the studs, reducing her gums to pulp. Then she adds, in a whistle of a breath: 'Why? Those old houses, they are like mazes.'

'But I'm going to tie every thread together,' I say. 'That's how I'll find my way out.'

It is a long, sleepless night on the Red Arrow train from Moscow to Leningrad.

'Your mother danced in the *Bolshoi ballet*?' asks Lev.

'When you say it like that, it sounds even less believable.'

'You should just call them,' he says. 'You can say, *I'm the daughter of Katerina Simonova*. Did she ever dance for you? Then you'll know.'

'I'm going to sound mad,' I say, but it's mostly mad because I don't think I've ever admitted like that to being Mum's child. I was always embarrassed by her, even when she was young and charming, because I didn't want to be another one of her sycophants, didn't want to seem as needy as everyone else. Then later, in England, I was even more embarrassed. Yes, I'm *Kate's* daughter, folks! Kate who sometimes wanders outside in her dressing gown and falls asleep by the postbox. Kate with her lemony complexion and cheesy breath and her stories, those stupid, awful, drunken stories, that she starts telling – *shouting* – to anyone within earshot: *In a faraway kingdom! In a long-ago land!*

But if she was never a ballerina, I think I would resent her less. I'd feel a bit sorry that someone would be insecure enough to lie to her own family about who she was. Maybe Mum couldn't bear who she was; maybe she didn't even know. Maybe that's why I never figured her out either.

273

'No, then?' says Lev.

'Yes,' I say. 'I'm Katerina Simonova's daughter.'

The taxi driver takes us along a sinuous route, as meandering as any of Leningrad's rivers, until we reach the Fontanka embankment. He deposits us in front of a three-storey mansion of dull-pink granite. Several of the first-floor windows are boarded up with plywood, and the stucco is coming off the façade, revealing the stone underneath.

The house calls little attention to itself – if I glanced this way from down this street, I might not even see it – yet it taunts anyone who looks closer. *I survived everything*, it's saying. *I'll outlive you too.*

I rattle the brass knob of the front door. Unlocked. Lev and I step over the threshold, into an empty foyer. I am reminded of the day Mum and I moved into our first apartment in England, how she ran her hand along all the walls and windows. She was careful not to touch any of it. Communing with the house, was how she explained herself. Because what people won't say, houses often do.

But the silence in here is steadfast.

Above our heads are the skeletal remains of a chandelier and a high, moulded ceiling of what looks like marble. In front of us is a staircase that leads to a dark upstairs landing. I almost want to call out for Zoya for reassurance that there aren't other ghosts in here, but I also don't want to awaken the house.

A door just past the stairs groans open. A woman toting a netted bag emerges, and when she sees us, she squeals, puts a hand over her heart. 'I'm the landlady,' she says, regrouping. 'Who are you?'

'Are these apartments occupied?' I ask.

'More or less,' she says. 'The top floor is full. The floor above me belongs to someone who is never here. Why? You need housing?'

'Yes. Housing.'

'You two married?'

'Newly-weds,' I say, and Lev snickers. 'My grandmother used to live in this house, decades ago, and I think there's something romantic about it. These ceilings, the windows, the view on the river, and I hoped we could just take a look. Right? Lyova?'

I don't think I've ever used his diminutive name before. The smirk leaves his face a little.

'Could we see the one you said was empty?' I continue. 'If the owner is never here.'

The landlady purses her mouth. 'I'm not sure. The owner is the writer, Alexey Ivanov. You've heard of him? He is an important man.'

What?

Lev steps in. 'Please,' he says to her, 'my wife is an orphan. She knows so little about her family. She only just discovered that her grandmother lived here. I don't know Mr Ivanov, but he might understand. Wanting to discover the past.'

'He might,' she says suspiciously.

Lev is already reaching around for his wallet. If I learnt to do it like that, I would get the best tables in all my favourite restaurants. Soon the landlady is handing him a key and saying she's going out to the shops, so *don't take any longer than that*. Lev begins to head up the stairs, but I stop on the bottom step.

'Thank you,' I say. 'I'll repay you.'

'Don't,' he says, without looking back.

The apartment is made up of several empty rooms, an unnerving contrast to Alexey's apartment in Moscow. Sunlight steals through the plywood, creating hints of colour here and there. The kitchen is barren except for the stoves, gone to grey, and a number of dinner tins, a reminder of what must have been, before there were cobwebs strung like banners across the ceilings.

'Look at this bedroom,' says Lev. 'This place hasn't been used for years.'

'I just don't get it,' I say. 'Why keep an empty apartment in Tonya's old house? Does he think she might come back here to live?'

'He can afford to keep apartments wherever he wants.'

I go to the far end of the room and touch the bare, powdery spaces where the wallpaper is coming away. It was sloppily glued. But that's not what's bothering me. I touch it a bit more, rub my fingertips, and pull at the paper.

There's something underneath.

Writing.

I pull harder. More writing. More and more, in a tiny Cyrillic script that is nearly invisible, except that it's clear now the paper was meant to hide it.

'What are you doing?' asks Lev warily.

'There's dates here.' I start to peel another panel of paper off the wall. 'Someone used this room like a diary. Look. *15th January 1942. 18th January 1942.* Look! It's everywhere! It's all the way to the window. It's—'

Nineteen forty-two.

The Leningrad blockade. This is a siege diary. Someone lived here, in this room, during the Second World War, when Leningrad was surrounded by the German army and cut off from the world. When a third of the city's population starved to death.

I wonder where the writing ends – and when.

'I don't think my cursive abilities are up to this,' I say, lowering my voice. 'Can you read any of it?'

Lev begins to read, also quietly. It takes me a full minute to realise that I already know what it is that he's going to say next. This isn't a diary. Maybe the dates refer to when the writing took place, but the text itself has nothing to do with the blockade. This isn't an account of a devastating winter in wartime.

This is Alexey's memoir.

The Last Bolshevik.

Word for word.

Alexey spent the blockade in this house. He must have written his memoir of the White Sea Canal while it was going on. It almost makes sense. *The Last Bolshevik* has the look, the feel, of something composed with restraint, with self-censorship even. Lev was right when he said not everything could be included. That not everything could fit.

Literally.

'Raisa,' says Lev.

'Yes?'

'I think this is the handwriting in your mother's notebook of stories.' He sounds like he doesn't want to say it. 'And in the memoir.'

277

'What?' I'm still in a daze. 'That's not possible.'

'With the same spelling, grammar mistakes,' he says. 'Only here they're uncorrected.'

My mind spins. I'm used to my mind spinning, of course, when I'm working. Juggling all the little bits and pieces at once, non-stop, until I get where I want to be. Right now the spinning goes something like: Either Alexey Ivanov didn't write *The Last Bolshevik* – or else he wrote everything. *The Last Bolshevik*; Natalya's memoir; and Mum's notebook of stories. *For Lena, beloved daughter*, is what it says on the inside cover. I assumed Tonya, Lena's mother, was the one to write that dedication, but it could have been her father.

Lena's father was a Bolshevik, is what Akulina said to me.

Valentin Andreyev.

Alexey Ivanov used to be Valentin Andreyev.

Under different circumstances, I might be telling myself: I was right. I knew it. I *knew* it all along, and I still might not know what Alexey really wants, but I'm going to find out, and I'm going to get there first.

But staring at these walls – at 1942, appearing over and over again – I don't tell myself anything. I don't say anything else to Lev either. I let my brain stop whirring, calculating. I'm done.

Now I know there are ghosts in this house. They should be the ones speaking.

Bombastic music plays over loudspeakers as we step back onto the Red Arrow, and Lev gives me a rueful smile. But it doesn't bother me. There's something about the overnight

278

train between Leningrad and Moscow that makes me feel as if we are leaving Russia in 1991 and entering some other era, and I don't know what the way back would be.

I take one of the top bunks and close my eyes.

Around nine, the attendant brings by some tea. Unable to sleep, I shimmy down and peek out the window, brushing aside the red curtain tassels that give our compartment a whiff of grand decay. The northern sky is the colour of a seashell. We're leaving the land of the White Nights. No wonder I'm feeling carried away by the romance of it, by the idea that there's some poetry, some symmetry, behind all of this.

'Still up?' Lev swings his legs off his bunk.

I gesture to the window. 'The light is beautiful.'

'Yes, when you notice it.'

I let go of the curtain and sit down on his bunk.

'I feel . . . I feel different,' I say uncertainly. 'When I was in that room, with the writing, something happened. I can't explain.'

'You don't have to,' says Lev.

There's no sound except for the rhythmic creaking of the train. *Chug-uh-chug-uh-chug*.

We are sitting so close that I can see flecks of gold in his eyes. Before he can say anything else, I turn back to the window.

Richard. Think of Richard.

Richard didn't impress me when we first met, in Michaelmas term of my first year at Oxford. He seemed like every other stuck-up toff in the place, with an accent that could shear a sheep and that bloody scarf he *always* wore. And he was *always* talking, in hall, in the library, in the cafe where he first really looked my way.

It was only after a few reluctant dates – I used him, admittedly, for nice meals out at first; who wouldn't, with my own suppers consisting of canned beans? – that I understood it wasn't just that Richard liked the sound of his own voice. He'd been taught to fill silences. I'd been soaking in them for years.

It felt like we were made for each other.

But are we made? Or do we make ourselves?

The sky over Russia does not reply.

'Raisa,' says Lev, but I don't turn around.

This sojourn to my homeland was never about Eduard Dayneko.

It was about closing the chapter of my life that included my family, Papa and Mum and Zoya, for ever. I would finish it off and be able to embark on my proper English life, beginning with marrying Richard, a proper English bloke. I'd be proper English Rosie all the way through. But instead of putting the Russian part of myself to rest, instead of expelling it, I've become more aware of its presence.

I haven't buried anything by coming here. I've brought something back to life.

Chug-uh-chug-uh-chug.

The silence between me and Lev is stretching to its breaking point, as it often does. But this time, unlike all those other times, I don't feel stretched out along with it. I don't want to talk any more on this journey, just in case we are travelling back in time. Maybe I want to be carried away a bit more. Just a little longer.

A HOUSE ON A WIDE RIVER

In a faraway kingdom, in a long-ago land, a princess returned to visit the palace where she had lived as a young woman with her former husband, the prince. This palace of a hundred rooms had been built by the sea, and was slowly sinking into it, but this did not trouble the princess. She had once been her husband's prisoner, within its walls, and she wanted to see the palace humbled and brought low. She liked that her dead husband's books had all been burnt, all his belongings stolen, all his tapestries ripped from the walls. She liked that it belonged now to the common people. And when it happened, solely by chance, that one of the hundred rooms was empty at a time when she needed a place to live, she decided to move back into it. Her new husband understood, because he had been prisoner once too, but in a different place, by a different sea. He understood that you have only truly escaped when you can freely return.

And so the princess lived once more in the palace by the sea, but it was no longer a palace by the sea. Those days were over. It was only a house on a wide river.

CHAPTER TWENTY-TWO

Antonina

Leningrad St Petersburg, late 1941

TONYA IS IN HELL. A WHITE, FROZEN HELL THAT REEKS OF turpentine. Or purgatory, because they are suspended in time, waiting for the Nazis to march into Leningrad, or else to grow restless and leave. In the midst of all this waiting, there isn't much to occupy their minds, so Tonya has begun to tell the twins the longest story she has ever told, padded with unnecessary details, frivolous characters. She started telling it in November one night over dinner and she is not finished. Katya and Misha hang on her words. Valentin acts like he might be listening but Tonya knows he isn't.

Lena is the impatient one. *For goodness' sake*, Mama, she'll say. *Just tell us how it* ends, *would you?* And Tonya wants to reply: *That's why I can't tell you, Lenochka, because as soon as you know the end, you won't have anything to wait for.*

Whatever Valentin has heard in his head since he came home from the White Sea Canal eight years ago, he is hearing it louder and louder as this blockade goes on. Maybe it's because of the cold. It is a *malicious winter*, as Mama would say. The kind that comes around once every few decades. Or maybe it's that Leningrad has been severed from the rest of Russia.

Just like the camps.

'Drink something warm,' Tonya says, pushing a glass towards him, across the kitchen table. She strains the same leaves every morning and the tea is duller than water. But drinking tea is a remnant of life from before the war, and she won't give it up.

He smiles distantly at her. Doesn't move. Tonya wants to throw the glass in his face.

Throughout the autumn there were air-raid alerts day and night, German aeroplanes humming, anti-aircraft guns whirring, people shouting, ducking for cover. Lena would hurry the twins down to the basement where they could huddle against the walls with their hands on their ears, and Tonya would try to hurry too, but she'd always look back and Valentin would still be there, at the top of the stairs. He would look at her without any fear in his face.

Without anything in his face.

Granite.

Valentin raises the tea to his mouth at last. He likes to use the glass with the crack along its rim. As he drinks, there is a button of blood on his lips. He does not seem to notice.

The luckiest of their neighbours were evacuated out of the city in summer, just after war with Nazi Germany was declared. Others Tonya has not seen in weeks, except for

Mrs Kemenova, who lives upstairs and has grandchildren the same age as the twins. In Tonya's small apartment, the other residents are either missing or dead. The bedrooms are empty again, the furniture unused, the beds untouched, the curtains closed.

Just the way Dmitry liked to keep them.

Often Tonya will go into the apartments downstairs and peek into what used to be the Blue Salon, or the study where Anastasia lived and died, or Dmitry's libraries and galleries, now partitioned into single-family rooms. She knows exactly why she likes to wander. It feels as if it's hers now, this house on the Fontanka, when once it was the other way around.

'This was where you used to entertain?' says Lena, when they go down together one day. 'But why was it called the Blue Salon?'

'It had blue wallpaper.' Tonya runs her fingers along the wall. Now the wallpaper is yellow and floral and chintzy. Cheap and dry. 'See, Lenochka, parts of the original paper remain.'

Lena scrapes a bit off with a nail. 'It's like a secret room under there,' she says. 'A secret world.'

Lena has been living with them for the last four months, and she and Tonya have grown closer than ever before. There was a rupture in their relationship when Lena was young, after Sasha left Otrada. As the years went by Lena threw herself into school, friends, her dream of becoming a doctor. The rupture began to mend when they moved to Moscow to be with Valentin, a move that was good for Lena, that challenged her.

But their closeness now is like this yellow wallpaper. From a distance, it looks smooth. Natural. Like it was always there. But it hasn't been. And Tonya is aware of how fragile it is; who knows all the things they still fail to confide in one another?

'I like the blue colour better,' says Lena.

It was Lena who dropped in one Sunday afternoon in June with the message: *Kiev and Sevastopol have been bombed by the Germans!* A week later Lena went to work digging slit trenches at the city limits. Every day she telephoned to tell Tonya that they should have Katya and Misha evacuated to a summer estate in the country. Most other young children had gone, by order of the Leningrad soviet, including the occupants of the children's home where Tonya worked. *You're much too sentimental, Mama!*

One day Lena called with something new to say: *The circle has closed around Leningrad. They've cut off the last railway—*

The line was cut off too.

Not long afterwards, Lena fell down, in those deep, dirty trenches, and broke an arm. She was sent to hospital, and then home, but her former apartment had been shelled, so she came to live with Tonya and Valentin. She still keeps the arm tucked into her side, still wears her sling.

Maybe nothing can heal in purgatory.

'Let's go back up,' says Tonya, even though Lena is clearly in the grip of the blue wallpaper, entranced by that old sea-surface pattern. Tonya never liked the blue, never cared that it was bespoke-designed or hand-painted. But she does think it would be better for there not to be secret worlds where nobody can go. Where Valentin now lives.

* * *

285

The story Tonya is telling the twins has no end. She can't even remember the beginning any more. She simply must keep telling it.

'You should have become a writer for children's magazines, Mama,' says Lena, after the twins are asleep. 'Like *Murzilka*. Better yet, you should publish your own collection of stories! One of those beautiful ones with the illustrated covers. I love those. Really, your talent has been going to waste at the orphanage.'

Tonya glances at Valentin, who doesn't seem to have heard.

'I prefer telling to writing,' says Tonya, briskly.

'I suppose I prefer reading to hearing.' A laugh rises to Lena's lips, dies there. For a second her face looks dull, blue around the eyes. Tonya blinks, and the blueness is gone.

They must have spent too long the other day staring at the wallpaper.

'Would you tell another one?' asks Valentin softly.

'Another story?' Tonya says, with surprise.

'Please,' he says. 'One of your older ones. One I would know.'

Tonya wants to ask him why. They're only silly, short, baby's-breath folk tales. It's folly, lunacy in fact, to think that any of them could ever be published. They don't adhere to the communist worldview, in which royalty is evil and the peasants and workers always vanquish their enemies, and talking animals only say the right things. Tonya has never been more tired of saying the right things. Of pretending as if all this is normal.

'A princess lived in a palace by the sea,' she says, because that is the only one he would know, 'far from the city, far from the people . . .'

286

Valentin has never asked to hear a story before. As if the thing that is consuming him is what wants to listen to her, and not Valentin at all.

On her daily errands, Tonya sees trolleybuses standing frozen in their tracks. The streets are lined with the bodies of those who died where they stood, half buried in snow; other corpses are hauled around in sleds, swaddled in white sheets. Tonya always pulls her facecloth higher and resolves to keep moving. Look ahead. Only look ahead. But she can't do that at home.

They are running out of food.

When Tonya enters the kitchen, she finds Lena alone, napping in the corner by the tiny handmade stove. Kerosene. They have run out of kerosene. They'll have to burn paper and books. Next will be the furniture. The parquet floors. Eventually the whole house may be fed into that stove—

Lena is yawning. 'Had a bad dream,' she says. 'Do *you* still get nightmares, Mama?'

Yesterday Tonya had to add toothpaste to their broth, to give it heft. Today she's had nothing from the shops. The breadline closed just a few people ahead of her: *Come back Saturday*, the sign on the door said. Yes, there will be less people in the queue on Saturday, but only because more will have died—

'Mama?'

'Nightmares,' says Tonya. 'Yes. Sometimes. Sorry, Lenochka, I have to go upstairs. I've just remembered . . .'

Tonya goes up.

Mrs Kemenova does not have any kerosene to spare. Tonya asks if her young grandchildren have visited lately and Mrs Kemenova says yes. Mrs Kemenova enquires after the family and Tonya says that Katya sucks her thumb for hours on end and Misha keeps to his play-world of trains and tin soldiers and Valentin is becoming a stranger and Lena's calm company is the one thing she can depend on, only she isn't saying any of it. She's only crying.

Mrs Kemenova's expression sharpens and she leaves Tonya by the door and then comes back with a tin of milk powder and says it should go to the twins.

'But what about your grandchildren?' asks Tonya unwillingly.

'I was being polite,' says Mrs Kemenova. Her tone sounds a bit like Valentin's, Tonya is only noticing now. 'They are dead.'

Tonya does have nightmares, those same dreams of Otrada, but she no longer thinks of them as nightmares because she is no longer scared. She knows that the girl with the ivy writhing below the skin does not mean her harm. The girl *helped* her. Saved the twins on the night they were born, by waking Tonya up.

Tonya wants to help the girl, too.

She must get into the house.

In the dreams, Tonya walks through the orchards as usual. Sometimes Sery follows and sometimes she even picks him up. He is light, limber. Not as he was in life. And there at the veranda they encounter Mama, but Mama never budges.

It is only recently that Tonya has begun to notice the *smell*.

She has never smelt anything in dreams before. It is trembly and sweet, like the air before a summer storm. Like burnt sugar. Like the volcanic black smoke that filled the sky on the September night that the Badayev warehouses, containing the majority of Leningrad's food stores, were hit by the Germans.

Tonya thinks the smell is coming from *inside* the house. But she cannot go any further. Not without getting through Mama.

That, she knows, is what Mama wants.

For Tonya to come closer.

Valentin stands by the bedroom window, a hand on the curtains, looking into the darkness. Tonya sits down on their bed, presses on the lumps in the pillow. They don't sleep in this room any more, because of the cold; they all sleep in the kitchen. Valentin is the only one who still spends time in here.

'You're so quiet, nowadays,' she says, struggling to sound carefree. 'Do you have no more views on the war?'

Before the shelling started, Valentin was full of opinions, and he would often try to engage Tonya in political debate – and fail. To Tonya's inexpert mind, Soviet Communism and National Socialism might as well be the same. All she knows is that whether it is aristocrats and peasants, politicians and citizens, or German bombers and Russian civilians, those above do not care for those below. Those below are always on their own.

If only he would try again.

'My hand hurts,' is what he says.

Valentin is missing the barest tips of two fingers on his right hand, too bare for most people to see. A terrible thought springs up, so fast Tonya can't help it, like a knee coming out of a socket: maybe Valentin *should* have died on the White Sea Canal, rather than have to live the rest of his life without everything he lost there.

'Lena's putting the twins to sleep,' she says, more urgently. 'We have time to talk.'

'You're not tired, *milaya*?'

'Of course I am.'

He turns away from the window. His eyes are bright. 'Then go to bed.'

'I'd rather talk to you.'

'About what?'

'About you!' She is losing the struggle. 'It's the Canal, isn't it? I know you have been thinking about the Canal, about whatever happened there. Please, you must tell me about it. You must let me in!'

'You don't want to be where I am,' he says.

Tonya refuses to lose him like this. Too much is already lost. She didn't wait for him all the years he was in exile only to surrender him now to the *thing* that wants him, the thing that shines in his eyes. 'My mother used to say that a memory is a foreign object in a body,' she says. 'You think it's part of you. Inherent to you. But as soon as you remove it, you see it for what it is. That's why Mama wrote in diaries all her life. If you get it out of you, it can't destroy you from within! But you must pull it out!'

'I want to,' he says. 'But I think sometimes that that's

290

all there is left of me, the memories. There's no more Valentin Andreyev. One day I'll wake up and I won't remember anything at all, you or the children or any of this—'

'If you're not strong enough to do it for your own sake,' Tonya interrupts, seizing on an idea, 'then you must do it for the people.'

'The people?' He says it like she is speaking a foreign language.

'No one has ever written an account of the White Sea Canal.' Tonya no longer cares how desperate she sounds. 'Maxim Gorky visited the camps at Solovetsky – and maybe the report he published of it was nonsense – but no one has ever written about the Canal. And now the Canal is finished! Nobody will ever work there again. If you don't speak up, the people will never know how it was. Never.'

'I don't know,' he says brokenly. 'Maybe.'

She will reach him. Somehow she will reach him.

'You don't have to decide tonight.' Relief tips over her body, tingles in her fingers. 'Just think about it.' She's shaking. She stands, heads for the doorway.

'Wait.'

She turns.

'When we were young, you spoke so often of your mother,' he says. 'Not much any more.' Valentin laughs, a lonely sound. 'We've both changed, haven't we?'

Tonya's toes curl in her stockings. All of a sudden she can picture Mama sitting at that vanity table, full of her strange wisdom. That waterfall of shimmery hair, those

291

black eyes, that painted mouth. Mama was breathtaking, the splendour of Mama was dazzling, but as the years go by, as Tonya looks back, she has begun to feel like it masked other things. So many other things.

One morning just after the New Year, which they did not celebrate with fir trees and presents as they usually do, there is something splayed at the top of the staircase, just past the corridor. When Tonya sees what it is, she has to look away. A neighbourhood cat, one of those short-haired breeds, a lanky, self-sufficient animal. Nothing like Sery, who was fat, fluffy, spoilt. Who died in his favourite spot by the veranda.

Tonya gathers the pitiful creature up in her arms. It's meat, only meat, and she would skin every animal in the city by now, to get her family through this winter.

In the kitchen, Lena is alone and awake, wrapped in blankets by the stove. 'A dead cat,' she observes. 'You don't mean that you're going to make us eat that?'

'Won't you help me prepare?'

'My arm's bothering me.'

Tonya turns to look at her daughter. 'Again?'

'Not too much.' Lena's face is contorted into an odd smile. 'I'm just comfortable where I am, that's all.'

There is an order of decline in families, people say. Babies die first, then the elderly, then the men, then the women.

So why is Tonya so afraid?

'I heard you vomiting last night.' Tonya rolls up her sleeves. She plunges her hands into the cleaning bucket, begins to rub them raw. She didn't hear; she saw. Lena retching, writhing, only for a teardrop of water to come up. As if she'd been vomiting all day. Lena did not even seem distressed, only climbed back beneath her blankets.

That despicable heap of blankets. They're making Lena look bigger than she is.

'Didn't you have a cat growing up?' says Lena. 'What was his name?'

'Sery.' Tonya wipes her knife on a dishcloth. The cat's eyes protrude from its face. She begins to slit the skin along the underside, moving up, and that is when she finds stitches, bristling against her thumb.

This cat was cut open once before. It has been resewn.

'What is it, Mama?' Lena asks. 'What are you looking at?'

Is she losing her senses?

No, there is something tucked into the cat's intestines. It is slimy, soaked. Tonya pulls it out and now everything may come up and out of her too.

It is a small porcelain doll.

She'd let Sasha convince her that the first doll, seventeen years ago now, was only the nasty trick of an angry villager. But no angry villager has left this one. With macabre curiosity she turns it over, but she already knows what it will look like. The colour of the eyes. The shine to the skin. The doll is smiling one of those weird, wide doll-smiles. It looks a bit like Lena's.

The cat meat does not last long.

A few nights later Tonya awakens and goes downstairs to the Blue Salon. She carries with her a cobalt-blue caviar

293

dish, a piece of a set left behind by neighbours. The night air simmers with promise. She starts by the window, without pausing to think. The wallpaper glue comes off in scraps, collects slowly in the dish. She moves from one strip to the next, and when she has gathered all the glue she can, she peels the paper from the walls. It comes off like clothing. As she goes, her pace quickens.

She has revealed the Blue Salon, but the telltale silver-blue wallpaper is no longer proud. It no longer sprays light like a prism. It is tired, missing in places. Torn in others. Just like everybody else. It does, in the end, look a bit like the sea, a bit like where the Baltic bleeds into the Neva Bay, where the gulf is full of rocky islands that hug the coastline, and around those islands are schools of fish and herds of grey seal.

Now she finally sees it.

Now she will destroy it.

Another layer of paper means another layer of glue. Tonya sits in the dark, scratching, pulling, until her fingernails begin to split. She will cook the glue in broth. She will burn the paper for fuel. She will do this in every room of the house; if only there were some use for bare walls.

But perhaps there is.

'I was transferred out of Solovetsky in autumn 1931,' says Valentin, in a monotone. 'My prisoner transport arrived in September at Soroka, a village on the southern edge of the White Sea, on the mainland. From here, they told us, the Canal would connect all the way to Lake Onega. Soroka is now called Belomorsk – but, first, I should explain. The White Sea is an inlet high in the north. It stems from the Barents Sea, even further north . . .'

Solovetsky, Soroka, Onega, Belomorsk, Barents.

The north is only a curtain of white to most people. They will already feel lost amongst these places.

'Should I continue?' he asks.

Tonya breathes into her hands. She's brought along a dozen ballpoints and a handful of fountain pens, courtesy of all the other apartments in the house. But their bedroom is so chilly everything is covered in a web of frost. It will take downward force to prompt the pens to roll ink onto any surface. There also seems to be glaringly little space for error. Once they write on these walls, they will be written on for ever. You can hardly get ballpoint ink off anything.

'I should be the one to write,' she says.

'Why?'

'You're thinking about the reader, Valentin. You must forget that there will be readers. You must think only about the story, to be able to close your eyes and go back there. If you don't go back – you can't leave. So I will be the one to write.'

'You don't have to do that.'

'I would like to,' Tonya says, ignoring a pinch of anxiety. She's done very little writing in her life. A few letters, a few lessons for the orphans. Nothing like this.

'Whatever you prefer,' he says.

Once upon a time, Valentin could make people believe in anything. Once upon a time, they were *both* storytellers. Her stories began far away and long ago; his began here

295

and now. Her stories had already happened, and his had yet to happen. She had nightmares of the past, and he had dreams of the future. He wanted to reach everyone in the world, while she was desperate to reach herself.

All the times when she looked at him, back then, and saw such hope, such light, it was because he was like a mirror, showing her everything that existed *within her*.

The walls of their bedroom appear naked, stripped of wallpaper. The layer beneath is bone-bleached, faded out. Much like Valentin. Tonya's hope all these years has been futile. He is never going to be the person he used to be. He will remain like this for ever, and every month, every year, he will become a little bit *more* like this, stoic and stilted, until the day she screams his name and there is nobody to hear.

But even on that day, she will still be here.

Tonya grips the pen hard.

'Close your eyes,' she says. 'Tell me what you remember.'

Valentin sits at the table with Katya on his lap. Katya is sucking on her thumb. *Tsh. Tsh. Tsh.* Misha plays alone in the corner. Lena lies on the ground by the stove. Her skin has gone dark red, the colour of currants. She keeps her hands locked over her chest.

I'm going to be a doctor, Mama. I'm going to save people!

Lena's few, feathery eyelashes settle like she's falling asleep. Tonya drops to her knees beside her daughter, takes Lena's hand.

It is hot as fire.

Just save yourself, Lena. Save yourself, save yourself, save yourself first.

But Lena has always been more like Valentin.

'Something's not right,' says Tonya, lifting her face. But there's no way to take Lena to any hospital. There are no more hospitals, at least none that she knows of, that weren't laid to waste by the Germans and that have enough staff to function. And it is the middle of the night. They would die of exposure, traipsing through the snow for hours, towards the hospital that does not exist. There are no trams, no cars, nothing.

It doesn't matter. Tonya and Valentin will carry her. Lena is leaf-light, since they are all starving. Tonya will find something, somebody who knows what to do. She will ask Mrs Kemenova to look after the twins. They'll—they'll—

'Mama.'

'Lena,' she says, 'we have to get you somewhere where—'

'My arm.'

'You've come down with something. We'll find help.'

'My arm,' Lena says again.

'Show me your arm.' Tonya yanks the blankets away, harder than she ever pulled any wallpaper, one after another. Beneath all those blankets is Lena, trapped in still more layers, coats, sweaters, nightshirts, and Tonya unbuttons and grabs and forces while Lena shivers, shivers even though she is piping hot, until they have reached a layer that Tonya can rip open and there it is, a lump that was once an elbow, wrapped poorly in dressings.

'I'm sorry, Mama,' Lena sobs, or maybe Tonya is sobbing, it's hard to tell, the tears falling like the bombs that once rained down on Leningrad, the explosions rocking the streets and the fires combing through the buildings. Tonya

297

was caught in it once, had to stop beneath an archway by the canals. The water was as black as pitch. The sky above was red, streaky, splattered with searchlights.

That is what Lena's arm looks like.

With tangible dread Tonya begins to undo the dressings. The smell is worse than the sight. Tonya knows, even as she is unwrapping, round and round, that there is something dead below. Her heart ceases to beat in rhythm. Her pulse is in her mouth. Her lungs contract with the breaths she cannot take. The final piece of dressing is adhered to Lena's skin, and when Tonya tries to ease it off, the skin breaks too, stringy and slippery.

The elbow is black. Slick as scales in some places, horsehide-rough in others. But black.

'Why did you not tell us?' asks Tonya, almost a shriek. 'Tell me what to do, Lena, tell me what to do!'

But Lena's eyes are closing again. Tonya shakes her by the shoulders. Shakes harder. *Wake up*, she screams, *wake up, I'll tell you the end of the story just like you wanted, only wake up*, and this is all Valentin's fault that Lena is like this, Valentin who only thinks of the *people*, because she can hear Lena's voice as if Lena has woken up, as if Lena is talking, saying, *It's nothing, Mama, I just didn't want to worry you, you should focus on the twins, it's other people that need you, not me—*

But she sees Valentin staring at her, and then he cracks too, like his favourite glass. He is wracked with silent weeping, sitting there with Katya still on his lap, Katya's mouth still clamped around the thumb. *Tsh. Tsh. Tsh.* It is the only sound.

'Lena,' Tonya begs her. 'Please, Lenochka, please don't leave me! Lena!'

Tsh. Tsh. Tsh.

'Lena!'

Lena's expression is knowing. Secretive. There is a hidden, hollow place inside everyone, and that is where they go right before they die. You cannot see it from the outside. But you can hear the echo. The time-lapse. Tonya has witnessed it a few times. At Mama's death. At Little Fedya's. By the time the echo reaches your ears, its source is already gone.

Lena is gone.

It is the longest February of Tonya's life.

There are a few hours of weak sunlight every morning, before the dark arms of winter close over Leningrad. There is nothing left to burn. There is no food in the larder. Tonya forces Katya and Misha to eat the old tea leaves, the ones from which she has brewed the last sliver of life. She eats one herself and it tastes like tar. She boils down her old shoes, the straps of her purse. Her remaining strength boils down with them. Misha no longer looks at his trains. Katya only works on her thumb.

Lena's body is kept in a different room. It may never break down.

The cold air of a *malicious winter* can preserve anything.

With Lena gone, Tonya writes on the walls more than ever. It keeps her hands busy, keeps her from fading. Valentin tries to stop her sometimes, says they've done enough for the day, touches her shoulder. She feels his fingers by her

299

clavicle. She is a sailor lost at sea, bones showing where she'd not known people to have bones.

'I believe that one day people will find this,' she says with difficulty. 'Will read it. But we won't be there to see it.'

He brings her into an embrace that feels new, it has been so long.

'There's something else,' he says.

Tonya licks her lips, chafed, bleeding. It no longer matters. Perhaps he stole food. Perhaps he cheated someone, shirked his work, or failed to help a fellow prisoner. Whatever it is, he has been reliving it, over and over again, so that he cannot see her, cannot see anything around him.

It undermined the person he thought he was; and so now he is no one.

'People should know the truth about the things I did, on the Canal,' he says, suddenly fierce, and for a second he sounds like the old Valentin. 'This story should be about that, too—'

'No,' she says, 'it's over, it's finished now,' and he buries his face in her hair and he speaks into it, says something that sounds like *Antonina*, the way he did when they were young. She is astounded, because she has long believed that the Valentin who liked to do that, to say her full name, never came home. That he was still out there on the Canal, in the water, looking out to the endless horizon as he always had.

How does a smell get in a place? Through the doors, like a person? Through the gaps in the sills? Through the windows, like light, like sound? Is it only a parasite, entering on the

300

back of something else, holding tight to a man's jacket, to a child's fingernails? Where do smells even come from, in the beginning?

The smell in her dreams *is* the beginning.

The beginning of the very first nightmare of Tonya's life—

Tonya blinks fast. Her brain hungers, strains for a point of reference. She looks around the kitchen, wallows in the silence. Nobody else has stirred. She shifts aside the blankets and gasps at the cold. It comes down like a set of jaws.

Has she dreamt of Otrada again?

Without knowing why, she goes out of the kitchen, down the hall, until she reaches the bedroom that used to belong to the Sitnikov family, where Lena's body is being stored. She uses a final shudder of strength to push open the door. The walls, the floors, are sticky with ice. Most of the furniture is gone, burnt to embers.

The body on the bed, under a sheet, looks like a stowaway on a ship.

The body is not her daughter. In fact, it is as far from Lena as anything on earth can be. It is the *reverse*. Tonya pulls on the frozen sheet. It cracks as it comes away. Her thoughts crack along with it, become jumbled.

She'll need the sharpest knife she can find to cut into the corpse.

She'll never be able to use the knife again afterwards. She'll never be able to tell anyone. But there's hardly anybody left to tell, anyway, and it's only the murder of people for food that is considered a crime.

Lena's body is in decent condition. As soon as Lena died, her elbow stopped dying.

Go on, Mama, Lena would say. *I would do it, in your place. For Katya and Misha.*

Go on.

You're too sentimental, Mama!

Tonya replaces the sheet and backs out of the room. Her legs buckle beneath her as she shuts the door hard. Only when she reaches the kitchen does she collapse against the stove, wracked with self-loathing. What good would it do, anyway? All that remains of Lena is skin on bone. It's not enough to keep the twins alive.

If they go another week, another two weeks, without food, the twins will die, and this winter will have taken all of her children.

Tonya slides down to the floor. The twins and Valentin are as skinny, as scrawny, as Lena was. Tonya, on the other hand, is thicker, rounder, than ever before. It is a funny thing that happens to some people before they die of dystrophy, according to the grim chatter in the breadlines: *Most* of us grow skinnier and skinnier, until our heads begin to bobble on the sticks of our bodies, but *some* of us blow up like balloons!

Tonya pinches her own thigh, through her stockings, and holds it. Waits for it to hurt. It doesn't. She moves her fingers along, down to her calves. Pinches more. It's not much, but there's something between her fingers.

Mama used to say that this body, this physical body, is only the costume of the soul. When you die, you slip it off. Tonya never quite believed it, because first of all Mama loved nice costumes, and second of all Mama was the vainest person in the village.

You see, Mama would say, *if you ever must sacrifice yourself for someone you love, it is no sacrifice.*

This, Tonya can do.

She will gouge out her own flesh and feed it to her children.

She must start right away, for it will be slow-going. The first cuts will be into her calves, her upper arms, maybe her buttocks. Wherever she can comfortably reach, so long as she can tend the areas quickly and hide them beneath her clothes. Much of the skin on her arms and legs is already disfigured by the marks she was born with; a few more will hardly make a difference.

Tonya's hands are steady as she stands.

Back in the Sitnikovs' bedroom, near Lena's body, she lays out a few rags. She does not go near Lena. She ties a piece of cloth as a tourniquet around her own thigh and bites into the end to avoid making any sound, but she might have used up all her screams on the nightmares, over the years, because she doesn't need it. The knife goes in soft, easy. The run of blood is slowed by the cold. She digs a small hole, carves it out. It looks like a spider bite, stings like one. Nothing more.

De profundis clamavi ad te, Domine.

In the kitchen, everyone is still asleep. The clock ticks, torments. Tonya waits on a pot of water, waits, stares, moves the pot around.

It is when she is stirring, cooking her own meat, bringing it to a boil, that she finally recognises the smell.

CHAPTER TWENTY-THREE

Valentin

Leningrad, St Petersburg, summer 1945

THE WAR IS OVER. PITER IS IN RECOVERY. THE BUILDINGS blasted out by shells are being rebuilt. Flowers bloom and bells chime. The evening is lush as Valentin and Tonya walk through the Summer Garden with the twins, picturesque enough that he feels there *must* be young lovers and old friends just around the corner, eating ice cream, laughing hard. There *must* be many more children than Katya and Misha, running and playing leapfrog by Krylov's statue as their parents smoke and read the papers. There *must* be plenty of people beyond the wrought-iron gates of the garden, headed to museums and cafes and university lectures.

There will be. Not quite yet.

'Do you know,' Tonya asks, 'that I no longer dream of Otrada?'

'No?'

'The girl is gone,' she says.

'The girl with the ivy?' he says cautiously. 'The one who would cry to you for help?'

'I can't summon her back.'

'Why do you think that is?'

'She's gone wherever dreams go, I suppose, when the dreamer is . . .' Tonya laughs. Valentin finds it a pretty but jarring sound, like wind chimes. She glances at the twins, who are tumbling over one another, yelping with glee, and then at Valentin. 'Ready to stop dreaming. To live.'

To live.

Valentin thinks of the writing on the walls. There is a beauty in the starkness of the story, the way Tonya has written it: *They die in the aid of no cause, at the altar of nothing and nobody. They slip beneath the water, and they find no reason to come up for air.* It makes him wonder if there was beauty in the starkness there, too. Of the sea.

One day they'll pick it up again, write a new version on paper.

'I have no more desire to look backwards,' says Tonya. 'Though I miss Lena, will always miss Lena, we have buried her. We've survived this war, and I'm ready to be happy, entirely happy, with you, with Katya and Misha, to live *our lifetime.*'

Or maybe it'll never be published.

He doesn't care.

He doesn't care about any cause.

He does not care about anything larger, anything further, than what is right in front of him. This one moment, with her.

'Yes,' he says, in awe. 'Let's have our lifetime.'

* * *

305

One day, when he returns to the house with Katya, they find something awaiting them on the doorstep. Katya gives a cry of delight, falls hard upon it: a doll, the painted, porcelain kind. A patch of hair on the back of the head is inexplicably shaved clean.

Valentin recalls that the doll found in the dead cat disturbed Tonya more than she would say.

I'm ready to be happy, entirely happy . . .

'Tell Mama I got that for you at the Passazh,' he says, and Katya nods solemnly. *Yes, Papa.* She hugs the doll tighter to her, and he has a brief, scalding flash of doubt. Like he has just made an irrevocable mistake.

CHAPTER TWENTY-FOUR

Rosie

Moscow, August 1991

THE RADIO GIVES OFF A GRATING HUM, AND THE announcer on Ekho Moskvy speaks too fast for me to keep up: *Emergency Committee . . . to save the Great Motherland . . . mortal danger . . .*

'It's a coup,' says Alexey. 'A coup by the old party elite, to oust Mikhail Gorbachev.'

I glance at Lev, who only draws on his cigarette.

'They're saying that Gorbachev has taken ill in the Crimea,' Alexey continues. 'And that Yanaev, the Vice President, will act in his stead.'

'What's this about an Emergency Committee?' I ask.

'It's made up of Gorbachev's political enemies. As I said, it's a coup.' He sighs. 'I have to make some calls. They might switch off the phone lines.'

Alexey utters this so casually that I don't startle until he's left the kitchen.

Switch off the phone lines?

The radio plays a quick jingle, and then stops. I fiddle with the dials. Only two stations broadcast in Moscow. It's not hard to jam everything.

Again, Lev only takes a drag. A deliberately long one, I would say.

'Will your family support this coup?' I ask.

'My father's involved.'

'You know that?'

'He and his friends have never come around to perestroika and glasnost. It's all been brewing for a while.'

But is this all it takes to undo those reforms? A reported case of the sniffles in the Crimea, and a bunch of Party and military officials can just steamroller their way to victory?

Lev still isn't meeting my gaze.

If he were in the OMON now, he would be working for the same people who might switch off Alexey Ivanov's phone lines.

Alexey strides back in from the foyer, exclaiming that Boris Yeltsin will not allow this to happen. The President has asked all concerned citizens to gather at Manezh Square, and calls for popular resistance—

Brrrring. Brrrring.

Alexey disappears again to answer the phone.

'I'm not my family, Raisa.' Lev stabs out his cigarette.

'I know that.'

'Do you?'

'It's for you, Rosie,' says Alexey, reappearing. 'Marina Petrovna?'

'I know her,' I say quickly. 'Thank you.'

On the phone, Marina immediately speaks in English. I get the feeling that there's someone listening in on her end. And there's always someone listening in on *my* end, isn't there?

Though Zoya's been quiet lately.

If I didn't know better, I'd worry something had happened to her.

'My husband and I discussed it over the weekend,' Marina says. 'Mikhail would like to know more about this man you suspect to be his father—'

'Meet me at Manezh Square,' I say. 'I'm on my way there now.'

By the time we get to Manezh Square, there's plenty of people already milling around, most of them looking bewildered. Some cheeky chap with a loudspeaker is helpfully informing everyone that it was all a ruse; that Yeltsin never intended or planned to have anyone meet up here. *Go home, my friends, go home!* I, for one, am tempted to take him up on this advice. The sky has split open overhead, and it's starting to rain. Just the right amount to dampen enthusiasm for a protest movement that doesn't look promising.

'Hurry up, Rosie,' Alexey yells at me, from somewhere in the growing mass of people. 'We have to lie down to stop the tanks! Let's go!'

Stop the *tanks*?

I can't see Lev anywhere. People press in on all sides, and the rain falls harder.

'We can't stop *tanks*! We can't just lie down!' I protest.

'Exactly,' he says, 'we can't.'

It's the last I hear from Alexey before he too slips into some crevice in the crowd. An awful sound begins to blare from across the square; it's the tanks that he knew would come, because he's endured a lifetime of this. Alexey is used to the people and the rain and the loudspeakers and the way the ground seems to ripple beneath our feet, like an earthquake, because nothing is certain any more. There is no foundation to this world. I might wake up tomorrow in a different one.

People begin to shout as the tanks burrow deeper into the square. Their noise is like thunder. *Please don't shoot! Don't shoot us!*

I can't imagine what possessed me to tell Marina to meet me here – they'll never find me – but I wish she would. I want to see a familiar face, because I've never been more surrounded and yet I've never felt so alone.

This.

This is why I'm with Richard.

This is why I want to be Rosie and not Raisa. Because *this* is what being Raisa feels like: small, confused, exhausted. Raisa always chooses the worst possible moment to be anywhere. The worst moment to open the door to the living room, to find her family dead, to *see*. But that's the thing, because she doesn't really. She doesn't understand any of it. She doesn't know who *that man* is; she doesn't know why Zoya and Papa are lying without moving like that; all she does know – and she just *knows* – is that she is alone.

Completely alone.

Why did you leave it?

I left it for you. You're my daughter . . .

A woman grabs my arm. 'OMON!' she exclaims. 'Over here!'

'I'm sorry,' I say in English, pulling away from her. 'I have to—I have to go.'

'Oh, excuse,' she says in dismay. 'Yes. Not yours.'

She means that it's not my problem, what's happening, and she's right. I have a British passport. I could squeeze all the way back across Manezh Square, because by now they've cordoned off the parts that are usually only for vehicles, and I could be back at Alexey's apartment in minutes. I could pack my things and hail a taxi and grab one of the last flights out before they shut down air travel and lock down the country, if that's where all this is headed, and why should I care if it is? So what if things go back to the way they were, if Gorbachev is pushed out and Yeltsin is defeated and all the reforms are peeled back? They can keep the whole country under martial law for ever if they want!

What's it to me? Why should I care?

Why can't I leave Russia right now? Why does it matter who Eduard Dayneko really is, or what he really did? What does it matter what Alexey really wants? Or who I really am? What more, what deeper, truth do I need?

Whatever we are looking for will not be there, was what Alexey said.

I don't even know what I'm looking for any more.

Maybe I never have.

OMON buses and tanks have already stopped in the square, but the surrounding protestors don't look angry or

311

scared. In fact, they're handing out food and sweets to the troops, who are just standing by, accepting these goody bags.

No shots are being fired.

The OMON have come over to the side of the people.

Lev is suddenly there, right in front of me, taking me by the hand. I can't hear a thing above the tanks and the crowds and the pounding in my ears. He seems to be glancing back, wondering why I'm taking so long to follow, why I'm resisting.

I'm no longer resisting.

Lev turns around and begins to say something, but he doesn't finish. He must see it on me. Something flashes in his eyes and then he's got my face cupped in his hands and I'm on my tiptoes and we're kissing, hard, with force. Without any hesitation. The wait has been too long. People push by, shoving and shouting, but somehow I hear him, feel him, speak. *That afternoon we were looking at the maps, when I looked up and I saw your face*, he says, against my mouth. *Vdrug mne pokazalos', chto ya prosypayus' posle samoy dolgoy nochi . . .*

It seemed to me that I was waking up from the longest night . . .

The tumult around us continues. We do not stop. It is almost painful, but we do not stop. I am bruised with it, nearly bleeding, the rain keeps coming, flooding, but I never want to stop.

The more time I spend in Russia, the closer I get to the truth, the more I know, the less I understand.

All I can do is bask in it, bathe in it, drown in it.

* * *

312

Something is bubbling on a stove. Coffee. I rub my eyes and prop myself up. *I'm in the cot.* Various items of clothing are strewn over the floor: my sundress, looking shoddy from yesterday's rain; my ballet pumps, layered in mud; my bra and pants, in a shy, shameful heap by the far corner.

'It's eleven.' Lev is in the doorway.

'You should have woken me. I should have moved to my own . . .' I say, weakly. 'Did Alexey . . . ?'

'Alexey never came home,' he says. 'He called and said he'll be speaking at the White House rally today at noon. He's asked you to attend.'

I got a full night's sleep.

I'd forgotten what that feels like.

'I'd—OK.' I'm still in a stupor.

'We'll pick up Marina and Mikhail on our way there. They called too.' Lev looks back in the direction of the kitchen, listening for the coffee. 'They want to make sure to catch you this time.'

I have to telephone Richard.

Richard with his soft, unruly hair and slightly hooked nose; Richard who walks with just a touch of a slouch, a shuffle almost. He looks, in any context, against any background, *comfortable*. And even when he isn't, nobody notices. Whereas anyone would notice Lev, and probably wish they hadn't. Even now there's no hint of anything that happened between us in his expression. If not for the branding-iron memory of it in my brain, I might think I had imagined the way we came in yesterday, saying nothing at all, like words would only ruin things;

the way Lev tossed his keys on the coffee table and lifted me by the waist, against the wall, like I weighed the same as the keys; the way my hands slipped beneath his shirt, feeling many more scars than I ever knew he had, in rivers all along his side and up and down his back, his years in the Russian military written all over him.

The way he never took his eyes off me, like he thought I might disappear into thin air if he did.

'Could you pick Marina and her husband up first and pop back round to get me?' I ask. 'I have to take a shower, and . . . change.'

'If you like.'

I wait until he's out the door, and then I pull off one of the many quilts that congregate around Alexey's sofa and throw it over my shoulders. I try out the floor; the rug is cold beneath my feet. The apartment seems chilly for high summer.

But it isn't Zoya.

Where has she *been*?

I wish that she *were* here. I could use an older sister right now, because although Zoya never seemed to care about much, she cared about boys. There was always some shaggy-haired would-be suitor sniffing around, making her giggle behind the closed door of our shared bedroom, while I would sit in the living room doing my schoolwork, hating the both of them: *I wish you would just go away, Zoya. Run away and never come back.*

'Are you there?' I ask aloud, but she isn't.

On the telephone, the operator puts me through to London, to one particular street in South Kensington where Richard's father, James, lives in his whitewashed five-storey townhouse, all on his lonesome. Richard's father hasn't had human contact with anyone except work colleagues and immediate family since the day his wife died. Both Richard and Charlotte have stopped trying.

Everyone has a story, one way or another.

James picks up. 'Hello, darling,' he says. 'Richie! Rosemary on the line.'

'Hi,' says Richard, coming on. He already sounds unhappy. 'Honestly, Ro, we're seeing what's going on over there, and I think you should come home. What are you still doing?'

'I . . .'

'Are you hurt? Is something wrong?'

'I'm fine.' I pull the blanket tighter around me.

Where will I go, when I get back to England? My flight leaves in two weeks. Term doesn't start until the end of September. I haven't made close enough friends in my life to be able to ring someone up and ask to stay on their sofa.

Could I really go back to Mum's apartment?

'Then what is it?' Richard asks. 'Are you coming home?'

'Not sooner than planned.' I can't believe I'm doing this. I'm cutting off the only real lifeline I have. The only person left who loves me.

But I need something else.

I need *me*.

I need to be alone.

* * *

I pull the door shut behind me and pop on my sunglasses. Today the sun is out, and the sky is a bright, liquid blue. No sign of yesterday's clouds. Lev is around front, standing by the driver's door of the Mercedes. Mikhail and Marina are in the back seat.

The effort to build barricades in the city centre has left the surrounding thoroughfares looking like a lawn dug up by dogs. We park quite far off and pick our way through the streets on foot. The flotsam and jetsam of mass protest is everywhere: abandoned umbrellas, boxes, discarded clothing, pieces of wire mesh, even fragments of concrete. The closer we get to the White House, the seat of the Russian parliament and the symbol of a burgeoning democracy, the more the mood of anticipation is heightened.

Today the people know what they want. Today they're going to get it.

Mikhail is sporting thick bifocals, and each time I look at him and Marina, I see him look back at me, his dark eyebrows wrangled together right above the rim, like the two of us just don't know what to make of one another.

We have reached the White House, where an enormous rally is taking place. Different speakers are appearing on the balcony, taking turns decrying the Emergency Committee. All around us, people are climbing onto abandoned tanks for a better view; tricolour flags are flying. Every few minutes, a chant rises from the crowd: *Russia is alive! Yeltsin, we support you!*

'Is he in good health, the man you think is my father?' asks Mikhail, addressing me at last.

'I'd call him sprightly. That's him!' I point to the balcony. 'He's there!'

Alexey Ivanov has appeared at the rail. He's holding a megaphone, though part of me doubts he even needs it. This attempted coup has aged him backwards, if anything. He looks younger now, beneath unforgiving sunshine, than he did in that cafe in Oxford.

'Is it him?' Marina asks her husband. 'Can you tell?'

We are all staring at the white-haired figure. A pall of silence settles over the crowd as he begins to speak.

Alexey's voice is so intense, so rich, that it feels almost like he's never stopped speaking, not since the last time he took the stage here in his homeland. He was a Bolshevik then; he is the last Bolshevik now. He's here to fight for his final cause. He's come all the way around, through a century of bloodshed and violence and dashed dreams, to arrive at this spot, to speak to these people.

He raises his hand and closes it into a fist and the crowd cheers. The skin on the back of my neck prickles. He lifts his arms upwards, towards the sky, as if he derives his conviction from the heavens themselves. I can feel myself being lifted up too, higher, lighter, than I've ever been.

'We will have our freedom!' Alexey shouts. 'We will never go back!'

The wind blows hard.

Go north, Raisa. To Vorkuta.

Zoya's voice.

You asked which way to go, she says. *Now go.*

She's never spoken to me like this, in complete sentences.

317

I whip my head around, as if she might be there, but there's only strangers behind me.

To Vorkuta, she says again, and then she's gone.

'No, wait!' I cry out. 'Zoya!'

Lev gives me a sharp look.

'My sister,' I babble. 'She was—she was—she said—'

'It's not him,' says Mikhail.

We all turn to him. His eyebrows have fallen back into place. He shakes his head.

'I don't know who that man up there is,' says Mikhail, 'but that's not my father. That's not Valentin Andreyev.'

PART FOUR

CHAPTER TWENTY-FIVE

Katya

Leningrad, St Petersburg, autumn 1948

KATYA IS TEN YEARS OLD, BUT SHE ALREADY KNOWS what she's going to be when she grows up: a ballerina. She tells this to anyone who will listen. Mama says that people are always listening, that she should be quiet sometimes, but Katya doesn't like staying quiet. And there *is* that story that Mama tells, about the handsome heir to the throne of the old Russian empire, the Tsarevich, who grows bored by the empty-headed ladies of the court and is drawn to the peasant girl who has slipped into the palace by chance, because she stands out from the rest.

Katya wants to be the one who stands out from the rest. She hopes her own Tsarevich is watching.

Katya has an older sister who died. It happened during the war. Mama and Papa have never explained how, so Katya thinks maybe Lena charged head first into enemy lines. Misha says that Lena probably died because she tripped on the street and hit her head on a rock. It makes

Katya want to hit him on *his* head. They fight a lot. Mama always says to *stop squabbling, kids*, which is unfair, because Katya is not allowed to say *stop squabbling, Mama and Papa*, when *they* do it.

If Mama and Papa are arguing and somebody mentions Lena by accident, then everybody goes quiet. She has a lot of power for someone who is dead.

One day Katya is snooping and she finds something unexpected beneath some of Mama's things. It is a small notebook. She thinks it might be an old diary and she gets excited because all she knows about her parents is from eavesdropping. Mama has never even explained how she and Papa first met. Papa is full of secrets too. Like the time he said that Mama's eyes reminded him of Lake Syamozero by night, a lake in the north between Lake Ladoga and the White Sea. Katya asked him whether the family could visit this place, but he said he would never go north again.

The notebook is not a diary. Just stories. They're short and there's not many of them. Katya is curious because Mama writes stories for magazines, but none of those begin with a note to the reader. And Mama usually writes on her typewriter, not by hand.

On the back of the cover there is one line.

For Lena, beloved daughter.

No mention of Katya. Just Lena.

Lena, who is not even here to read it.

Katya feels so betrayed she almost can't believe it. But it's right there. In ink.

No, she thinks savagely, no, it's not written in ink, it's written in pencil. And pencil can be erased. And before she knows it she's found an eraser and she's starting to erase it. Katya is allergic to rubber and later her skin will itch and her eyes will hurt but it's worth it, because now at least nobody will ever know, even if this notebook is published too, that Mama only loves one of her daughters.

Lena, the dead one.

Misha often makes fun of her dolls, but Katya has caught him playing with them before. Having a tea party. She's never said. She's been blessed with a tremendous talent for dance, while Misha doesn't have much talent for anything, and it would be cruel to tease him. When he teases *her*, she simply looks past him and pretends that she is staring down an auditorium of people – not just any auditorium, but the big one, in Moscow – and holding her pose for however long it takes before the curtain falls.

Katya has a collection of at least fifteen dolls, and of these, three are made of porcelain. The porcelain ones are special and thrilling because they come from an unknown person. A secret, mysterious gift-giver. They are left on the doorstep, and small gifts are always hidden inside. Katya found the gifts by exploring the doll and discovering a circular, removable portion of the scalp. The head is hollow and large enough to store pieces of candy and toy rings and with the second doll, even a silver spoon.

The gift in the last doll was the most thrilling of all. Katya pried off the wig of hair, removed the circle carefully, and reached into the head. Nestled behind the eyes was a miniature ballerina figurine. A *ballerina*.

She has her first fan.

It is a little embarrassing and she would never, ever admit it to Misha or to the girls at school or to anyone who is alive, ever, but she daydreams sometimes about whoever it is that leaves the dolls. She daydreams that it's a youngish sort of *he*, and that he makes them himself. Maybe he even made the ballerina. Katya's not sure how such things are made, actually.

She asks Mama casually if she can visit the famous Lomonosov Porcelain Factory and Mama laughs.

I'll take you if you explain why, says Mama.

This leads to Katya showing her the ballerina, stupidly, which Mama shows to Papa and Papa says he has no idea where it came from, but Papa *does* know the three porcelain dolls were left at the front door, and Mama didn't know, and soon Katya is confessing to everything, tearfully and tragically, even to the daydreaming.

But Mama does not confiscate the porcelain dolls. Instead, Mama and Papa get into the biggest fight of their lives. Katya and Misha cower in the living room while they shout at one another in the kitchen and Misha doesn't have to say it, because she's already beating herself bloody with it.

This is all your fault, Katya. This is all your fault.

For the first time since Katya can remember, Mama does not come at bedtime to tell a story and give a kiss. Papa comes instead, and Papa doesn't tell good stories so he reads something boring from a book, not that anyone is listening. Katya turns away when he leans in to kiss her cheek so that he can't feel her tears.

Mama and Papa seem only to speak in whispers now. Dasha at school says it means they're likely to divorce and they don't want anyone to know yet. Misha says if that's true, then it's Katya's doing. Her and her dolls. Dolls are for *babies*, Misha says, and Katya yells that she's seen him having the odd tea party and that if they're making rules about dolls then dolls are for *girls* or isn't that right? And he turns red around the ears and he says, *I wish you weren't my sister*.

He says things like this all the time but this time it feels like he means it, because she hates herself too. Mama and Papa are divorcing because of her.

Katya isn't sure how she came up with the plan, but it's taken her long enough already. She is going to run away. The family will be happier without her. Mama and Papa won't have to divorce. She is going to go live with the doll-maker. Somebody who creates beautiful treasures, who treasures *her*. Maybe he can do other things, too. Draw. Paint. Sculpt. Anything with his hands. He'll have enough talent of his own that he won't mind when she has to do busy-ballerina things, like perform on the Big Stage. Like tie up her ballet shoes.

She doesn't know much of what ballerinas do, besides that.

She adds *A Ballet School* to her list of places the doll-maker should take her to visit, right underneath *The Lomonosov Porcelain Factory* and *Lake Syamozero*.

The only problem is that her plan requires money, and she has none. Nobody she knows has much money except maybe Vitya at school, who brags a lot, but she's not about to ask *him*. He's a skinny, weaselly schoolboy. Nothing like the doll-maker.

Katya thinks and thinks, makes lists, doodles in her schoolbooks. She can't bear to sell the dolls; the doll-maker might never forgive her. She watches Mama working one day on the Underwood, typing hard, oblivious to her presence – see? They might not even notice when she's gone – and then inspiration strikes. It just hits her right as she's standing there.

Maybe this is how the doll-maker feels when he adds just the right glob of paint to the right spot on one of his masterpieces. It *must* be. After all, they were both born to be artists.

Mama's editor is called Vladimir Stolypin. Katya's family have been to their home for dinner many times. Vladimir and his wife Anna weren't able to have kids. Katya knows this because she once heard Mama and Papa talking, saying that Anna Stolypina was told she will never have a baby and for some reason this made Mama sad, which seemed silly because Mama and Papa have had three children, including Lena. *Three*. That's nearly enough that they could have given one away to the Stolypins.

Katya walks there after school with Mama's notebook of stories in her hands.

The Stolypins are at home. They seem distracted. Maybe they have guests coming for dinner. Katya shouldn't delay.

She says she's brought a notebook with stories she's written and she'd like to sell them to the magazine, please. Anna Stolypina looks stiff at this, like she might need to use the toilet. Vladimir Stolypin patiently asks to see the notebook and Katya congratulates herself on how he won't realise it's Mama's because it's handwritten. He reads only a page or two, which she finds disappointing, and then he says: *Are you sure you wrote these?* And she confirms that she did.

Katya, says Vladimir, *please be honest.*

Her lower lip wobbles.

Anna Stolypina takes a look at the stories. She asks, *Did your mother write these, Katya*, and Katya bursts into tears. She does break easily, she's noticed. Anna comes over and puts an arm around her and says that everything's fine, it's just that these particular stories aren't meant for kids.

Katya thought *all* stories were meant for kids.

Vladimir Stolypin clears his throat and says he's going to hold on to the notebook for the time being. He says maybe there's something to them after all. His wife looks surprised. He asks if Katya can come back next week, a different afternoon, to talk with some friends of his. Katya nods happily now. Her tears have dried. She'd love to talk. She loves talking.

There are three men sitting in the Stolypins' living room when Katya visits the next time. Vladimir Stolypin must have many friends. Katya doesn't have even *one* real friend at school. Misha is the opposite. Well liked. Funny. He says *she* will never make friends until she stops telling everyone she is going to be a prima ballerina, and she feels chilled on the inside when he says this.

One day, Katya, she promises herself, *they're all going to adore you. They're going to hang on your every word like ornaments on a tree.*

Like how Vladimir Stolypin's friends are doing right now.

They don't resemble Mama and Papa's friends. They are dressed like they want to match. There was a time when Mama dressed Katya and Misha to match. In fact, these men do seem to act like twins, or in their case, triplets. Katya notices how they steal glances at one another, speaking in their own silent language. She and Misha have their own language, or they used to.

'So, Yekaterina,' says Triplet #1. He has a face that is girlish, almost pretty. 'If we may ask a few questions . . .'

'Please, call me Katya,' she says regally. They see her as equal to an adult, she can already perceive this. A lot of people call her 'Katenka' without even asking and she *hates* that.

'Your mother is Antonina Lulikova, is that right?'

'She only goes by Tonya.'

'And your father is a man called . . . Anatoly Radakov.'

'That is my papa,' Katya says proudly.

'Of course it is.' Triplet #1 smiles and she beams in return. 'Now this notebook, Katya, I want you to take it and put it right back where you found it. Alright? But it *is* interesting to us, and you deserve a reward. We can come by your home and—'

'No! You can't.' Katya flushes. 'I just need—I want to sell it.'

'Oh, yes. I see. It's a secret.' He holds a finger up to his lips. 'But we are good at secrets. In that case, don't tell your parents about this meeting between all of us, eh? We'll contact you again through Comrade Stolypin right here and arrange something. But just be sure to put the notebook back.'

Something in her stomach turns at this. She doesn't like how he said *Comrade Stolypin*. Mama does not call her editor Comrade Stolypin. But on the other hand, Triplet #1 probably does not know that Anna Stolypina cannot have kids, and Mama does.

Where *is* Anna Stolypina?

'Thank you so much, Katya,' says Triplet #2, speaking for the first time. He is an older, horsey version of Triplet #1. She feels annoyed. She didn't say *he* could call her Katya.

That night Mama comes in to tell a bedtime story as usual. Mama is radiant when she tells stories, like starlight. But Katya wonders why, whenever Mama is like this, she has a terrible urge to say her older sister's name, just breathe it out. *Lena*. It must be because she wants to hurt Mama, deep down. Because she is a bad person. Because she's never been as wonderful and amazing a daughter as Lena was, and Mama and Papa will never love her the way they did Lena.

But that is all about to change.

After Katya runs away, *hers* will be the unspoken name. *She* will take Lena's place in the family. The perfect one. The immortal one.

* * *

When Katya gets up for a drink of water, she sees light beneath the door of the kitchen. Mama and Papa are still awake. They are finally speaking in normal-volume voices.

Mama says: *The notebook was missing, for almost two weeks. And now it's back.*

Katya goes closer. She stands behind the door.

Papa says: *You think Katya took it?*

Mama says: *I know she did.*

But why? Curiosity?

Yes, probably. I'll keep it in my pillowcase from now on. She doesn't mean badly.

No, she doesn't.

But I've been feeling uneasy. Because of the dolls. Because you lied to me.

I'm sorry, Tonya. I . . .

Have you read the papers? There've been more arrests lately. We should be more careful, not less. We don't know what the dolls mean. Or who is watching. I'm scared, Valentin. I think we should move. Or at least go away for a while.

Come, don't be frightened. We're together, Antonina. That's all that matters.

Katya pauses with her hand on the knob. She has never heard anyone call Mama *Antonina*.

And who on earth is *Valentin*?

Who *are* these people?

Two nights later Katya is awoken by a *thump*. Misha, in the other bed, sits up straight. *Thump*. Neither of them speak. *Thump*. Mama bursts into the room. She gets everyone out of bed. There are people in the apartment. They are standing in the hallway. They're in uniform, with dark-blue caps, red stripes. Papa is there too. Misha whimpers that he has to pee.

The uniformed men have their shoulders pulled back and their chests stuck out. They say to go to the living room, to sit down on the sofa.

Katya sees Misha's expression and she knows it mirrors her own. That's what twinship is good for.

'What are they looking for?' asks Misha fearfully. The men are overturning everything on Mama's work desk, in Papa's bookshelves. They flip through the books. They shake out a drawer. They pull up the rug. They look bored. Mama doesn't answer.

Katya isn't sure how she knows, but suddenly she knows.

They are looking for the notebook.

They have been sent here by the Triplets.

Katya put it back where she found it, like the Triplets asked her to do, but now it's in Mama's pillowcase. Should she reveal where it is? Then they'll take it and go away, and all this will be over. Mama can just recreate the stories from memory later—

Mama's gaze is on her. Katya wonders if Lake Syamozero ever looks like *this*, like the bottom of a well. Mama shakes her head in a such a small way that maybe she didn't shake it at all. Her hair, down around her shoulders like this, looks like satin. Now Katya doesn't want to say Lena's name, or dim Mama's radiance. She doesn't even want to run away to the doll-maker. She just wants to climb onto her mother's lap like a baby and hold on.

The apartment is a mess. The intruders leave the same way they came. *Thump, thump, thump.*

Katya hears Mama exhale like she's been holding her breath for years.

Saturday. Mama's best friend comes to visit. Katya loves Aunty Vika. Every year the family visits Aunty Vika at her dacha a few hours away where she has a piano that takes up half a room. When Aunty Vika plays on it, her fingers move so fast they are nearly invisible.

'Aunty Vika!' Katya cries out and Misha comes running too, and Aunty Vika squeezes both of them hard. Then she shoos them away and says that she's here to talk to Mama but as soon as *that's* over she'll come find them and hear how everyone is doing. *Boring Adult Stuff first*, she says.

Katya loves Aunty Vika.

Katya hovers as Aunty Vika takes up her usual place in the kitchen with her usual cup of tea while Mama hangs laundry on the line. Aunty Vika looks over and winks and Katya slinks out of the room.

She sits outside against the wall. Waiting. Should she tell Aunty Vika about her plan to run away? Though the plan has lost some lustre over the past few days. Ever since those strange, stompy men came through. Katya felt oddly protective of Mama and Papa while sitting on that sofa with them.

At first it really is Boring Adult Stuff. Katya is considering getting up to play or going outside to pass the time until Aunty Vika is done, but then Mama says—

'We've decided to go away for a while. Do you think I'm overreacting? People say it can't ever be as bad as it was ten years ago. But they came here, Vika. They were *here*.'

Katya can't move. She didn't think Mama and Papa were serious, the other night, speaking of leaving Leningrad. Where is there to go? Dasha at school has family in Siberia and says it is a wasteland. Dasha says her cousins have farm animals sleeping inside their house with them. She swears that they still think there is a Tsar, one who's not human, but a *god*. Katya can't imagine that the people in such places have heard of something as sophisticated and high-minded as the ballet.

How will she ever attend a Ballet School or perform on the Big Stage?

How will the doll-maker find her again?

'There's something I must confess, before it's too late.' Mama's voice sounds funny. 'It's been on my mind so often lately, every time I read the news of another arrest.'

Katya feels dizzy. She isn't sure she wants to hear this, either.

'Something I did, back then.'

'Tonya,' says Aunty Vika, a warning.

'I was the one who denounced Pavel.'

Pavel. Another name Katya has never heard. Another name, no doubt, with a secret history, like *Lena*.

Like Valentin.

'All these years we've been friends now . . .' Mama is crying. 'Your father was executed because of me. He's gone, because of me.'

Katya feels like she has frozen solid.

332

'I knew,' says Aunty Vika. 'But I forgave you.'

Aunty Vika is just sitting there letting Mama cry, from the sound of it, but that's who Aunty Vika is. She lets people be themselves. Whenever Katya tells her she's going to be a ballerina but nobody else believes, all Aunty Vika says is: *You're already a ballerina, Katya, and don't let anyone say otherwise.*

'Some things are unforgivable,' says Mama, through her tears. 'Sometimes I think that if anything happens to my family, it's a fitting punishment for everything I've done, all of it unforgivable.'

Unforgivable.

'If anything were to happen to you and Valya, I would look after the children,' says Aunty Vika, but somehow that word of Mama's, spoken like that, *unforgivable*, still rings in Katya's ears. It goes on so long she begins to worry she will never stop hearing it.

In the middle of the night there is another *thump*. Katya closes her eyes and hopes it's only Misha falling out of bed. It is not. It's the men in uniform again. This time they find what they are looking for: Mama. Mama's hair still looks like satin, even when someone else's fist is in it. Katya and Misha watch from the doorway and Katya feels that this is a nightmare. This must be a nightmare. Misha is crying so hard he cannot stand up; he has to bend. It all happens so cleanly it's hard to believe these are the same people who made such a mess, last time. The door clicks behind them.

The look on Papa's face is unlike anything Katya has ever seen on anyone's face before.

CHAPTER TWENTY-SIX

Rosie

Vorkuta, August 1991

On the train journey from Moscow to Vorkuta, I am joined at Arkhangelsk by a forty-something fellow with a jolly, jaunty look about him, a bit like a baby animal.

'Do you know,' he says, 'that we will soon pass the line between the tundra and the taiga?'

'Really? Can you tell where that happens?' I ask.

'If you're paying attention. The railway up there was built by gulag prisoners,' he adds. 'From Vorkuta. It was one of the circles of hell.'

Jolly and jaunty indeed.

'That's where I'm headed,' I say, feeling claustrophobic in our small compartment. 'What's it like now?'

He scratches his sideburns. 'Bedevilled, by its own history,' he says. 'When I moved into my current home, there was graffiti on the front door. *You want coal? I want freedom!* is what it said. Vorkuta's in the middle of a coal basin. My mother was a prisoner in the Rechlag special camp – she worked in the mines. Almost everyone still in Vorkuta is a zek, a former prisoner, or a descendant thereof.'

My mother was a prisoner. It seems so incredible that such people could have survived what they did. But in a way such experiences were ordinary, weren't they? Millions lived through the same things. They just don't say.

'What is the Rechlag?' I ask.

'The river camp,' he answers. 'Maximum security, for political prisoners and terrorists. Established in 1948. Short-lived. But then, the whole Gulag system was dissolved within a few years of Stalin's death in '53, of course. My mother never left Vorkuta. Still lives up there.'

Out of habit, I have the urge to ask if I could talk to his mother, but instead I nod and give what I hope is an affable smile.

Not a living archive.

As we travel on, he tells me what to expect in Vorkuta: Large, airy avenues, like a European capital. Old billboards boasting slogans like *Glory to Those Who Work in the Polar North!* Nowadays Vorkuta has cinemas and schools and a launderette and bronze statues, just like any other Soviet outpost.

'But the temperatures are extreme,' he says glumly. 'There's no equilibrium. Not between summer and winter, nor between past and present.'

We cross the line. It's not as dramatic as he described, but in a way it's even more unnerving as a result. I've missed the best time of year for wildflowers, but a few stragglers in eye-popping reds and yellows are hanging on, adding a welcome dab of colour to the flat, endless tundra. Other than that, there is little out the window but empty space. A few 'reindeer fences' and solitary bushes dot the horizon.

The summer in the Arctic is almost over. The days will grow shorter until they disappear. This desolate land will freeze over and freeze its secrets with it, as it does, year in and year out.

I don't know what I'm doing here, but that must be a feeling a lot of people have in this place.

My travel companion shows me the hotel he manages, just by the train station. He offers to take me on a short tour, starting with Moscow Square, past the statue of Joseph Stalin. He tells me readily about the construction and renovation that never seems to cease, evidenced by workers digging holes around every corner. We keep going all the way to the outskirts of town, where a muddy lane lined by small, dark huts leads directly to a barbed-wire fence.

Beyond that, I know without asking, is the location of a former camp, even though there is nothing there.

At one of the huts, the door opens. Standing there is a woman in a roomy gingham dress, waving at us with enthusiasm. Her hair is tucked into a red bandana. I can't imagine that her home or this road are going to last much longer than they have done, and as if to emphasise their use-by date, we hear the nearby sound of shouting, drilling and banging, of something being taken down.

'My mother, Ilana Konoreyko,' says the hotel manager. 'Do you want to meet her?'

'I don't want to bother anyone.'

'Not at all,' he says generously. 'Please. She loves company.'

'If you're sure.'

Ilana's home is hot and damp, and the seat I take has a flat cushion that moves around on its own. Ilana knits with nimble-looking hands as we make small talk.

'Moscow?' she says warmly. 'You've come a long way.'

'She's interested in the camps, Mama,' interjects her son.

'Oh,' I say hurriedly, 'but we don't have to talk about—'

'I don't mind.' She smiles at me. 'What would you like to know?'

'Who you were,' I say, after a moment. 'Who they all were.'

'Me, I was only twenty, studying art, about to be married. They arrested me because of one of my paintings, is what was said at my trial. They never said which one. But I am Ukrainian, that was also unhelpful.' Ilana sets down her knitting and touches the knot tied at her throat. 'I arrived in 1948. First year of Special Camp Number Six. Some thirty thousand men, but only a thousand or so women. There are some pictures I have now, in fact, that I could show you.' She puts out her hand and her son produces a pair of large-rimmed glasses. 'Now, the album is—'

I wait patiently, but now she's looking right at me. Blinking fast, behind the eyeglasses. The expression she's had so far has worn off.

'Your eyes, your face,' she says. 'They are distinctive.'

She doesn't mean it as a compliment.

'Sorry,' says the hotel manager, sounding confused. 'Mama, if you're getting tired—'

'I'm not *tired*.' Ilana pushes the glasses further up the invisible bridge of her nose. 'I just have an excellent memory, that's all, and she reminds me of someone I knew. Anyway, never mind. Let's see.'

Mum used to tell me and Zoya a bleak little tale that began in a cemetery in the far north. It was summertime, she'd say. All the coffins had bobbed to the surface. They'd been buried above the permafrost, and when the active soil layer thawed and washed out each year, they re-emerged. Every grave was marked by a wooden cross, and every cross had a plaque with a name spelt out in copper letters . . .

While listening to this story I would whimper, imagining a decomposed grave with the lid coming off. Mum only chuckled at me.

You didn't know that, Raisochka? In the north, everything rises.

Everything finds the light.

'This someone,' I say. 'You knew Tonya.'

The hotel manager looks back and forth between us.

'I think I'm related to her.'

Ilana nods, accepting this. 'I'd believe it.' She pauses. 'Tonya lived in my barracks. She and I weren't close, but she was known to everyone. She was the resident storyteller. Told her yarns in exchange for extra food and whatnot. I know she had young children – she spoke of them often. Something with a K . . . ?'

'Katya.' It burns my tongue.

'That sounds right.'

Tonya is my grandmother. And she was a prisoner here. A political prisoner, when all Zoya and I were ever

338

told about our babushka was that she was long dead. Zoya might have asked once for details, and Mum started describing a dumpy woman who smelt of walnut cookies and herbal tea, before dovetailing into another anecdote that was clearly made up.

Why? Is that what Mum thought we wanted, just more and more fairy tales, one on top of the other, until nobody could tell where any of them began or ended?

'Is that why you've come to Vorkuta, for your family history?' asks Ilana. 'Many people do come now for this purpose. But how tremendous that you met my son on the train!'

'Do you know where Tonya went, after you were all released? After Stalin died?' I ask.

'Released, indeed.' Ilana cracks her knuckles. 'They opened the gates, but the law then was that we had to remain here as civilians. Now that they permit us to leave, it's too late. When you're older, you will understand.'

'Tonya stayed here too?'

'Tonya died,' says Ilana, gently now. 'She was hauled off to the infirmary, in 1950 or so, with something in her lungs. Never came back.'

And there it is.

I sit back and fold my arms to hide my ridiculous self-pity. After all, at my age Ilana was a prisoner. I'm free to leave Vorkuta today. But the casket has slammed shut. I had a grandmother and then I didn't. I found Tonya and then I lost her again.

I wanted the truth and now it's all I have.

I just can't help but wonder how an answer, something that fills in a blank space, could feel this empty.

At the kitchen table, Alexey is bent over paperwork. He does everything with a younger man's ease, but his legs are apart, his trousers rising up, and I can see the white hair and marbled skin of his ankles. When he smiles, his face crinkles like tissue.

He pops his pen into his mouth. 'There you are.'

'I know who Kukolka is.'

Alexey doesn't seem surprised. He pulls the pen from his mouth and shifts his attention fully over to me.

'Mum never said anything about her mother,' I say. 'I don't know why she kept it secret, but she did. You're looking for Tonya. Who are you? And why did you really hire me?'

Alexey rubs at his chin. 'It would be better to find her. Once we find her, then we can talk.'

'She's dead, Alexey.'

'You can't know,' he says, steely-eyed. 'No one knows. She was arrested in 1948. There's no record of her after that.'

I can't help myself but step back. Alexey doesn't move forward. The walls of the kitchen seem to constrict, pull inwards, like a pair of lungs. The weirdest thing is that he still doesn't seem any different. Even now that I know everything between us has been built on lies, he still looks the part of Alexey Ivanov, scholar and historian and writer and speaker. Gentlemanly and distinguished.

'Who *are* you?' I ask.

'Most people just called her Kukolka before I came along, you know.' Now he smiles. 'You could say that I'm the one who made her.'

CHAPTER TWENTY-SEVEN

Katya

Leningrad, St Petersburg, autumn 1948

THE NIGHTMARE REFUSES TO END. MAMA IS GONE. KATYA and Misha stay home from school. Papa cannot go to work, and spends all day locked in the living room. Aunty Vika comes to stay, to help. One afternoon Aunty Vika makes honey cake and sits with Katya and Misha in the kitchen.

'As you know, your mother has been arrested,' she says.

'But *why*?' Misha demands. 'Papa won't tell us anything!'

'I'll tell you everything I can,' Aunty Vika says. 'Somebody your mama knew professionally gave her name to the secret police. He claimed she wrote a notebook of short stories filled with anti-Soviet content. Maybe he just made it all up, maybe he just wanted to divert attention from his own family, but unfortunately—'

'It's *your* fault!' Misha whirls on Katya. 'Stupid Katya! I know you stole Mama's notebook! I saw you with it! You *showed* it to someone, didn't you!'

'Stop it, Misha,' says Aunty Vika.

'She showed it to someone!' he shouts. 'Is it whoever you scribble about and drool over in your schoolbooks, you pathetic idiot? That one! Didn't you!'

Katya feels herself breaking again, just like she did at the Stolypins'.

'Schoolbooks?' asks Aunty Vika, like that is the point of all this.

'The one who sends her *dolls*,' Misha sneers. 'Katya's in *love*!'

'Mikhail, enough! Katya, what is he talking about?'

Katya shakes her head and sniffles.

'Forget it then. Now, listen to me, both of you. You're ten, soon to be eleven years old. I'm being honest with you, and I need you both to be honest with me.'

Katya pulls her legs up and rocks herself. It's OK, feeling like this, it's OK. This is how it'll feel onstage one day, too. Pure nerves. Pure fear. Pure terror. You just have to keep a hold of yourself until the curtain falls, Katya. That's all.

Aunty Vika looks lost for a moment. 'Yes.' She takes a deep breath. 'Now, your mother. We don't know what's going to happen. But in the meantime, don't say her name. Ever. In any conversation, with children or adults. We can't know who's listening, or what anyone wants. We don't know whom to trust. Your best chance to have your mama back home is never to speak of her. Is that clear?'

Katya and Misha are both crying now. Katya tries to take his hand. They used to hold hands a lot. It used to feel like they were one person. But he crosses his arms, stuffing his hands beneath his armpits. Like he'd rather cut them off than touch her.

Unforgivable.

One day Aunty Vika has to return to her dacha to get something and she forces Katya and Misha to go to school again. At least the other kids give Katya a wide berth. Misha goes off with his friends afterwards and Katya goes home and there is nobody there. The door to the living room is open. The room still smells of Papa. Katya walks around anxiously for a few minutes and then makes a snack and then falls asleep in bed and then Misha is hollering her awake and says *Aunty Vika is back now, where's Papa? Where is Papa?* Misha is pale and sweaty. He looks sick.

'I don't know,' Katya says uncertainly, 'he wasn't here when I got home from school.'

'Then where *is* he?' says Misha, and she worries that he'll shout again, but he doesn't. His eyes are so wide they may pop from his face.

Aunty Vika calms everyone down. She's found a note from Papa saying he's gone to help Mama. Katya reads the note and it makes no sense. Aunty Vika says that Papa has been through a lot in his life. *He spent almost a decade in the camps, before you two were born*, she explains. This is the word she uses: 'camp'. *Lager.* Katya and Misha are both confused. *The way our neighbours go camping in Novgorod?* Misha asks.

'No,' says Aunty Vika. 'Labour camps for political prisoners. Your mama's arrest may have reminded him of

344

this, and he isn't—himself right now. But he loves you both. He'll come back.'

'When?' says Misha.

'I don't know.'

When Katya gets back into bed she can't fall asleep, of course, because she spent the whole afternoon sleeping. She has the feeling – no, stronger than a feeling – that Papa left because of her. Because he too knows the truth. *She* caused this. She brought this upon the family. Just like she brings it upon herself, what the other girls do to her at school. *Your face is too pretty, let's help*, they say, as they yank her hair and spit in her eyes and hold her down to kick her, and Misha sees this, sometimes, but he doesn't come to her defence. He acts like it's not happening. He acts like he doesn't know her.

Nobody knows her. She is alone.

Katya misses Mama and Papa so much that it feels like nothing will ever be right again. She slips the notebook of stories out of Mama's pillowcase and hides it in hers instead. She doesn't dare to open it, to look at it, because she'll cry on the pages and destroy all the writing. She's just keeping it for when Mama comes back. But Misha says she isn't ever coming back. It's been weeks now. Maybe more than a month. Misha is getting tougher. Mouthier. Katya is turning softer and weaker. But it's always this way with twins, people have said. They'll *always* be opposites! One will be quiet and the other loud. One will be serious and the other silly.

One twin will be good, and the other will be bad.

* * *

Today there is a new porcelain doll. It has been left outside like the others. Katya is relieved that Aunty Vika and Misha weren't the ones to find it. This doll is beautiful. Absolutely perfect.

There is a message inside the head, on a piece of paper.

Katya, meet me today in front of the Kirov State Academic Theatre. You will know me by what I am holding – it will be just for you. I can wait there until 6.

The doll-maker has never used her name before.
He knows who she is.
He wants to meet her.
He wants this to be real.
It is more than real. It is *fate*.
Katya stuffs the note back into the doll and she sweeps up her other porcelain dolls into one of Papa's old suitcases, with her clothes wrapped around them. She's just about to leave the apartment when she remembers Mama's notebook. She doesn't *want* to take anything else. The dolls are heavy enough. But somehow she cannot leave it. It's OK. She'll toss it out one day. She'll toss everything out, this whole ugly horrible pointless *unforgivable* life of hers – *unforgivable unforgivable* – and she will never, ever look back.

CHAPTER TWENTY-EIGHT

Valentin

Moscow, autumn 1948

'YOU DON'T UNDERSTAND ME,' VALENTIN INSISTS. He can smell drink on his own breath. 'My real name is Valentin Andreyev, and I am a traitor to the State. You'll see for yourself, in my file! You've arrested *her*, but I'm the guilty one! You need to let her go! *Listen to me!*'

'Uh-huh. Wait here, Comrade Radakov . . .'

Valentin has already been handed off twice. He is about to be handed off again. Why aren't they arresting him on the spot? He twitches in his chair. His head hurts. Everything hurts.

'Comrade Radakov?'

Somebody new, and far more important. Good, thinks Valentin, a senior officer can better fix this. The man in front of him is ageing, balding, broad-bellied but skinny in strange places. The hollows of the cheeks, for one.

'Can I get you something to drink?' asks the newcomer. 'Water, perhaps? No, coffee.' A shout down the hall, and then the door is shut. The two of them are alone. 'Sit down,' says the man.

Valentin wasn't aware he had moved from the chair. 'I'm glad to talk to someone else,' he spits out. 'My wife has been wrongly accused of anti-Soviet crimes. Her name is Antonina Lulikova. You must release her. I'm the guilty one. I'm telling you, I'm telling everyone, my name is Valentin Mikhailovich Andreyev. I was born in St Petersburg in 1896. My father worked in the Kirov—'

'I understand.' The man holds up his hand. 'But let me tell you who *I* am.'

Valentin presses the flat of his palm against his own temple.

'I know Antonina. I brought her in as an informant in 1937. Maybe she mentioned me to you? Alexander Ozhereliev?' A flash of teeth, stained like glass. 'Or just Sasha?'

Valentin shakes his head. 'Please,' he says. 'You need to believe me. The evidence is in my file!'

'I do believe you. But the problem is, you see, I got rid of your file ten years ago, so that no one else would investigate you. My official finding was that it was only rumour that Valentin Andreyev had survived Solovetsky and was living in Moscow, and what's more, that this rumour was being used by your father-in-law, Pavel Katenin, as a cover for his *own* crimes. For example, an anti-Stalinist newspaper of which he was editor.' A short pause. 'Don't know what's holding up the coffee. Do you want a cigarette? You are green around the gills.'

'Yes,' croaks Valentin.

Ozhereliev gives him a cigarette. Valentin lights it, lets the smoke fill his lungs, lets it blunt the feeling of everything else.

'Pavel Katenin was a much bigger fish than you,' says Ozhereliev. 'And I was the one to get him. There were internal purges here in our offices around that time, and I believe that getting him saved me, Andreyev. Helped me rise.'

'Pavel was not the editor of any newspaper,' says Valentin raggedly.

'No, but you were. Your own words were used to convict him.'

Valentin cannot draw enough air to respond.

'*The still water is where the devils live,*' muses Ozhereliev. 'Have you never felt this, when looking at Tonya? She turned him in to save you.'

'No,' says Valentin, 'she would not have done that.'

'Go home to your children, Comrade Radakov.'

'No,' Valentin shouts, 'no, she did not do that!'

'Give my best to Lena. She'll know me, at least. And your twins, they're how old by now . . . ?'

An image of Katya and Misha flashes through Valentin's mind. The man is right. Valentin has to get home. But then he remembers *Lena*, Lena lying still by the stove, and then he thinks of Pavel with a hood over his head, the cane cracked in two, and a firing squad and someone counting down and he doesn't even know if that's how Pavel died but it still can't be true, none of this can be true, he has to find Tonya, has to go to Tonya, she'll explain, she'll make the memories go away—

'Tonya has been sentenced to twenty-five years,' says the other man. 'I tried, truly, but there was nothing anyone could do. Oh, here comes the coffee.'

His head. His *head*. He tastes mud. His face and hair seem to be caked with it. Valentin has no idea where he is, outside this mud puddle. Was he on his way home from somewhere? Has he missed his *marshrutka* again? He'll have to take a late one, and Tonya hates that. He is always missing things by an hour here, a day there. He's never missed this badly, though, because he's ended up in a village, downtrodden and dreary.

There is no sign for Leningrad.

Valentin rubs the mud out of his eyes. On the other side of the road is a vegetable stall, set up on somebody's front porch. The word *Grocer's* appears in big letters on a placard propped up against a tree stump. A bearded man sits in a rocking chair, whittling away at something.

Valentin rasps a greeting.

The man must be the grocer himself, because he puts down his whittling, selects a vegetable stalk from the table, and bites down into it. He looks at Valentin with keen brown eyes. His grey hair is cut slackly around the ears. As he eats, pieces vanish into his beard.

'You've been there all night,' the man says. 'Ever since the coach dropped you. You were dead drunk, but I've the thing.'

The grocer reaches behind the tree stump, produces a bottle of spumy liquid. Valentin doesn't know if it's water or worse. He staggers over and holds it to his lips.

He coughs, looks around. The sun is rising over the trees, turning everything golden. Valentin takes another drink, and then he remembers how he got here.

Tonya told him the way to Otrada.

Made him memorise it.

'Is the year 1924?' Valentin asks.

The man's bushy eyebrows are furrowed. 'You need rest, my friend,' is his answer.

'I've come to meet her.' Valentin laughs and laughs, a beefy bellow. 'I made it. I'm here.' There is a pair of *babushki* staring at him now from across the lane. They frown, their faces shaded by age. He wipes the laugh off his mouth.

'Steady,' says the grocer, 'why don't you come inside and my wife can make you something hot to eat—'

'I should have gone with her, when she asked,' says Valentin. 'I should have stayed with her. I should have boarded the train in Moscow, with her. But I'm here now. We're going to be together. I just have to find Otrada.'

Valentin brushes away a branch, ducks his head to avoid another. The sunlight has receded, caught like a fly in the web of foliage overhead. There's the creek at last, high and pounding, the banks being skinned by the hard current. The path continues from the other side of the water. Valentin takes off his shoes and socks. On the wet stones he slips and nearly falls. He can't feel his toes, the few he still has.

Tonya, I'm coming—

The path leads down to a lake, a perfect hand-mirror. Past the lake lies a birch forest. Valentin goes around and into the trees. They give off a dainty, disorienting, butterscotch smell. He reaches out to touch one and grimaces. The bark feels like human skin.

Tonya, I'm here—

Day has bled to evening by the time he comes upon black iron gates. Valentin's headache has returned with a vengeance. He stumbles through, onto a wide walkway that is flanked by willow trees. They tickle his shoulders, whisper in his ear. The walkway ends at a large house of indistinct colour, the exterior marred by dry, cracked plates. The front entrance is a modest set of wooden doors.

Tonya, wait for me—

Valentin presses against the doors. Just inside, the floor feels like moss. His feet sink low with every step. He hears Tonya's voice at last. She is here. They have found one another.

Run, Valentin, run!

He moves forward blindly, testing everything with his hands, into the cavity of the house. Something will give way, he thinks. Something will open up and he will fall back into his everyday life, his normal life, and he will wake up next to Tonya.

Valentin searches the house for hours. He can't locate the front door, and the pain in his head is sharp as a needle.

He finds himself at the deepest point anyone can go: the conservatory.

Tonya won't be in *here*. This is the place she sees in her nightmares, and anyone might, for its high glass panels are coated with must and mildew, and the smell is some unspeakable mix of rotting teeth and the exotic sweetness of jasmine. Valentin breathes through his mouth. He is stupefied by the sight of the vines. Thick as pit vipers, they cover the walls and the floors and the beams, obscuring the shallow dome of the roof.

Except in one place, and he sees why.

Bones.

He has seen enough bones to know them anywhere. The vines have left these wretched remains alone, keeping to a distance that is chilling. Valentin approaches, his heart high in his throat, his headache worsening still. It is the decaying maw of a human skeleton; the flesh is gone. He cannot begin to think how long it has been here, sealed in tight.

Something is sown over the bones. *Paper.* Also disintegrating, but still intact. He reaches down for one of the limp sheets.

9th January 1904
My husband does not like that I use her. It's been
my mistake, waiting this long.

The moonlight filtered through the vines above is not enough for reading on. Valentin fumbles for his lighter. Its flame is weak but sufficient:

28th August 1907
My husband tells me that I should not expect
Kukolka to spend her life here. That our daughter
will have to get married and go away.

15th February 1908
Pregnant again.

20th May 1908

We did the ritual today, but Kukolka woke up in the midst of it. In the morning she did not appear to remember, but my husband's misgivings about how I use her have grown. He spoke again of how we will have to give her away one day.

I will never allow it to happen.

A sound echoes in the darkness around Valentin, and he drops the lighter.

It catches on the paper, which begins to flicker. The edges soften, the flames spreading, moving, as alive as the vines. Valentin puts his sleeve over his mouth. The glass walls tremble. The vines begin to strain and slither as if trying to get away, but there is no way out. If there were, there would be no skeleton here.

Run, Valentin, run!

Smoke is rising to the top of the dome. If the flames reach the house, it will burn like a pile of kindling, all of that old, dry wood. But it was an *accident*. He didn't mean to drop the lighter. He has a bad hand, damaged fingers.

Or maybe it wasn't. Maybe he wants to destroy this place. To destroy everything, because he has always been the one to destroy everything.

He has *missed* Tonya, the way he misses his appointments, his buses. Only he has missed her not by a minute, an hour, or a day, but by an entire lifetime.

I just don't know if you can have both—

Can't live two lives, you mean?

Be serious, Valentin!

I'm more serious than I've ever been. We'll be together soon. Nothing will keep me from you—

Valentin wants to put his hands over his ears, to block everything out, but he knows he can't block out what isn't there. It's happening again, after all these years. He is falling into the abyss in his mind. He thinks he sees a face bending over him, pale as the moonlight, but he is already on fire. He no longer cares. He feels nothing. He is there again, in exile. It is the only place he has ever belonged.

CHAPTER TWENTY-NINE

Rosie

Moscow, August 1991

ALEXEY SAYS HE PREFERS TO SPEAK ON THE BALCONY, so we go outside. Until now I've not seen him smoke, not once. He does it with a small tremor, like he might have been addicted in his youth, and his thin shoulders relax. We stand at the balcony, and he holds the rail with one hand for support. He's going to speak, but it's going to be without his usual rhetorical flourish.

'I met Tonya in 1914. She was fifteen. I was twenty-four. I wasn't looking to marry. But she was . . . well.' Alexey sounds resigned. 'And her parents were neglecting her. She was uneducated, untamed, undernourished. I married her, and I gave her plenty of freedom to roam, in Leningrad. I tried hard. All I wanted was to take care of her.'

'You were her husband?'

'I *am* her husband, Rosie. We were jumped in the street, the year of the Revolution, by a bunch of Bolshevik hooligans. They stabbed me.' Alexey says it with disdain.

'I got lucky. Didn't go through any important organs. But Tonya left me for dead, and following that incident, after I recovered, I realised my methods for looking after her were inherently flawed. I opted for surveillance.'

'Surveillance?'

'I watched over her from afar.'

'But why?' I ask, intrigued in spite of myself. 'If she didn't love you, if you couldn't be with her, what was the point?'

'To make sure that she was alright! She was part of my collection, Rosie. You cannot just let the crowning piece of your collection be egregiously mishandled and misused by amateurs, by the ignorant.'

I know I shouldn't ask. 'Collection of . . . what?'

'My collection of precious and beautiful things. I already had several dolls, as it happened. But I learnt that Tonya couldn't be kept in a room like the others,' he continues. 'She was too special. So I let her go, though every so often I would come across another worthy addition, another doll like her, and I would send it to her. To keep the collection together, you understand. You would recognise these additions. They sit in your mother's living room in England.'

Dolls. *Dolls.* Somehow the more he says, the less I can react. I can't move from the spot.

'I never cared for Tonya's firstborn. Lena. Too much like her father.' Alexey waves a hand dismissively. 'But Katya, your mother! I watched her closely, and she *liked* that. It was her nature. When Tonya was arrested, Katya came to live with me, in fact.'

'Mum lived with you,' I say, in disbelief.

'Oh yes. She was ten years old at the time. But she wasn't how I imagined. She was needy and unhappy. In the end – when she was sixteen or so – she ran off with some boyfriend,' he says, a bit stroppily, 'and that never stopped. Boyfriend after boyfriend. Even after she married your father. Even after she had children.'

My mind reels. Alexey was watching us too. All of us. Did I ever notice him in the background? Did I ever sense somebody there? But I reckon he was an expert at it, by then. Sticking to shadows. It's just too much, all of this, all at once.

'I just—can you stop,' I say. 'Stop for a moment—'

He doesn't. 'Such a shame when Zoya died,' he says. 'But I tried to make the best of it. To watch over you, next. When your father and sister were killed, and you and Katya left Russia, I decided to follow you two abroad. To defect.'

Defect. That word again. It's so heavy. Like Mum might have dropped into one last curtsey on a grand Moscow stage, before grabbing my hand as the curtains fell, enveloping me in a black cloak and hurrying us outside to meet the taxi that would whisk us away to freedom. *Take us anywhere; take us to our new home!*

We never arrived at any new home. The last home Mum ever made for me was already behind us.

'I used *The Last Bolshevik* to do it,' Alexey goes on. 'The dissident networks got me out after it was published in the west.'

'You plagiarised the writing on the walls,' I say slowly. 'In Tonya's Leningrad apartment. Is that why you bought it? So people wouldn't find out?'

He clucks. 'Yes, I broke in once, years after that house was vacated, just to see if there was anything left behind worth taking, and that was when I found the writing. I purchased the apartment as soon as I had the means, but only to *preserve* that writing, Rosie. To make sure it would never be destroyed. And it was always my apartment anyway. My house. I hope you see that I've only gone to such lengths because of how much I care! I even made my presence known to Katya, in England, hoping for a fresh start, but she refused to let me meet you. She'd only take my money. I paid your way to Oxford.'

I'm starting to feel light-headed. 'I got a scholarship.'

'No. I organised it all. *The Last Bolshevik* brought me fame and fortune, and I tried a lot of things to help. But your mother was beyond help. You know it best, of course.'

The night air swallows the remainder of the smoke. Alexey doesn't light another cigarette. He's nearing the end.

'I lied about a lot of things,' he admits. 'I was the one who put the map of Popovka into the notebook. I knew Akulina Burzinova would see your face and mention Tonya. Little ways to draw you in; little things that would bother you. I know what kind of person you are, Rosie, because I've watched you all your life.'

I try to speak but it comes out as a laugh.

'Tonya was strong,' Alexey says thoughtfully. 'A survivor. Your mother was weak. A victim. But you, you're more like me. We have no moral high ground, make no judgements. We see other people only insofar as they are useful to us. We take what we want. Nothing else matters.'

It's the last thing I want to think about right now, but I'm reminded of Lev, only a few nights ago, how still he was for a second, his eyes shining into mine—

Is Alexey right? Do I just take what I want?

'That's my life,' Alexey concludes. 'I've been honest now.'

Yes, if you can call this a life, one spent on the margins, chasing a single thing from start to finish.

Is this who I am? Who I want to be?

'I was always going to tell you everything. Maybe not this soon. But now we can do it together,' he proclaims. 'We can find Tonya. With our combined skills and minds, we can uncover the truth at last—'

'Why did you destroy Tonya's photograph, the frame?' I ask bluntly. 'I found it in the rubbish.'

'What do you mean?' Alexey asks, clearly astonished. 'I would never do such a thing. I don't believe in mindless destruction. I'm a curator!'

'But if it wasn't you, then who . . . ?'

Zoya.

I keep the thought at bay.

'Tonya's dead,' I say. 'She was sent to Vorkuta after her arrest. She died there.'

'That's impossible.' He shakes his head. 'How could you know that? I couldn't find a trace of her after 1948. Nothing.'

'I'd tell you how, but it's, well, it's impossible.'

'It's not true.' Alexey's voice wavers. 'She was a *doll*! She wasn't a person! Not like the rest of us! She was Kukolka! She's out there, Rosie, and we can still find her! Let's finish it, and you can know everything you've ever wanted to know! Don't you see?'

I do see. All those long explanations; all those justifications. They sounded almost rational, here or there, but they were a cover too.

This is Alexey Ivanov.

'*You* told me,' I say, 'that whatever we are looking for, won't be there.'

'Rosie, please,' Alexey pleads. 'Wait a moment – just give me a chance!'

I turn away. Alexey can't do anything to me, or anyone, any more. Maybe he had full control, once. Maybe he was dangerous. Maybe there was a time when being watched by him meant hardly enough room to breathe, let alone move. But if there was ever such a time, it's over, because now he's just an old man wedded to an illusion of himself. The only thing that could give him any power is my fear.

And I am not afraid.

A few days later, after I've moved out and into a hotel, the news is in every paper. Alexey Ivanov gave one last, stirring speech in front of an immense crowd in Red Square. He moved everyone present to tears. The very next morning he was found dead in his bed. People have a lot to say about his death: As peaceful and silent as his life was turbulent and momentous. An ending worthy of a national hero. Here was a man who opened himself so that the world could see in.

That's what they'll continue to say, unless one day I choose to speak.

* * *

Lev is at the wheel of his own car this time, a rickety Lada. There's no radio and the window cranks are stuck in place. In the aftermath of the failed coup, the city feels sluggish and drowsy. Many Muscovites have decamped to their summer getaways, to sun-soaked beaches, to blissfully airy dachas. And yet the traffic moves no faster through the city centre. The cars proceed like cells trying to squeeze through a thickened blood vessel. I rest my head against the fraying seat belt.

A vehicle behind us honks its horn.

Raisochka . . .

Zoya. Oh, no. Later, please.

Raisochka!

Tell me the truth, I say. *Did you kill Alexey? What are you capable of now?*

No! You don't understand. Let me explain, she says.

I sit upright, ignoring Lev's look of concern. *I know it was you, the broken frame. What do you want from me, Zoya?*

Alexey's been stalking you all this time! A sudden outburst, and she sounds more like the Zoya I used to know. *I just wanted you to see what he was! I wanted to free you!*

Maybe so. But she's been stalking me too. I want to yell at her, to scream so loud the windows shake—

And that's when I understand at last.

I've always thought I wanted Zoya to go away. I thought I was tired of the memories and the mysterious scents and the looking over my shoulder until my neck aches. But I don't think it's just her clinging to me; it's also that I've been clinging to her. And the harder I cling, the longer this goes on between the two of us, the more powerful she becomes. The more she can touch and move and feel things in my physical world. The more we are able to communicate. The more the line between life and death will be blurred, and neither of us will ever be able to fully experience either one.

The harder it will be, ever to stop, until the day comes when I'm not able to tell myself apart from her.

'We have to turn around,' I say to Lev.

'Where to?'

'I need to talk to Eduard Dayneko,' I say. 'I need to talk to my father.'

Dayneko looks tired and greasy, like he's just emerged from a pub brawl, but he lets me in to his apartment. I'd been expecting something dark and minimalist, the decor of my hotel room, but what greets me is what I ought to have expected instead.

This isn't just the hovel of a murderer. It's also an art studio. The windows are letting in an evening breeze with a nip to it, and just enough light for me to see everything he's working on. What *is* missing is normal furniture. He has no chairs, no sofa, no television stand, no wall-to-ceiling *stenka*.

'Do you want to sit down?' he says.

I sit down on one of his stools and keep my handbag between my legs. 'Thank you.'

Dayneko takes a seat on another stool.

'Tell me about your organisation,' I say. 'In the *mafiya*.'

'It's family run,' he says, out of the side of his mouth. 'It's good money. That's how I still have time for my artistry.'

He looks over at me. 'I could teach you, if you're interested. Painting lacquer. The skill was taught to me when I wasn't that much younger than you. It might be nice to have someone to carry on the tradition.'

Maybe he really is from Fedoskino.

I think of my papa.

Papa was always rumpled-looking, not slovenly, not dirty, but run-down, even for a relatively young man. He looked safe. He didn't have Eduard Dayneko's grey eyes or Eduard Dayneko's jawline or Eduard Dayneko's gift for turning murder, among other things, into an art form. And Mum in her youth wanted anything more than she wanted *safe*. She liked to teeter on her tiptoes. She liked to know she could come crashing down at any moment.

Lucky her. She did, and she brought us all down with her.

'But that's not why you're here, of course,' says Dayneko. 'You're here because you still have questions. You ran off too soon, last time. I spoke too soon – I should have prepared you better.'

'It's true that I needed time.'

'I've told you everything, Raisa.'

The steam over my own tea is dissipating; the breeze is growing stronger. I don't have another night to spare.

'It's not why I'm here,' I say.

'Are you here to kill me?'

I laugh.

'You *are* my daughter,' he says. 'After all.'

I can tell from the way he says it that he thinks he's wrong-footed me again, the way he did in the marketplace of the Vernissage. He thinks he's always seen me coming, before I even get there. He's always known before me when our paths would cross.

But he hasn't foreseen this.

'I might be your daughter. But my father is dead,' I say. 'And I'm not here to kill you, or to hear your side again. I'm not here to learn your art. I came here to let you go, but as I'm saying this, I think I already have.'

I still remember Mum's own version of the tale of Koschei the Deathless, the immortal. How he falls in love with a married woman. How he comes up with an idea: *this woman* would be the new and better object in which to store his eternal life.

They have an affair, the woman falls pregnant, a daughter is born.

Koschei lets the woman and her husband raise the child, but he still wants to warn his daughter that her powers, like his, can be dangerous. One night he decides he must tell her who she is. He goes to the family's home when he thinks she is alone, but he miscalculates. Her human father and siblings are at home too, and as soon as they see him, they begin to beg for their lives – until the noise rouses the youngest member of the family.

Koschei's daughter.

When she comes in and sees all this happening, she closes her eyes and begins to cry. And maybe because of her terror and her confusion, or maybe because she's still partly asleep and not quite awake, the power within her rises on its own.

And kills them all.

Except that Koschei the Deathless cannot be killed.

He's carrying his knife, as he always does. It's the only time he ever feels human: when he takes a life. His daughter still has her eyes closed, is still crying. Koschei panics and stabs the dead bodies of the rest of her family, so that she'll think that *he*, this unknown intruder, has murdered them. So that she will never know what she has done.

She opens her eyes and they see one another, for the first and last time.

And then he vanishes into the night, never to return.

The end.

Now I understand that this story was about *that man*, about that night. Now I know Mum was trying to tell me about it in the only way she knew how, and it wasn't that she didn't want to talk; it was also that I couldn't hear.

What relationship this version has to the truth, I will never know. There's no code for me to break. There's no problem I can solve. This is all I will ever have, and for the first time, I don't need anything else.

A fairy tale is good enough, because that's all the past is, in any form.

Just stories. The ones that we tell ourselves.

Another ride through Moscow with Lev in the Lada; another snarling knot of traffic near the city centre. We are headed for supper at his parents' dacha. As we drive, I watch a host of sparrows take to the sky. They blot out the strongest rays of the sun. Lev and I have not said much to one another since we spent the night together. He's waiting for me to speak. Maybe he's prepared himself for what I might say: That it's almost September. That I'm going home. That I'll remember him fondly.

I'm about to tell him about my final encounter with Eduard Dayneko, but I find myself remembering that old line that Mum loved, from *War and Peace*.

Patience and time; they will do everything . . .

The first time I heard them, I took those words to mean that I just needed to *wait* for my opportunity, and I would have every answer I wanted. But maybe it actually meant that patience and time would fight *for* me. They did the work so that I didn't have to. So that by the time I was there, sitting with a killer, looking into a face that reminded me a little of my own, it was already done.

I had healed without even knowing it.

Mum read *War and Peace* to me again, a year or so later, this time in translation, and I liked it even less in English. I can still picture her in that nightgown, hear it swishing by her ankles as she sits at my bedside. I can hear her reciting: *It is possible to love a person dear to you with human love, but only an enemy can be loved with divine love . . .*

I remember I stopped Mum at that spot. I couldn't keep up. I'd heard enough.

She shut the book. Seeing how irritated I was, she said that we would start a new story the next day, but of course we didn't. Mum wasn't someone who moved on easily. The next night we picked up right where she left off.

It's time, now. It's time for me to start a new story.

The car slows as we approach a turn.

'I'm not engaged any more,' I say.

'Ah,' says Lev. 'I see.'

The words are as slight, as insignificant, as the way he reaches for my hand and laces his fingers through mine, just for a second, before he has to change gears again. But this may be the first time in fourteen years that I find myself in the present moment without anything else hanging on, and right now, I could be weightless.

'You're leaving Moscow?' says Colonel Ivan Vasiliev, folding his hands on his desk. 'But of course. You must have missed home.'

'I have,' I say. 'I've missed home.'

'I've been trying to contact you,' he says. 'I left several messages at the number you provided. Someone picked up once, but there was no sound.'

'I didn't get any phone messages from you,' I say, slowly.

He clears his throat. 'Well, you're here now.'

I ignore the thorny sensation along both my forearms. 'I just came to say goodbye. Why have you been trying to reach me?'

'As I attempted to tell you last time, Raisa, before we were preoccupied by your . . . request, there's something we must discuss.' Vasiliev unfolds his hands. 'It's about your sister.'

'About Zoya?'

'You know I've always felt responsible for what happened to your family, and so I've respected your mother's wishes.' He sighs. 'But now that Katya is gone, it falls to you.'

'What does?'

'What to do with her.'

'What to do with . . .' I let the seconds pass. My heart thuds. 'What are you talking about?'

He rubs his eyes hard. 'So Katya never told you.'

Raisochka . . .

I ignore Zoya's whisper.

'Since that night, your sister has been on life support at a facility here in Moscow, at my discretion. They feed her, keep her breathing, and so on,' Ivan Vasiliev says, expressionless. 'In a way, although unresponsive, she has shown remarkable strength. But there is no hope that she will emerge from her coma. There was never any hope.'

Zoya?

Yes, it's true, I'm afraid! Zoya says. She laughs, just a tinkle of it. *Tell this man you want to keep me as I am, OK?*

But—

It's the only way I can keep coming to you like this, Raisa. Otherwise . . . A note of anxiety in her childish voice. *Otherwise I'll be really gone.*

'You don't have to decide at this moment,' says Ivan Vasiliev. 'I can also arrange for you to visit her. Your mother refused, despite my . . . strong urging.'

Mum couldn't even say Eduard Dayneko's name. Of course she couldn't visit.

I've always wondered, deep down, why she and I had to leave Moscow the way we did. Whether, if we stayed, Eduard Dayneko really would have hunted us down and killed us too. Maybe the colonel earnestly believes so; maybe it was better not to take the chance. But I don't believe it. Not any more.

We left because all Mum ever knew how to do was run away.

I could visit Zoya. I should. Maybe I will. But would it *be* her? Zoya's not lying on her back in some soulless medical facility, her body hinging on the verge of decay, her lungs being inflated by a machine, her blood being pumped by something heartless. She's not unresponsive and unconscious and at the mercy of strangers. Zoya's here, all around me, and she always will be, in every sweet scent that drifts by on the breeze. It doesn't matter if we can speak or not. I will always be listening.

And for the first time it occurs to me: she's not my older sister any more.

She's my *younger* sister. I grew up. She's still a child. She was never given the chance to be anything else.

'It's been long enough,' I say. 'I want her to be at peace.'

No! Raisa!

'Katya found she could not make that decision,' says Vasiliev. 'If you wish to take more time . . .'

No! Zoya shrieks. *No, I don't want to leave you!*

No, of course she doesn't. She never had a real mum or a father who paid enough attention; she must have felt so alone all her life. Zoya deserves a parent at last, and I'm the only one left. I'm the only one who can tell her that it's going to be OK. Even if I spend the next six months – the next year – the next sixty years – wishing I hadn't done this, I must do it anyway.

She is my pain, and I am hers. We have both been holding on too long.

You will never leave me, Zoya, I say, *and I will never leave you.*

Please don't. Zoya's crying. *Is it because of what happened with Alexey? Because there's more that I can tell you, now that we can finally talk like this! Don't you see? More that I can help you with—*

No, I reply. *I understand what happened with Alexey. I know you wanted to free me. And now I am going to free you.*

On the aeroplane, as Moscow fades into the distance, I find my mother's notebook and flip all the way to the end. Lev and I have read the whole thing now, though somehow I don't think the last story was meant to be the last. Whatever the final one really is, it's not here.

I'm about to put the notebook away when I suddenly remember the short note on the first page.

A Note for the Reader
These stories should not be read in order.

There *is* one story left for me to read, and now I am able to read it on my own.

The very first story.

THE SNOW WAS PORCELAIN AND
THE RAIN WAS GLASS

In some faraway kingdom, in some long-ago land, the snow in winter was porcelain and the rain in autumn was glass. The summer sun was honey, spreading itself over the tablecloth of the earth, drizzling into a small grove where a young princess sat by a creek. She tried to catch the fish that skirted by with her bare hands, but the fish were laughing, and each time she missed, she laughed too.

'Princess!' came the cry through the woods.

She dug her toes into the fatty soil of the bank.

'Princess!'

She got to her feet.

'Princess! Come!'

She'd forgotten that today was a special day. Today her mother, the Queen, would take over from the cooks and make something herself, and whether it was soup or sturgeon or chocolate torte, she would lavish it with spices and serve it on her best bone china. The two of them would eat alone, for the King would remain in his glass house, tending his roses. After this meal, the girl would go to sleep, but it was not the sleep of royalty, which ought to be smooth and untroubled, with dreams as delicious as any chocolate torte.

No, the princess would be lured into something else, something deeper, and she would wake up the next morning with bandaging around her arms and legs and an ache in her forehead even tighter than the bandaging.

Tonight the Queen made fish, and the princess had little appetite for it. When her mother's back was turned, she fed her portion to the palace cat, who rested by her feet. Then the princess fastidiously scraped the bottom of her bone-china bowl and told her mother how very delicious it was.

Very soon, the princess felt herself falling into the sleep that was not sleep.

But when she woke, she was not in her bedroom. She was in the palace kitchen. A pot simmered on the hob, and from it, a smell filled the room, of acid and char and table sugar. It was sweeter than the aroma of her father's roses, and heavy as fog.

The girl knew she would never forget it, this smell.

She tried to stand.

'Why is she awake?' the King asked. 'She's awake! Look!'

'It doesn't matter,' the Queen replied.

'But we can't—'

'We must.'

The King held the princess down, while the Queen brandished a knife, saying that she needed to cut out her daughter's living flesh; to eat it. The Queen had lost so many babies, and was now pregnant again. This was the only way to save the unborn child; the Queen had seen it in a dream.

The princess had to give a little piece of herself so that her sibling could live. But only a little. And once the baby was born, the Queen promised, they wouldn't have to do this any more.

The princess looked towards the window and saw there the face of the palace stablehand. He had always been kind to her. He would surely save her.

Please, she mouthed at him. *Help me!*

He looked afraid.

Please! she cried, with all her might. *Come back! Help me!*

When the girl woke again, she was in her own bed, in her own beautiful bedroom, on her own embroidered sheets. She felt the hard wrappings on her elbow, just like the end of any other special day. She felt a headache like the tip of a knife.

Just like always.

She could not remember the night before, but she remembered screaming. Maybe it had been another of her nightmares. Later her mother would give her something to take that would make it better. The Queen knew where all the best things grew in the forest, that could take away troubled thoughts, take away pain, take away memories. Take away all feeling.

The princess went downstairs and found her parents. She asked them if they'd slept soundly, or if they'd been bothered by another of her nightmares, and they said they hadn't been, and the girl believed them. She believed that in this land, the summer sun was honey and the snow in winter was porcelain and the rain in autumn was glass. She believed that her life was a fairy tale, and her house was a castle, and she was its princess.

But there are no fairy tales, dear Reader.

Not the one she was told, and not the ones you have just read.

CHAPTER THIRTY

Antonina
Vorkuta, 1949

'LOOK AT THAT SNOW,' SAYS THE NEW OCCUPANT OF the hospital cot next to Tonya's. 'I've never seen any like it.'

Tonya keeps her eyes closed. Country snow is what it is, up here. Bright and furious, looking like a quilt. If you could die against any backdrop, you might choose this, and she is dying. The doctors suspect it is silicosis, but they don't know what's in her lungs. It could also be fluid, or a soft bundle of coal dust.

Or the ice of that first winter of the blockade, still lodged inside her.

'You must be tired of it,' the woman continues. 'How many winters have you been here?'

'It's my second,' says Tonya. 'But my lungs won't last another.'

'Is that what the doctors say, darling?'

The word plays on her memory. She has not heard it in so many years; she is no longer even sure of its meaning.

Tonya opens her eyes. Her companion's face looks melted, like candle wax, the green eyes tainted by jaundice. The hair that frames the face is dove-white. The only thing that Tonya recognises is the small silver cross that sits in a fleshy fold of the other woman's neck.

The Countess Natalya Burzinova.

'This can't be,' says Tonya, but a spurt of laughter escapes her. Of course it is. 'How long it's been, Natalya Fyodorovna – I did not know your voice.'

'Do you know what I have tattooed on my arm, Tonya?' Natalya asks, as if their meeting after twenty-five years, in a place like this, is not astonishing in the least. '*I do not regret. I do not shed tears.* I've been in and out of prison, you see, these many decades, so many times I've lost count, and one must have tattoos to fit in. I'm not a political like you, darling, and they keep shipping me around. In a few weeks I'll be going to a new prison down south. Or I would be, if my organs weren't failing.' A pause. 'You could say I'm getting out in my own way.'

Tonya turns to her side, resting edgily on her weaker hip. Natalya Burzinova is all that is left of the world into which Tonya was born: Otrada, Mama and Papa, Imperial Russia, Princes and Princesses and Counts and Countesses. The Bolsheviks might have stormed the Winter Palace, but they did not witness the true end of that era. It is only ending now, in the form of a diminished figure in a filthy cot at the outer limits of the earth.

Tonya will be the one to witness it.

* * *

'Tonya,' comes the fervent whisper at night, 'Tonya, are you sleeping?'

Tonya pulls her thin sheets up to her chin. She is shivering down to her toes. But she senses those two wolf-eyes upon her, gleaming in the darkness, like all the life that remains in the Countess is concentrated there.

'I do have regrets,' says Natalya, huskily. 'I have so many regrets, but my biggest is that I let down my daughter, that she believes I do not love her. Everything else I could live with now, die with now, but that! That Akulina despises me.'

Tonya feels a wretched flutter of pity. 'I'm sure Akulina does not despise you—'

'She does. I found her, you know, after you and I met at Otrada. I tried to make her understand, but I couldn't. She said I killed Little Fedya and that as far as she was concerned, I died during the Civil War as everyone said I had, and she had had no mother since.' Natalya pauses to draw a breath, a hitch. 'You despise me too, of course. But we can help one another. We can make an exchange. I'll do something for you, if you do something for me – fair is fair!'

'You think there's time left for exchanges?' says Tonya. 'Look around!'

'Not for me, no. But you!' Those eyes burn like emeralds. 'If you don't die soon, they'll move you back to your section, and you'll die quicker there. You must get out of Vorkuta, darling, and then you may have a chance to live. I can help you!'

They might have pumped something into Natalya for the pain, and it now courses through her, reviving old synapses, making sleep impossible, making her delusional. 'And what would I do for you?' says Tonya, to humour her.

'If you survive, you will write my memoirs,' says the Countess.

'I do not know your life enough to write your memoirs.'

'I will tell you. And how much is there to know? You remember the old days too! The parties I used to throw, the music, the gossiping, the fun! You remember what it was all like! Tell my story for me. So that Akulina might read it one day – might read it, and know me.'

It is an absurd idea. Absolutely absurd. Tonya shakes her head as well as she can.

'Take this.' Natalya reaches to her neck, unclasps the silver necklace.

Again Tonya shakes her head, vigorously this time. The cross looks smaller, shrunken, in Natalya's hand. No longer where it belongs.

'Take it,' Natalya commands. 'Even if you won't help me, this necklace can still be of use, if you're sent back to camp. You can trade it away. You wouldn't believe all I've done to keep hold of it – but it's worthless to me now. Take it. Allow me this peace of mind.'

Tonya wants to refuse. Wants to say that there is nothing, nothing that will make up for what Natalya did, but she also remembers the day she confessed her greatest crime to Viktoria, sobbed, fell to her friend's feet: *I denounced Pavel*; *unforgivable*; and Natalya is still holding the necklace, obviously using up her final vestiges of strength, and Tonya takes it. Just takes it. It's a locket. It opens to reveal an inscription, a spidery line.

'I do miss the old days.' Natalya's eyes have lost their gleam. 'If only I could return. Just for a moment. See it all again, knowing what I know now.'

'I can help you return,' says Tonya. 'Close your eyes.' She doesn't know what she's about to say. *I do not regret. I do not shed tears.* She likes it. She will choose to believe it. She hears herself talking, as if she is another listener, as if she could fall asleep now, for ever, but the story would carry on without her. As if it has a life of its own. 'In a faraway kingdom, in some long-ago land . . .'

CHAPTER THIRTY-ONE

Valentin

Popovka, Tula province

VALENTIN SITS IN THE ROCKING CHAIR AND ROCKS. Nelly is moving around, keeping busy. She says *are you hungry* and he rocks. They have buried Kirill this morning, and Nelly will not sit down. She flits back and forth like a bird. She asks, *Do you remember when Kirill found you, all those years ago*, like she wants to reminisce. Valentin doesn't remember. He knows he was in and out of consciousness for weeks after Kirill Vladimirovich, the grocer, pulled him from the flames at Otrada. By the time he had recovered his own name, months had passed.

He has never recovered much else.

Nelly is hard to pin down today. Still moving. Valentin doesn't try to intrude. He has never fully understood their kindness, Kirill and Nelly, taking in a disabled stranger. *Life's funny*, Nelly is saying. She never had children. Couldn't get pregnant. But now her husband's gone and there's still somebody here for company. Life is funny.

Valentin rocks, rocks, rocks.

He never had children either. Or if he did, he hopes, assumes, that they can't even remember him. It's for the best. Look what a burden he'd be, like this. Unable to do any work but simple physical labour, chopping wood or rigging a fishing line. Only able to speak in incoherent bursts. Always rocking.

Twenty-five years. Twenty-five. He doesn't know why he remembers this detail, better than anything.

Twenty-five years in the north; that's a hundred years anywhere else.

She will have died there, and he will die here. They will never have a moment of deliverance. Life is funny.

And so he rocks.

CHAPTER THIRTY-TWO

Raisa

Moscow, January 1993

A PAINTED SIGN FOR A BOOKSHOP IS A BEACON IN THIS heavy snowfall, and I duck inside, shaking the flurries off my jacket. The shopkeeper looks up from her novel and assesses me.

'What are you looking for?' she asks, grudgingly.

'I'm just browsing.' I'll find something to buy. The foreign currency in my bag is probably worth more than the entire shop right now, with the collapse of the Soviet regime in December 1991, and subsequently the economy.

I turn to the shelves behind me. This might be enough books even for the likes of Mum, which reminds me that I still haven't properly cleared out her apartment. I now plan to sell it, but I know I have to decide what to do with her things, and if I can in good conscience get rid of her bisque dolls. I often can't help thinking that I should have had them cremated along with her.

As I sweep a finger along the titles, one of them stops me.

The Snow Was Porcelain and the Rain Was Glass.

It is a hardbound book with a hand-drawn cover, written by someone called Antonina Larionova. I flip it open.

A Note for the Reader
These stories should not be read in order.

I blink for a moment just in case, but it is exactly what it seems to be. A printed, *published* version of Mum's notebook of stories. I check the front matter: *Published in 1985.* How is this possible? How can there be another copy? Not just another copy, but this eye-catching volume, rebound and reworked and reimagined, replete with *pictures*?

Antonina.

Tonya.

I check the dedication page. *To my children*, it says simply. I can see the snow falling ever harder outside. The shopkeeper is back in the world of her novel, making satisfied noises as she turns the pages.

I start to read.

All the stories have been lengthened and polished, and several new ones appear. The final story in this copy is entitled 'The One and the Other'. It's set at a gulag camp, in which a political prisoner called The One is struggling to survive the harsh winter. In hospital, she encounters, to her amazement, an enemy that she hasn't seen in decades.

This former nemesis is called The Other.

The Other is serving a sentence for multiple murders and is only in transit between prisons. She's due to be transferred to another facility in the south, but she knows she will die before any transfer. The two women make a pact. The One will tell stories about their lives before the Socialist Revolution, before the fall of the Tsar. About the luxury, the magnificence, the way Imperial St Petersburg glittered like the gems around the throat of the Empress Alexandra.

Stories that help the Other forget her pain.

In exchange, the Other will enable the One to take her place when she dies. *Fair is fair*. They will bribe the orderlies, trick the guards. And that is what happens: The Other dies. The One, in her place, is transferred to a different prison. In warmer temperatures, without hard labour, her lungs recover and her body heals and her strength returns.

But – the twist!

Joseph Stalin dies soon after, and the dismantling of the entire Gulag system follows. The vast majority of the political prisoners of the USSR are quickly released – except for our main character. The One is now destined to pay for crimes she did not commit. To serve the full sentence of her oldest enemy.

In the low afternoon light, dressed in murky-green camouflage, Lev looks like the stranger he used to be. He drops his sports bag on the kitchen floor and meets my gaze. Even if we've been writing regularly, it's been almost a year and a half since we last laid eyes on each other, and in that time, the end of the USSR has left behind untold wreckage.

This is his parents' dacha in the suburbs of Moscow, the address through which we've been corresponding. A modest

385

home surrounded by vegetable boxes. His mother was here when I arrived, but now she's out, and I've been pottering around, unpacking my bags, left to twisty thoughts.

Whether Lev's return to the OMON will have changed things between us.

Whether we are part of the wreckage too, me and him.

As if I've said it aloud, his expression grows quiet, pensive. *Things haven't changed at the top as much as people think*, he wrote to me not long after Christmas 1991. I was in Oxford, anxiously watching replays on telly of Mikhail Gorbachev's final address to the nation as General Secretary. *My father still has a lot of influence.*

I didn't blame Lev's father. If I were him, I'd want Lev back in the OMON too. I'd want as much as possible for things to be the way they used to be.

'You've come,' is his greeting.

'Of course I came.'

He approaches. My heart begins to hammer. I can see those golden specks in his eyes. 'A month?' he asks.

'A month. I'll have to spend some days working.'

'Me too. Although . . .' He reaches for my hand. 'I'm leaving the OMON. I haven't told my parents yet – I haven't told anyone. I have a lead for a job in Leningrad at one of the district police precincts. It's criminal investigative work. It's just training, but I wanted to tell you in person, because I was inspired by you. By everything we did.'

'You mean St Petersburg,' I say, smiling up at him.

'St Petersburg.' He grins, and then he kisses me. For a few minutes we're only kissing, but I know I have to say it now, before anything else happens, before we make any promises or plans. He knows full well that I've been a bit frightened, with the events of the past few years, by his role in the OMON. I don't want him to do it for my sake.

'You might miss the military,' I whisper. 'Once it's really behind you.'

Lev draws back. His eyes don't leave mine. 'I will miss it, in some ways,' he says. 'But there are always a hundred lives not lived. There will always be a hundred paths I did not choose. And this is the one I do.'

With every blast of wind my teeth clink together like coins. The snow on the streets has turned to sludge, but there's enough of it to bury a person alive. At the corner, an old woman is hawking home-made potato cakes. I've seen other old women and other tables, at the mouths of the underground walkways, outside all the metro stations. Their pensions are gone; their money is worthless. What happens to all the people who *can't* bake sugary treats? How do *they* survive in the New Russia?

Lev glances at the door to the cafe and back at me.

I can't return to knowing nothing. I can't live in stasis either. That means the only possible place to go is in *there*.

Opening the door to the cafe is like opening a portal to another dimension. The fragrance of coffee and pastry; enough electric heaters running that I might melt. The hostess slinks over to us, catlike, with eyes set too far apart and pointy ears to match. She shoots a smile at Lev.

From the moment I saw it, I liked the way Antonina Larionova's name rolled, just like Zoya's old nickname for Mum. *Katerina Ballerina*. We spoke quickly on the telephone and when I said I would pay for a meal, if we could meet in person, she directed me here. I anticipated it would be somewhere with a snide waiting staff. I anticipated feeling out of place. But I don't feel out of place at all.

There she is.

There she is, sitting quietly at the only occupied table, dipping a spoon in and out of a cup.

By now I am used to ghosts. I have heard them here in the capital, in the laughter of the children playing with their wooden sticks on the frozen Moskva. I have glimpsed them in the teenage girls outside the shops, with their all-knowing smiles and unmistakable airs. These ghosts live on in everyone; I can see them everywhere. They don't scare me.

But I did not expect to see the ghost of myself.

Not here, not like this.

This woman is what Mum would have been. What I will one day be.

She is silver-haired and tiny; her smile is open-mouthed. Friendly. She wears round tortoiseshell glasses, and I can feel her eyes on me. The past is beginning to slip in through every crack, through every crevice, coiling around us. Now that we have found each other, it will never let us go.

'It is you I am waiting for?' she asks, in a wispy voice.

Somehow I am able to move towards her. Lev follows. Her smile changes. She is seeing what I see. Now I notice that there is something flowy, something faraway, about her. It is the same quality I often observed in Mum, and I thought it was simply *foreignness*, a person living in an adopted country, but it's not. It has no name.

'Who are you?' she asks.

I know I've ambushed her. I look mutely at Lev, but he shakes his head.

'Who are you?' Again, harder this time.

'I'm Katya's daughter,' I say. 'I'm your granddaughter.'

We talk about her time in Vorkuta. It is the safest territory to cover, that vast land that is so far from this cafe it could be just another one of her fairy tales. A place where, as my grandmother says, in a country where there was always somebody watching, she and the other prisoners were finally all alone.

Tonya arrived in Vorkuta in autumn 1948, via what she calls the Pechora Mainline. She describes carriages divided by steel netting, bloodsucking flies that dug into everything they landed on. The air was thick as syrup. She was assigned to a camp section, a *lagpunkt*, upon arrival. At night creatures with many legs would scuttle up and down her body. To this day she doesn't know what they were.

She dreamt nightly, she says, of escaping the barbed wire, of running away into the tundra. But the tundra took no prisoners at all, and anyway there was not much time for dreaming. In her *lagpunkt* the sirens went off every morning at four. The guards took headcounts before the women ate breakfast, bread that tasted like pebbles, imitation tea. Then the daily trek to the mines. She remembers the punishing wind. Her bunkmate's southern drawl. The handful of criminal prisoners huddled by the kerosene lamps, gambling, growling at the others. The barred windows of the barracks; how it made her long even more for that wide-open tundra.

Then, she says, came the first snowfall, and her cough.

That is where she stops.

In spite of the depressing tale, my grandmother burns bright, somehow, with hope. She looks like the kind of person reporters might interview on *Vremya* about the future of Russia. You look at her and you want to be part of the story too.

It makes me wonder if there was ever anyone who saw deeper than that.

'So, Raisa,' she says. 'Now I understand. You're the one who met Misha during the August Coup. He said that there was an English girl who reminded him of Katya, that he never got a good look because she was in sunglasses. I did not think anything of it at the time. When you lose people, you see them everywhere.'

'Misha. You mean – Mikhail Katenin?'

'My son. He was adopted after my arrest by a family friend.'

'Mum had a brother,' I say, more for my own sake.

I'm struck by the thought that if Alexey had not been so blind to everything but Tonya's female line, his collection of *dolls*, he could have followed Mikhail Katenin instead. And that might have led him straight to Tonya.

'Misha said that this girl had convinced Marina of a peculiar theory.' Tonya smiles serenely. 'That a famous dissident historian was in fact his father. They even went to see this man speak, and only told me later.'

I take a deep breath. 'I now know that Alexey Ivanov is *not* Valentin Andreyev—'

'Alexey Ivanov is known as a decent public speaker.'

The smile cools. 'But that's not hard, with practice. A voice is only another kind of costume. And people are easily distracted by costumes.'

I recoil a bit from her gaze. 'You know who Alexey is?'

Was.

'After they told me, I was curious. I bought his book, and that's when I realised.' Tonya continues softly: 'But I didn't care. I've been living in hiding anyway, more or less, since I was released from prison. It was in 1964, the year Khrushchev was deposed – the beginning of a period of renewed political repression, of persecution. I reunited with Misha and tried to adapt to a cautious, quiet life. Larionova is not a pseudonym – I remarried, though my husband died soon after. I then spent most of my time writing. I didn't know how to find your mother, and I believed we would never see her or Valentin again. Though Valentin was already gone, in a way, when Misha and Katya were children.' A youthful flush appears on her cheeks. 'My Yekaterina.'

Yekaterina. Katerina Ballerina. Something fills my chest, blocks my breath. I grope helplessly in my bag for what I want to give her: Mum's notebook. *Tonya's* notebook. She is its author. Its rightful owner. I can't find it, so I start to pull everything out, place it on the table. The usual: keys, wallet, ticket stubs.

'What is *that*?' Tonya says, in an entirely different voice, one that suggests her other one was only a *costume* too.

I think she must have spotted the notebook herself, but she hasn't. She's sliding something out from under my wallet.

It's the crinkly old rag that I received from the old man in Popovka a full year and a half ago. It's so sheer I didn't even realise it was still in there.

'Oh,' I say uncertainly. 'That was a gift.'

Her dark eyes blaze at me. 'A *gift*?'

What is going on? Have I done something offensive? I glance at Lev, who looks just as bewildered. Tonya holds the thing at a distance that suggests it smells bad. She waves it at me like I should take it back, burn it, bury it.

'A gift from whom?' she demands.

I suddenly can't answer.

'We were in Popovka,' supplies Lev. 'A villager gave this to Raisa.'

'A villager! Who?' she says, not even questioning why we were in her tiny two-horse home town, of all places, to begin with.

'I don't remember.' I hesitate. 'Wait. Kirill, I think. I saw a letter on his table.'

'It can't be the Kirill I used to know. He'd be well over a hundred. He and Nelly must have had a son. I hope so.' Tonya turns the rag over. Over again, staring at it. She is still searching for whatever answer we've failed to give. 'I haven't seen this handkerchief since I was seventeen years old. It belonged to my mother-in-law. I must have brought it with me when I moved back to Popovka.'

'We would have asked him more, only he was a little confused,' I say, because it's clear that my grandmother is still unhappy. 'The villager, I mean.'

'Confused?'

'He kept repeating lines of that wartime song, "The Blue Kerchief".'

'Oh, I know that one very well. Look,' she says, 'look at all that you've brought with you, Raisa. I can't believe that you're here. I can't believe that we are sitting here together. Come. Come closer.'

I am shocked to see that Tonya's eyes have blurred with tears. She lets go of the handkerchief at last, reaches out for my hand, and puts it on her face. I see a glimmer of a different smile, my mother's smile, through her tears, through mine, as if Mum is still here. Right between us. Right where she has always been.

Tonya tells me what the notebook was, what it did. What Mum did with it. My grandmother is not interested in having the notebook back and tells me to keep it. Today she and I are perusing a few tables in a makeshift marketplace where people have put their whole lives for sale. We pass a table of porcelain figurines, and she stops to admire them. Some stand adorned in enamel, soaked with glaze, while others are a raw and naked white. One is a ballerina in a tutu with a pink bodice, her arms raised high above her head, hands not quite touching around the top. Her pink ballet shoes are laced around the ankle.

Katerina Ballerina, preserved in time.

I think of the burden, the guilt that Mum must have carried from girlhood, when she was too young to understand. I always thought she was glory-seeking and attention-addicted. Self-absorbed and selfish. Maybe she was. But I don't think that's how I'll remember her any more.

CHAPTER THIRTY-THREE

Antonina

Popovka, Tula province, February 1993

TONYA TOUCHES A SMALL SPOT ON THE CAR window, rubs away the condensation. It is raining, a fresh-smelling rain that only happens this time of year. Raisa, who is at the wheel, has said little on the way. Her friend Lev appears cramped and unused to the back seat of the car. At least he doesn't wear the maroon jackets of the new Moscow gangs. At least he does not call Tonya *baba*. In fact, she likes the way he smiles at her granddaughter, even if he does not smile at much else.

'Sorry, I'm still learning to drive. This was where we met the old man who gave me the handkerchief,' says Raisa, stalling the engine, and Tonya peers through the slashing rain.

Nelly and Kirill's former home, indeed.

Tonya has a terrible flicker of doubt, remembering the last time she ever stood on the outside looking into this place. Nelly refusing to come out to say goodbye, still working on that horrid shawl, longer by then than the creek, and as easy to drown in. Kirill standing on the porch, saying that he would visit, help her fix up Otrada, but he never came. Sasha waiting for Tonya on the other side of the lane, eating a melon rind, spitting out the seeds; Lena, writhing in Tonya's arms, wanting melon for herself.

They are all gone. Except for her, and whoever awaits inside.

'Do you want us to come in with you?' asks Raisa.

'No,' says Tonya, 'even if there's nobody around, I'd like a few hours here on my own.'

'Hours?' says Raisa dubiously. 'It's raining quite hard.'

It's why they've made this trip, so Tonya can feel this rain, can breathe this air, can touch this earth. She will walk all the way to Otrada; she will never be coming this way again. She's begun to think this is what she always needed, to go home one more time, before she dies.

She hasn't told Raisa this, of course.

'I've seen worse in February,' says Tonya, already opening the door.

Raisa shouts something from behind, but Tonya doesn't turn around. The weather this time of year can indeed be strange. Changeable. There was unusually good weather *one* February, long ago; it was warm enough to draw people from their homes and out onto the streets. Warm enough that she can still feel it on her skin, seventy-six years later.

Tonya approaches the porch. There is a rocking chair, as Raisa said, but there is nobody in it.

'Hello?' she calls out, glad for the shelter from the rain. 'Hello, is anyone home?'

No answer.

'Hello,' she tries once more, 'I'm sorry to disturb you.' She reaches into the pocket of her jacket for Anastasia's handkerchief. Once lighter than air, it is a bit gummy now. It's lived her lifetime too. 'Are you the son of Kirill Vladimirovich? Your parents were friends of mine. I'm just passing through, and wanted to—'

The door opens.

'It's raining,' says the person in front of her.

'Don't you know me?' Tonya cries, and then claps a hand over her mouth. Of course he doesn't know her. She's hallucinating, the way those kids used to when they poked around Otrada, seeing spooks. Everyone sees spooks around here. How wrong she's been, coming all this way! Maybe the appearance of Raisa in her life made her think she could dare to face the past once more, but she can't, she *can't!*

He is squinting at her.

He can't *see* her. He is blind, or as good as blind.

'Let me inside,' says Tonya, shaking, 'I'm so cold,' and he opens the door just wide enough for her to come through. The door shuts behind him. The house is much as it always was. The stove, the crawl space where she used to lie, the shrine to St Nicholas, now an icon corner, the jars by the window, right where Nelly used to keep them. This *is* the past. Tonya has entered it, and this is where Valentin has been waiting for her, all this time.

Perhaps he first came here looking for her.

'Valentin,' she says, and the name has a taste, a texture, 'it's me. Tonya.'

'Have you lost your way?' he asks, like he doesn't understand.

So this is what has happened. This is how he is.

But she always knew it was going to happen. The White Sea stole too much from him, and people do not regenerate like that. She knew that one day they would be looking right at one another, and he would not remember her, not recognise her, not smile at her, not tease her, not hold her, not even touch her.

And she is prepared.

'No,' she says. It seems like the rain is still falling, even indoors. She brushes the water from her cheeks. 'I've found what I'm looking for.'

'You know where to go?'

'I'm already there.'

Her answers seem to dissatisfy him. His clouded-over eyes look through her and he says again: 'I don't know you, comrade.'

'It doesn't matter if you know me.' Tonya squeezes the handkerchief. 'I have some time. Why don't I tell a story?' He's shaking his head, but she wants to keep talking because otherwise she won't be able to start again. Her eyes are too full, her mouth is too salty. 'Far away,' she says, 'and long ago, was a kingdom where a princess lived in a palace by the sea, far from the city, far from the people. One day she escaped the palace walls, but she didn't know which way to go. She walked all the way into the kingdom—'

'Stop,' he whispers.

'When she overheard a voice that captivated her—'

'Stop.'

'Alright,' she says, ruefully, 'you never did like my stories that much.'

'No,' says Valentin, 'that's not why.'

'Why then?'

'I've heard it,' he says. 'I've heard it before.' He looks at her again, and whatever he sees, it's enough. 'I've heard your voice.'

Tonya lets go of the handkerchief. She goes to him, embraces him, puts her head against his chest. His breathing is harsh and uneven. His arms close around her but it could be for support, to be able to stand. *I have loved you longer than anyone*, she wants to say, *and I will love you longer than everything that has just ended, longer than any of this around us will last*, but she can't speak any more. She made the mistake of stopping. Valentin says something into her hair, *Antonina*, or maybe nothing, maybe it is only in her mind. But of all the things that have only been in her mind, her stories, her fairy tales, her dreams, of all the endings she has ever imagined, she could not have imagined this one.

But wait. It is not the ending.

Today is not the last day. Today is the first day.

EPILOGUE

I RETURN TO MUM'S APARTMENT. I GO THROUGH HER POST and breathe in her scent. I turn to her collection of porcelain dolls, and even though they still terrify me, I find the courage to pick one up. I set it down again quickly. As always, the big blue eyes do not blink.

But they *should* blink.

The doll that Eduard Dayneko left on our living-room sofa was this same kind of doll, with these same blown-glass eyes, but when I was carrying it around Moscow, I noticed that its eyes *did* blink. Up and down, open and closed, whenever the doll was moved from standing to lying or back again.

Why don't these eyes do the same?

I pick the doll back up. I turn it around and upside down. The wig falls off. Beneath the wig, on top of the doll's bald, stained scalp, is a large circle. Not just a circle, but what looks like a segment of the head. It was not accurately replaced by whomever last opened it. Feeling as though I am conducting an autopsy, and against my own better judgement, I pry the remainder of this odd circle loose.

The hollow head has been stuffed full of paper.

This is what's wrong. There is a small pendulum behind the eyes, held down artificially by the volume of material. Without it, the pendulum swings once more, and the doll can blink. See, Mum? I've fixed it for you.

I turn my attention to the paper.

The same thing is written on every single sheet, each one dated, spanning years and years.

Dear Mama, please forgive me.
Katya.

I put the doll's head back together as best I can and I put the wig back on too and I put the doll with the others, lying her down so her eyes can finally close. *There you go*, I say, talking out loud. *There you go. It's all OK. You can rest now.*

AUTHOR'S NOTE

THIS AUTHOR'S NOTE IS FOR ANYONE (LIKE ME!) WHO enjoys learning the stories behind a story, but a quick warning first: spoilers abound!

I have always been, and will always be, obsessed with family secrets. My grandfather, for example, had a very clear line that separated the two parts of his life: 'before' a traumatic historical event (the Chinese Communist Revolution in 1949, which he fled) and 'after'. He never spoke of the 'before', and he died before I ever got up the courage to ask him about it. In the final years of her life, I tried to ask my grandmother about her childhood, growing up in the Japanese occupation of Taiwan, but she would only talk around it, defaulting to stock anecdotes that had already been told infinite times and essentially crystallised – she'd use the same words, even the same hand gestures! Older members of my family have always tried to give the impression to younger members that their lives didn't start until the younger ones came around, but the result is not quite that impression. Rather, a gap. And a gap, as Rosie discovers in this novel, that leaves space for the imagination.

The Porcelain Doll is a novel about stories hidden between the lines. About the unsaid, unspoken, unformed, unfathomable. The context of Stalin's Russia, in which people were forced to keep secrets, to hold their tongues, to lead performative lives, in a number of ways, lends itself to such themes. But it is also a novel about mothers, daughters and granddaughters. It is about a girl who discovers that what happened before she was born not only made her family what it is, but made her the person she is, too.

Below, I discuss my sources of inspiration for individual characters in the novel, as well as a few other notes.

Alexey

Alexey is my own creation, and not based on any one person in particular. However, as I was drawing up the character, I was inspired by the case of Slawomir Rawicz's memoir *The Long Walk* (1956), which describes his escape from a gulag camp and his subsequent, and harrowing, journey to freedom. It was much later determined that there was no evidence of an escape by Rawicz – in fact, there was evidence to the contrary, namely that he'd been released. Whatever the truth of that case, when a story is good enough, when it's told convincingly and movingly enough, people want to believe it.

There are a few superficial similarities between the life of the writer Alexander Solzhenitsyn and that of Alexey (anyone familiar with Solzhenitsyn may already have noted this). Alexey's seminal work is published in Europe (as a lot of things were); he's then forced out of Russia and eventually invited back. I simply found this turn of events convenient for the plot of *The Porcelain Doll*, however. Alexey is in no way intended to resemble or recall the real-life figure of Solzhenitsyn, whose body of work on the Soviet camp system is tremendous.

Tonya

I have a lifelong interest in fairy tales, as well as myths, urban legends and magical, eerie stories in general. Alexander Afanasyev's *Russian Fairy Tales*, published in the mid-1800s, is one of my favourite compilations of such stories. It includes the tale of Vasilisa the Beautiful, a girl who defers to the wisdom and resourcefulness of a magical talking doll she carries in her pocket. In my view the doll is the real 'human': it thinks, acts and makes decisions, and it does it all in the service of someone else. In *The Porcelain Doll*, Tonya is the eponymous 'doll', but the real doll is Alexey: beneath his shiny, heavily curated public persona, there's no substance.

Fairy tales have a particular allegorical power, one that partly lies in their simplicity and structure and in familiar lines like 'far away and long ago'. The Soviets knew this, and churned out and distributed tiny fantastical stories, often a spin on traditional tales, as part of their propaganda machine. These 'corrected' fairy tales have always been fascinating to me: The 'right' ones implies that there are wrong ones. What do you do if you're writing the wrong ones?

I invented the stories in Tonya's notebook; they aren't based on pre-existing folk tales. Some of them represent moments in her life, such as her marriage to Dmitry, while others are political (the monster from the sewers is the Bolshevik Revolution; the king who makes it rain is Stalin), but all of them are intended to reflect a bigger reality than is shown. Given that any perceived slight or criticism of the regime could have devastating consequences (and often did), Tonya would have known that her stories could not be published officially. She wrote them 'for the drawer', as the common phrase *pisat' v stol* is usually translated. I expect that, after her release from prison in the 1960s, she would have attempted self-publication via the dissident underground.

Some of the most famous Russian books of the past century enjoyed a considerable shelf life as *samizdat* or *tamizdat* (material smuggled and published abroad). In the span of a few years in the 1980s (when Tonya herself finally achieves publication), innumerable novels that were banned or censored in previous decades were finally published in the USSR, from *Lolita* to *Dr Zhivago* to Eugenia Ginzburg's *Journey into the Whirlwind*.

There are places in Tonya's narrative where I took a degree of poetic licence, and I want to highlight some of these. Firstly, there are several historical details that have been taken or altered and then rewoven into the world of *The Porcelain Doll*. For instance, I used elements from the Romanovs' private rooms in the Winter Palace for the interior of Tonya's house on the Fontanka. The name Popovka comes from the real-life home town of Prince Georgy Lvov, and Otrada from the abandoned (and gorgeous) real-life house Semenovskoye-Otrada, both in Tula province. In his letters to Tonya, Valentin writes *wait for me*, deliberately an echo of the title of one of my favourite poems, 'Wait for Me' by Konstantin Simonov, who also gave his surname to Rosie's character.

I took further liberties elsewhere. For example, Tonya moves back into a communal apartment in the house on the Fontanka with Valentin, years after leaving Leningrad. From a logistical point of view, although this would have been possible, it is admittedly unlikely. Likewise, the difficulty of moving around from city to city is understated in *The Porcelain Doll*; Valentin's reference to using connections to obtain a propiska (a residence permit) for Leningrad is about as much detail as I go into. It is true that connections – any connections – in Soviet Russia were worth their weight in gold. (An additional note: Valentin returned home in secret, but typically ex-prisoners were not permitted to settle in big cities.)

In the Siege chapters, Tonya feeds part of herself to her children. She considers the important distinction in Russian between murdering someone in order to eat them (*lyudoyedstvo*) and eating the flesh of someone who is already dead (*trupoyedstvo*). Cannibalism did take place, with women most likely to engage in the practice, but I want to emphasise that it was not a defining feature of the Leningrad blockade. For the vast majority of people, it was not part of their experience at all. For Tonya, however, it is a turning point because the smell of her own flesh cooking finally allows her to confront her repressed trauma and abuse at the hands of her mother. As smell is linked to memory more so than any of our other senses – odours are able to trigger extremely vivid memories long after an event – this is also how I wanted Zoya to start to communicate with Rosie.

I still remember the first time I read in Anne Applebaum's *Gulag: A History* (2003) that within the world of the Soviet labour camps, a gift for storytelling (or entertaining of any kind) could help a prisoner survive. I always knew that Tonya's storytelling would be her ticket out of Vorkuta. However, while movement between the camps was fluid and the system quite chaotic, the Monte Cristo-style swap between Natalya and Tonya is not based on any real-life case I have come across. (That doesn't mean it didn't happen!)

Rosie

Many Soviet writers became practised at lining their work with subtext. One popular theory that I've always enjoyed is that Dmitri Shostakovich, the famous composer whose popularity with Stalin ebbed and flowed, *encrypted* his compositions, adding or using a secret code through which he could get across an anti-Soviet message. (For the curious, it all began with the editor's introduction to Shostakovich's memoirs, *Testimony*.) Rosie's memory of her father discussing the idea of writing code into a piece of music, or into other mediums, reflects my fascination with this notion.

Valentin

Valentin's 'work' is left unspecified to avoid having to delve into the dense political history of the Russian Revolution and its aftermath. To give some context: in my view, Valentin was connected prior to his arrest in 1924 with the Left Opposition (in short, he was a Trotskyist), and was actively involved in a plot against Stalin. In the years Valentin spent in exile, however, organised resistance to Stalin was effectively wiped out, punctuated by the imprisonment of Martemyan Ryutin and his supporters in 1932 (aka the Ryutin Affair). For the late 1930s, I again left unclear what Valentin's 'work' consisted of, and/or whether some of it might be solely in his mind. Certainly if he was organised and clear-headed enough, pockets of leftist opposition to Stalin could be found, but this is open to interpretation.

I drafted the character of Valentin with several real-life figures in mind, including Viktor Serge (author of *Memoirs of a Revolutionary*) and Eduard Dune (*Notes of a Red Guard*), among others.

To Conclude

My usage of diminutives (Maria turns into Masha/ Mashenka/so forth) is limited, on purpose. I also often forgo the formal address of first name + patronymic (Alexander

Petrovich, Alexandra Petrovna), again for simplicity's sake. I opted not for any official system of transliteration from Cyrillic to the Roman alphabet, but for what I hope is sheer readability, turning what might have been Dmitrii into Dmitry, and Aleksei into Alexey. (I also kept popular English spellings, i.e. Yeltsin.)

If you've read all the way here, I want to let you know that I put something into this novel that isn't necessarily 'seen'; just for fun. In *The Porcelain Doll*, there are several hints/allusions to Tolstoy's *Anna Karenina*, none of which are explicit or identified. If you have read it, or if you ever do, see if you can spot any or all of these tiny homages!

ADDITIONAL NOTES

ALL THE ENGLISH-LANGUAGE TRANSLATIONS FROM Russian text in this novel (with one exception, noted below) are my own. All mistakes are my own.

The line Rosie remembers about 'patience and time' from Tolstoy's *War and Peace* is found in Book 10, Chapter 16, in the English-language version. The line about 'divine love' is found in Book 11, Chapter 32.

The line of poetry in the epigraph is from Sergey Yesenin's poem 'Mne Grustno na tebya Smotret'. I first came across the line in the English-language version of Varlam Shalamov's *Kolyma Tales*, in a slightly different translation. I would like to recommend Shalamov to anyone interested in camp life, especially as it makes an interesting contrast to Solzhenitsyn.

The text of Natalya's tattoo – *I do not regret, I do not shed tears* – is also Yesenin's, from the poem 'Ya Ne Zhalelyu, Ne Zovu, Ne Plachu'. This is the most commonly used and reproduced (if not exactly direct) English-language translation. Yesenin took his own life in 1925.

Finally, in Tonya's earliest chapters, the dates are given according to the Julian [Old Style] calendar. It was my preference to keep the months as they would have been then, to the characters involved.

ACKNOWLEDGEMENTS

M Y THANKS GO TO EVERYONE AT ALLISON & BUSBY. Thank you sincerely Lesley Crooks, for believing in this book, Claire Browne, Christina Storey and Sara Magness, for their incredibly hard work and support, and Christina Griffiths, for the stunning cover.

Thank you to my agent, Sharon Galant, for being such a tireless champion of my work, and to Thomasin Chinnery, for helping me navigate the world of book contracts.

I'm grateful to Michele Rubin, who spent over an hour on the phone with me discussing the very first, messiest version of this book, and Helen Corner-Bryant, for her insightful feedback and vote of confidence. Wendy of the Caledonia Novel Award has been so supportive; thank you for the utter thrill of being shortlisted.

No writer is an island – thank you to Eleonora and Catherine for being the best writer buddies anyone could have, for endlessly reading and critiquing, for the laughter, camaraderie, zoom chats, wine tastings, and generally being the sounding board for everything I do now. My fellow past and present members of Critters, Felicity, Sue, Charlotte, Melissa, and Marcelle, thank you so much for your inspiration and wisdom. An additional shout-out to the writers I know via social media who have been so generous with their time, and to the book bloggers and book community, who so energetically read and promote books.

To friends who have helped along the way, thank you: Samna, for the lovely photos, coffee sessions, and for being such a loyal reader; Sasha, spasibo bol'shoe, for answering all my questions; Valia, for being my point-person in London; Sabine, for your enthusiasm from the earliest days. Samangie, needless to say, I don't know where I'd be without you. Thank you for everything.

Words are inadequate, but thank you to my parents for their boundless patience and generosity; Collin, for the most fantastic song; my children, for being the sweetest, most eager, most amazing people; and thank you Steffen, for so many things it would take a whole other book to list them, but especially for keeping me well caffeinated.

KRISTEN LOESCH grew up in San Francisco. She holds a BA in History, as well as a Master's degree in Slavonic Studies from the University of Cambridge. Her debut historical novel, *The Porcelain Doll*, was shortlisted for the Caledonia Novel Award and longlisted for the Bath Novel Award. After a decade living in Europe, she now resides in the Pacific Northwest with her husband and children.

kristenloesch.com
@kristenloesch